Bridal Pact

Book One of the Warriors of Phaeton Series

Leora Gonzales

DEDICATION

I would like to give thanks to my family and friends who have been supportive while I stumbled through writing my first book.

Special thanks to my friend Andrea. A bumper sticker brought us together but wonder twin powers keep us going strong. Tina, you have become a close friend and I will never get bored talking to you. Your talent, life experience and generous heart make you an amazing woman. Plus, you get bonus points for putting up with Richard…that's kind of a big deal.

Most importantly, I want to dedicate this to my husband. I was lucky enough to find a man who is super smart, loving, hilarious and also diabolical. When I said that I wanted to write but had no computer, I had no idea he was going to surprise me with a new laptop. There went my list of excuses. Touché, Richard. Touché.

CHAPTER ONE

Poppy Williams jerked awake at the sound of police sirens. Sitting up in bed as if she'd been electrocuted, she looked around for a minute. What the hell was going on? Confused from sleep, Poppy blinked a few times to focus her eyes. The amount of sun streaming through the window could only mean one thing.

"Holy fucking shit!"

Not only had her alarm not gone off but she'd apparently overslept by more than an hour. Scrambling from under her comforter, Poppy stumbled and ending up face-planting on the floor by her bed, landing in a pile of shoes.

"Motherfucker!" Now she was not only going to be late for work, she'd have a shoe imprint on her forehead.

Snatching her phone from the nightstand, she hit the icon to call work. When all she got was a busy signal, she tossed it onto the bed and ran to her closet to find some clean clothes. After getting dressed with a speed she thought would impress the Flash, she moved to the bathroom to clean up her face.

The only way to tame her curls would be to start over with a shower and since that wasn't an option she pulled her hair back and piled it into a bun on top of her head. As she brushed her teeth, she tried to smooth down some of the curls around her face.

"Stupid hair," Poppy muttered. She actually loved her long curls but only when she had enough time to tame them. Glancing into the mirror one last time, she took in her image. Standing at five foot three, she had some serious curves. Poppy normally weighed herself every morning out of habit and knew the one hundred and eighty pounds that showed on the scale would make most women cringe. She however had decided long ago to accept what seemed to be her "normal". No, she took that back. She not only accepted herself, she liked herself.

Leaning forward to make sure she didn't have toothpaste on the side of her mouth, Poppy took a second to clear the sleep from the corners of her brown eyes. Another good thing was that she appeared closer to twenty-three than the twenty-seven years she was pushing.

She'd wasted enough time in the bathroom and raced to the door where her other shoes were. Slipping them on as she walked caused Poppy to almost fall for the second time this morning. As she redialed the office, she noticed the time at the top of the screen. *Well shit. Why weren't they answering?*

In her hurry to get out the door, she barely missed slamming into the man blocking her path to the stairs. She brushed by him at the last minute, narrowly avoiding knocking both of them over. She stopped dead. Something wasn't right.

Work forgotten, she saw almost all her neighbors were standing on the open-air staircase. That was when she remembered what had originally woken her up.

Sirens.

Walking back a step to the man she assumed was her loud next-door neighbor, she asked, "Is one of the buildings on fire?"

When he didn't answer her but instead simply stared across the parking lot, Poppy turned around to see what had everyone in a trance.

"What the fuck?!"

Not believing her eyes, she blinked a couple times and then pinched her arm for good measure.

There, hovering in the sky, was a strange plane. Studying it closely, she realized, no, that wasn't a plane. It was some sort of ship. A bright, shiny silver ship like something straight out of the movies. Just floating in the air as if it were guarding something, it cast a shadow over a few of the buildings it hovered above.

Poppy jumped when a hand clasped her shoulder hard from behind.

"Didn't you see the news?" Her neighbor was still staring at the ship with a panicked expression on his face.

"What? What news?" Shaking her head to clear it, she blinked a few more times and whispered, "What the fuck is going on?"

"It's aliens. There are aliens…aliens…"

As his voice trailed off in disbelief, Poppy looked frantically around, trying to figure out what was happening.

Every single neighbor on her floor was out on the stairs watching the strange ship hanging in midair over the buildings in front of her. Some people were whispering, quite a few were crying, but most of them were just staring in shock at the ship.

Poppy tried frantically to unlock her phone with fingers that were now slippery with sweat. Finally getting to the screen she needed, she punched the icon with her sister's picture on it.

"Pixie. Answer the phone, Pixie." Poppy heard the voicemail pick up and immediately hit End to dial again. How dare Pixie not answer the phone when there were aliens? *Aliens!*

"Poppy!" Her sister's voice had Poppy breathing a sigh of relief.

"Pixie! Are you seeing this?" Poppy peered over the rail on the stairs to see a police car circling on the street beneath her third-story apartment. She covered her free ear to drown out the siren that was continuously wailing. Poppy strained to hear what was being said.

"Stay indoors. Do not panic. Stay indoors." The words were being repeated from the emergency vehicle in between the siren blaring.

Poppy walked back toward her apartment door even as the rest of her neighbors stayed where they were.

"Pixie? I can barely hear you. What did you say?" Poppy struggled with the door to her apartment with one hand, holding the phone with the other.

"Poppy, the ships…they're everywhere…it's all over the news."

In between crackles she could hear sirens on Pixie's end of the line as well.

"Hang on." Finally getting the stupid door open, Poppy ran to her TV to turn it on.

When the screen flickered, it was all Poppy could do to keep breathing. The live shot from the news crew showed not just a single ship but dozens of them. Simply hovering over the city.

As the news alert showed different cities reporting the same phenomenon, Poppy felt her stomach sink.

"Poppy? Are you still there?" Pixie's voice wobbled over the phone.

"Yeah, Pix, I'm here. Are you at home?" Poppy had the undeniable urge to get to her last remaining family member and make sure she was safe. From her window she could see the police cars still making their rounds on the busy street. From what she could make out, traffic was blocked up and down the road. Fuck. There went that idea.

"Yeah, I was watching the news before I went in to work. I tried calling your office but I couldn't get through."

"Well, at least you had the news to prepare you. I missed my alarm and almost mowed a guy down on the stairs. I didn't know what was happening until I saw that thing in the sky." Poppy took turns peeking out her window at the commotion below and walking back to the TV.

"What the fuck are they?"

Pixie started talking again but Poppy shushed her.

"Shhhh, Pix, they're having a press conference."

Turning up her TV to drown out some of the outside noise, Poppy sank down onto her living room floor. The local news switched over to a national broadcast. She held her breath as she stared at the screen, watching the president take his place behind a podium. He managed to appear calm and collected despite the panic and confusion out on the street. Holding up his hands to quiet down the reporters shouting questions from all directions, he focused directly on the camera.

"My fellow Americans, do not be alarmed. Many of you have been watching the news reports this morning regarding first contact that has been made with an alien species. The truth is that we are no longer alone. In fact, we have never been alone. This race of beings has also made us aware that they are not the only ones in the unknown depths of space. The safety of all Americans is our number-one concern. After our initial contact, we have started negotiations with their leaders.

"While we speak with them, we ask that citizens stay calm. There is no need for panic. We have ascertained that they are here on a peaceful mission and the ships that many of you have seen are there for observation purposes. During this time we ask that nonessential businesses stay closed today and we recommend that citizens stay inside until the streets have cleared. For your safety and others, please only call emergency services if they are truly needed. The State Department also asks that concerned citizens do not try to disturb the ships, which are protected by force fields. Air travel has been suspended except for military flights, and there will be a press release announcing when commercial or private planes will restart."

Poppy took in a huge gulp of air when he stopped speaking. Her mind was whirling, trying to absorb her new reality. Aliens. Motherfucking aliens.

The screech in Poppy's ear was loud and obnoxious but managed to knock her out of the funk she'd fallen into, hanging on the president's every word. Still holding the phone to her ear with her sister on the line, Poppy tried to swallow to clear her throat.

"Did you see that?" Pixie asked.

"Yeah."

"Holy shit," Pixie breathed out.

"No joke. So…wait…you can't come over. I'm here alone, Pixie, and this is freaking me out." For some reason, Poppy felt on the verge of tears. Overwhelmed, she blinked a couple of times to clear her eyes.

Pixie was the only family Poppy had left. After a car accident had claimed the lives of their parents five years ago, the sisters had been closer than ever before. Poppy had begun to rely on her older sister more the past couple of years. It was hard not to. Pixie seemed to have her shit together. While Poppy worked at the front desk in a medical office, Pixie held a managerial position at a successful restaurant. She had to admit, she was slightly jealous that Pixie had a chance to use her college degree and make decent money doing it.

Whoever thought to major in history was an idiot, and that pool of idiots happened to include Poppy herself.

"Poppy, I can't. There are actually barricades blocking my street."

Poppy could hear Pixie fiddling with the loud blinds in her living room. "I know, Pix. I'm sorry… I'm just having trouble taking this all in." She dropped down onto her loveseat and kicked off her shoes to think for a second.

"Is Brian home or had he already left for work when all this shit happened?"

Brian was Pixie's live-in boyfriend of two years. Her sister seemed to be on the verge of becoming Brian's fiancée at any time, if the rumors were true. All their mutual friends hinted Brian seemed to be acting a little sneaky and might have spent some time at a jewelry store recently. Poppy was happy for her sister's success, both in work and relationships. Although she'd prefer not to have to confess to it, she did sometimes feel a little envious.

"He'd left but only made it down a couple blocks before there was a wreck. By the time he turned around, he noticed people were stopping their cars in the street to get out and look at the ships that'd become visible."

"Become visible?"

"Yeah, Brian said he was driving down the road and then a ship just appeared in front of him in the sky. He said it didn't fly down, just popped up out of nowhere."

Poppy leaned her head back and tried to calm her nerves.

"Well, Pix, at least you have Brian there." Glancing wryly at her front door, she added, "I may have to keep company with my loud and obnoxious neighbors. I spoke to them for the first time in two years."

"Once they reopen the streets, you can come here and stay with us," Pixie offered in her "big sister" voice.

"Yeah, I may have to do that. This whole thing is so unbelievable." Poppy was now talking more to herself than to Pixie.

"Hey, Pops, Brian just came in. He's been standing in the front yard watching everything. We're going to keep watching the news today. Call me in a little bit to check in, okay?" Pixie waited for her sister to agree before saying goodbye.

Without the phone to cling to now, Poppy glanced around the apartment, listening for noises from outside. Nothing but sirens wailing with the continued, "Stay indoors. Do not panic."

"Well shit."

CHAPTER TWO

For the next week, Poppy stayed inside her apartment. The doctor's office she worked for had cancelled patient exams and told her not to bother coming in until she received a call when they'd reopened. That meant that Poppy was using her vacation time, which sucked for a couple reasons. Like many of her friends she lived paycheck to paycheck. She had a little savings, but that amount tended to be enough to splurge on a dinner out every now and then. It was definitely nothing to live off.

Between calls to check in with Pixie, she tried to become more familiar with her neighbors. She quickly came to realize her fellow apartment dwellers could be lumped into the "crazy Floridians" group. Poppy was relieved that she hadn't felt the need to become friendly before the whole alien invasion. These people drove her nuts. Her first clue to the crazy they subscribed to was apparent when on the second night she heard gunshots in the parking lot and peered out to see the man she'd talked to previously, now with a dangling bottle of Jack in one hand and a handgun in the other. As he fired shots up at the ship closest to them, he yelled, "Come and get me!" This lasted until someone called the police. After some shouting back and forth, Poppy finally had some peace and quiet when they Tasered him and he was arrested.

Poppy felt slightly guilty when thinking back on it. As the shenanigans had been happening outside her window, she'd popped a bag of popcorn and sat watching as if she were at the movies. Who could blame her though? She was getting tired of watching the news and this was more entertaining than cable TV. It seemed every channel claimed to have "inside" information about their space invaders. There were stories being leaked that ranged from missing women who were believed to have been abducted and probed to the aliens being blamed for climate change.

As Poppy sat in her living room flipping through the channels, her phone rang.

"Hey, Pix." Apparently it was time for her morning check-in.

"Hey, Poppy, how's the status quo?" Pixie asked. This was obviously getting old if that was her opening line.

"Oh you know, the usual… An alien knocked on my door today to try to convert me to some freaky alien religion, my neighbor went gun shopping again, and I'm pretty sure I'm down to my last roll of toilet paper," Poppy quipped.

"Hardy-har-har. Very funny." Pixie's tone went serious. "These news broadcasts are still freaking me out. Did you hear they believe twenty missing women have been connected to the aliens?"

"Pix, c'mon now. I'm sure the last thing on their minds was coming down here to steal women. The last lady who was interviewed about being abducted was wearing a tinfoil hat. She was a total nut ball." Picturing the woman in question from the news report caused her to laugh. "But I was being honest about the toilet paper…I have half a roll left and no paper towels. I'm going to need to leave my apartment soon."

"Poppy, from what I've heard, people have been going out with no problem. You're not too far from the store. You should be able to go pretty quick and be right back."

That thought made Poppy frown. She hated Mega Mart. It was sometimes fun to go in the middle of the night and people-watch if she was really bored but actually shopping there was no fun at all. So what if everything was super-cheap? The crowded aisles were hell to navigate with their wonky shopping carts that always tended to lean right no matter how many times you switched carts.

"I'd rather drive across town and take my chances at the Super Store than go to Mega Mart during the day, Pix. You know I hate that place."

Pixie let out a snort of laughter. "So you're telling me you'd rather take a chance being abducted by aliens than go two miles to Mega Mart?"

"Hellz yes, bish. That's how I roll."

Both sisters loved to curse. In fact, they tended to make an art of it and used bad language in every sentence they could. When they were bored and drinking, they'd try to create new words just to mix it up. "Bish" was one of those words. According to Pixie it was like calling someone a bitch but with a little love thrown in. They used it so frequently their phones had stopped autocorrecting it when they texted each other.

"Hey, what's Brian up to?" Normally Poppy could hear background noise when talking to her sister but this call had been surprisingly quiet. Brian was the type of guy who tended to make noise when he was simply sitting down doing nothing, so she could tell when he wasn't around.

"Well, he decided to go in to the office today. Architecture apparently waits for no man...or alien," Pixie deadpanned then started giggling. "He actually sat on our porch last night and stared at the ships for a bit."

"Ummm...why?"

"Because he said that the curves and engine placement on them were 'fascinating'. I swear he's such a goofball sometimes. He went in to mock up some drawings apparently and left me here."

"Hey, is he still acting weird?" Propping her feet up on the table, Poppy twirled a curl that had managed to escape from her bun.

"Yeah...a little. Since we've been hermits this last week, he hasn't disappeared on me but he seems nervous about something."

"You mean, other than aliens?"

"I don't know. Before all this happened he was really secretive about where he was. For a minute I thought he was cheating but then Becky said she'd seen him browsing through rings downtown at a jewelry store..."

"You mean engagement rings?" Poppy took pride in needling her sister. Pixie was the type of person who was superstitious when it came to anything and everything.

"Don't say that! You're going to jinx it!" Pixie interrupted quickly.

"So, not to say he *is* going to propose, but if he did, would you say yes?"

Poppy already knew the answer even before she asked the question. Pixie was nothing if not predictable. While Poppy had floundered with school majors and then entering the workforce, it seemed Pixie'd planned everything out from the time she was in high school. The next step for her would obviously be marriage and then the two-point-five kids complete with a white picket fence and perfectly blooming flower boxes.

"Of course I would. We've been dating for two years and living together for one. Why wouldn't I?" By her tone, Pixie obviously had no doubt that her life plan was a sound one.

"Well...do you luuuuurve him?" Poppy sang obnoxiously into the phone.

"Yes, why would you ask that?" Pixie was starting to sound offended at the questions.

Poppy thought for a moment and decided to go for broke. It wasn't that she didn't like Brian. He seemed like a great guy: stable job, stable salary, stable sense of humor. That was the one thing that bothered her. He was plain toast when she had always imagined her lovable sister with someone who had a little more spice.

"I like Brian. I really do." Pausing to try to make this as gentle as possible, she chose her words carefully. "When you're together...you seem different. You don't laugh as much or crack jokes. When we are alone, we say 'fuck' about a million times and laugh so hard we snort. It's sad when my sister seems to lose a little bit of her spunk when her boyfriend is around."

There, she'd said it. Now she was full-on twisting the curl in her hand as she waited for Pixie to say something. Anything.

"Poppy...Brian is a great guy. He's loyal and sweet. And he has a great job and would make a wonderful father. We aren't getting any younger, you know. Plus, we've been dating for two years."

"I know. I just don't want you to settle for someone because he's comfortable, Pixie. I want you to have some passion in your life. Are you passionate about Brian? I know when you first started dating you seemed so happy and then it seemed as though the more you settled in, the more boring it got."

Poppy sat quietly while waiting for her sister to absorb what she was saying. Pixie was obviously doing the same thing since there was silence on her end as well. After a few moments with neither of them talking, Poppy decided to let it go.

"I just want you to be happy. And if you love him, then you're happy and I'm happy for you."

"Great. So let's all be happy and drop the subject, okay?" Pixie had apparently had enough of the Brian discussion so Poppy changed it quickly.

"So, the big question is…toilet paper at Mega Mart or across town? The bonus is that I can stop for food across town on the drive back and not have to eat canned ravioli again." She pulled on a light jacket. Florida weather was a little chilly in January so her winter gear consisted of a thin jacket and a scarf.

"Well, hell, if we're basing your decision on a repeat of canned ravioli then by all means go across town and get alien-napped. Just don't call me when they pull out the probes." Teasing Poppy for her ability to make decisions based on her stomach, she added, "But I do want you to call me first thing when you get home. Okay?"

"Of course, sister dear. Hey, by the way, when are you going to go back in to work?" Zipping up her jacket, she made sure she had her wallet in her purse before heading out the door.

"The restaurant reopened this afternoon with a bare-bones staff. I'll need to go in tomorrow and figure out payroll in the morning but today I'm taking the day off. Brenda is there acting as manager on duty so I don't have to worry too much."

After scanning the stairwell to make sure everything was quiet and no little green men were hiding, Poppy jogged down the steps to her late-model Honda. "Isn't Brenda the chick who's been causing problems lately?"

"Yeah, but it seems we only have issues when she tries to do paperwork. I swear, I spend more time fixing her fuck-ups than it would have taken me just to do whatever it is myself to begin with."

By this point, Poppy had reached her car and climbed in. "Okay, Pix, I'm in my car and I'll call you when I get back."

"Gotcha. Drive carefully. Brian said people are still watching the ships more than the road, so pay attention."

Poppy ended the call with their customary air-kissing noises and started the car.

"What the *fuck*?"

According to her gauge, someone had managed to steal most of her once-full tank of gas. Seriously? Poppy couldn't believe it. *Breathe in and breathe out, Poppy. Fuck breathing!* she thought, banging her hands on her steering wheel. She leaned forward and rested her head against the car horn. There went fifty dollars and hello, side trip she hadn't anticipated. Poppy ran through a list of the gas stations on her route and figured she had enough to get to one at least.

What a bunch of assholes.

CHAPTER THREE

Two miles into her drive across town quickly changed Poppy's destination. All four lanes of traffic had come to a standstill due to an accident that had Poppy cursing and smacking her steering wheel. Poppy made a quick U-turn. Praying she had enough gas to hit the station next to Mega Mart, she crossed her fingers.

The gas station was packed with what appeared to be a bunch of crazy doomsday preppers who seemed intent on emptying the station tanks. "Who needs ten cans of gasoline?" Talking to herself seemed like better entertainment than anything since the radio had turned into nothing but more news. Recognizing the ten-can gasoline man as her gun-toting neighbor made Poppy flinch.

"Yeahhhhh… I might want to stay at Pixie's for a while."

Once Poppy had finished as quickly as possible, she headed for the store. The parking lot resembled a reenactment of Black Friday. There wasn't a space for what seemed like a mile away from the doors and figuring it was faster to just park than to try to stalk someone walking to their car, she pulled in and hopped out.

If she'd thought the parking lot was full, then she was shocked to see how busy the store was. There wasn't a free cart in sight and most of the shoppers were leading multiple carts around on squeaky wheels. She picked up the biggest bundle of toilet paper she could see and walked to the frozen food to check out her options. Obviously no part of the store had gone untouched by the people who were creating their own stockpiles.

She suddenly felt the hair on the back of her neck stand up. Someone was watching her. Juggling the large square of toilet rolls in her arms, she turned to scan her surroundings. The men standing at the edge of the frozen food section were the only ones paying attention to her. The distance between them was far enough for Poppy to tell they were pretty big in stature, but she couldn't make out any details. They seemed clean and were all wearing leather pants and plain tops. All four men seemed to have similar shoulder-length hair but one wore his hair longer than the others, in dreadlocks pulled into a low ponytail on the back of his head. Maybe a rock band's tour bus had broken down or stopped for supplies? Now wanting to see if they were anyone famous, Poppy moved down the freezers until she was in front of the cases with desserts.

Trying not to stare, she took in the gorgeous men in front of her. She saw one of them whisper to the other three, who nodded at him. The whisperer turned to face the others, his back now to Poppy, giving her the chance to take in what was a totally magnificent ass. Too far away still to see what color their eyes were, she nevertheless figured the guys must all be related. Upon closer inspection, the men all had similar features and two had tattoos on their temples. Definitely a rock group. That bad-boy hair, leather pants and now tattoos could only point to that. They also seemed not to be calling attention to themselves, keeping out of the way of anyone shopping but also checking out the crowd.

As Poppy was bumped by another shopper, her grip on the toilet paper loosened enough for it to fall out of her hands. At the sound of it hitting the floor, the men all glanced over to where she was standing and the closest smiled at her. Her stomach tightened at the bright white teeth that were flashed at her. Her cheeks were bright red when she smiled back stupidly at the leader of the group. Turning away to face the freezer, she rolled her eyes to the heavens. *That's just great. Getting the attention of a hot guy by dropping an extra-large bundle of toilet paper.*

Poppy had wasted enough time and snagged a pint of ice cream from the case in front of her to go with the sad-looking frozen dinner she was juggling. Damn. Just her luck that the men had left while she'd had her head stuck in the freezer case. On her journey to the front of the store she kept her eyes peeled but didn't catch another glimpse of the group.

During the trek to the checkout lanes she had a feeling she was being watched, but didn't spot the men from earlier, so brushed it off. She'd been in her apartment too long. Obviously she had cabin fever if she was this paranoid. If there was anything she needed to worry about right now, it wasn't some fine-looking men at the store. She really needed to focus her worries on her crazy neighbors. In particular the one who liked to stockpile not only guns but cans of gasoline. Yep, mind made up, Poppy was going to pack a bag and head to Pixie's tonight come hell or high water.

Getting home was easier said than done. People were so concerned about the ships there seemed to have been an accident that then had led to more, until it was like a life-sized version of bumper cars on the main roads. It was afternoon by the time she reached the safety of her apartment.

Poppy called her sister and left a message. "Hey, Pixie, I'm home. I think I'm going to come over to your place in a bit. I saw my neighbor at the gas station earlier and with the amount of gas he's hoarding, I figure it might be safer there than here. I would rather be cautious than be the next news story. I can already see it now. Boring, single, lonely woman dies in explosion due to Florida idiots. Anyways, I'm heading your way as soon as I pack a bag. See ya in a bit."

She was on the road again when her phone rang.

"Hey, sis, I'm on my way now." Hating to talk while she was driving, especially with all the morons on the road, she wanted to hang up quick.

"I got called in to work. Go ahead and use your key. I'll be home in a bit after I fix whatever Brenda managed to fuck up in the ten minutes I left her in charge."

"Mkay, love you."

Within an hour she was pulling into Pixie's neighborhood in a subdivision on the other side of Jax. Pixie lived in a nice residential area where she and Brian rented a house. Brian's car was in the driveway. What the hell was he doing home early?

Not bothering to knock, she used her key and walked in. Dropping her bag by the front door, she heard footsteps behind her.

"Pixie, what are you doing home?" Brian's deep voice sounded confused.

Poppy and Pixie resembled each other quite a bit. Both had the same rounded figure, even though Pixie had two inches on Poppy in height. The sisters also shared the same hair color, cut and length, except Pixie's curls tended to be better behaved than her own. Poppy and Pixie always joked about the humidity of Florida, using levels in their "hairdicator". Poppy liked to think she was normally at stage "fluffy" when Pixie referred to it as "fuzzy".

Turning around to make a face at Brian, she teased, "Brian, you can't even tell the woman you love from her sister. Tsk-tsk."

Brian stood before her red-faced, wearing only his boxers. Poppy had to admit that he was attractive. Plain, but still attractive. His dark-blond hair always seemed to be combed perfectly and he had a nice smile. Standing at five foot ten, he was well-built, which Poppy knew came from using the gym at the local health club. Scanning Brian up and down, Poppy noticed even his boxers were boring.

"Pixie said I could come over and stay for a bit. It's a long story that deals with a man wearing a wifebeater, and a barrel of gas. Enough about me though." With one hand propped on her hip, she gestured to him with the other. "What are you doing home? Pix said you went in to work today."

Brian ran a hand through his blond hair, which of course fell back into place perfectly, then smiled uncomfortably.

"I haven't been sleeping well, so I took a half day to come home and catch up on some z's." He hefted her bag from the floor. "Let me take this to the guest room and get some clothes on."

Pixie took the bag from him, nodding her head in the direction of the master bedroom he'd come from. "No no no, if you came home to sleep, then go back to bed. I'll just read or watch TV until Pixie gets off."

"I can keep you company, seriously." Brian snagged his phone off the kitchen counter as Poppy ushered him back to his room.

"I'm a big girl, Brian. Seriously. You are tired anyways. Plus, I didn't mean to bother you. Do what you planned on doing today and get some sleep." Poppy detoured to the guest room to drop off her stuff after making sure he had followed her advice.

As she walked back by the master bedroom, she heard Brian on the phone.

"Yeah, Poppy just got here."

He must be calling Pixie for her. Poppy proceeded to get comfortable on their big and relaxing couch. Stroking the empty space next to her, she thought, *Hell, yeah, I need one of these.* Smiling at the thought of fitting this gigantic couch into her tiny one-bedroom apartment, she kicked up her feet and lay back. As she drifted off to sleep, she wondered when Pixie would be home.

A few hours later, Poppy jolted awake to the feeling of someone tickling her feet.

"Goddammit, Pix!" Poppy kicked out a foot and caught Pixie on the leg. She giggled as she avoided another hit.

"Hey, at first I was just trying to move your legs over. Then I figured your lazy ass needed to be woken up." Pixie laughed, plopping down on the couch next to Poppy, and pushed her hair back off her face with a tired sigh.

"What are you doing home so early?" Poppy glanced at the clock on the DVR. "I thought you'd be longer."

"There was a news alert saying a press conference is scheduled for six o'clock today so I wanted to get home in case the roads got bad again." She punched Pixie lightly on the shoulder. "Plus, Brian called me and said that you came home and caught him in his boxers. He was worried about his virtue."

Leering at her sister, Poppy cackled dramatically, "I want your boring boyfriend…and your fluffy couch too."

Pixie giggled at Poppy's witch impression and then reached over to take her hand. "I've missed you this week, Pops. I was worried about you alone at your apartment."

"Awww shucks, sis, so nice of you to care about little ol' me. I worried about me too after witnessing the idiocy that the entire state's seemed to subscribe to recently. On a serious note though, I missed you too."

"C'mon now, let's figure out what's for dinner before we glue ourselves to the TV."

The sisters worked together seamlessly in the kitchen. Spinning around each other to get to the fridge and the sink, they fell right into the routine they'd perfected when they were younger. Soon the smells of Mexican food roused a groggy Brian from the bedroom. This time he happened to be wearing clothes.

"Hey, that smells really good," Brian greeted them, kissing the top of Pixie's head. He stole a slice of avocado off a plate as he watched them finish up.

Swatting his hand away, Pixie chastised, "Stop sneaking food. I was lucky they had this at the store today. That place was almost bare. You wouldn't believe how crazy people are acting. Shelves were cleared through the entire store." She moved the plate and lined it up with the rest of the fajita mixings Poppy had already arranged.

Poppy set some dishes down on the counter. "C'mon, guys, the news is about to cut to the press conference," she said, motioning for everyone to make up their plates.

The three of them filled plates and shuffled to the living room to eat on the couch.

The President cleared his throat before speaking. "My fellow Americans, we appreciate your patience during this last week. I know many of you have questions and I will do my best to answer them. We have met with the aliens' leaders and have new information for you. They are called Phaeton Warriors. This race is highly advanced and was able to clearly communicate the reason they have come here. First, I want to assure you that they are not here to do us harm. The State Department has deemed them not a threat, and in actuality, we have discussed how they can help our country. They have not only been willing but eager to come up with ideas for our future that will impact not only our generation, but the generations to come. Our scientists and engineers are currently meeting with the Phaeton Council. Their technology is astounding and so advanced we have no doubt that we can solve our current energy crisis as well as implement new medical advancements that may end the spread of AIDS and some cancers. We are negotiating with them now and will continue to do so until we reach an agreement for their assistance in dealing with these issues that are currently costing millions of people their lives every day."

As the president stepped back from the podium, Pixie and Poppy both leaned back in their seats. Poppy glanced over at Pixie.

"They can cure AIDS? And cancer?"

"Pops, that's amazing. Think of it…these aliens could literally save millions of people." Pixie sounded as excited as Poppy felt.

Both girls had some friends and family members who'd been able to overcome cancer but a few of them had succumbed to the disease eating at their bodies. A few years ago their last surviving aunt had passed away after multiple rounds of treatment for breast cancer. Both of the girls had felt the blow as if it were their own mother. Aunt Tilly had been their last link to their parents and had resembled their mother so much they'd felt as though they were losing more than their aunt.

"And don't forget the energy crisis," Brian mumbled around a full mouth. "I wonder if that means we wouldn't need to rely on foreign oil?"

"Hmmmm…" Pixie looked as if she'd wondered that herself. "Hey, he said we were negotiating… What do we have that they need? If they have all this technology, what does Earth have?"

Thinking back to her nutball neighbor, Poppy blurted out, "I can safely say that Florida has an abundant amount of idiots we can send them."

"Well, it doesn't appear like he's going to say anything else tonight. Let's put on a movie. What are you in the mood for?"

"I vote for comedy," Poppy piped up.

Brian shrugged, indicating he couldn't care less what was chosen.

The three of them settled on the couch and relaxed as much as they could. All of them had vetoed anything with aliens or zombies since that hit a little too close to home right now, even if it was done jokingly. Making popcorn and relaxing with Pixie turned out to be exactly what Poppy needed. Since this was a movie they'd seen before, the girls talked throughout, which annoyed Brian.

"Hey, fussypants, why don't you go to bed and get some more sleep? You're really grumpy tonight." Pixie patted Brian on the shoulder.

He shrugged. "Well, since you two won't stop yapping for me to hear, that's probably a good idea." Laughing when Pixie swatted his butt as he stood up, he nodded a good night to Poppy.

After he left, Pixie reached for the remote and turned down the volume. Twisting sideways on the couch, she stared at her sister.

"How was your trip to the store?" Leaning on an elbow, she mimicked Poppy's pose.

"How do you think any trip to hell would be? The torture started in the parking lot and lasted through the checkout line." She smiled and tapped her chin with her fingers. "I did see a couple hotties though."

"Were they stockpiling like everyone else?" Pixie reached down for her soda and took a large gulp, waiting for Poppy to answer.

"I don't think so, they didn't have carts or anything and just seemed to be watching the chaos unfold around the frozen food section." Grinning, she waggled her eyebrows. "I think maybe their tour bus must have stopped there, because they were wearing leather pants and all had long hair. Super. Hot."

Laughing at Poppy's version of an eyebrow wiggle, Pixie set her now empty can back down. "I don't think there are any concerts around here. They were probably just passing through." Pixie stretched back and reached her arms over her head with a groan. "I don't know about you, Pops, but I'm beat. I haven't been sleeping for shit this past week. Is it okay if I hit the sack?"

"Yeah, I think I'll head to bed soon too. I've had trouble sleeping myself. You going in to work tomorrow?"

"Yeah, I have to finish some paperwork, but then I should be able to head out early. 'Night."

Once alone, Poppy wandered over to the living room window and peeked through the blinds. Yep, the aliens were still there. What could they possibly want from Earth?

CHAPTER FOUR

The next morning Poppy woke up after having slept fairly decently. Tossing on a pair of her ever-present yoga pants and a T-shirt, she thought she'd take a walk in the neighborhood. Being cooped up this last week had not agreed with her and she needed fresh air. The first thing she saw outside was a ship floating above. Having watched the news all week long, Poppy knew that the ships had not actually done anything other than hover above the cities. It was time to get back to her normal life. Who knew how long this would last, and Poppy had things to do and people to see. Patting her pocket to make sure she had her phone, she walked down the driveway and started along the sidewalk.

After walking around the subdivision for about thirty minutes, she felt the skin on her arms tingle. Pausing to peer around, she didn't see anyone but felt that maybe she should turn around to head back to the house. As she did so, she caught sight of an idling car at the stop sign. It was what she would normally refer to as an "FBI-mobile". The large black SUV had completely blacked-out windows and after Poppy stared at it for a couple of moments, it moved down the street at a slow crawl.

That was weird.

Poppy checked the mail before going into the house. It was amazing that they had been delivering all week long. *The USPS delivers—rain, shine and even during alien invasions.* Giggling, she pictured that motto on their badges. Tossing the letters onto the counter for Brian and Pixie to go through, she sat on the couch and flipped on the TV. Since every channel seemed to be showing news twenty-four hours a day, she thought she'd watch it for a little bit before giving up and tuning into cable.

Seeing a red banner pop up on TV caused Poppy to reach for the remote and turn the sound up.

"The president has called an emergency press conference, please stay tuned."

Hearing the door lock click, Poppy glanced over to see who it was.

Pixie dropped her bag on the floor and flopped down on the couch next to Poppy.

"What's going on? I heard the emergency broadcast noise in my car and had to turn off the radio before my ears started bleeding."

"I don't know yet. Apparently the president's called an emergency broadcast."

Both women hushed as the president walked onto the screen to take his place at the podium.

"My fellow Americans, negotiations have concluded with the Phaeton Warrior race. After speaking to their council of leaders, we have learned that the Phaeton race has been surviving by using cloning. Unfortunately the science that they have used has resulted in a low female birth rate. For their species to survive, they have been searching on other planets for potential mates.

"The State Department has decided to initiate a 'mate match' for single female volunteers to apply for what we are referring to as the 'Bridal Pact'. In exchange for these volunteers, we will be able to use the Phaetons' medical advancements to save American lives. We will have access to a new fuel source that will all but eliminate our need for oil, both foreign and domestic. And we will also have the protection of their military from other species that may discover Earth.

"This is not a draft. It is completely voluntary. Women who apply will be compensated for filling out an application and signing the contract. We want to assure you that your safety and the safety of your sisters, daughters and friends will be our number-one concern. We are working on a profiling system with national dating sites and the Phaeton Council to make matches, similar to what many of you have used in the past to find companions. As of right now this is only open to women who fall within certain criteria but might be expanded after an initial trial period passes.

"Please keep an open mind and know that the safety of our citizens and country is our top priority. Women wishing to volunteer or obtain more information can contact their local Intake Centers, which will be listed by state following this news conference or found at bridal-pact-dot-state-department-dot-gov. This is an exciting time for our country and its people."

Poppy and Pixie were totally silent for about two seconds after the speech ended. Almost in unison they turned toward each other with their mouths open.

"Holy fuck," Poppy whispered, unable to believe what she'd had heard.

"Yeah. Holy fuck," Pixie couldn't help but repeat after her sister.

"They want women!" Poppy was still having trouble wrapping her mind around it.

They both jumped with a startled scream when the front door opened and Brian ran in.

"Did I miss it?" he panted out between breaths.

"Where the hell have you been?" Pixie asked, holding one hand to her heart as if making sure it was still beating.

"I went for a jog and lost track of time." Bending over to catch his breath, he continued, "The guy down the road yelled at me from his porch that the president was speaking and I needed to get home, so I hauled ass back." Wiping sweat off his face, he waited for the women to say something.

"Well?" he prodded when they were silent.

"They want women," Poppy blurted out.

Brian raised his eyebrows in confusion, sat down next to her and threw an arm over her shoulder. "What?"

Finding the remote that had fallen in between the cushions, Poppy hit the rewind button. After the entire speech had been replayed, they all sat in silence, staring at the TV.

Poppy took the silence as a chance to let the possibilities run through her head.

So many diseases could be eradicated. The US wouldn't have to fight for oil anymore. Alternative energy sources to stop climate change. So many possibilities…and they wanted women in return.

Poppy was brought out of her thinking when Pixie nudged her shoulder.

"Hey, did you hear me?"

Shaking her head at her sister, she waited for Pixie to repeat herself.

"I asked, do you think they've been taking women all along and those tinfoil crazies were telling the truth?"

"It sounds as if they are searching for ways to reproduce. I can't see that abducting a sixty-year-old lady would work and guessing her age at sixty is me being kind. How many women do you think are going to apply?" Pixie wondered.

"Who in their right mind would apply?" Brian laughed out loud at the thought.

"Brian, did you not hear what he said? They have the ability to cure cancer. New energy sources that we could use. The possibilities are endless."

"They're going to get a bunch of crazy people applying and that's all."

When Poppy made a face at him, he teased her, "What, Poppy, are you going to apply for the Bridal Pact?"

"Well, why wouldn't I?"

When Pixie choked on the drink she'd been taking from her water bottle, Poppy patted her on the back and kept talking directly to Brian.

"I could apply if I wanted to. In fact, it doesn't sound like a bad idea the more I think about it."

"Now, hold on right there. Everyone needs to calm down. Poppy, you're not applying. Brian, shut up and stop egging her on." Pixie stood up from between them on the couch and moved toward the kitchen.

Poppy started thinking out loud. "I have a shitty job. I have an even shittier apartment. My car has over two hundred thousand miles on it. My savings account consists of five hundred dollars minus whatever I spent the other day at Mega Mart. I haven't had a boyfriend, or even a date for that matter, in the last six months. What's stopping me?"

Poppy blinked at how fast her sister was able to move to stand in front of her.

"Pops, are you serious? You'd apply to marry one of them?"

Pixie's anxious face had Poppy automatically wanting to reassure her she was just joking. Instead she decided to answer her truthfully. "I don't know. Maybe."

Pixie lowered herself to sit on the coffee table in front of Poppy. After they'd been eyeballing each other for a moment, Pixie broke the deadlock. She grinned at Poppy and waggled her eyebrows. "What if they have two dicks?

Seeing that her sister was trying to distract her with humor, she went with it and smiled back. "The more the merrier?"

Both women erupted in laughter as Brian stood and threw his hands in the air. "You two are crazy. I'm going to take a shower. Figure out what you want for lunch so we can eat once I'm cleaned up."

Pixie moved from the coffee table to the couch beside Poppy. "You won't really apply, will you?"

Poppy shook her head. "I was just thinking out loud, Pix. But you have to admit, what they can do is amazing."

"Yeah, it is."

Watching the news broadcast for a while longer, the women talked about ideas for lunch before settling on going out for Chinese food.

Once Brian was ready to head out, they all piled into Pixie's SUV. The Chinese place Brian preferred was close by and only took about ten minutes to get to.

Getting a table was fairly easy even though the place was crowded. A quick five-minute wait and they were sitting down with menus while groups of people were talking loudly around them. Every once in a while, Poppy would hear "aliens" or "bride" pop up but she didn't want to eavesdrop too much.

Brian dominated the conversation over lunch, talking about his work as if he were a heart surgeon saving lives. That was one thing

Poppy had never liked about him. Everything he did was crucial. Every meeting he took was with important people. Blah blah blah. It was all too much for Poppy to take sometimes.

Pixie was quiet through almost the entire meal, and Poppy knew she herself was the reason. She hadn't meant to worry her big sister when she'd mentioned applying for the Bridal Pact. Poppy wasn't even sure what these guys looked like, for goodness' sake. They could be two feet tall with green skin and bulging heads.

Trying to come back to the present, Poppy listened to Brian drone on and on about work. She'd have to go back to her apartment soon. There was only so much of him she could take. Unlike Pixie, she had a limit on how long she could listen to him and not think he was a total douche. Throughout lunch, she tried to participate in the conversation, or at least Pixie's portion of it, but for some reason, she couldn't get the thought of the Bridal Pact out of her head.

CHAPTER FIVE

Poppy ended up moving back to her apartment after staying with her sister another week. It was either go home or smother Brian in his sleep. She figured that might piss off her sister for some reason. Getting back into a routine seemed to be what everyone else in the world was doing. In the two weeks that had passed since the last presidential press conference, people were once again going to work, mowing their lawns and pretty much ignoring the spaceships.

Major cities had opened Intake Centers in previously vacant office buildings to gather applications for the Bridal Pact. The first time Poppy had seen a government commercial asking women to apply, she'd been shocked. It played out like a political campaign ad, pointing out all the reasons to apply. It seemed to be working though since the news had shown a few ladies being interviewed on their way into the Intake Centers.

The only thing that Poppy wasn't able to get back into the routine of was work. She'd been fired shortly after the office reopened. Apparently being late too often had pissed off the higher-ups and while they'd been closed with all the alien hubbub they'd reorganized the office to eliminate her position.

Searching the classifieds didn't give her much hope either. Poppy was told she was overqualified for most positions or needed a better degree for others. Damn history major. It was getting her nowhere fast. Deciding to call Pixie and see if she wanted to get together for dinner seemed like the way to cheer herself up.

"Hey, Pix, wanna come over and veg? Maybe order a pizza?" Poppy hoped Pixie said yes since she hadn't seen her sister since moving back to her place. Apparently Bonehead Brenda couldn't do anything right and Pixie had ended up working late nights fixing problems that she'd created.

"Sure. It actually figures that my one night off Brian ends up working late. Do I need to stop for a movie?" Pixie asked, sounding as if she were shuffling papers around.

"Nah, I have the newest Simon Pegg one already. Pizza okay or would you rather order something else?"

"Pizza sounds good. I can be there in…thirty minutes?"

"Great, bish. Drive carefully." Hanging up the phone, she flipped on the news to see another presidential speech was going to be televised in an hour. Poppy wondered what bomb the man would drop on the American public this time.

Studying her feet propped up on the small table, Poppy decided to paint her toenails while waiting for her sister and listening to the news. A few minutes later, while blowing on her now hot-pink toenails, she glanced up to see her doorknob jiggle. Hopefully that was her sister and not Gas-Can-Man, which was what she now called her crazy neighbor. When the door opened to show her frazzled-looking sister, she stopped blowing and smiled at Pixie.

"You seem stressed. You okay?" Poppy waddled with her toes up to the door to give Pixie a hug.

"Yeah, just tired. Work has sucked balls. Big, big, big balls." Pixie pulled a hard cider out of the fridge, cracked it open and took a huge gulp.

"Nice of you to complain about your job while I don't have one," Poppy teased. Humor generally helped knock Pixie out of a funk.

"You know I could get you a job, right? Just let me know and I can get some hostess hours for you," Pixie offered in between gulps of her now almost empty drink.

"Yeah…no. Can you imagine us working together? We would definitely move from bish to bitch pretty quickly. Plus, I'm pretty sure with my tendency to say 'fuck', you'd have to fire me the first day." Shuddering at the thought of having her sister as her boss, Poppy shuffled past her to get a bottle for herself.

"You have a point. But maybe I can help you check around. I have some connections with our vendors. Maybe one of them is hiring."

Both women headed into the living room to collapse onto the tiny loveseat.

Pixie tipped her bottle at the TV. "What are we watching?"

"Oh, there's supposed to be another presidential address in a little bit. I wanted to watch it before we started the movie. Tell me what happened today at work, I need the comic relief after my bust with the classifieds."

Pixie soon had Poppy laughing with what she now referred to as Brenda's Blunders. "Pixie, why don't you fire her already?" Poppy felt it was a fair question considering Pixie had obviously given the woman multiple chances.

"I'm thinking I may have to." Making a face that showed this was going to be an issue, Pixie huffed. "She's making more work for me and messing up orders left and right. I just feel bad. She was my friend before I hired her but now I can't stand to see her after-hours and she seems to be honestly trying. When I have her do things in front of me, she follows instructions perfectly. It's when I leave that mayhem ensues."

Poppy and Pixie both grew quiet as the news flashed to the presidential news conference. The president was now not alone at the podium; four men stood to his side. Almost spitting out her cider all over her coffee table, Poppy sat up straight and pointed at the TV.

"Oh my god!" she yelled, making Pixie jump beside her.

"What the fuck, Pops? You scared the shit out of me."

"It's them!" Poppy was stunned at what she was seeing. Unable to believe her eyes, she stared harder at the TV.

"It's who?" Pixie yelled in frustration.

"It's the Mega Mart rock stars!" Poppy now stood to get closer to the TV.

"What the fuck are you babbling about?" Pixie was blotting at the cider she'd spilled on her shirt when Poppy had startled her.

"Oh my god. Remember the hot guys I saw at Mega Mart? I told you about them watching everyone, and, and about their leather pants. I swear to god, it's them!" Frantically pointing again at the men standing next to the president, she hopped up and down. Being able to see them clearly now, she realized how fucking hot they were. They were much taller than the president, who happened to be a little over six feet himself, and they were buff. All four men were broad in the shoulders but seemed lean everywhere else.

"Wow. They *are* hot," Pixie said, eyeballing each of the men and fanning her face.

Hell yeah they were smokin'. These men were the entire package. Strong jaws, great hair, and boy, did they fill out leather pants well.

"Shhhhhhh, he's talking."

"Good afternoon, everyone. I am happy to introduce you to some members of the Phaeton Council. Many of you have questions regarding their species and they are here to answer those inquiries." Stepping back from the microphone, he gestured toward the man closest to him.

"Holy. Fucking. Shit." Poppy was having trouble breathing.

These were the aliens. And she had seen them. In person. And they were *hot*. Not just a little hot, but *really hot*.

While her brain was trying to play catch-up, Poppy sat stunned at what was in front of her. Not able to make a sound, both women were glued to the TV. As the camera panned to the man closest to the president, Poppy almost drooled over the gorgeousness filling the screen. When he started talking in a deep voice, she felt like melting into a puddle on her couch.

The Phaetons who were representing their race took turns answering questions that had obviously been pre-screened for the conference. Poppy threw all thoughts of little green men right out of her head. If this was what the aliens looked like, what the hell was she waiting for?

When the conference ended, Poppy and Pixie still both sat stunned.

Finally clearing her throat to move the frog that seemed to have appeared there, Poppy could only say one thing. "Wow."

Pixie nodded enthusiastically. "Exactly. Wow."

"They are gorgeous...and not...alien-y." Poppy was still trying to connect the dots as to why they'd been at Mega Mart. When people had been told the aliens were here to "observe", she had assumed they were watching from their ships. It hadn't even crossed her mind they would have been walking around among humans. Of course, at that time, she had imagined they wouldn't appear "normal". Aliens were supposed to be green, dammit! Not smokin' hot guys tempting Poppy into doing something she knew Pixie would think crazy.

Seeing the expression on Pixie's face that always came right before a lecture, Poppy quickly popped in the movie to take her sister's mind off the aliens. Since the DVD was one Poppy had seen before, she knew she'd be able to at least pretend she was watching it while her mind whirled with the possibilities of a sexy alien man in leather pants.

That evening, after Pixie had left and Poppy had locked up her apartment, she did something that had her hands shaking. Poppy logged on to the State Department website to view the application for the Bridal Pact. There had obviously been quite a few visitors to the site. The system crashed twice due to high traffic issues before she was even able to click on the link. Not wanting to take a chance of having to start all over, she quickly hit the Print button on her laptop.

She reasoned, "It's not like I'm going to fill it out. I'm just curious about the questions."

After scanning the paperwork she now held in her hands, Poppy admitted some of the questions were pretty invasive. Setting the stack on her nightstand, she tried to get some sleep. After an hour had passed with Poppy tossing and turning, she finally turned to the packet of papers that was keeping her awake. She picked up the application and walked to the kitchen table.

"For fuck's sake, this is going to drive me batty."

She reached for the cup of pens she kept on the table. Clicking a pen several times, she took a deep breath and read the first page.

Bridal Match Questionnaire

Please complete the following thirty pages. Any questions that you are unable to answer please mark as "unknown". Please answer all questions listed. Potential matches are based on your answers, so honesty is extremely important. Upon completion, please return this form and all signed documents to the nearest Intake Center and you will then be assigned a human liaison for the rest of the application process. Please be aware that if your last physical examination took place over thirty days ago, you will need to have a new exam, including a Pap smear and blood tests, prior to being assigned a liaison.

Name: Poppy Williams
DOB: September 20, 1987
Blood type: Unknown
Weight: 180 pounds
Height: Five foot three
Living relatives: Pixie Williams (sister)
Parents: Deceased
Children: None
Medical conditions: None known
School history: HS diploma and college BS
Own or rent your home: Rent
Allergies: Seasonal and cats
Medications: Birth control, vitamins, and OTC allergy medication
Number of previous sexual partners: Two
Date of last sexual encounter: Six months ago
Last medical exam: Six months ago

After filling out the first portion, Poppy rolled her shoulders and dropped her head back. "Pixie is going to fucking kill me."

CHAPTER SIX

Poppy awoke the next morning thankful that she didn't have a day job to go in to, considering she'd slept like ass. Cracking her neck to loosen the knotted muscles, she looked at the papers next to her bed. After she'd tried to fall asleep for the second time, she'd given up and reached for her vibrator. Her "pocket rocket" had been her best friend lately and the only outlet for sexual release she'd had in six months. Picturing the warrior from the press conference, Poppy had no problem going off like a rocket alone in her bed. In fact, she could have gone another round if she hadn't been so damn tired.

After tucking her little friend away in the nightstand, she'd stared at the papers resting on the tabletop until she'd fallen asleep. Poppy's dreams had been riddled with thoughts of aliens and the man she'd seen yesterday.

Deciding she'd stretched enough, Poppy crawled out of bed and glanced around her room. Her apartment was small and plain and that included the bedroom where she stood. Her furniture had seen better days and was the stuff college kids bought until they got "real jobs". Poppy's problem was that she'd never gotten a real job. Particleboard was the material of choice at her place.

Kicking a T-shirt on the floor out of her way, Poppy mused out loud, "I'm really going to do this."

She decided she might as well get it over with and dialed Pixie.

"Hello?" Shuffling papers accompanied Pixie's greeting.

"Hey, Pix. Do you think you can come over tonight?"

"I should be able to. What's wrong?" "Big Sister" mode seemed to be second nature to Pixie.

"I need your help filling out an application." Hoping Pixie would assume Poppy had found something in the classifieds, she left it at that.

"Sure. Want me to bring dinner? I can order whatever the special is from the restaurant and head over straight from work."

"Sounds good. Text me when you're on your way." Hanging up quickly before Pixie could ask any questions, Poppy decided to get showered. Then she planned on getting as much of the application filled out as she could before her sister came over later.

By six o'clock that night, Poppy was on pins and needles. Pixie had messaged saying she was on her way and Poppy set out the paperwork on the kitchen table. A majority of it had been easy to do herself. She had come across some problems when needing to answer family medical history though, which was where Pixie would come in handy.

Poppy's phone buzzed, signaling a text message had arrived. *"I parked. Need you to open door. Hands full."*

She smiled, knowing Pixie had probably ordered them a feast. When her stomach growled, Poppy realized she'd been so keyed up all day she'd forgotten to eat a meal and just snacked on a granola bar and some fruit. No wonder she was so hungry.

Opening the door to see Pixie making her way up the stairs, she yelled out, "Faster, bish! I'm starving here!" Laughing when her sister tried to give her the finger while holding food bags, Poppy opened the door wider to let her sister pass.

"God that smells good. What did you bring me?"

"I got a couple orders of lasagna and some salads...along with tiramisu."

"Do you have anything to drink?" Pixie asked as Poppy opened the takeout containers and dished up their food.

"I should still have some cider in the fridge. Get us each a bottle." Poppy put their plates on the small bistro table that they ate at and moved the paperwork sitting on the table closer to her plate.

Pixie sat down in the other chair and the women dug in to their food as if they hadn't eaten in years. Between mouthfuls of cheese and sauce, Poppy mumbled, "Your restaurant has the best food ever."

"I know. I've gotten a little sick of it though. I try to only eat there once a week now. Plus, my ass was getting mad at me every time I ate there. I think I've gained twenty pounds since I started that job."

Poppy rolled her eyes at Pixie. "You weigh less than I do, and your ass is fine."

Watching Pixie fiddle with her fork, Poppy had a feeling that something was wrong.

"What's up, sis?"

"I don't know. It seems that since I gained a little bit of weight…" Pixie stopped when tears filled her eyes.

"What?" Reaching across the tiny table, Poppy gripped her sister's hand.

"Brian doesn't seem too frisky lately, that's all." Rubbing her nose, which was now running, Pixie looked everywhere but at Poppy. "And he's been working all the time. Do you think he's avoiding me?"

Poppy squeezed the hand she was holding and smiled at her sister. "Don't be an idiot. Brian loves you and I'm sure he's just been really busy at work lately." Shrugging, she went on, "If it really bothers you, though, you need to talk to him about it."

"You're right." Gathering up their empty plates, Pixie gave Poppy an affectionate shoulder bump as she walked by. "Where's the application you needed help with?"

Poppy took the last gulp of cider from her bottle and decided now was the time to pretend she had balls. Big balls.

"Well…first I want to let you know that I've thought about this a lot," Poppy started.

Pixie stopped what she was doing and turned her attention to Poppy. Eyebrow raised in question, Pixie waited.

"And I've decided to apply for the Bridal Pact." The words rushed out of Poppy's mouth so fast they slurred together.

"I can't believe you're actually going to do this!" Pixie yelled.

"Okay, Pix, calm down. I've thought this over for a while, and it makes sense." Holding up her fingers to tick off her points, Poppy began her prepared speech. "I have no job. I have a shitty apartment.

You are my *only* family. And I haven't had a successful date for a while now. I'm lonely. You have Brian and I have nobody. I'm starting to feel like the third wheel every time we go out somewhere. It's uncomfortable and depressing." Stopping to take a breath, she then said in a softer voice, "Something's got to give, Pix. I'm a step away from going to the doctor and getting something to make me feel better about just being me… That's not good."

Both sisters sat staring at each other, each one hoping that the other would give way first and blink. Pixie must have read the determination on Poppy's face, because her face softened and she nodded once in understanding.

"You're right, Pops. I just worry. If anyone has thought this through to the point of obsession, it would be you. Tell me everything and don't leave even one tiny detail out. I have to know what's going to happen if you get selected and how to find you if I start to wig out." Pixie took a huge sip of another hard cider she'd snagged from Poppy's almost bare refrigerator. "And by the way, I am going to need something *sooooo* much stronger if I'm going to be able to process this. Do you have the stuff to make 'ritas?"

"I think I'm out of the mix, but I might have straight tequila somewhere in the cabinet. We should probably try to stay sober though if you're going to help me out with this packet," Poppy pointed out, waving it in the air before setting it down.

Getting herself another cider from the fridge and grunting over the stubborn cap for a second gave Poppy the time she needed to compose herself enough to figure out where to start. She picked up the Galactic Bride Welcome Packet off the coffee table again.

"Okay, it says here women are compensated based on how much of the actual process they complete." Poppy had to admit that the money was a nice touch. With the resources they'd been spending on trying to secure other energy sources now freed up, the government was able to pay debts and more importantly pay brides to apply.

"I get ten thousand dollars for completing the application and signing the contract and that's even if I don't get selected! Do you know how many bills that can pay off?" Poppy pulled out some papers from her welcome packet. "See here. It says if I fill out all questions, provide a doctor's report and sign the contract, then the first portion of the stipend is mine as long as everything is verified."

She sorted another paper from the stack and found the FAQ sheet the Intake Center had included in the packet. "This says that the aliens have implants to be able to speak English as well as other languages and I'll have the option to get one as well in case I want to understand their language. Well, I guess that beats the hell out of me flunking out of Spanish, like in high school." There seemed to be so much information to go over in this packet that her head was starting to spin a little.

"I really need your help with the medical part. It asks some stuff about family medical history on the second page that I wasn't sure of."

"What kinds of questions are these?" Pixie asked, skimming the first part of the packet.

"You know, the normal…age, weight, height, sexual experience…" The last couple words were mumbled into her bottle of cider and of course that was the part Pixie decided to latch on to.

"Did you just say 'sexual experience'?"

"Pixie, c'mon now, you know the whole reason they're needing brides is to procreate. You can't be surprised that it's a question on here. It really does make sense. Plus those aren't the questions I need help with. I'm pretty sure I can recall all of my dismal sexual experience on my own. The harder questions are the ones I got stumped on. Do you know if Mom or Dad had any medical problems before they died?" Poppy asked in a calm voice.

"No, they were healthy as horses. I'm not sure about our grandparents though. So what else other than medical crap do you need help with? This bundle seems huge. There has to be at least fifty pages of questions here. Why didn't you just fill this out online?"

"Because my crappy laptop decides to shut down every thirty minutes no matter how much charge it has and after that press conference with the hotties on it yesterday, their website keeps crashing. I actually prefer paper though anyway. It's easier for me to flip back and forth. It is a lot to digest, but they probably have a bunch of questions to weed out the crazies and make sure the matches are as good as they can be. The more questions there are, the more I actually feel like this might work."

By this time, Pixie had moved on to the last cider in the fridge.

"Let's open up that tiramisu you brought," Poppy suggested.

Pixie nodded. She'd chilled out a little between the last cider and this one, and Poppy was sure she was going to ask for a smoke break on the deck when she realized Poppy wasn't going to change her mind. Pixie and Poppy were both emotional smokers. When the shit hit the fan, the cigarettes came out.

Poppy decided they could eat their dessert straight from the to-go containers. She headed back to the living room to see Pixie gathering her stuff up.

"Sorry, Pops, stupid payroll problem at the office and of course it has to be cleared up tonight before it can go for auto deposits tomorrow. I can be back in an hour or two depending on how much my assistant has fucked it up." Blowing air kisses as she walked, she was already reaching for her phone again, most likely to yell at whoever'd messed up the payroll.

Poppy ended up filling out the rest of the forms on her own that evening. She admitted that her sister had not been necessary for her to do it. Poppy had really just used that excuse as a way to break the news of applying to Pixie. Her plan that her sister would be more supportive if she'd felt as if she were involved in the process must have worked, because Poppy had expected a much bigger protest from Pixie.

Poppy cleaned up the rest of the kitchen and got ready for bed. She set the completed packet down on her nightstand and smiled. Hopefully, having finished it would give her a chance to relax. She gazed up at the ceiling as she lay down, her belly fluttering at the thought of the future and having her own handsome warrior to keep her company at night. Letting out a sigh, she reached for her bedside drawer. As she picked up the vibrator from inside it, she admitted, "I know who I'm going to be thinking of tonight."

CHAPTER SEVEN

Driving up to the Intake Center in her ancient Honda, Poppy noticed the building was flooded with protesters outside its front gates. After parking, she jogged up the steps, hoping this would be a quick trip in and out with no lines. For one thing, the grocery store was calling her name since she wasn't in the mood for leftovers and all her hard cider was gone.

The armed guards waiting by the door made her pause in her steps. All of a sudden the building seemed much more daunting.

"Do you have an appointment, miss?" one of the guards asked.

Her yoga pants and *Star Wars* T-shirt didn't make her seem as if she were there on business. Pixie would have been totally right about the jeans and nice top today. She hated it when Pixie was right.

"Ummmm…yes I do. I mean, no I don't, but I'm just dropping off my packet to the office," she stuttered, taking in his military dress and intimidating gun.

"We will need you to walk through the security zone and also see your ID for the sign-in sheet." He opened the door and steered her to the area indicated. Her apprehension at all the security she was seeing made Poppy rethink her decision.

"Miss? Miss? You need to keep moving through security." The loud voice was coming from one of the desks located in the security area.

Poppy walked to the counter just past the entrance and smiled weakly at the guard sitting there.

"Good afternoon. I'll need your ID and also a signature. Are you just turning in your packet?" He nodded toward the folder Poppy was clutching to her chest.

"Yes, sir, I am. What's all this security for? Did something happen?" She could feel she was being filmed and glanced up to see cameras on the ceiling about every ten feet.

"Unfortunately, we received a bomb threat last night. The State Department has decided that we need to up our security so they sent in the National Guard until private security measures are implemented. The protesters showed up last night right before the bomb threat so my money's on them being the ones behind it, but better safe than sorry. I'll also need to check your purse and take your cell phone while you're inside."

After walking her through a set of metal detectors, he handed Poppy her bag and ID and pointed to the elevator she needed to take to turn in her papers. Nodding at her to continue moving on, he turned to the next woman coming in behind Poppy.

She hurried to the elevator. Once on the third floor she found the correct door and walked inside. An older woman was sitting at the desk facing the door, sorting papers. She smiled warmly as Poppy walked up to her.

"Welcome to the Intake Center, miss. My name is Suzie. Is that your application to turn in?"

"Yes, ma'am. I finished it last night. I still haven't had a chance to get my physical yet but I wanted to get the ball rolling."

"Poppy? Is that your legal name or a nickname?" Suzie peered up over her glasses with another smile.

"Legal name, ma'am. My parents weren't exactly traditional with naming their daughters. My sister's name is Pixie. I think they may have been closet hippies." She smiled at Suzie and noticed that all the other folders on her desk were also applicant packets. "Can I ask how many applicants you have so far? What are the chances of being selected?"

"Well, so far we have about thirty at this center. There would be more but the protesters have scared some women off and then our computer system was hacked and some applications deleted. So it's actually a good thing you filled out a paper application, otherwise you would be needing to go over all this again."

Poppy smiled again and said, "You know, if I don't get selected, maybe I could apply for a job here? It seems like you could use some help with this stuff and I have office experience."

Suzie leaned across the desk and patted her hand. "Well, aren't you just a sweetie! It actually isn't too bad. I just scan all this in and don't actually have to read or retype any answers into the program. It's pretty simple but it does set me back a bit when somebody fudges with my computer." She started flipping through the packet and noticed the dates of Poppy's last medical exams. "Do you have appointments set up for these or would you like to use our physicians on the sixth floor while you are here today? We can bill your insurance."

"I didn't know there was a medical center here. I thought the whole building was just an Intake Office."

Suzie walked around the desk and reached for a pamphlet in a clear holder on the wall. "Here, sweetie. We have doctors available that take most insurances so our applicants don't have to wait for appointments to become available at their family doctors. The doctors here are all certified and working through contracts with the State Department. Would you like for me to see if one is available?"

"Sure, I'd just planned on grocery shopping so I can even wait a bit if they can't fit me in immediately. I haven't even called my doctor yet to see when the soonest he could get me in was so this would help me out." Poppy searched for her cell to text her sister before remembering it was at the security office. "Can I borrow your phone? I need to call my sister and let her know I may not be out of here when I said I would."

Suzie smiled and said yes while marking down a room number on a card. "Just hit which line you want to dial out on and go from there. They have an opening in about thirty minutes so your wait won't be long."

After calling her sister and leaving a voice mail, Poppy took the elevator to the medical offices and proceeded to wait for her appointment. Heck, even if she didn't get selected for the program, at least she'd be able to get her physical out of the way early this year.

One Pap smear, physical exam and blood draw later, Poppy was heading back to Suzie's desk. Amazingly enough, the medical reports had already been sent down to Suzie by the time the elevator brought Poppy back to her office.

"Okay, sweetie, I just have to notarize these items and you will be assigned your liaison. Any questions that you have they can answer. They will have a packet of information for you to go over regarding the different Warrior breeds you may be matched with. This is information that the Phaeton Warrior Council has put together so you could learn something of their culture and be somewhat prepared for your match."

Suzie had been skimming through Poppy's paperwork and stamping and signing away when she paused for a moment. She looked up with a smile. "And, sweetie?"

"Yes?" Poppy asked, trying to get over the feeling that things were moving way faster than anticipated.

"Good luck!" Suzie followed her words with a wink.

The top piece of paper Suzie passed her was a welcome form with Poppy's liaison's name.

Valerie Bennett. *Well*, Poppy thought, *Valerie had better be prepared to answer a shitload of questions.*

* * * * *

Valerie actually ended up being a woman close to Poppy's own age. She had brown hair with red highlights Poppy was sure had never seen a frizzy day. Wearing a tailored white button-up top with a pencil skirt, she appeared professional yet sexy. Poppy studied the outfit in admiration, knowing that if she didn't get selected for the Bridal Pact, she would want to invest in an outfit like hers for job interviews. After introducing herself with a firm handshake and a warm smile, Valerie led Poppy to an office down the hall, her heels clicking as she set a quick pace.

"So, I'm sure you have many questions and by the expression on your face you're overwhelmed. Maybe we should do this over coffee," Valerie quipped with a grin.

"Dear god yes. I didn't plan on doing anything but turning in my paperwork today. All of a sudden I have my doc's appointments out of the way and I've been here almost three hours."

Poppy flopped into the chair on the other side of a large mahogany desk. Accepting a cup of coffee from the personal coffeemaker Valerie had on the table behind her desk, she took a sip and tried to relax.

"Okay, Poppy, you have the hard part done already. Suzie is actually scanning your questionnaire now. Once it's uploaded, the system will start to sort your answers and match them with a potential husband. Suzie noted that you were interested in your odds of being selected. Well there are only about one thousand applicants in the US and we have about ten thousand profiles from the Warrior Council submitted so far." Valerie said this so matter-of-factly Poppy didn't immediately digest what was said.

Then it hit her. *Ten thousand* warriors.

"Did you say ten thousand?" Poppy's gulp was extremely loud in the quiet office.

Valerie smiled and held out some papers. "Yes, we have ten thousand so far and are actually expecting about three times that amount when we've finished with their profile intake. Apparently they used a lottery system to figure out who would be the first warriors to apply for brides. They didn't want to overload the system from the get-go so they're going in groupings of ten thousand. When the first group is matched, we'll move to the next lottery group and go from there. Our hopes are to have enough volunteers to accommodate their large number of profiles. We've been open for a while and the small amount of volunteers is discouraging but we hope once we have our first successful matches, others will follow."

Poppy realized she was still holding the papers she had taken from the liaison and began to go over them. *Warrior Breeds* was printed at the top. "Suzie mentioned there were different types of warriors but I didn't really let that sink in… What does that mean exactly?"

"Well, simply put, their society is made up of different classes of warriors. There are the scientists, diplomats and military breeds, from what we gather. The scientist breeds make up their doctors and engineering warriors, then the diplomats are usually all political figures, and well the military breeds...that's pretty self-explanatory." Valerie started pulling up pictures on her computer and tilted the screen toward Poppy.

"Military breeds are the larger of the race, normally at least seven feet tall and bulky. Among their society they're called *Skrammon*. They still fight physically in battle so they're built for it in height and bulk. Most of the profiles I've seen show they have tattoos around their temples and dreadlocks."

The computer screen showed a darkly tanned man who seemed attractive even though he was different from anyone Poppy had seen before.

"The *Healson* are the diplomats of the group. Most of them are political figures and are known for being keen negotiators when it comes to arguments. They're the ones who developed the lottery idea when it came time to figure out who would get the first shot at matches."

The screen now showed a slightly smaller, lean warrior with shorter hair and no tattoos on the temples. The alien's height was still listed as six foot ten, so height must be something they all shared across the board.

"The *Brakken* warriors are the science guys. They make up the majority of the doctors, engineers and teachers of the race. They are extremely smart but also strong. We've been told they're always tinkering with things and can fix almost anything."

Tall, dark and handsome popped up on the screen. This warrior's skin was slightly darker than that of the previous two, more of a cinnamon tone versus what Poppy would have called an African-American skin tone. He had similar tattoos on his temple, but they seemed to be higher on his forehead than the previous Skrammon breed and this warrior was smiling in his photo.

"Will I get to choose a preference when it comes to my match? From what I've heard so far, I'm not sure how well I would mesh with a politician or a warrior." Poppy was trying to absorb as much as she could but felt a panic attack coming on. Considering she'd expected to be shopping the freezer section at the local grocery store right about now but instead had her profile whizzing through the government database made her feel nauseous all of a sudden.

"I'm so sorry, I spaced out. Can you repeat everything you just said?" Poppy smiled weakly as she tried again to relax. "I honestly didn't expect this to happen so quickly. I had just planned on turning in the packet today…not actually completing the whole process in a couple of hours, and now I'm a step away from instant alien husband."

Valerie smiled and tilted the computer screen back around. "Take a couple deep breaths. I'm sure you feel like you want something stronger than coffee but this is all I have right now. My job is to make sure you are comfortable and informed throughout this whole process. I hope we can be friends through this. You are my sole concern right now. Liaisons are assigned only one applicant until the process is completed so all my focus is on you. That includes knowing when you need a breather or even a drink.

"Are you ready to continue?"

At Poppy's small nod, Valerie started again. "Let's go over the contract portion of the bridal packet. Most people have those questions first so we can knock those out of the way early and I'm sure it'll make you feel better." Valerie walked around her desk and took the chair beside Poppy.

"Once a match is made, we will notify you within twenty-four hours. At that time, you will need to start getting prepared for a meet-and-greet. At the meet-and-greet, you'll meet your warrior and at that point a thirty-day clock will start. The thirty days is essentially a trial period where you will go and actually stay with your match on the aliens' spaceship. You are not required to have any type of intimate contact during the trial period."

Valerie paused for a moment as if she were trying to find a way to say something she didn't really want to say.

"We encourage you to find out if you are 'compatible' but the government is not putting pressure on you or any of the other

volunteers to do anything you're not comfortable with. If you want
to explore …physical attraction then that is between you and your
match. There is a small US military presence on the squadron ships
and you are not only encouraged but expected to report to the US
representatives there if you're feeling physically threatened, even if
this is coming from your match."

"So no sex unless it's consensual. Got it." Poppy knew the next
words out of her mouth were going to cause her to turn bright red.
"Do they know how to…you know?"

Valerie smiled and said very matter-of-factly, "We've been told
they've been monitoring Earth for quite some time and that includes
watching cable broadcasts to try to assimilate. I'm sure if they've seen
some of the shows on the cable channels I watch then they have an
idea even if they haven't actually practiced before. You do need to
know that physical contact like hugging or common friendly gestures
are generally not done there. Being an all-male race means that they
generally have physical combat training, but holding hands and
hugging aren't something many of them have ever done or actually
seen unless it's been on TV."

Poppy let out a long breath and wondered again, *What am I getting
myself into?*

"You are clearly overwhelmed. Do you want to keep going, or
make an appointment after you take a couple days to breathe? If you
have any questions I will answer them or find answers for you. I also
want you to let me know before you sign the contract if you have any
doubts regarding the process. Do you want me to keep going or
break for the day?"

"Honestly? Yeah, I probably need a break, but my sister is going to
grill me later and if I don't have some good answers, she may kill me.
Let's keep going. Can you explain what happens after the thirty
days?" If she was going to do this then she was going to pull up her
big-girl panties and go for broke.

Valerie continued, "After thirty days, if both parties are satisfied
with the match, then you will enter into a spousal contract, which is
essentially their version of marriage. At that point, they will want
physical relations to begin. Getting pregnant is essentially the brass

ring in this program. I need to let you know they don't really have divorce on their planet but we have had them add it into the spousal contract. However if you do get pregnant then you're expected to give up your parental rights and leave the child with them if you wish to return to Earth. They were adamant they don't trust us to care for or protect their young if one is born. It is very important you make sure this is the path you want to take, considering this will potentially involve your future children."

Poppy could feel the tension in the small room. She understood Valerie was trying to stress the weight of her decision and was grateful she wasn't getting anything sugar-coated.

Valerie took the pause as a time to gather a couple papers from the desk in front of them. Handing Poppy something that resembled a deposit slip, she continued.

"Also, your first portion of the stipend will be deposited later today and the second part when you're selected. After the thirty-day trial period, if you marry, you will receive half a million dollars. You can do anything with that money. Pay off bills, gift it or even invest it. However, we wanted to warn you there's a limited number of personal possessions you can take with you once you leave. Space on the crafts is limited and apparently it's easier to buy new items when you arrive than transport them across space to their home planet. You will be expected to live there with your spouse. We're working out a clause that may allow volunteers to come back if they have a death in the family but so far the warriors are not very happy about that. Their goal is to protect you and whatever child or future children you might carry. Let's just say that the recent bomb threats have made them very antsy regarding our security."

"Wait. Did you say half a million dollars?"

"Yes, the government feels that's a reasonable compensation for your sacrifice. We also have paperwork showing that if you do come back to Earth, the money will be tax-exempt. We do ask that you keep that number to yourself. We want women to volunteer and make an honest go of this. If it gets out that we're offering such a large sum, we could have the wrong type of people apply. I will need you to sign a nondisclosure agreement before you leave."

Poppy took a sip of her now-cold coffee and thought for a minute. That actually did make sense. Hell, if she'd known she'd be getting that much money, she would have been much more eager to apply. She also knew some of her friends would dump their so-so boyfriends and apply as well.

"So what would I do with all my stuff?" she asked.

"I would actually be in charge of getting it into a storage facility for you for your trial period. At the end of the thirty days you can decide if you want to sell it, pick through it, or we can auction it off for you and deposit the money collected." Valerie handed Poppy more paperwork and pointed out a spot to sign. "If you want me to take care of everything then sign here. Otherwise we'll assume that you'll have family or friends take care of your possessions. You don't have to decide what to do with your possessions right now but this just authorizes me to set up a storage container and movers after you pack your initial bags you want to take."

Poppy signed the marked spot, knowing that Pixie was too busy to worry about packing and storing her belongings. Poppy didn't have much in the one-bedroom apartment and she figured if she did get past the thirty days, a majority of it would be donated to a shelter since it was all cheap stuff.

"I do actually have a question…what did you do before you became a liaison?" Poppy asked.

"Oh, I was a social worker before I applied here." Valerie's smile tilted to one side. "Honestly, I had a hard time with the social services aspect."

When Poppy cast her a questioning look, she added, "I couldn't handle seeing the tough stuff, you know? I loved being able to help kids but in the end, the state had the final say even if it was something I didn't agree with. That part is hard and I wasn't prepared for it, even though I thought I was. I had actually been planning to go back to school, maybe getting my law degree, when I saw an ad for a liaison position. So…here I am."

Smiling with understanding, Poppy handed Valerie back the paperwork and pen after signing the nondisclosure agreement.

"It sounds like you actually have all this job down pat. Do I now just wait and see what warrior name pops up as a match?"

"Essentially, yes. We will contact you, but before you leave I need to remind you of the nondisclosure agreement you signed. We'll be closely monitoring all your calls and emails. This is for everyone's safety. If there are any threats, we'll know about them immediately and be able to take care of them. Also, you are not allowed to speak to any press unless you've spoken with our people and been given a script to read. It's very important that during this initial test run we control all information going out and coming in. I don't know if Suzie mentioned it, but we had to eliminate some candidates who did their questionnaires online. When the hackers released the information, it created a frenzy of death threats and also media blitzes on those applicants. They're considered compromised since we don't know if they're going to be getting paid from outside sources in exchange for information now."

Poppy stood and nodded her head. "Okay, mum's the word and all communication is monitored so watch what I say. Gotcha."

Valerie followed Poppy out of the office and handed her a business card as they walked toward the elevator.

"My card has all my contact info, including my home and cell numbers. If you have any questions, and I mean *any*, please call me. I'll call you once I find out about the match. Once that happens we won't have a lot of time to get things done so it might be a good idea for you to start deciding what you would want to take to the squadron ship sooner rather than later." Smiling at Poppy, she pushed the Down button. "It was wonderful meeting you. You aren't going to regret this."

As Poppy stepped onto the elevator and started the trip down to get her phone and sign out, she kept thinking, *Please let Valerie be right. Don't let me regret this.*

CHAPTER EIGHT

Poppy had barely made it home when her cell phone started ringing.

"Hello?" she gasped, trying to catch her breath. Those three flights of stairs took it out of her normally and that wasn't counting when she had to juggle groceries as she climbed.

"Poppy? This is Valerie. You've been matched!"

Valerie sounded extremely excited and the words echoed in Poppy's head. Matched? Matched! Holy hell, she was matched!

"Already? I thought this was going to take a couple days... Are you sure this is right? Could the system have made a mistake?" Poppy was so stunned that the jar of sauce she had managed to get to the counter rolled right off it and into the kitchen sink.

"The match came through right after you left and since it happened so quickly, I asked myself the same thing...but Poppy, they double-checked it and ran it through once more. It picked the same warrior. The only thing I can tell you right now is that your match is a Healson Warrior and you will be meeting him as soon as we can get our ducks in line. He's very anxious to meet you."

"Healson? Isn't that the diplomat class? In all honesty, I was kind of hoping for a Brakken—I don't know anything about being a politician's wife. The only time I vote is when it's time for presidential elections." She managed to pull out one of her barstools and lean against the counter until she got her legs working again. Holy crap. A match. Her brain was having trouble processing this.

"Don't worry about that. The system knows how to do its job. It's our job to trust the programming."

"But…I guess I just didn't expect…holy shit," Poppy stuttered, still in shock.

"Poppy? Are you okay? I really wanted to tell you in person but I was so excited I couldn't help myself. You're actually one of the first five women matched. Can you believe it? I'm so happy for you. This is amazing. We need to start getting things going so you can meet and greet and start the trial period. Did you talk to your sister yet?"

"Um no…I actually was planning on cooking her dinner to go over all the info tonight and let her know that the schedule's been moved up since I had my exams today. Now I'm going to have to tell her I already have a match. She's going to kill me!" Poppy breathed in and out heavily.

"Calm down, Poppy. Everything is going just like it's supposed to. Just a little faster than we anticipated," Valerie said in a soothing voice.

"And the trial period? When does he want to do the meet and greet? I haven't even started packing anything. What about stopping my mail and paying my bills? What about—"

Valerie interrupted the mini-breakdown Poppy had decided to have. "Poppy. Listen to me. I am your liaison. I am here to help. I can even meet with your sister if you need support when breaking the news. Don't worry about your mail. I'll take care of that when it's time to set up the storage facility. That goes for any bills you have due as well. My job is to make this process as easy as possible for you, both mentally and physically. Do you need me to head your way to help with your sister? I can be there in about an hour."

"No, I can talk to Pixie myself. I may need to call in backup though if she starts asking questions about things that I don't remember paying attention to. Or if she tries to strangle me," Poppy said, reaching in for a cider from the sack. Taking a rather large sip, she asked, "Can I call you back tonight if I need you?"

"Absolutely. I'm here to help any way I can. We want to set up the meet for tomorrow morning. Can you pack tonight after talking to your sister? I want you to focus on getting your stuff together and talking to your sister. Call me as soon as she leaves so we can figure

out a time you can come in. You may want your sister with you.
There's nothing saying the family can't meet your potential husband."

Poppy nodded and then realized that Valerie was unable to see.

"Okay, wish me luck. Pixie's a pistol. And, Valerie?"

So many questions were running through her head but she did
want to get one thing out to the liaison, who was now seeming more
of a friend than anything else.

"Yes?"

"Thanks. I may be shocked right now but I'm also actually excited.
I really appreciate you calling me and helping get all the small stuff
out of the way. I just can't believe this is happening."

"You're welcome, Poppy. I'm so happy for you. I have a good
feeling about this."

* * * * *

Breaking the news to her sister was actually easier than Poppy had
expected. Pixie was somewhat preoccupied and had mentally checked
out of the first part of the conversation. It wasn't until Poppy said
she'd already been matched that Pixie decided to check back in.

"What the fuck did you just say?" Pixie dropped the piece of garlic
bread she'd been preparing to shovel into her mouth.

Poppy tipped the bottle of wine and topped off Pixie's glass yet
again. Not a bad idea to keep Pixie tipsy if she could help it. Liquid
courage for herself actually wasn't a bad idea either and she decided
to fill up her glass with her favorite sweet red wine. Now that she was
thinking about it, did aliens have access to alcohol or should that be
one of the things she packed to take? That was definitely on the call
list for Valerie later.

"I was saying that I was matched today. Yay!" Poppy said with a
gigantic fake smile and raised her wineglass, hoping her sister would
follow her lead.

"Poppy— Poppy— Fuck! I don't even know where to start! Are
you sure you have a match? I thought these things took weeks or
months. This is too quick—are they going to try to take you away
from me tonight?"

"Pix, what's going on with you? I went through the first half of the meal answering all the questions you had yesterday and you didn't even pay attention. Are you okay? Plus, you're about to cry…you never cry. And what do you mean, 'take me away'? You act as though I'm going to get snatched off the street. You have a life, sis. I don't. You have a great job and boyfriend. I don't. I can't even get a cat in this stupid apartment to become the crazy cat lady. I need this. Or, at least, I need to see if this will work."

Poppy pleaded with her eyes for Pixie to understand where she was coming from. She knew she was on the verge of tears herself but knew also that if she cried then they would both start blubbering. When her sister took a deep breath in, Poppy braced herself for more yelling. She was very surprised when Pixie spoke in a small voice.

"I am happy for you. I think this is a good thing…at least it's something you need to do to knock yourself out of whatever rut you have been in. These problems at work are grating on me and it's as if Brenda is fucking up on purpose. I don't know why she would do that, but it's making me crazy. Maybe she wants my job…or she's just an idiot and because we're friends she thinks she can get away with all these mistakes. Brian is still acting weird and when I tried to talk to him last night he brushed me off."

Shaking her finger at Poppy, Pixie smiled. "And don't even mention getting a cat and being a cat lady. You're allergic to them, you loon." Pixie took another sip of her wine and continued.

"I just normally have all my shit together and give you advice. All of a sudden you're making life-changing decisions without me. I know we don't see each other as often as we could, but when you leave I won't even have that chance. And what if this guy is a nut ball? Or a crazy wife beater?"

"Drink your wine, sis. First, he's never had a woman to beat so I doubt he's abusive. According to the FAQ sheet women are revered because there are so few. Second, if I feel threatened in any way, there are people who I can talk to. They would bring me back immediately and the trial period is over. Also, our profiles were matched, so if he is a nut ball then I guess I'm one too."

Poppy allowed a small smile to creep over her face when Pixie snorted a laugh into her wineglass.

"You are obviously a nut ball. And so am I apparently because I'm happy for you. How long do we have before you have to go meet Mr. Warrior?" Pixie grabbed the piece of bread on her plate and popped the entire thing into her mouth.

"Well, that's the other thing I needed to tell you. I should meet him tomorrow morning to start the trial period." *And three, two, one, detonation.*

"What!" The word was somewhat muffled by the carbs and garlic flying out of Pixie's mouth but Poppy understood her loud and clear.

"Apparently he's really excited and we're meeting tomorrow morning." Before Pixie could start protesting, Poppy held out her fingers and started ticking off her arguments. "My liaison, Valerie, will be in charge of bill paying, mail forwarding and also hiring movers to take this stuff to storage. Which reminds me, I need you to take the family photos to your place for safekeeping. If this works out, I'll most likely donate all my crap to the women's shelter, so grab anything you really want to keep, and if I come home, I'll just steal my shoes back."

"Wow, you really do have all your shit together." Pixie sat there stunned with bread crumbs all over her shirt. Grabbing the bottle of wine, she chugged a couple gulps straight from the source and peered around the apartment.

"How come you're so calm right now? I would be losing my shit," Pixie finally asked once she'd demolished about a glass and a half via the bottle.

"Honestly, I've had mini-breakdowns all day." Poppy gave Pixie a sheepish grin. "Valerie is a lifesaver and they've thought of everything to take care of for me so I don't have to worry about that. I guess I'm too excited to be upset really. I mean, I've waited for something awesome to happen to me and I think this is it. I could be married in a month, Pix! *Married!* I haven't had a steady boyfriend for a couple years and my dates have all been losers. What if this man is truly my soul mate and he just happens to come from another planet? I could be getting pregnant soon—that was something I couldn't even think about before because I didn't even see the possibility of meeting anyone."

Poppy could tell what Pixie was thinking. By now she had to realize that nothing was going to change Poppy's mind.

"You're right, Pops. I am happy for you. It sounds like you're happy with your decision." She smiled and yelled as she turned to run down the hall, "I just hope that you're going to be happy I'm taking those shoes I've been wanting to steal for months now!"

Poppy laughed as she jogged after her crazy sister. Pixie was right—she *was* happy with her decision. Nothing could pop this happy bubble she had created for herself.

CHAPTER NINE

The next morning came sooner than Poppy expected.

"Are you ready?" Pixie asked, cradling a to-go cup of coffee.

"As I'll ever be…and you'd better have gotten me a cup too. My coffeemaker broke this morning and I haven't had any caffeine since I finished the first pot." Poppy stood and cataloged what she'd scattered on the floor. Three suitcases and one duffel bag, courtesy of Pixie.

"Did you say you'd already had a pot of coffee before you broke it?"

"Yeah, I couldn't sleep so I got up at four and made a pot. Then the coffeemaker decided to break on me like the piece of crap it was. And don't give me that look. I can't take your judgment this early in the morning."

She walked to the bathroom to get the smaller duffel she'd filled with her toiletries. Shampoo, check. Deodorant, check. Tampons, check. Birth control pills, check, although she wasn't sure whether she would need them or if she was even allowed to take them with her. She only had one week of pills left, so surely it wouldn't be a problem. Endless amount of hair ties, check.

"Damn, Pops, you pretty much packed every single piece of clothing you had. Couldn't you at least leave some of the yoga pants?" Pixie laughed when Poppy pretended she was going to throw the small duffel at her. "Just kidding, jeez." She set her cup of coffee down on the nightstand and jumped over a bag to give Poppy a hug. "You still sure this is what you want to do?"

"Absolutely. I think packing helped me step over the 'I don't know' feeling that may have been floating around inside my head. Pix, my life literally fits into these bags. Everything else is disposable." Poppy turned around and scanned the room again. "Is that pathetic?"

"No, Poppy. It's not pathetic. You just haven't set down roots yet. I would be in the same place if I hadn't met Brian." Pixie brushed a kiss on Poppy's cheek. "It's time to go, slowpoke. We need to leave in the next ten minutes to be there on time, and that means we can't get you a coffee if you don't hurry. I'll grab this bag and head down to the car, so don't keep me waiting."

Pixie jumped as Poppy smacked her ass on the way out the door. "Let's hit the road then. I have a new life waiting for me."

One cup of coffee and a drive through traffic later, Pixie was pulling up to the Intake Center. The building appeared more militarized than the previous day—if that was even possible.

"I can't believe you had the balls to go in there and apply, Poppy. Those guns are freaking me out," Pixie said, leaning forward to stare out the window.

"Apparently they had a bomb threat and the government flipped out. Do you think we just leave all the luggage here and they'll come out to get it when I leave? I don't want to walk through all those protesters carrying all my stuff."

"Yeah, let's just head in and figure out what they want to do."

As the girls walked up to the doors, the protesters began to sneak steadily closer with their signs.

"C'mon, Pops, let's keep moving."

"Why does that guy have an anti-gay sign? That literally makes no sense." Shaking her head at her sister, Poppy moved faster up the steps, trying not to trip on the stairs and yet at the same time unable to take her eyes off the crowd that was slowly descending on them.

"Ummmm…maybe because he is crazy. Hurry up, bish. They're getting closer," Pixie murmured as she grabbed Poppy's arm and tugged to increase their pace. She let out a sigh of relief when the guards opened the doors enough for them to enter before quickly slamming them shut on the protesters.

"Whew, that was kind of scary, Poppy. I didn't realize there were going to be protesters." Pixie had wide eyes by now and her hair was beginning to frizz. They always joked the higher the stress levels, the more frizz popped up. It was the "hairdicator" that both the girls laughed about when they noticed one was getting poofy.

After checking in and heading up to Valerie's office, they were late. Valerie's office was locked and there was no light shining underneath the door.

"Crap, we're about twenty minutes behind. Do you think Valerie thought you were a no-show and went to tell Mr. Awesome you changed your mind?" Pixie had begun to refer to Poppy's alien with different monikers ever since the great shoe raid of last night.

"I hope not! You already took all my good shoes, and the only thing I have left waiting for me at home is a broken coffeepot and crappy furniture."

"Maybe we should look for her?"

"Maybe she's looking for us?" both of them said at the same time.

"Jinx! You owe me a Coke. Let's go find your new BFF and meet your big green guy."

Pixie and Poppy linked arms and had just started walking down the hall when they heard raised voices.

"I cannot believe I am doing this. Not only do these humans risk the security of our females but apparently they cannot even find them!" This was practically yelled by a fairly deep voice. "And did you *see* my match? Her intake picture was not very attractive. What if I am unable to go through with this?"

"Calm down, Wheaton. They said she might be running late because of the crowd outside. And her liaison told me she hadn't planned on getting photographed yesterday so she may not be that bad in person. I am sure everything will be fine."

Hearing heavy steps walking across the room, both women outside stood stock-still and kept listening.

"You are one of the senior Council members and need to be an example for your men. There seems to be some discontent that you were one of the first matched. If you show displeasure at your fortune, we may have a riot on our hands. We need to show these humans how grateful we are for their generosity. You remember our previous failures with the women we took…"

At that last tidbit of information, both Pixie and Poppy gasped.

"There you are!" Valerie's voice seemed to sound directly beside Poppy's ear, which caused both girls to jump into the air with a squeal.

"Holy shit, Valerie! Don't sneak up on people. We were searching for you and nobody was in your office." Poppy was still trying to take in what the men in the room had meant when they had said "women we took." That didn't sound good.

"Are you ready to meet your future?" Valerie said with a huge smile and hugged Poppy.

"Yes, I think so." Poppy was still dissecting what she'd overheard. Unattractive? What an asshole. And on the same note, thank god she'd decided to look a bit prettier today. Her hair was down in curls, her makeup on, and she was wearing her "nice" jeans with a pretty top. "Nice" meaning no stains and a newer style.

"I'm Pixie, by the way." Pixie elbowed Poppy when no introduction came about. "My sister's running low on coffee this morning and is a little spacey." She smiled over at Poppy and said, "Get it? *Spacey?* I crack myself up."

Valerie smiled at Pixie. Pixie always made people smile with her stupid little jokes and the fact she really didn't operate with a filter. She always watched what she said if it was going to hurt somebody's feelings but in situations like this she pretty much said whatever popped into her head.

"Your warrior is right through here. I have his basic profile and it says his name is Wheaton. He happens to be a senior Council member so this means you might be able to come back once in a while on diplomatic visits. Well, ladies, let's go."

"Wait!" Pixie reached for Valerie's arm just as she went to open the door.

Both Poppy and Valerie froze.

"We need to freshen Pops up a bit. Let me give you my earrings and some lip gloss. From what we overheard I would say that we need to knock his space boots off."

"Overheard?" Valerie asked with a confused face.

"Yeah. Apparently Star Lord in there thinks Poppy isn't up to snuff. But a little tweaking here and she'll be perfect." Pixie took off her earrings, handing them over to her sister. Digging in her bag for the makeup case she always carried for her multiple glosses, she quickly found what she needed. Pixie had the idea that a women should always carry an array of shades because the right gloss could make it seem like you were wearing a full face of makeup even when you weren't.

Rubbing the gloss on her lips and smoothing her hair back over her shoulders to let the borrowed earrings be seen, Poppy straightened her top and made sure it was lying just right. Then she took a breath for courage and nodded to Valerie to go ahead and open the door.

After knocking twice, Valerie opened the door and ushered the women into the room. The space was set up like a standard meeting area, with a large table placed in the center and a bank of windows on one side. Two men were facing the window but turned and started walking toward the door as the women entered. Both were dressed in some sort of leather outfit that resembled something Poppy had seen on a sci-fi show. They also had similar hair: shoulder-length, black with a slight wave. She'd originally thought Johnny Depp was the only one who could pull off that hairstyle but apparently aliens were the exception. Her gaze locked on the taller man on the right and he returned her stare. His eyes were such a vivid green they seemed to glow against the dark tan skin tone and black hair he was blessed with. Poppy started, realizing that this was the same man she'd seen when shopping.

"Holy shit."

Pixie immediately started giggling, which knocked Poppy out of her little mental vacation and she realized she'd said that out loud. Instead of being embarrassed, she giggled too. Pretty soon Valerie was also smiling and trying to hide her laugh behind her hand while clearing her throat. The men were confused for a couple moments but the sound of the women's laughter must have been contagious, because they both smiled and Mr. Green Eyes raised an eyebrow in Poppy's direction.

"Is 'holy shit' good? Or bad?" he asked as they stood in front of the three women.

"Totally amazing in this case," Pixie breathed out while staring at the men. It was now Poppy's turn to elbow Pixie.

Wheaton had to admit he was relieved when he first caught a glimpse of the human woman, Poppy, in person. His packet contained a grainy picture that looked as if she might have been mid-sentence when the picture was snapped and her hair had been a jumble of what appeared to be fuzz on top of her head. Prior to the women entering the room, Wheaton had not held back when speaking of his concerns to Dathrow. Other than Poppy not physically matching what he had hoped and expected, her questionnaire was also causing some concern.

He was unsure what her college degree actually qualified her for, but her work history did not seem to be the ideal for a Council member's bride. He had already decided to tread carefully when it came to how much exposure she would have regarding his work. Her file appeared to indicate she seemed ill-equipped to handle being matched to someone as prominent as he was. Now that he could see her in person, he admitted there was an attraction there. In fact she was almost completely different. Maybe she had been ill when the original picture had been taken? He exchanged a quick glance with his friend that conveyed his pleasure at the surprise that was his new bride.

Dathrow seemed to be staring at the woman accompanying his bride. Wheaton could tell they were family, since they seemed to share many physical characteristics. Both women had similar hair, although his bride did have more curls, and the two women had similar body types and coloring. His bride seemed to be slightly heavier in weight than the woman next to her, but Wheaton was surprised to note that he preferred her softer shape.

"Gentlemen, this is Poppy and her sister, Pixie. Poppy was our applicant selected for your match, Mr. Wheaton." Valerie now turned and handed the paperwork to his friend—who, Poppy also happened to notice, was pretty delicious-looking as well.

Wheaton cleared his throat and stepped closer to her. He was now close enough for her to smell his natural musk, which she had to admit smelled delicious.

"Just Wheaton. Not Mr. Wheaton. Poppy, it is wonderful to meet you. We have been very fortunate to have made a match so quickly and I am very excited to show you your new home. This is my warrior brother, Dathrow," he said with a nod to the man standing beside him. Wheaton reached for her hand in what Poppy assumed was supposed to be a handshake but he squeezed too hard and almost shook her arm out of its socket.

"Yikes, Mr. Muscles, calm it down. You break it, you buy it," Pixie muttered.

Wheaton turned to Pixie and held out his hand to shake hers as well and she waved, pretended to cough into her hand and mumbled something about germs, which had him glancing at her in confusion.

Valerie and Dathrow had moved away and were now going over paperwork while the other three stood staring at each other.

Pixie walked toward the snacks on the side of the room and muttered, "Don't want to be a third wheel."

"Poppy? I had read that was a flower. Are you named after a flower? And Pixie? Isn't that another word for 'fairy' or a candy? We are still trying to adjust to the language and our translators seem to have the most trouble with names." He rubbed his right earlobe, giving her a slight smile.

"My mom did like the flower, but she didn't say I was named after it. I believe she had a friend in college who she stole the name from." Poppy smiled back at him and couldn't help but stare into his eyes. He really did smell wonderful—almost like sunshine and leather.

"I've see you before…at Mega Mart," she said in a rush, unsure if he remembered.

Wheaton studied her for a moment and then nodded slowly. "I remember you. You were carrying paper and getting food items."

Her face turned red with embarrassment. He had seen her buying enough toilet paper to stock the Duggars. "Why were you there?"

"We've been running shuttles down to Earth to acclimate to human culture. Most Phaetons simply ride in a big black automobile to watch the way your society runs. When we did the same, we noticed many people heading to that large warehouse and were curious to see what they were doing there." Smiling slightly, he quirked his eyebrow up. "Most people did not notice us. Some asked for us to sign paper, which we did not understand."

Poppy couldn't help but giggle at the vision that created. "They probably thought you were famous. I actually thought you were a rock star until I saw you on TV."

Now he seemed entirely confused, so before he could ask what she meant, Poppy continued, "The leather pants made you look like someone famous, that and the long hair." She couldn't help but brush the tips of his hair that were resting on his broad shoulders.

She glanced to the side of the room where Pixie was eating some cookies while staring at her as if she were watching a movie. Turning slightly away from Wheaton, Poppy mouthed, *Cut it out*, which made Pixie laugh and shovel another cookie into her mouth while she wiggled her eyebrows.

"Soooo…" Poppy didn't quite know what to say as she gazed up into Wheaton's eyes.

"Would you like to sit and have a beverage? They placed food items in here for us to eat while waiting for you."

He placed his hand on her back to guide her to one of the chairs at the table. Poppy felt the heat from his large hand above her waist and goose bumps popped up on her arms. Holy cow that was electric. He moved the chair out for her to sit and sat in the one next to it, but moved closer and leaned forward as if he were going to tell her a secret. She angled her head so she could hear him better when she realized he was simply breathing her in. Her eyes closed as she tilted even closer to his mouth.

"You smell wonderful…and your hair, it appears so soft. May I touch it?" His nose was now pressing against the side of her neck and their chairs were as close as they could be.

"Well, it seems only fair…I touched yours." Grateful she'd left her hair down today, she nodded while trying to swallow past the dry lump in her throat. She heard a soft sound and realized it was a whimper that had come from her.

Instead of him simply touching her hair, which was what she'd expected, he put his hand on the back of her neck and threaded his fingers into the strands at her nape. Giving it a slight tug, he pulled her head back and moved his nose down her neck, causing her to let out a noise she hadn't heard herself make before. Whimpering? Since when did she whimper?

Another noise, this time coming from him, had her opening her eyes.

"Did you just growl at me?" she whispered.

"I rumbled. It's a sound our race makes when we have certain emotions," he said in a husky voice.

"Your rumble sounded an awful lot like a growl." Poppy's lips were almost touching his, they were so close.

"I am sorry if I scared you. We don't have much physical contact unless we are training or in combat. I find touching you, even just your hair…arousing." He licked his lips while staring at hers.

Poppy felt as if they were in a bubble of their own inside the large conference room. She could hear the buzz of the lights overhead and also her sister talking to Valerie. Every once in a while she could hear Dathrow murmur something but it all seemed fuzzy, almost as if they were huddled together in a dimly lit bar instead of in a brightly lit boardroom.

"Wheaton. Wheaton!" Dathrow was now standing behind their chairs. "I have been trying to get your attention for a couple moments now. Your cheeks seem flushed. Are you feeling well? We can have a Brakken ready a medi-unit for our arrival on Squadron One if needed." Dathrow seemed more like a concerned parent wanting to hover over a sick child than the warrior she'd first seen him as.

Wheaton slowly untangled his fingers from her nape and with one last neck squeeze, he rolled his chair back and cleared his throat.

"I apologize, Dathrow. I was speaking with Poppy and trying to measure our compatibility." He reached up to rub his neck.

"Well, you guys were compatible as fuck from where I was standing."

Pixie of course took that moment to pipe up.

"Wheaton, I need your mark on these papers for the trial period to begin. Valerie will collect Poppy's mark and then we need to leave. Apparently the knowledge of our presence has been leaked and the angry people out front have grown louder." Dathrow motioned Wheaton away and Pixie plopped into the chair that Wheaton had vacated.

"Holy shit, Pops. I thought he was licking your neck from where I was standing. And I'm pretty sure I saw your eyes roll into the back of your head." She looked at Valerie and smiled. "I guess we don't have to worry about them being attracted to each other now, do we?"

"Nope, I don't think that's going to be an issue at all. Poppy, did he steal your ability to speak? You've been sitting there with your mouth open since we interrupted your...moment." Valerie placed a hand on Poppy's shoulder, about to give it a little shake.

"No, I'm fine. I've never felt anything like that before. Ever. Like *ever* ever. I think he blew my circuits there for a minute. Did you hear him growl? It literally made me shiver. I need some cold water." Poppy sat there stunned and fanned her face with a hand.

She had never felt that type of physical response to anyone in the past. It had almost felt that if he breathed on her a bit more, she could've had an orgasm then and there. She felt so overwhelmed that she could probably start laughing hysterically any time now. The only thing that stopped her was the fact Wheaton and Dathrow were talking but still watching the women from their side of the room. Meeting Wheaton's eyes from the distance, she smiled at him and when he smiled back, she couldn't help but let her smile grow.

"Well, my mind's made up. Let's sign this stuff and get my trial going." Poppy had a huge smile on her face by the time she signed the trial forms.

Pixie sat there tapping her fingers on the table while Poppy signed the forms to leave Earth. It hit her all of a sudden that her sister was actually doing this. *Poppy was leaving.* And she wouldn't be coming back if that hunky warrior had anything to say about it. She didn't want to be selfish, but that's exactly how she felt. Pixie looked at her sister—really looked at her. Poppy had smiled more and seemed more alive in the past fifteen minutes than Pixie had seen her act in the past two years. She knew about the dismal dates Poppy had sat through: since they were sisters they talked about everything. Wine had a way of making sisters talk pretty openly, including the fact Poppy had become way too attached to her vibrator and she was sad that her friends were getting married and having babies while she sat at home and watched the History Channel. Speaking of babies…

"What about my future niece or nephew? Will I ever get to see them? Hug them?" Pixie asked in a sad voice.

Valerie crossed to stand behind Pixie and put a comforting hand on her shoulder.

"Pixie, they have a system similar to Skype so you'll be able to talk to your sister by video whenever she's available. Also, we're trying to work out the kinks regarding family visiting. I'm sure you can tell that security is a major issue but maybe we can work out some sort of pass for you to visit if the match works out and you want to visit Poppy and her family. I'm actually unsure if Poppy will be on the ship once the trial passes if she decides to enter the spousal contract. From what I gather, they may go back to their home world to live if he isn't needed for diplomatic missions on the squadron. I can find that info out for you as soon as possible though."

Pixie and Poppy stared at each other, the papers forgotten. Pixie reached for her sister's hand and held it in a tight grip.

"I love you, sis. I'll support you no matter what you decide but I'm going to miss you like hell."

Tears were now falling down Pixie's cheeks and Poppy could feel hers start to fall as well.

"I love you too, Pix. I'm so excited about this but I know this isn't easy for you. I'll make sure that I try to call you as much as possible and I'll talk to Wheaton about you being involved with our family, if that actually happens." Poppy smiled. "I have a really good feeling about this though. It's as if my entire body lit up when he touched me."

"I could see that from the cookie bar, Poppy. I'm pretty sure everyone in the room could see that," Pixie said with a wry grin. "Well, let's not waste any more time… It's time for your future to start, sis."

CHAPTER TEN

On the shuttle ride up to what she assumed was Squadron One, Poppy had tears running down her face. She was probably a runny-nosed mess considering how much she was sniffling. Even she had to admit she wasn't a pretty crier. Their departure had been anticlimactic. Her car had been brought around by Valerie and unloaded in a guarded lot where a shuttle was waiting disguised with a cloaking device. Wheaton had not touched her again except for a guiding hand on her back when she'd hesitated while walking.

Dathrow, who had been following the couple, strapped himself into a chair behind them while Wheaton worked on something similar to a tablet computer. He hadn't spoken to her since their close encounter in the boardroom. She assumed he might have been embarrassed by his strong physical reaction since Pixie had used their goodbyes to tease him about some growling she had heard. She'd also whispered something when walking by him to leave the room after ten minutes of hugging and clinging tightly to Poppy.

Poppy hadn't been able to hear the exchange since Valerie had distracted her with questions about her luggage. She would have to ask him about that when they had a moment. The last thing she needed was Pixie threatening to cut off a body part or something along those lines. Her sister's overprotective instincts were something Poppy was familiar with. Pixie had once been suspended from school for cold cocking one of Poppy's tormentors in their school cafeteria. Following the knockout punch, she had then dumped the contents of his food tray onto his prone body before walking away like a boss. The scene had been both terrifying and amusing at the same time.

Poor Simon had never been able to recover his manly reputation after being felled by a girl almost a foot shorter than he was. Glancing at Wheaton, Poppy grimaced. She definitely needed to talk to him and find out what her sister had said.

As the shuttle moved toward Squadron One, Poppy peered out the window in the front of the ship. Watching clouds move past in what seemed like puffs of smoke, she felt her stomach drop when they reached high enough that darkness eclipsed her view. Pretty soon the sky was lit with stars and Earth was behind them. A pang of uncertainty hit her. Had she made the right choice? Glancing around the shuttle at the men beside her, she realized it was too late to change her mind now.

As the ship docked on Squadron One, Poppy reached for Wheaton's hand but he turned away and started speaking to the pilot. She wasn't sure why she had reached for him, except everything seemed so foreign she felt she wanted to cling to something, or someone, even a little bit familiar. After a couple moments, Wheaton walked out through a door, leaving Poppy to pick up the duffel she carried with her. Deciding that she wasn't going to stand there watching his retreating back, she turned to the other man standing with her. Dathrow stood with his hands crossed behind his back, quietly studying her.

"Poppy, please follow me. I will take you to your quarters to settle in," Dathrow stated.

"Ummm…where's he going?" Poppy finally asked as Dathrow started walking quickly out an automatic door.

"He is going to a meeting. He will be back to your quarters when his business is finished." Dathrow was now moving very quickly down a lit hallway. Everything seemed extremely bright, as if it was lit by bright-blue bulbs. The gleaming walls were reflecting light to the point of making her eyes hurt slightly. Poppy struggled to keep up with her fast-moving companion while her eyes adjusted. The hallways were like something right out of a movie. Everything was so shiny and the smooth metal corridor had to be a bitch to keep clean. Remembering her disastrous experience with stainless steel appliances was enough to make her cringe when she caught her reflection on the walls.

Their walk was spent in complete silence. Dathrow did not explain where they were walking or what they were passing. He simply moved silently, barely letting her keep pace with his long strides. Taking an elevator to another level, Dathrow turned and waved his hand at a door. Poppy watched the movement with curious eyes. She didn't see any type of handle on the door itself and wondered how it opened. It took Poppy a minute to figure out he had been moving his wrist over an almost unnoticeable pad next to the opening. Catching a glimpse of the silver band around his wrist light up, she realized it was acting as a remote to the door when the pad blinked with the same color light. Interesting. Hands-free entry. No wonder there were no fingerprints on the walls or other doors she had seen.

Dathrow gestured to his wrist when he caught Poppy's curious glance. "Wheaton will be back later to take you to get your band fitted. He suggested you watch the videos he has loaded onto his viewer to learn some of our history and culture."

Poppy stepped inside the room and turned around to ask how to do that when the door swished closed and she was alone.

"Well shit," she said to the empty room. "What the fuck do I do now?"

Exploring the quarters, she found the bathroom with a shower that seemed fairly easy to use. After setting out her toiletries in the small space, she walked back to the living area. The apartment consisted of two rooms. The living room had a small kitchen with a peninsula coming out from the wall to separate it from the main area. On one side of the room was a small white leather couch and the opposite wall was blank with a large screen flanked by electronics.

"Okay...video...video...where could you be?" Talking to herself was apparently going to be her only company this evening so she might as well go for broke. "Helloooo....maybe this button. Nope. Maybe this one? Nope." Pushing random buttons on the wall was probably not the smartest thing to do on a spaceship, but things didn't seem to be blowing up so she was going to keep going. "How about this one? Ah ha! Score."

A video system popped up onto the blank wall space opposite the couch and she wondered if it was touch screen or there was a remote. After fiddling with the wall, she figured out it was some type of touch screen. Everything was marked with odd symbols, so she hit the one that was listed first. A movie was starting up so she sat down and got comfy. Then she almost fell off the slick white couch. Holy shit! This was porn! And not even good porn, but really cheesy, cheap porn. How could a woman function with fingernails that long? Okay, wrong video. *Way* wrong video. Selecting another movie, she found yet another porno. Seriously? What was wrong with this guy? Apparently he had the libido of a teenage boy if all these videos were pornos. By her count she had another fifty to go.

Twenty-five videos later, she found something that appeared to be a history program. This must have been what he was talking about, because the men resembled some of the warriors she had seen on the Intake Center screen. Unfortunately for her it wasn't in English, so she wasn't going to get anywhere by watching this. Well that was a total fail. After an hour had passed and she had nothing to do, she took a fleece blanket out of her duffel and snuggled in with her e-reader and iPod.

She awoke to the feeling she was floating and realized someone was carrying her. Smelling leather and sunshine, she understood Wheaton was back and carrying her into the bedroom. She must have fallen asleep while reading. How much time had passed? As she became more awake, she realized she was actually pretty hungry.

"Food," she said in a sleepy voice, patting Wheaton's shoulder.

"Food? Did you not eat?" He stopped walking toward the bedroom.

"How the hell would I have eaten? I was left here not knowing what to do and couldn't figure out how anything would work. Where's the fucking fridge?"

"I apologize. I meant to return sooner. The meetings kept me longer than I planned." He turned around, carried her back to the living room and sat her down. "Stay and I will get you food."

He turned and busied himself at a small counter. Poppy took this time to try to clear the cobwebs from her head. Watching him move was like watching a dance. He was extremely large but moved silently back and forth at the small counter. No movements seemed to be wasted. Wheaton turned toward her with a plate piled high with french fries and a cold sandwich.

Wheaton was hoping to distract Poppy with food while he figured out how to explain his earlier absence. When he had left her after the ship had docked, he could tell she was directing anger his way. On the ride to Squadron One, she had reached for his hand at one point and he had felt almost frozen in place. His earlier episode—when he had nuzzled her neck and rumbled—had been so out of character for him it was enough to cause him concern and he had decided to visit the med center to have a scan run to make sure he had not contracted an Earth disease during his visit.

Her tears on the flight to the ship had upset him, which added to the fear that something was wrong. When she had reached for his hand and he had felt a warm tingle followed by his chest feeling heavy, he had quickly found a med pad and placed a request for a regen bed immediately. When he had left Dathrow to take care of his new bride, Wheaton had gone to get scanned from head to toe. The regen bed had come back showing normal scans on all fronts, so he was stumped as to what was happening. At the very least it was disconcerting.

"You have regular food here?" she asked, taking the plate from him. Apparently she was hungrier than she had thought. She practically snatched it from him as if she hadn't eaten in a week.

"Yes, we took classes to become familiar with common human foods. We have a generator that will make almost any food item once it knows the base components. We just have to assemble it when complete. Once you get your band, I will program your favorites so the generator will know what you desire." Wheaton sat next to her on the small couch and watched her eat.

"Dathrow mentioned a band, but I don't understand why I need one," she said between bites.

Wheaton held up his arm and showed her the silver wristband that was thicker than a bangle but narrower than a cuff that graced his wrist. She saw small colored lights blink off and on.

"All of the brides will have a band on their wrists similar to this one. It is your identification and will also give access to portions of the ship." He added, "It will let others know you have been matched and mated so you will not be approached by single males searching for a mate."

Now her stomach was full, Poppy was unsure what to do. She almost wished she had more to eat so she could keep her hands and mouth busy. "What was your meeting about?" she asked.

"Nothing to concern you. Would you like to start physical relations now?" he said, standing up and reaching out his hand to assist her.

"Wait, what? Physical relations? We barely know each other…" Poppy turned red and the now lead weight of the sandwich she'd wolfed down made her feel sick.

"You seemed eager for my touch earlier, and I did not think humans needed to know each other for sexual intercourse." Wheaton seemed confused and placed his hands on his hips. No doubt according to everything he'd studied, this was the point where clothes came off and the physical contact started. She let her face tell him he'd assumed wrong. In a big way.

Poppy stood up and mimicked his stance. Then she poked out a finger and pointed it at his chest.

"Hold your horses there, buster. I may have acted…receptive…yeah, *receptive* earlier, but I don't sleep with strangers. You're pretty much a stranger. I mean, hell, you just left me here. What am I saying? It wasn't even you who walked me here, it was that Dathrow guy and all of a sudden you're done with your 'meetings' so you want sex? Well that isn't going to happen tonight!" Her voice started getting louder and she was literally poking Wheaton's chest.

"You are angry that I left? I explained that I had a meeting." Wheaton obviously had no idea how pissed she was getting, because he then added, "Do you want sex or not?"

Hell. No. She stepped back to put space between them, and basically to also get away from the temptation to stroke the chest she had been poking just a second earlier.

"That would be a no. We will not be having sex until I figure out if I like you or not. And speaking of sex, what the hell are you doing with all that porn on your TV?"

"The sex videos are educational. We believed humans were aware of the lack of females on our planet. Were you not told?" He raised an eyebrow in her direction.

"Of course we were told! I wouldn't be here if you didn't need women. I just meant, that's a *lot* of porn," she huffed out. Poppy had a feeling this was going to be a long conversation and she was pretty tired.

"Also, those are *not* educational. Granted I'm not one who's had really good sex but all those people are faking it. At least I'm pretty sure the women are. They don't look like they're enjoying it at all. It's completely unrealistic!"

"I do not understand. That sex is not real?" He really did seem stumped and was staring at the blank wall as if it was going to give him answers.

"Wheaton….those are people paid to have sex for entertainment. It's all about the sex part. Not kissing or cuddling or….well…anything really that a woman would want. I mean, some of the stuff is probably nice but those women there are acting. Those moans are most likely not real."

Oh boy, if she was going to have to be the lead once it came down to them actually consummating this thing, then it would be like the blind leading the blind. Her experience with an actual living breathing male was fairly limited and she had never been able to climax during intercourse. Most of the time it had been afterward, either by herself or with the help of the men she had slept with using her trusty bullet vibrator on her.

"Kiss? Cuddle? I understand the words but do not understand how they relate to sexual intercourse for procreation."

"Well, it's arousing for one…you know, ummmm…gets the juices flowing." At his blank stare she then mumbled, "Okay, so no you don't know. Since this isn't even an issue tonight we can talk about it when I'm not in a food coma and tired on top of that. Can you just show me where to sleep and we can talk more tomorrow?"

"You will be sleeping with me." With that he again picked her up off the couch and carried her into a room that she had assumed was the sleeping quarters but where she hadn't seen a bed.

Wheaton holding his wrist up to the door caused a bed to fold out from the wall. Poppy recognized a Murphy bed and it was pretty large too. At least if she had to share a bed it would be with enough space to not have them on top of each other.

After Wheaton set her down on her feet, Poppy excused herself to go to the bathroom area to get a sleep shirt. Hoping it was enough to cover her without her being embarrassed, she walked back into the bedroom.

Poppy guessed embarrassment wasn't something he would experience, because standing next to the bed was a very naked Wheaton. He was also very aroused.

"Holy fuck," she whispered as she stopped in her tracks.

He was a sight to behold. His body was something women dreamed of. Lickable abs flowed into a strong set of shoulders and arms in one direction and then into the vee of his hips and sturdy legs in the other. Standing there staring at him, she noticed he had minimal body hair, except for a small trail that went from his bellybutton down to his groin and then a dusting on his legs.

"You use a lot of 'holy' words. My translator doesn't process some of them. 'Fuck' is translating as a slang term and earlier you said 'shit', which was translated as excrement. Can you explain?" Wheaton was now fully facing her with his hands on his hips. He stared at her as if she were wearing too many articles of clothing and the only thing he could concentrate on was figuring out how many layers he would need to peel off her before they were able to sleep comfortably.

Poppy on the other hand was completely unable to think at all. He was *ripped*. And not just ripped but also very blessed in the privates department. Her sister would be high-fiving her right now if she'd been able to get a peek at the manly goodness in front of her.

Figuring out she needed to not stare so hard, she tried to move her eyes away from the beauty in front of her.

"Ummmmmm….you have no clothes on," she was finally able to say even though her mouth was dry.

"We do not sleep in clothing. Why are you wearing that large cotton garment? I wanted to see my bride." He walked toward her as if he were prepared to take her shirt off. "Why do you step back? I can assist with taking off your garment."

He reached out again and Poppy was too stunned to move as he whisked the shirt over her head. Pausing for a moment to rub the garment between his fingers, he hummed to himself before tossing it aside.

"Fuck! I sleep in clothes, Wheaton! Give that back now!" Her arms had automatically gone to cover her chest.

"Clothing inhibits reproduction. There is no need for it. I understand you want to wait for intercourse but we will sleep prepared in case you change your mind." He lowered his hands to the band of her underwear. "These are attractive but you will not wear them."

"Hell yes I will. You keep your hands to yourself, mister! People wear clothes to sleep in. There's actually a whole line of clothes just for sleeping in. I also happen to like to wear those clothes during the day sometimes…okay, most of the time. But they're comfortable, dammit. And will you stop that?" she snapped while trying to knock his hands away.

"You will not wear these clothes in our sleep unit. I want to inspect you and become familiar with your body. I believe I may need to self-pleasure tonight. If you need to do so also it will be easier without this fabric covering your pussy. That's what they said on the videos… Is 'pussy' a correct term? My translator kept saying it meant feline but I think it may not be working when it comes to certain portions of your language."

With that last part of his statement he had literally shocked her still. He had her panties off and tossed into the corner before she knew what was happening. Nudging her legs open, he ran his fingers over her lower lips.

"This hair is not as soft as the hair on your head, but it is short and neat. Do you groom yourself here?"

"Ohmygod, what's happening right now?! I can't even process this." Poppy buried her face in her hands as she felt his fingers run up and down her cleft. "That tickles. Knock it off!" Her words earned her a soft smack right on the front of her pussy. "Did you just smack me?" She had dropped her hands and was staring wide-eyed at the man now kneeling before her. He was essentially at face level with her privates and she was mortified but for some reason was unable to move away. That could have also have been attributed to the fact he'd moved his hands to her ass, where he cupped and started kneading her skin.

"You told me it tickled and to 'knock it off'. I translated that you wanted me to tap you. I have seen that in the videos." He winked and then skimmed his eyes down her bared skin. "I think you may be mistaken and the videos are realistic. We have already performed many of the actions that I witnessed in the images and from your lubrication you are showing arousal." He looked up, smirking, and licked his lips. Seemed his mouth was practically watering at the thought of licking her pussy.

"Okay, time out." Pausing to smack the top of his head, she shouted when he didn't stop. "Hey! I said time out. I didn't say you could put your mouth there! Back up. Back. Up," she said through clenched teeth when she felt his breath get close to her lower lips. She wasn't mad at him and her anger was coming from embarrassment more than anything.

"I'll sleep naked. That's fine." She was already naked in front of him so that door had already been thrust wide open, no point in trying to hide what he'd been face-to-face with. Literally. When he reached for her again and moved to speak, she shushed him up quickly with that finger he'd gotten poked with earlier.

"Do. Not. Talk. Only listen. We will *not* have sex tonight. You are *not* allowed to touch me unless I give permission. That includes taking off my underwear in the future. And no smacking me anymore. Well…at least not right now. I didn't mind it too much, so we can negotiate that in the future when the time comes. *Comprende?*"

Poppy had never had the chance to experiment with anything kinky but from what she'd gathered so far, Wheaton didn't seem at all shy and seemed eager to do whatever she let him get away with.

"I cannot translate that word," he said, crossing his arms. "But fine, we will not partake of intercourse this night. Would you like to explore my body?" he said, lying down on top of the cover on the white bed.

"Explore your…? Ummmm…sure," she said with a smile. She wasn't about to pass up the opportunity to touch the type of body that was usually only viewed in a fireman's calendar. Trying to ignore the fact that she was naked as a jaybird, she stumbled to the side of the bed.

He tossed her a small grin. Getting an unencumbered view of her body, he was very happy that Poppy had been matched to him. Some of the other warriors who had seen his new bride on the transport had given him pitying looks and he had not only felt anger but had actually considered hitting a few of them. The more he talked to her and discovered her little quirks, the more he liked her. Her plush little body was a bonus. It was also a bonus that his body seemed very grateful for, if the throbbing in his cock was an indicator.

"Are you going to stand over me or would you like to recline while you do it?" He folded his arms behind his head to give her complete access.

"Oh, well I guess I can lie down too. Yeah, I can do that." Acting like this was something she'd done a millions times before, she lay down at his side. Hmmmmmm…where to start. Taking her hand and running it along his chest, she felt his stomach muscles tighten up.

"Did that tickle?" Poppy asked in a breathy voice she didn't recognize as her own.

"No, it felt nice. Do it some more," he whispered in a soft voice but didn't move again. She felt he was trying not to scare her off. He probably knew her sexual experience was limited, with only having had two partners in her past.

Stroking his chest and tracing his nipples rewarded her with a breath from his chest that expanded his torso. Taking her fingers and running them up and down his stomach muscles, she decided to count and discovered his six-pack was more like an eight-pack. By the time she was happy with her exploration of his upper torso, she moved her way down with a shaking hand when it came to the gorgeous vee of his hips. Those were something she had only seen in a magazine and she was drooling at the fantasy of tracing that area becoming a reality. Pulling her hand back and making a fist so she wasn't tempted, she made a decision…one her lady parts wasn't too happy about.

"I can't believe I'm saying this, but I think I may need to stop if I'm going to hold to the no-sex rule." Biting her lip, Poppy could not believe she was going to stop touching the superb manliness in front of her. She felt as if she were going to have to sneak off to the bathroom to masturbate. Clenching her thighs together, she realized, yep…definitely time to stop.

Wheaton could tell Poppy had been holding herself away a little. And when she had leaned forward to trace his chest, it took all he had in him to not take her hand and roughly drag it lower.

"Go ahead and rest then. I need to self-pleasure." Unfolding his arms from behind his head, he lowered them to his waist, bumping her now hard nipples that were close to his side. He started stroking his cock in a relaxed twist and pump of his hand. Watching her face as he did it, he was aware that she could feel the rumble coming from his chest.

Dragging her gaze away from his strong hand, she noticed his gaze on her breasts. Poppy's nipples were already so painfully tight she could feel them start to tingle. As the rumble get louder and deeper, she scooted slightly closer so her breasts were touching the arm that was now moving faster with his stroking hand. The action was basically allowing him to rub her nipples without actually doing so with his hands. Poppy peeked back down at his hand as he came. She had never wanted to place her lips somewhere so badly before. In fact, she hadn't really ever been a fan of oral sex but watching him stroke his cock made her want to lick every place his hand touched.

Trying to control his breathing and his movements, Wheaton knew he would be unable to hold back his climax. Her hard nipples bumping his arm with every movement and the scent coming from the haven between her legs were enough to push him over the edge quickly.

Wheaton rumbled loudly as he felt himself come. Instead of closing his eyes, he watched her face. Her own gaze was glued to his now-softening erection and he was satisfied she seemed to still be on the edge. If watching him self-pleasure had that effect on her, then he would make sure to do it every night. She would not be able to hold out too long before she gave in, if her pink cheeks, rough breathing and red lips were anything to go by.

He rolled slightly away from her, reached into the bedside cubby and pulled out a towel to wipe his hands and abs. Poppy felt as if she were panting and one second away from saying "fuck it" when he tossed the towel down onto the floor, waved his bracelet at the headboard and rolled to his side away from her.

"Good sleep, Poppy."

She heard a sigh and then nothing.

Well holy shit. Poppy rolled onto her side facing the wall and punched her pillow a couple times. Wanting to scream into it but figuring that would scare Wheaton, she compromised with whipping the cover out from under her neglected body and kicked it a couple times for good measure. She tucked the cover around her shoulders, her mind racing as she tried to calm her breathing and her body. Why had she said no sex tonight? For the life of her, she couldn't think of one damn reason.

As Poppy tried to get some sleep, she kept thinking of everything that had happened that day. It seemed like a whole week had passed since she'd had her first cup of coffee that morning and she'd need to be on her game tomorrow. She willed her body to calm down and eventually drifted off, but not before she felt Wheaton's arm slip around her waist and cuddle her closer.

CHAPTER ELEVEN

The next morning came way too soon if the sleep in the corners of her eyes was an indicator. After a cup of coffee from the generator, Wheaton had been all business when he'd laid out some plans for the day. First thing that was on the list was getting Poppy acclimated to life on the ship. Wheaton had taken her to get fitted for a bracelet, which Poppy still had yet to be able to figure out. Inspecting the device, she was unsure how to take it on and off. After she'd fiddled with it a couple times, Wheaton pointed out it was not meant to be removed. Ever. It was sealed onto her body and was waterproof so there would be no need for it to be taken off. When she asked about what would happen if her arm swelled, he said that the medical unit would be able to remove it with a special tool if needed.

Their next stop was to get her translation device implanted. Wheaton explained that normally the ship's doctors would fit it, but they were in meetings, so a communications officer would do it. A chip being inserted into her head was something Poppy had been nervous about but she had to admit, the device was pretty nifty. She had felt a small pinch at the back of her ear and voilà, she could apparently understand their language. Reading it was still a no-go but understanding the voice commands would help her figure out her surroundings a little better. Wheaton's chip allowed him to speak English but with her now chipped as well, she would be able to speak with warriors in their native language. After Poppy was outfitted, Wheaton walked her around the ship for a tour.

Exploring the ship was an eye-opening experience. Squadron One seemed to be endless and Poppy was awestruck whenever they went by the glass that separated her from space. They toured the dining hall, the recreation room, the med center and the media area. Even though she walked the entire ship, or what felt like the entire ship, she still felt slightly lost. Every single hallway seemed the same and was marked with symbols, which she figured were signs and room numbers, but that was about it.

Poppy was having an interesting morning, but so far it had been disappointing in regards to her soon-to-be husband. She wasn't sure what his problem was but Wheaton was acting like a robot again. The horny guy she'd become familiar with the night before had disappeared. When he spoke to her, it was as if he were conducting more of a formal tour than showing his girlfriend around. The few times she'd reached for his hand he'd pulled away or moved at the last minute. Hoping that he was simply uncomfortable with physical contact in front of the other warriors and not taking it personally was hard. Many men they'd passed had given her a simple nod to say hello but there hadn't been one smile or handshake. She was hoping the coolness from him was a cultural thing.

Poppy was really trying to give him some leeway but their alone time before they went to get errands done had been no better. He hadn't spoken to her when they woke up...no "good morning", no smile...nothing. After dressing, he'd walked to the kitchen area while she finished up. She was finishing putting her hair in a bun when she noticed a familiar smell: coffee! Poppy practically sprinted to where Wheaton was standing. Without ceremony, she snatched the cup he held out in his hand.

"Thank you, thank you, thank you." Before sipping the coffee, she saw that he'd already doctored it for her.

"How did you know I took my coffee with milk and sugar?" she'd asked after a moment of surprise.

"It was on your profile." With that being said, he'd turned to the door. "Please follow me. We will get your band now and I have time to give you a tour." Not even waiting to see if she followed him, he'd walked right out the door.

Hoping they could have some time together this afternoon, she was thinking of "get to know you" questions. Excited about being able to grill him about his favorite things and what it was like growing up on his planet, she made a mental list. During their walk back to their quarters, they were stopped by another warrior in the hallway. Giving Wheaton privacy, she moved over to the window in the bright hallway. Everything was so beautiful up here. So clean.

While Poppy was gazing out toward the stars, Wheaton took his own time to study her as he talked with the other warrior. Being around her this morning was causing him some trouble. He liked her company but had made a decision last night that he would not get further attached to her until she had made up her mind about staying. The last thing he wanted was to form either a physical attachment or even a more personal one and then have her leave. Walking her around that morning, he had spent more time watching her than where they were going.

Wheaton had not really been in favor of her receiving a translation device. Knowing that it would make her time on the ship easier to manage, he relented to the directions of the Council but he was not going to encourage her to talk to the other warriors. He had only been with her for a short time but he felt proprietary over her time and attention. If he was in a meeting, he would prefer that she stay in their quarters and wait for him.

Wheaton trusted very few warriors with his new bride. Dathrow had been his warrior brother for many years and had accompanied him on multiple missions. Thorne was another warrior he trusted, a Council member who had been in favor of the Bridal Pact but who had shown no interest in applying for his own. When it came to friends, there were only a select few who shared that title.

"Poppy?" Poppy jumped when she heard Wheaton's raised voice, realizing he'd been trying to get her attention.

"My presence is needed in negotiations. Thorne will escort you back to our quarters."

With that small statement, Poppy was staring at Wheaton's back as he walked away from her.

So here Poppy was. Sitting alone. Yet again.

Not knowing how late he would be back, she decided to make herself some food. Using the food generator was easy peasy now she understood how it worked. With a full stomach and her e-reader, she found her iPod and scanned the music. She felt she was in either a Liz Phair or Patty Griffin mood. Griffin won out and Poppy was soon rereading one of her books with her favorite songs on in the background. Before she knew it, she was drifting off to the sounds of Griffin's soothing voice ushering her to sleep.

Waking the next morning to a buzzing noise, she was still on the couch. And her neck hurt. Apparently Mr. Wonderful hadn't made it back to their rooms yet. Wondering what could have kept him gone for so long, Poppy heard someone moving around in the other room.

"Hello? Helloooooooo?" Poppy called out as she followed the noise. "Wheaton? What are you doing here?"

"These are my quarters. I sleep here," he said in a very matter-of-fact voice while pulling on his boots. Somebody seemed crabby this morning. Had he wanted to spend more time with her before they…pleasured themselves, and been disappointed she'd fallen asleep on the couch?

"What time did you come in this morning?" Leaning against the bedroom door, she watched him.

"Morning? I arrived last night after you had fallen asleep," he said, completely oblivious to her annoyance.

"Why didn't you wake me up? You just let me sleep on that tiny couch?" Now she was really peeved. She walked toward him to stand toe to toe. "What happened to carrying me to bed like the first night?"

"You are now aware of where the bed is placed. I assumed you fell asleep there on purpose." He walked past her into the kitchen area.

Wheaton did not have time to argue with her this morning. Between the meetings yesterday, where he seemed to answer endless questions about his new bride, and his lack of pleasure last night, he was not in a good mood. At the Council meetings it seemed that half of the Council was trying to figure out how to get him out of his match and the other was applauding his luck in being assigned a bride so quickly. There had been a few members who did not understand how a diplomat could be assigned someone who on paper was not compatible with a government official. Wheaton had to admit the doubts that other warriors expressed had made him question the match even more than before.

"Seriously?" sputtered Poppy. Wheaton seemed completely oblivious to the anger she was feeling and that was starting to piss her off.

"I am always serious," he deadpanned, appearing unsure why she questioned him.

"Yeah, I'm getting that. The polite thing to do would have been to let me know you got home…and the carrying to bed would have been nice also." Did she sound as if she were pouting? Poppy hated people who pouted.

Wheaton turned to face her after making himself a drink. Staring at it for a few seconds, he placed his cup back on the counter. "I do not understand the interaction you want. Did you want to procreate last night? I have a small amount of time if you would like to do so now."

If Poppy had been angry before, she was even angrier now. She was silent as she stared at him for a moment. He actually had the balls to appear hopeful at possibly getting some sex. Poppy was done. *Done.*

"Wheaton, we need to talk. And I need you to listen." Walking over to the couch, Poppy waited for him to follow.

"I really have to go, Poppy. There are many items that need my attention this morning." He turned toward the door to leave.

"Wait, you have time for sex but not talking?" Stunned at what she was hearing, all she could do was just stand there staring at him.

"Yes. Sex is more important than talking so I would have made time." And with that he simply turned and walked out the door.

Wheaton thought it was better to leave before he did something to make her even more upset with him. Considering he did not know what had set her off in the first place, that seemed like a solid plan.

As the door closed behind him, he tried to think of what could have angered his new bride but was quickly distracted when he ran into another warrior in the hall. Going over meeting notes for the day, his mind was occupied more with items that would need to be discussed and less with his prickly bride. Hopefully tonight would be better and she would calm down enough to explain why she was so upset. Even better would be if she completely forgot about it and they moved to physical relations. As he walked with the warrior away from the door, he thought he heard a loud huff come from their apartment but must have been mistaken. She couldn't be that angry, could she?

In the apartment, Poppy stood glaring at the door. *What the hell had just happened?* Wheaton had to have known how angry she was, right? She did understand that he had limited experience with humans but the emotion of anger was broader than just her species. He had essentially brushed her off and acted as if she were only there as a physical vessel when he needed her.

Poppy let out a frustrated scream. Not only had that douchebag left her alone again, but he hadn't even realized how not cool that was. She'd better try to calm down before he came back, whenever that may be, and try to figure out a way to communicate to him she wasn't going to be treated as an afterthought. This was supposed to be their bonding time, dammit! How was she supposed to bond with someone who only showed up when she was sleeping?

Staring at the door, she had one word running through her head. *Fuck.*

For the next three days, Wheaton and Poppy saw each other in passing. Barely any words were spoken and the physical contact and any "exploration" they'd had the first night didn't happen again. Poppy did wake up snuggled into him but going to bed alone sucked. She had a feeling she would actually fall fast and hard for him if given the opportunity. From what she was able to see of Wheaton, she could tell he was honest, sincere, and loyal to his warrior brothers. A day didn't go by that he wasn't busy with everything he needed to do and Poppy admired his work ethic. It made some of the boyfriends she'd had in the past seem like the losers they were.

Listening to the *Rain* album on her player, she sat on the couch and decided to have a pity party. The album was a compilation of music Poppy always listened to when it rained outside and she felt blue. Poppy had to admit, when she wallowed, she went all-out. The only difference was that she didn't have Oreos to gorge on or Pixie to call and complain to. Thinking about Pixie ended up being the push to make her actually start crying. As hot tears tracked down her face, she had never felt so alone in her life. Closing her eyes and leaning her head against the back of the couch, she didn't notice anyone behind her until she felt a finger trace a tear on her cheek. Opening her eyes, Poppy glanced up into Wheaton's concerned face.

When Wheaton had walked into their quarters, he had been taken aback to find Poppy looking so miserable on the couch. Thinking she might be feeling unwell, he walked closer until he noticed that she was crying. His first experience with her tears had been when she was sad as she was leaving Earth and her sister, and his gut clenched to realize that maybe she was missing her old life. Walking up quietly so he didn't startle her, he touched her face.

"What is wrong?" he asked. Since she still had her headphones on she couldn't hear him but was able to read his lips. Taking off her headphones, she tossed her player onto the table in front of her.

"I'm sad," she whispered, wiping her face on her hands.

Wheaton might be dense when it came to humans but he could tell she was sad. He wanted to know *why* she was sad. She had food, clothes and entertainment to keep her occupied in their rooms when he was gone. Unsure if he should even ask what was wrong, he did and braced himself for the answer.

"What happened to make you sad?" Wheaton moved around the couch until he was sitting beside her.

"Wheaton, I'm not happy. I don't think this is going to work out…maybe I should contact Valerie and make arrangements to end our trial period early."

Wheaton felt anger when he thought of her leaving. He had not seen her much during her stay so far, but the time that he was able to spend with her left him craving more. The only thing that had kept him back was his earlier idea of not becoming too attached.

"Tell me what to do to make you not sad. You cannot leave me," Wheaton said, reaching for her.

She shook off his hand and stood up. Poppy was annoyed he was deciding now was the time to talk. Were tears the only way to get through to the big lug?

"Do you realize this is the first time you've touched me in three days? We barely talk and I think the last thing you said to me was when you asked me to move out of your way so you could leave yesterday."

Deciding it was always easier just to rip the bandage off quickly, she spat out the thoughts that had been tumbling around in her head since her second day of solitude.

"I don't think we are a good match, Wheaton. You act like you can't stand to be around me and I'm lonelier here than I ever was on Earth. At least back home I could still see my friends and Pixie…and visit dogs at the shelter." With a sad smile she continued, "I'm totally isolated here and I haven't been able to talk to her on that video thingy because our timing doesn't line up. I'm just really unhappy." Craving some sort of physical contact, she leaned into him as she started crying.

Wheaton stiffened up for a second as if he were uncomfortable with the contact and then reached over to hold her shoulders. Putting his arms around her, he leaned his face toward the top of her head while she rested her face against his chest. After a few moments she stopped crying but didn't move away. This was the only interaction she had experienced with another person in three days and she was going to soak it up while she could. Tilting her face to the side so she could breathe easier, she felt his arms tighten as he took in the scent of her hair.

Wheaton felt the warmth of her body and relished the contact. Even if her face was puffy and leaking, he had to admit this contact was better than if she left and he had absolutely none. He had, unknowingly, made his bride feel unwelcome. Not having a human before, he had been unsure what their care involved. Realizing that something needed to change to convince her stay, he thought for a couple moments.

"This is nice," he whispered, his breath moving her hair slightly.

"This"—she stopped to swallow hard—"this is what I was missing. I need someone who will be present...someone who'll talk to me and ask questions and just generally care if I'm there or not. I can't be ignored...I refuse to be ignored." She looked up at him with a determined expression on her face, no matter how much it hurt.

He moved one of his large hands to her face and her cheek to wipe a stray tear away. "This hurts me. Please don't cry again. I don't understand why, but it makes me upset to see you sad." Wheaton compared watching her cry to being hit in the stomach. For some reason it made him feel sick and angry. He felt the need to make her stop and fix whatever was the cause. Realizing that he was the cause made him feel awful.

When Wheaton had originally been matched with Poppy, he had questioned the program. Sure there had been a glitch for it to say his potential bride was a medical office worker when he was a diplomat, he had asked the science sector to check into the matching algorithms and make sure they were working correctly. But Wheaton no longer questioned his match. Not one bit. In fact, he'd had no doubts shortly after they had met but his previous complaints had stirred up enough warriors so now an official investigation was being conducted.

The last thing Wheaton wanted was Poppy to know he had doubted their joining in the beginning and that he was the reason there was a problem with the Bridal Pacts. Talking and laughing with her was the one thing he had started to anticipate toward the end of the day. Prior to her arriving, Wheaton had thrived on government meetings and negotiations. And now, some Council members had even questioned his commitment to his race because he called for shorter meetings and had defended his innocent little mate when she was disparaged.

Gazing into her face, he took in every detail of her upset visage, wanting to replace it with a smile, but actually being able to accomplish that seemed like a huge task.

"Will you do something for me?" she asked quietly while she searched his face.

"Anything," he answered, hoping he was able to do whatever it was quickly and it wouldn't involve her leaving him to do so.

"Listen to this music. I think it will help you understand what I'm saying...how I feel." Reaching for her music player, she took her earbuds and placed one in his ear and the other in hers. Selecting a couple songs from Patty Griffin's *1,000 Kisses*, she started playing the music. "Just listen," she whispered in his free ear.

Three songs later he finally got the point. By this time, Poppy was basically sitting on his lap with her head against his chest as they listened. When the track ended, she gently tugged the earbud from his ear.

"It sounds so sad," Wheaton said, gazing deep into her eyes. If this sad music was comparable to the way he'd made her feel, it made him want to punch himself in the mouth. How had she sat here feeling like this for days?

"It's supposed to," Poppy said, staring into his eyes just as intently, seeming to realize he finally got it.

His hands, which had been rubbing her back in a comforting motion, moved to cup her face.

"I don't want you to feel that," he said before his mouth slanted across hers. Wheaton vowed to himself the pain and loneliness she was feeling right now would never be caused by him again. He was realizing his happiness was hinged on her own. "I should explain..."

Pausing for a moment to suck in a huge breath, he realized he owed her the truth. "After our first night together I made a decision. A decision I now think was the wrong one." Catching her gaze, he cupped her cheek in his palm. "I thought it would be best to not get too close to you, in case our match ended up not being permanent. I could not imagine it being easy to get over the feel of your presence if I let you fully into my life and then you decided to leave. Now I realize that I was pushing you away and that is the exact opposite of what I wanted to accomplish. I will fix this if you will let me."

Poppy had sucked in a deep breath before he blocked it with his mouth. His lips sucked lightly at hers while he cradled her jaw. Poppy slid her hands up to his face, tracing his cheeks, before running her fingers into his hair. Slow and deep. Consuming and drowning. Wheaton felt himself get lost in the kiss. His hands left her face to run down her back to her bottom. He rumbled into her mouth while licking at the seam of her lips. Unable to stop his hands from massaging the plump cheeks within his grasp, he then pulled her hips forward to grind against his erection. Breathing hard, he struggled for control as he pulled away.

"Will you stay?" he asked softly.

"For now," she whispered back.

Relief hit him in a wave. If she had said no, he was not sure what he would have done. Wheaton knew he wouldn't have let her go but was unsure of how he would have convinced her to stay. Seeing their position on the couch, Wheaton smiled at her and twisted his hips a bit to call attention to it.

"I would like to take you to our sleeping area." Wheaton smiled at the blush on her face that replaced her now gone tears.

Leaning her forehead against his shoulder, Poppy hugged him and then scooted off his lap. She studied his face and he wondered if she could read that he was not only listening, but also absorbing.

"I would like to talk more first. A couple hours ago I was ready to pack my bags. You can't keep me at an arm's length and expect this to work. We need to have some time for ourselves. I know that you work hard but if you want me to stay then we have a lot to work on. From the small bits I've been able to be around you I can already tell you I like and admire you." Poppy paused, cupping his cheeks. "And our physical chemistry is off the charts. I have never felt the desire that you make me feel. I'll stay for now but we need to get to know each other better. What do you say we start over?"

Wheaton nodded, pleased she was giving him a second chance to make up for ignoring her for so long. From what he had been able to see of the woman Poppy was, he was grateful for the chance to make up for the mess he had made. She was truly a wonderful woman and it was time she knew he recognized that.

"We have lots to talk about." Holding out her hand, she said, "But that doesn't mean we can't cuddle and talk at the same time."

Smiling, he followed her into the bedroom. "As long as you remember we will be doing this naked. You wore clothes the past few nights and I assumed you were cold because I wasn't present. There will be no excuse tonight," he teased, happy that she was giving him another chance.

"Deal. But this time, I get to undress you too."

CHAPTER TWELVE

Their truce lasted through the following week and then the next. Poppy could tell that Wheaton was consciously trying to include her into his daily routine. She started a tradition of good-morning kisses, which he usually tried to make into all-day kisses. Not that she minded. The companionship she was receiving now was like night and day compared to the first few days here. Wheaton talked about his childhood, his life on the ship, home world and hobbies, which were all fascinating to Poppy. From what he described, Poppy realized he must have had a very lonely existence and his warrior friends were brothers by choice. She talked about her love of dogs but how she wasn't able to have a pet, while he had trouble understanding the concept of an animal living with him. There seemed to be no subject that they couldn't talk about, except his work.

Whenever she asked questions regarding his time away, he would steer her attention to another subject. They ended up spending a majority of their time together alone talking and getting to know one another. He had taken her on more in-depth tours of the ship and she had watched him spar in the rec room with other warriors when he had the opportunity but she never had the opportunity to talk to other warriors. Wheaton seemed to want her to himself and for right now she realized she was okay with that since she wasn't too keen on sharing his attention either. The two exceptions were Dathrow and Thorne. She had talked to them a couple of times when they stopped to ask Wheaton questions or have him sign papers.

In the evenings, Wheaton now made sure they shared their meal and talked. Some nights he would connect her music to the speaker system in their rooms and listen to her eclectic playlists. Their names always stumped him though. She smiled, thinking about the long discussion they'd had when she tried to explain Hootie and the Blowfish. He didn't seem to like any music that was too moody, which meant she had to sing to Adele during the day when he was gone. One day when he'd come back from a meeting, he caught her dancing around the room to ABBA and laughed when she ended with a bow. Dancing with him was fun and she loved to see him smile as she tried to teach him some moves. His dancing always came out like a fighting stance, but she didn't care. He seemed to be enjoying himself and that was all that Poppy cared about.

After their dinners, she started showing him some of her favorite movies. He, of course, loved the action movies with explosions but also paid very close attention to the mushy movies she picked out. Watching him concentrate on the TV screen, she realized he was studying the interaction of the characters. Wheaton would now reach for her hand or put his arm around her shoulders when they walked up and down the gleaming metal hallways. Chairs were pulled out when she went to sit down and he stood when she entered a room. He'd quickly become one of the most attentive boyfriends she'd ever had.

Late evening had become a time both of them had begun to anticipate. Cuddling without clothes but keeping sex in the "not yet" category made Poppy feel like a teenager. It was during their naked times that they asked each other the real personal stuff. They talked about what they liked and didn't like. Poppy wasn't a prude but lack of experience had dented her confidence a bit. Wheaton had explained they had "pleasure ships" the warriors visited but he also had been nervous about what would happen when his bride arrived, which explained the porn. She was curious about the Pleasure Sector but did not necessarily want to hear about it from her future husband.

Poppy asked him how many children he wanted to have and his response had been sweet when he said, "The number you bless me with will be the perfect amount." Soon their discussions led to touching and touching led to some heavy petting and full-body kisses but that was as far as it went. Wheaton and Poppy had decided to wait until they were positive their match was permanent before having full intercourse. Wheaton had not been too enthusiastic about the decision but grudgingly admitted it made sense. Poppy was no longer taking her birth control pills, and risking a pregnancy when they were still feeling each other out seemed too risky.

Thinking back on the past few weeks and smiling to herself, Poppy realized how much she already cared about him. She was positive that Wheaton was "it" for her and she was anxious to call Pixie and run some stuff by her. Pixie tended to be the thinker of the sisters, something that Poppy had used for her benefit when it came to relationships.

Anxious now for her call to her sister, she got the screen ready. Setting up the com units had actually been a harder thing to do than either one of them had figured. They required special permission via a Council vote to contact Earth. Final decision was that the Council would allow "calls" as long as they were monitored. Poppy was unsure what they thought might be said but she wasn't going to ask too many questions considering she had gotten her way.

Seeing Pixie's face fill the screen made Poppy tear up.

"ET, phone home. ET, phone home," Pixie deadpanned.

"You're so stupid, Pix," Poppy said with a smile.

"Damn, Pops, I've missed you! You look great, by the way. I assume the humidity is controlled up there, considering that's the best I've ever seen your hair behave."

"Ha!" Poppy snorted. "Sometimes you're such a bish. I've missed you too." Poppy grinned into the screen.

"Seriously, is everything going well with Mr. Tall, Dark and Green? Do we need a code word in case I need to hijack a ship and head your way for a jailbreak?" Pixie whispered while covering one side of her mouth, as if that would make their conversation private.

"Everything is going really well. I'm happy and Wheaton is great. We had a couple speed bumps the first few days but that's been worked out...it's actually really great right now. We talk all the time and I've decided I'm staying," she blurted out in one gust of air.

Wow, Poppy realized that saying it out loud wasn't as scary as she imagined. She really *was* happy. And she couldn't imagine being this happy without Wheaton. She didn't want to say that her happiness hinged on him but she knew that he was the main reason she was happy. His smiles, laughter and touch had become addictive.

Pixie sat with an expression on her face that was hard to read. Poppy couldn't yet tell if she was happy or sad at the decision.

"So you're staying, huh?" Pixie asked.

"Yes, Pix, I think I'm in love with him," Poppy said softly.

Pixie looked as if she might cry. Poppy shifted her eyes away from the screen. If one cried then the other wasn't close behind and she didn't want to be sad about her decision.

"I could tell this was coming, Pops." Poppy glanced back at the screen to a smiling Pixie, who was now wiping her eyes.

"Really? You're not mad?" Poppy asked, trying to read her sister's expression.

"How can I be mad? All I want is for you to be happy and from everything you've told me over the last couple weeks you are definitely happy. I've never seen you this happy before, Poppy. Truly. I'm very happy for you, I promise," Pixie said in a voice Poppy could tell was serious.

"Now, on to the most important question..." Pixie got on her serious face.

"What?" Poppy asked.

"Have you guys done the nasty yet?" Pixie asked with a laugh and a lecherous leer.

"Ummm...not yet. But I think it's coming soon. I'm ready and I know he's ready. We've just been trying to take things slowly." Poppy paused, noticing Pixie was eating a bag of chips. "Everything okay with you, Pix? You only eat junk food when you're stressed out," she asked, nodding to the bag her sister was holding.

"Yeah, just work shit. Brenda is fucking everything up and I've had to spend a lot of extra hours at work fixing her mistakes. You know I don't want to fire her, we're old friends, so I'm super tired. Add to that Brian being a dick lately isn't helping. I was hoping to tell you I was engaged with this call, but he didn't propose on our anniversary so I owe you ten bucks for losing that bet." Pixie frowned and dug deeper into the bag of chips.

"Sorry, babe, that sucks. He will though. I remember you said he was working on the plans for a new building and was stressed with work too. Did he at least take you out for a nice dinner?"

Pixie rolled her eyes. "Yeah, we went out but it was to that Chinese place. The place which, by the way, I am now totally sick of."

"Yeah, I can see that getting old really quick. Did he get you flowers or anything?" Poppy felt like maybe she was digging to find something good that Brian had done but there was a high probability he had totally schmucked out.

"Don't you remember, sis? Flowers are a waste of money," Pixie said in a deep voice, imitating her boyfriend, who had indeed, apparently managed to screw up their anniversary.

"Well shit, Pix. I got nothing. I thought he would have done something special, even if it was small." Poppy was disappointed on behalf of her sister.

"Oh, but he did," Pixie said sarcastically. "He got me a gift card so I can get new work clothes at that posh place on the Plaza. You remember the one where I can't fit into anything in the store unless we are talking about earrings or socks." Pixie raised one eyebrow, showing how pissed-off it must have made her.

"Well…maybe you both need a vacation?" Poppy suggested, trying to change the subject before she witnessed her sister losing her shit.

"Meh, nobody on Earth has time to take a vacation, Pops. I couldn't imagine leaving work right now. Nobody would get paid and the place would probably burn down if I left for more than twenty-four hours…" Pixie seemed as if she were at her wits' end but was trying to shake it off. "Time for a subject change before I go crazy. Let's talk about something that everyone wants to know. Give me the nekkid details on Big, Buff and Galactic."

When Pixie waggled her eyebrows like a lunatic, Poppy burst out laughing.

"Damn, Pix, I miss you," she said, her tone serious, once she could stop laughing.

"So, no details? That's not very nice. We're sisters. Sisters are supposed to share everything. Just hold up the fingers of how many inches you are getting in this deal. Give me something! I need to live through you since I haven't had any with Brian for the last month." Pixie held out her hands as if she were measuring. "This much? This much? Dear god, Poppy, if my hands get any farther apart, I'm going to tell them you may need medical attention when you finally give him a chance at your pants."

"Jesus, Pix, I'm not telling you. I will tell you that he is blessed. Very, very, very blessed." She smiled and wiggled her own eyebrows.

"Oh my god, don't do the wiggle. You look ridiculous. Only I can pull that off," Pixie said with a giggle.

After the girls chatted for a bit longer about random daily happenings, they were interrupted when Poppy heard the door swish open.

"I'll let you go now, Pix. Wheaton is home. Call you later, okay?"

"Sure thing, chicken wing, and really…I am very happy for you."

"Thanks, Pix. I'm happy for me too. Now to tell my big guy." Smiling at her sister who was grinning back at her, Poppy felt calm and ready to face Wheaton.

"Love you. Muuuwahh." Pixie waved and then disappeared.

Turning to greet Wheaton with a smile, Poppy saw immediately he was upset. He had a "tell" when he was upset, and right now it was glaringly obvious.

"Wheaton, what's wrong?"

"How do you always know when something is wrong?" he asked, getting a drink from the kitchenette.

"You clench your jaw really hard and I can see the vein pop up in your forehead…and don't change the subject. What happened?" Pixie walked up behind him and wrapped her arms around him from behind.

Letting out a big sigh, Wheaton said, "We have to put a halt on bride collection for a bit and the warriors who have not been selected are upset. I am worried we may have a riot soon if the cause does not get resolved quickly." Turning in her arms, he hugged her back. "Did you have a nice talk with your sister?" he asked, hoping to distract her.

Poppy stared at Wheaton for a few moments in silence. She could tell what he was trying to do. She studied his face, hoping he would open up about his Council work at some point. He was always so secretive it was starting to drive her nuts. Poppy figured he dealt with things during the Council meetings that she wouldn't understand but she would feel better if he at least tried to let her into that part of his life.

"That was another subject change. Why is there a problem with getting more brides? Maybe I can help," Poppy suggested.

"This is nothing you can help to do. It is technical."

He dismissed her offer so offhandedly she instantly felt her hackles rise.

"Wheaton, look at me. I'm not useless. I've read all my books, listened to all my music over and over and will slowly go crazy if I don't get to do something around here. And I will take you with me if that happens. Tell me what's happening." Tapping her toes with her hands on her hips, Poppy stood waiting for him to open up, even just a little bit.

"I cannot talk about it right now, Poppy. It is classified…but when I am able I will let you know what is happening. There was nothing more for me to do in the meetings today so I decided to spend the afternoon with you. Did you want to play that game again with the little hat and money? I am going to win this time—I still believe you cheated," he teased, seeming anxious to change the subject.

Knowing that he had successfully distracted her, she smacked his arm.

"I did not cheat at Monopoly! You just had bad luck with the dice."

"I will still be watching you closely. How was your talk with your sister?" He knew how much she enjoyed her vid sessions with Pixie and sometimes Val.

"Well, it went really well. I actually told her I was staying," she blurted out. Hoping he was on the same page as her with their relationship, she held her breath, waiting for his reaction.

"Thank your god!" he yelled, hugging her tightly. "I have been waiting for you to tell me your decision."

"So, you're happy? You want me to stay as much as I want to stay?" Poppy hated that she sounded so unsure of herself but this was an either-go-big-or-go-home moment.

Smiling at her, Wheaton cupped her cheeks. "I want you to stay so much, Poppy! You have made me happier than I can ever remember being these past cycles. I have a hard time imagining my mornings without our kisses and cannot imagine what I would do without your presence in my life."

She bit her lip in nervousness. "I was actually thinking we could...maybe we could...you know since we've decided I'm staying."

"Sex?" He said the one word on a whoosh of air and his entire body stiffened at the possibility of actually extending their physical relationship to the culmination.

"Sex." Poppy felt her own nerves tighten at the thought.

Before Poppy knew what was happening, she'd been picked up in a fireman's carry, laughing as he practically jogged to the sleeping area. Her stomach bounced on his shoulder until she was back on her feet beside the bed they had reached.

"Finally!" he said, quickly stripping her of her T-shirt and yoga pants. He had once told her he appreciated that she wore light clothing that was easily removed.

"Hey, mister, I think I have been very generous in the touchy-feely department, so knock it off." By this time, her shirt, bra and pants were off. The only thing left was her panties. "And why am *I* practically naked and you still have all that leather on?"

Poppy smiled at the look of triumph that Wheaton wore once her clothes were removed. Propping her hands on her hips, she stared at him with a stern face.

"Because you are beautiful," he answered, hooking his fingers in her underwear and pulling them down her legs. "And you have been very generous. I appreciate the help with self-pleasuring you have been giving me daily…although when I think about your help I feel the need to self-pleasure again." He moved his hands quickly, undoing the buckles and zippers on his own outfit. Once he was completely nude, he tugged her to the bed.

Poppy took a minute to take in all the glory before her. Wheaton was so beautiful. He didn't seem to have an ounce of fat on his body and his skin was tight over the perfect amount of muscles that graced his frame. Right now she was focusing her attention on his cock though. The past week she had felt it, stroked it, licked and sucked it but she was finally going to be able to feel it fill her. She could almost feel her pussy clench on the empty space she needed him to be in.

"Speaking of self-pleasuring…did you take the batteries out of my vibrator?" She'd noticed them missing after the second night he'd helped her use it. If he was going to masturbate then by god she was going to do it also.

"Yes I did. I don't like that tool. If anything is inside you, I want it to be me. You may use your own fingers but if you want to be filled then I will be the one filling you."

Gripping her hips, he pulled her under his body while parting her legs with a knee. So after realizing her toy did more than just buzz, he'd decided to take action and get rid of the competition.

"Seriously? You seemed to like my vibrator when I let you use it on me…" Parting her legs so he could nestle into the vee of her body, she felt his cock settle against her mound.

Moving his head down her neck, he breathed in her scent. "I am always serious. And yes, I did enjoy watching the tremors of that piece of plastic drive you crazy. It was only when I realized that you could insert it into a place I had not yet had the privilege to enter did I decide to disable it. Granted, it is nothing compared to my body but it still made me angry at the thought. Can we kiss now for sex? I have been wanting this since I first scented your neck on Earth." Licking her collarbone and nuzzling her skin, his tongue left a path of warm fire that had her arching into his embrace.

"Hellz yes. Please continue."

Shifting until his arms were under her back, he hooked his hands on the top of her shoulders to hold her steady. Completely under his control, she shivered. She was trapped in his embrace and loved it.

"Thank you, Poppy. I do not believe you understand how happy this has made me," he said in a voice that sounded like he would rumble at any moment.

"I want you, Wheaton. Kiss me already," she whimpered against his lips.

All of a sudden his mouth was on hers and she seemed to have no air but was somehow still breathing. There was no way she could keep her eyes open against the onslaught of his mouth. Raising one leg up to rub against the outside of his muscled thigh, she sighed into his kiss.

Taking the sigh as permission to enter deeper, he tangled his tongue with hers. Plucking at her nipple, he rumbled deep in his chest. "I cannot wait until these are full of milk for our young," he said against her mouth. The visual apparently excited him so much he started rubbing his hips harder against her. The tip of his cock left a damp trail on Poppy's stomach as she rubbed back. His skin felt so hot against hers.

Holy shit, this was amazing. His fingers, his mouth, his everything. Poppy raked her nails lightly down to his muscled ass. Doing some gripping and kneading of her own, she took the moment when he moved his mouth to her breast to gasp for air. Nipping and suckling at her nipples, he took turns going back and forth…apparently not wanting one to get jealous of the other. Poppy glanced down to see him staring at her. He let go of one nipple with a *pop* and gently blew air over it, which caused it to get so hard she felt a slight pain prickle the tip. He brought two fingers to his mouth and licked them while still holding her gaze.

She reached for his hair to drag his mouth back to hers just as his fingers made it to their destination. Parting her sleek folds deftly and circling around her clit, he made a couple steady circles before sliding one finger into her.

"You are so tight…and hot," he murmured against her lips, seemingly anxious to finally be able to delve into her depths.

"May I lick you?" he asked.

"Fuck yeah." Poppy groaned, adjusting her body. Her legs opened wider to accommodate his shoulders as he moved down, kissing and licking his way past her stomach and hips.

Wheaton smiled against her skin. He loved the way Poppy talked. Sometimes she would make up words or say, "Pardon my French" after a tangent, and he thought it was adorable. He had started learning within a few days that "fuck" had many meanings. She used the word almost constantly when she was talking, from times when she stubbed her toe, to when she caught glimpses of him naked.

Once his mouth reached her pussy, he checked to make sure she was watching him. Wheaton gave her a sexy grin before spreading her lips open with his strong fingers. Nuzzling her clit for a moment before using the tip of his tongue, he pulsed with steady pressure off and on against her nub. He took breaks from the pressure to suckle at it. She leaned her head back and moaned loudly. The taste of her was addictive, making his taste buds crave more. The thought of being able to suckle at her whenever he desired was heady. A vision that pushed him to the edges of his already strained control.

She gripped the sheets in her sweating fists. Poppy heard herself moaning like a porn star. Wheaton had turned her into a porn star!

A nip at her outer lips made her jump and she looked down her body at him. His green eyes were watching her closely, almost glowing.

"Pay attention," Wheaton said against her flesh, wanting her full focus on him and what he was doing.

Gripping Wheaton's hair, she pushed him back down. "Oh, sweetie, you have *all* my attention. I promise," she moaned as he continued his assault.

His tongue and lips were driving her crazy. When he added his finger to her sheathe, she felt her toes clench. Holy fuck, his fingers were starting to go lower. Continuing to lick and nip, he had one finger in her pussy and rubbed another digit against her ass. That pushed her completely over the edge. It felt so dirty and oh so good.

"Ahhhhhhhh!" She exploded against his mouth and everything went to white noise in her head. Her legs began to twitch and her stomach clenched and unclenched as her orgasm flowed through her. Trying to catch her breath, she could feel her heart practically beat out of her chest and had a fleeting thought of a heart attack before she came back to the present.

Moving up her body, Wheaton placed the tip of his cock at her opening. "Ready?" he asked, his lips glistening from her pussy. He licked his lips, staring down at her hungrily.

"God yes," Poppy said in between panting for air.

With a thrust of his hips, he plunged all his inches at once into her swollen folds.

"Fuuuuuuuck," Poppy groaned, feeling the stretch of her body adjusting to being stuffed as it had never been before.

Wheaton's entire body was covered in a light layer of sweat and his chest was rumbling as he started thrusting into her welcoming body. Obviously unable to help himself, he tucked his head into her neck as he whispered into her skin.

Unable to focus on what he was saying, Poppy concentrated on the cadence of his rhythm. Moving her legs up around his waist made him go deeper and start to rub a sweet spot. On every down thrust, his pelvic bone hit her clit and made her tighten around him to the beat of his thrusting. Her hands had been clutching his back at first and now moved down to his ass as if she could keep him thrusting in the delicious rhythm he had begun.

"Ohhhhh god. Wheaton!" she yelled as she started to come. Her pussy fluttered as it tried to clench and hold on to the cock now pistoning in and out of her. Moving her face toward his shoulder, Poppy nipped and bit hungrily at Wheaton's sweaty skin until she felt her tremors slow.

Wheaton had been waiting for her to come again before letting loose. He increased the power of his thrusts and gripped her tighter as he moved faster. Her entire body shook as he growled out loudly and flooded her with his warm fluid.

"Poppy... Poppy...that was perfect," he said, his arms threatening to collapse. Catching himself, he lowered his body to the side.

As he pulled out, Poppy felt a warm trail dampen her leg.

"I think we need a towel," Poppy said huskily without raising her head.

"I think we need a bath," he replied with a deep chuckle.

"Wheaton?"

"Yes?" Settling his head on the pillow next to hers, he moved his hand to link their fingers.

"Best. Afternoon. Ever," she deadpanned.

"I agree," he said back in the same voice.

Poppy and Wheaton started laughing at the same time.

CHAPTER THIRTEEN

Poppy's morning started out with a bang when she awoke to a very aroused Wheaton cuddled against her back. Stretching with her arms over her head made her let out a groan. Maybe she should hit the rec room and work out. If her muscles felt this sore after a night with Wheaton, she must be really out of shape. Even though he was stiff against her backside, he was actually sleeping. One little wiggle out from under his arm and she was rolling off the bed, in the smoothest motion possible, to not wake him.

After taking care of her morning bathroom ritual, she walked into the living area to make some tea. Waiting for her cup to cool, she noticed a blinking light at the doorway. She had learned earlier during her stay that the light indicated there was a message waiting. Poppy decided to listen to it. She would feel guilty letting him sleep in if he was needed by the Council.

"Wheaton, we must speak immediately." Poppy recognized Thorne's voice. Her entire body froze when she heard the next part of the message. "You were correct earlier regarding the current bridal matches being wrong. We have found there is a glitch in the programming system on Earth's end and it is skewing the matches. Thankfully, the concern you have regarding your own match alerted us to the discrepancies before more of our warriors were matched. The brides that are currently on the squadron ships will be transported back to Earth immediately. The Council has decided to have bridal contracts dissolved as soon as possible."

Poppy couldn't breathe. Feeling what was in her hand slip from her numb fingers, she had barely enough time to move her toes before the cup and hot liquid hit the floor with a shatter.

"Poppy?" Glancing over her shoulder, she saw Wheaton standing bare-chested, leaning against the door frame. Concern was evident on his handsome face.

"What are you doing up so early? I was hoping to share our morning kisses."

Tears filling her eyes, and a tightening in her chest, Poppy cleared her throat. "You have a message," she said as calmly as she could considering her world was crashing around her.

"Thank you. I will listen in a moment. Come and give me my morning kiss." He reached out a hand as if to draw her into his embrace.

Poppy held out her hand to stop him from moving closer. "No, you should really listen to it now." Scooting past him, Poppy walked back into the bedroom. As soon as the door swished shut, she began to frantically gather her possessions into her duffel. She was pretty sure she was a mess by now but didn't want to take the time to wipe her face.

"Noooooo!"

Poppy jumped, hearing Wheaton yell the tortured sound from the living room. Hearing his bare feet run back to the bedroom had her pausing in her packing. She took in the vision of him blocking the opening she was prepared to walk through.

Wheaton felt as if his heart was being ripped out. He could not believe how foolish he had once been. Thinking that the mess with the bridal matching was over, he had brushed off some of the other Council members when they'd approached him about it recently during their meetings. He had not considered that they would try to take Poppy away after he had let his own concerns go. As she gathered her belongings, dread filled him to the bones and his mind raced. There had to be a way to fix this.

Wheaton folded his arms across his chest. "You will *not* leave me! I forbid it!" he said loudly, widening his stance as if to physically trap her in the room.

"Wheaton, I can't talk to you right now. I need to pack." Poppy gritted her teeth so she wouldn't start sobbing.

"You are not packing. You are going to listen to me." He moved into the room.

"Stop right there, asshole." Holding up her hand to stop him in his tracks, she said, "I heard that entire fucking message, and from what I heard it sounded like you doubted our match. Since when, Wheaton? Since the first time you met me? When I decided to not have sex with you immediately? How about last night, when you finally got to fuck me? Huh? When, Wheaton? When?!" By this time, Poppy was screaming at him. Her voice sounded hoarse to her own ears. She felt the harsh strain from trying to hold back tears.

As she zipped her duffel closed, she saw another pair of her pants on the floor. Bending down to pick them up, she didn't notice Wheaton come up behind her until the last moment. He grabbed her from behind and trapped her arms at her side to whisper into her ear, "Calm down, Poppy. Calm down and listen to me. Please."

"I will not fucking calm down, Wheaton. This is one gigantic clusterfuck. When will they come to get me? I still need to gather up my stuff from the living room," she said, standing stiffly in his arms.

"Poppy, you are not going anywhere. Please, you cannot. Let me explain what that message meant. Just listen," he pleaded, rocking back and forth in an effort to soothe her.

"Fine, you can talk, but don't expect me to stay once you're done with your little speech," she bit out.

Moving slowly as if to not startle her, he bent and slid his arm under her knees to pick her up. Carrying her into the living room, he sat her on the couch and stood beside her with his palm out.

"Please touch me, Poppy. I am addicted to your contact." Searching her face with sad eyes, he held his hand out.

"Wheaton, just talk. I woke up so happy and then heard that message. I'm trying really hard not to lose my shit right now." She ran her palms down her face to wipe away the now cool tears.

"Let me start at the beginning then." Rubbing his face as if to prepare to say something she didn't want to hear, Wheaton took in a deep breath.

"Please do," she prompted sarcastically.

"When I first found out that I was matched, I did not react very well. I only entered the pool to be an example for my men. My life was organized. I had my work with the Council I needed to focus on, anything else was a distraction in my opinion. I felt that I could better serve my warrior brothers from my Council seat, not by becoming one of the first husbands. I was perfectly content with my life but understood my duty to my brothers when my profile was pulled. We were all surprised in truth at the initial speed of the matches." He watched her closely, seemingly trying to make her understand. Pausing to swallow hard, he sat down on the couch.

"The time frame was suspicious to a majority of us. Our profiles were extremely detailed and although our matching system was built by our best engineers it did not seem plausible for it to find us life mates within such a short time frame. I questioned it at that time, before I ever left the ship to go to Earth. It had nothing to do with you personally. When I scanned over your sheet, it did prompt me to further question our compatibility. With you having no political experience, I was unsure how you would adjust to life with someone of my standing. When I viewed your picture I saw a soft and smiling woman. A woman who had an honest face that showed her emotions. A woman who, on paper, did not seem like someone I wanted in my life."

"You're absolutely right, Wheaton, we have nothing in common. This is a waste of time." Slapping her hands on her legs to stand up, she then said, "Can you find out when they'll return me home please? I need to be able to tell Pixie when to pick me up. Fuck! I need more than Pixie to pick me up, I'll need to find a place to live."

"Will you shut up for one second and give me a moment to finish?"

Stunned that he not only yelled at her but used the words "shut up", Poppy plopped back down onto the couch.

"Did you not hear anything I just said? I said that I questioned the speed of the match…I'm sure you did as well," he said, pointing a finger at her. Poppy did remember saying something about how fast it was to Valerie… Crap, he was right.

Nodding slightly for him to go on, she crossed her arms over her chest and waited for him to continue.

"Poppy, I may not have *wanted* you in my life at first…but I now realize how much I *need* you in my life. In the short amount of time that you have been here, you have made me smile, laugh and feel more than I ever have. It is scary and not what I expected or even wanted but I cannot let that go now that I have had a taste of it. Your face does show your emotions. It is a face that I look forward to staring at every moment that I have free. The preconceived idea of what I had in my head regarding a political bride was forgotten not long after you arrived. Please do not make me go back to the silence I had before you came and started yelling 'fuck' at me. I do not believe I could survive that." The last words were said on a whispered breath so quietly she barely caught it. His breath seemed to catch in his throat as he waited for Poppy to do or say something.

"Wheaton, from what Thorne said on that message I'm not even sure it's my choice. He made it sound like all the brides are going back. What if they make me go? No matter what we do, it may not be our choice." Poppy slid her arms around his body. The anger that she had felt when she heard the message had been forgotten during his speech.

She wasn't sure what her options were for staying but she did believe what he said. Maye he'd had questions when they first met, but now he wanted her to stay as much as she wanted to. Her head hurt when she thought about this mess. Hoping to draw some comfort from him, she held on tight to draw in in some calming breaths.

Hugging her back tightly, he kissed the top of her head and breathed in her scent.

"Let me talk to Thorne. I am on the Council. They cannot take you away from me…at least not without a fight." Hugging her back just as tightly, he paused and then continued, "I need to listen to that message again."

At that moment, the door chimed, indicating a visitor. They both stared at each other grimly.

"Well hell, they didn't waste any time at all."

"Sit down and I will get it. Remember what I said. You are not going anywhere," Wheaton said in a voice that screamed finality.

Opening the door with his wrist, Wheaton stood back with his arms crossed like a barrier to the world. Poppy was surprised to see not only Thorne but also Dathrow and Valerie standing in the opening. Valerie seemed just as emotionally drained as Poppy felt.

"Val!" Poppy walked over to Valerie, mindful of the still broken glass on the floor, to give the frazzled-looking woman a hug. Shortly after her arrival on the ship, Poppy had started speaking to Valerie by video conference often and they had become close friends in a short amount of time.

"Oh my god, Poppy! I'm so sorry for this mess." Val was on the brink of crying as well as she hugged her back.

"You're doing about as good as I am right now, aren't you?" Poppy said with a teary smile. Stepping back, she linked hands with Wheaton.

"This is one hell of a mess," Val heaved out with a sigh. "From the handholding I'm assuming you're not happy with the news?" She gestured to their linked hands.

"*Hell no!* We think the match is perfect and had already decided I was staying before we heard the voice message this morning. What's going to happen?"

"Maybe we can sit for a moment and discuss the situation?" Dathrow suggested in a somber voice.

"Yes please, sorry. I didn't mean to have y'all stand in the door." As Poppy moved to let them pass, Wheaton tightened his grip on her fingers.

Thorne and Dathrow sat while motioning for Valerie to speak.

"Okay…well…it seems there was a bug in the matchmaking code," she stuttered out. "Apparently, they ran the matches again and a different warrior popped up as your match, Poppy. It's a huge mess. Many of the liaisons are taking heat for it even though we had nothing to do with the actual programming of the system." Val cast a glance at Thorne and Dathrow before continuing. "We've been accused of matching the higher-ranking warriors over the others, and now the higher-ups on both sides want to wipe the slate clean and start over."

Wheaton stepped forward, tugging Poppy with him. "No! I am keeping my bride. She is my match no matter what the system says."

Thorne stood and started pacing. "Wheaton, it's not that simple. The Council is pushing to send the previous brides home and start over. Not only that… Wheaton, there is another situation that ties into this."

"Thorne, just say it. This can't get any worse," Poppy said with a sigh.

"Poppy, Wheaton has been assigned another bride," Thorne said quickly as if to lessen the blow.

"I want *no* other bride!" Wheaton shouted, startling Poppy.

"Well, fuck. I guess it *could* get worse. What do we do?" Poppy glanced at Val, who she knew even without asking was on their side.

"Well, right now, we're really trying to figure out what we *can* do." Val let out a watery sigh, as if she might cry again. "Can I talk to you in private, please?"

"Wheaton?" Poppy glanced at him. "I'm going to take Val into the bedroom and talk for a minute. Can you see if there is anything that you can get out of Thorne and Dathrow?" When he was about to protest, she said, "Val is on our side, sweetie. She may have an idea she wants to run by me before saying it in front of another Council member."

"Fine. Do not take too long. We might not have much time together. I do not want to waste a moment." Releasing her hand, he sat next to Dathrow and huffed.

Clutching Val's arm and leading her into the bedroom, Poppy hoped she had a couple tricks up her sleeve to figure out how to fix this mess. Clusterfuck indeed.

CHAPTER FOURTEEN

Sitting on the bed, Poppy put her head in her hands. Feeling as if she were taking hit after hit with no breath in between, she tried to calm herself. She looked up at a shuffling of papers to see Val digging through her bag.

"Tell me you can fix this, Val. Please…I can't leave him now. I'm pretty sure I'm totally in love with that man, and I don't know what I'd do if I have to leave." Swallowing back tears, she prayed that Val had a plan.

"What have I always told you, Poppy? I am here for *you*. Not only because it's my job but because we're friends." Val smiled, finding the paper she was searching for. "And I think I've found a loophole."

Thank god. "Tell me now. What is the loophole?"

Valerie sat next to her, holding out the original Bridal Pact forms Poppy and Wheaton had signed before this adventure had started.

"Here, the pact agreement says that unless you fear for your physical well-being or either party requests that the trial period ends, then you are required to spend your entire thirty days on the ship while finding out if you're compatible. Specifically being that the 'parties' are you and Wheaton, *not* the Council or the bridal service. The trial period can *only* be dissolved by the Council if you are a threat to their security." She paused with a smile. "Essentially they don't have a right to tell you to leave unless you're stealing secrets or you threaten their ship or their society." She pointed to the paragraph that held the info.

"So this is our plan then? It should work, right?" Excitement was evident in Poppy's voice as she quickly scanned to where their signatures were. It felt as if she had signed these forms eons ago instead of just a few short weeks.

"Yes," Val said with a relieved sigh.

"Well then, why did you want to talk in private?" Did Val have suspicions about the other warriors that were with Wheaton?

"Thorne is on the Council….and the Council members are the ones that are pushing for the matches to be dissolved, Poppy. Not Earth." Lowering her voice as if the men had super-hearing, she whispered, "Earth doesn't really want it known that we made such a massive mistake. We're still trying to get brides to apply and it's not going too well. A new anti-alien movement has formed since you left. They're basically using the same mindset that people used against different races marrying back when blacks and whites first started mingling. It's hugely racist but gathering a lot of followers and the protests are a huge deterrent to anyone even coming in and filling out our forms. The Intake Centers have had bomb threats almost daily and the protesters have gotten violent toward anyone entering the building. We have even had our cleaning people threatened as they come and go."

Valerie stood and cast Poppy a questioning glance.

"How well do you know those warriors other than Wheaton? Are they anti-human?" She crossed her arms and said with a huff, "Because let me tell you, there are some pretty anti-human Council members. They tried to stop me from coming up to see you. I couldn't take the chance of having you come back to Earth since we have more leverage with you still on the ship. Especially considering my loophole, if you had left then they could have claimed that you dissolved the trial period. There are definitely Council members working against us. I just don't know who yet."

Poppy thought long and hard on that one. She had met Thorne maybe four or five times, and he had been nice, if not civil toward her. She had originally attributed it to him being a warrior though. Dathrow she had been around more and he seemed very friendly and even eager for his own bride from what she could tell. They hadn't had much time to talk but from what she could gather Wheaton trusted both of the men.

"I think they're both friends of Wheaton's so I would hope they're on our side. I know Dathrow a little more than Thorne but overall I don't know. They're both polite to me and haven't said anything outright about my being here. If I had to assume, Dathrow is more trustworthy than Thorne but that's only because he has talked to me more. I think I make Thorne a little nervous. He admitted I was the first human he has ever met so it could just be that."

"Well let's go lay our cards on the table and see what reaction we get from those big guys. Their faces should tell us whose side they are on." Valerie strode toward the door, her walk determined.

"Val?" Rushing to catch her before she opened the door, Poppy reached out.

"Yes?"

Poppy pulled her into a massive hug.

"Oomph," Valerie puffed out, the squeeze of Poppy's hug taking the breath out of her.

"Thank you so much. You're a lifesaver," Poppy whispered into Val's shoulder.

Smiling, Val hugged her, patting her on her back. "Poppy, I am here for you and only you. No matter what."

"Well then, let's go. Time to see who our friends are." Waving her wrist over the sensor, Poppy went to share their news with Wheaton, who had hopefully been able to weasel some info out of the other two while she and Val had been planning.

* * * * *

Wheaton stood immediately when Poppy and Val reentered the room. Tugging Poppy into a hug, he breathed her in as if he had been separated from her for days instead of minutes. Talking to his friends, he had realized the situation was indeed more serious than he had originally thought. Knowing that he would not let Poppy go, he was prepared to fight no matter what it took. Dathrow and Thorne had said they would stand by his side when he went against the Council. They both admitted that he had indeed been acting differently since the arrival of his bride. But instead of viewing his change in demeanor as detrimental to his work, they considered it a benefit to their changing society. For too long, the Phaeton race had been in an emotionless cycle. Simply cloning new warriors so they did not die out but not making any advances in their own society. Existing just to simply exist had become their daily lives. Wheaton saw nothing wrong with his change and neither did the men who were here to help him.

"Thorne and Dathrow are on our side but there are Council members who oppose our union," he whispered into her hair.

Hugging him back and resting her cheek on his chest, she whispered back, "I think Val has found a loophole. Don't worry, big guy. I'm not going back without a fight either, and she's in our corner."

Leaning back from the hug, he cast a glance at Val in confusion.

"She's not in the corner, Poppy. She is standing in the center of the room," he said very matter-of-factly.

"It's a figure of speech, you goof. I meant that she's on our side and she'll help me stay," she said, her words coming with a smile.

Still holding her to his chest, he turned his head to address Val. "Thank you for covering our corner, Valerie. It is much appreciated. We will not let them take her." He had only met Valerie a few times but if she was willing to fight for them then he would owe her for the rest of his life.

Valerie tried to hide a smile at his words and nodded.

"Okay, fellas, here's the game plan." She had the contract in her hand and sat on the couch while setting it on the table in front of her. "I'll go over with you what I proposed to Poppy. I think we have a shot at making this work."

The men crowded around Valerie to see what she was pointing to. Going over the fine print of the contract with the warriors, Valerie seemed to make allies out of both Thorne and Dathrow. After listening to her explaining the ins and outs, they all leaned back except Thorne.

"Let's not discount the sway that Demascus has upon the Council just yet. He is starting to lean toward the Verge in ideals lately when it comes to Council voting. He was completely against the Bridal Pact when it was originally proposed and has since been hunting for ways to make humans seem inferior to the rest of the other Council members," Thorne said with a sigh.

Poppy glanced around the room and asked, "Who is this Demascus guy, and what the hell is a Verge?"

Thorne and Dathrow nodded to Wheaton as if he needed to be the one explaining things. Wheaton now regretted his decision not to discuss his work with his bride. Like it or not, Poppy was going to get a crash course in Phaeton politics.

"First, Demascus is what you would call an 'asshole'." Wheaton paused to make sure he had used the word correctly. At Poppy's nod he continued. "He opposed Council policy to establish our breeding program. It will help if I explain the Verge first though. The Verge are warriors who decided that cloning was the best solution to our dwindling numbers. They are not only anti-human but anti-breeding with anyone outside the Phaeton races. Years ago, the Council decided to search for species that were compatible and from the onset the Verge has been very vocal against it. Verge warriors believe that our species should not be diluted with lesser traits and remain pure."

Thorne decided to take that moment to chip in. "According to your history channels, they would be like the man named Hitler and his Nazi warriors, but without the mass murder. The Verge believe our race should be kept pure to the point of insanity. Our science has shown that any additional cloning at this point would be detrimental to our genetics. There is only so much cloning a culture can sustain before negative effects start happening. We have warriors who are smaller than our predecessors. We also noted a loss of our natural abilities and strength. Let us not forget that a race without women causes problems among male warriors for obvious reasons." He coughed into his fist, seeming embarrassed. A quick glance around the room showed that everyone got the gist.

"The Verge still trade with the Pleasure Sector but see no reason to find a breeding alternative. That is actually another issue that is negatively affecting our men. Missions to that sector are rotated to accommodate as many warriors as possible. However our race has a higher male population than they are able to serve. We have seen cases of females being sold on the black market and used as sexual slaves to those who can afford to purchase them. We have heard rumblings of the Verge possibly trading in slavery to appease their needs without regard to our laws."

The men became quiet for a moment, looking grim at the thought. Poppy sat silent, her mind absorbing all this new information. There was still one question that was bothering her though. "Okay, let's get back to Demascus. What does he have to do with the Verge?" Poppy asked when nobody showed signs of continuing the story.

"Demascus had a clone brother who was the originator, or 'father', to the Verge warriors. When the Verge decided to split off from the Phaeton world, we understood their need to do so and respected them. They did not recognize the advances our race needed to make and we did not agree with their ideals. Deciding we wanted no war between warrior brothers, it was a peaceful separation. Many expected Demascus to follow his brother..." Dathrow trailed off and shot Wheaton a glance.

Wheaton nodded at Dathrow, turning toward Poppy.

"What was that about, guys?" Poppy asked, trying to figure out what was going on.

"The Council is comprised of our strongest warriors from each breed. They are what humans would call politicians. The Verge have adopted a similar caste system for their own Council. Demascus would not be automatically guaranteed a Council position with the Verge. A politician of his standing would be unwilling to give up the power he has over our Council. If he defected then he would have to work to regain a position of such importance. We have talked about it and have come to the conclusion that he may have also stayed to sway the Phaeton Council to the Verge way of thinking," Wheaton said to the women. Looking at the men, he said, "They need to know what we may have ahead of us."

With a grim nod from Thorne to continue, Wheaton took Poppy's hand in his again. Holding her hand seemed to calm him and he paused as if he'd take what peace he could for the moment.

"We have no idea how far Demascus's reach extends. He may have a majority of the Council convinced that the breeding contracts are a bad idea after the matches came back flawed. Most Council members keep quiet when he speaks. Since he has been a member of the Council for years, he holds quite a bit of power...his name alone holds leverage during our meetings. Many are afraid to go against him for fear of retaliation. Those who oppose him generally do so quietly as to not cause trouble for their own standing."

Noticeably uncomfortable, Wheaton continued on, "When I initially had doubts, Demascus asked quite a few questions. He already had access to your profile and fueled my concerns when it came to how you would fit into being a Councilman's wife."

Wheaton cringed, waiting for Poppy to say something. Anything.

Poppy thought for a moment and chewed her bottom lip. She admitted she herself had had the same doubts when she'd found out she'd been matched to a politician. She couldn't throw stones when she'd been in the same place, could she?

"Why did the Council approve the matching in the first place if he is anti-human and has so much pull?" she asked.

Dathrow chose that moment to share his views. "We have searched for many cycles...years...for a species compatible for breeding mates. Most warriors understand the lack of females cannot go on much longer. We have other species we can mate with but none that we can breed with. And even those are limited. Humans are the closest we have found to match our biology. The discovery of humans was so well received it forced Demascus to maneuver quietly instead of openly opposing the idea. He did not want to be the one who stood in the way of us having women for our own and children from those unions. His opinion was not a popular one on the Council so he remained quiet but warned that the pact with Earth would lead to our downfall. If the pact worked then he would be able to say that he voted in favor of it. If it failed then he could remind members of the concerns he had against it."

"Ever the politician," Val said with a wry smile.

"I get it. So how do we go about letting the Council know I'm not going anywhere? This Demascus person has no idea who he is dealing with if he thinks he can bully us for his own agenda." By this time, Poppy had her hands on her hips and was ready to go to battle.

"I would call for a Council meeting immediately, Wheaton. It would be better for you to call the Council meeting before you are summoned and need to defend yourself," Thorne said with a nod.

"I agree," Wheaton said.

Flashing green lights suddenly lit up their bands. The men exchanged startled glances, each of them seeming surprised.

"Ummm, guys, what does that mean?" Valerie asked.

"It means the ship has been called home and we will leave Earth's orbit immediately," Wheaton said with a questioning glance at Thorne.

"I was not aware we were going to depart today," Thorne said with a frown then smiled at Poppy. "However, this means that you will not be able to go to Earth regardless of the Council ruling. We are only able to shuttle between certain distances and the trip home will be too far to transport you back to Earth. Once the ship is mobilized, nothing except mechanical issues will stop our voyage. Our planet is three weeks away according to Earth timetables so we know for certain we now have more time until you can physically leave."

"Well hell, that's good to know. Are you still going to call a meeting ASAP or wait a bit?" Poppy asked, relieved that she would have more time regardless of what the Council ruled.

"I am unsure what time 'ASAP' is, but I will still call one immediately. It is better to get this taken care of than to continuing worrying about it. Do you feel the same?" Wheaton asked with his brow raised.

"Yep, big guy. Right now my stomach is still turning at the thought of having to leave. I don't want this hanging over our heads any longer. Call your guys together so we can get this done." She leaned up to give him a quick kiss, which turned to a slightly longer one once their lips touched.

Valerie clearing her throat was the only thing that stopped the impromptu cuddling Poppy found herself in. Glancing at the three people watching them with varying degrees of smiles on their face, Poppy decided she would be a good hostess and offer them something to drink or eat while they waited for a meeting she was dreading.

CHAPTER FIFTEEN

Poppy was relieved when Wheaton said they had a few hours before the Council meeting would start. The extra time gave them an opportunity to go over all the information Val had brought with her. Wheaton needed to go and feel out some of the other members to see who might be allies in case Demascus tried to cause shenanigans during the meeting. According to Valerie, it seemed pretty cut and dried, but Dathrow seemed worried even though he kept his mouth shut. Poppy could tell Wheaton was worried. He kept stroking her hand and had essentially been glued to her side for the last few hours. She had to pry him off her to visit the bathroom and he had been chagrined when he realized where he was following her.

Poppy's stomach churned as she walked to the Council room. The hallways seemed brighter and longer than ever before. Hoping she didn't puke in front of everyone was one of the concerns running through her mind. For all her tough talk back in their quarters she was worried she was going to lose her newfound happiness. She had never been one to have amazing luck and she was hoping whatever good juju she had out in the universe would kick in right now.

Thorne, Dathrow and Valerie were all walking ahead of Wheaton and Poppy. She took in the fact that Thorne stayed between the other two at all times, and if her eyes weren't deceiving her, he had also taken a whiff of Valerie's hair a couple times along this seemingly endless trek.

Coming to a set of bright double doors, the group stopped and Wheaton turned to Poppy.

"Poppy, remember that I will not let you go. No matter what you hear today, nothing is going to change that." Wheaton picked her up into a hard hug. He gazed at her as if he had forever in their future no matter what happened.

"Don't worry, you two. We will present Valerie's loophole and this should be over soon," Dathrow said with an expression that didn't necessarily seem like he believed what he was saying.

A group of warriors were standing behind a large table inside the Council room. At Wheaton's entrance, the men turned and revealed the small man who had held their attention. His smarmy looks were exactly what she'd expected when the warriors had described Demascus. She wasn't disappointed in the villain-like appearance he presented when he introduced himself with a sly smile.

"Well, I should have assumed this meeting had been called by you regarding your human problem."

Poppy could only describe his approach as a slither as Demascus moved closer. Wheaton managed to keep Poppy by his side but angled himself so he was shielding her slightly.

"Demascus, this is my bride, Poppy." Keeping a firm arm around her, he motioned to Mr. Smarmypants.

"Poppy, this is Council Member Demascus."

Without letting go of Wheaton, Poppy stretched out her hand for a handshake out of reflex.

Staring pointedly at her hand, Demascus sniffed and said, "Wheaton, apparently you did not receive the notification that she is *not* your bride."

Poppy could see a mean spark in his eyes but didn't want to say anything yet. Wheaton had explained that usually Council members were the only ones allowed to speak within the room, and she was only to respond if they spoke specifically to her.

Wheaton tightened his grasp around her and said in a very cold voice, "Demascus, we have decided that the alert does not apply to us and since we are both more than happy with our match we are prepared to sign the bridal contract immediately." He enunciated every syllable so as not to be misunderstood.

Poppy took in the stunned look on Demascus's face and smiled inwardly. The man was obviously one of the warriors who had been affected by cloning. He was tall for a human but a good foot shorter than the others in the room. Moreover he was pale and she was unable to tell what breed group he belonged to. With his obviously receding hair slicked back into a low ponytail, he was completely creepy. When he smiled, he reminded her of a used car salesman she had once dealt with who called her "little lady" and "sweetheart" the whole time while trying to sell her a lemon. Even if this hadn't been the Council member she'd spent the afternoon being schooled on, she wouldn't have liked him anyway.

"I don't think I heard you correctly. Councilor Wheaton, this is not your choice to make. The matches are null and void as they were incorrectly made on Earth. Your bride is not your bride." Glancing to his side, he nodded at a few Council members who seemed to be listening in on the conversation.

"Let us rule and then your little human can go back to her world," he finished in the most condescending tone she had ever heard.

The men seemed to know that they were ready to begin and took their seats. Poppy would have been unsure where to go, but Wheaton directed her to her seat and took the one next to her with Valerie flanking her other side.

"Council members, it has come to my knowledge that my mating is being challenged due to a glitch in the matching profiles, and the brides are being transported back to Earth," Wheaton addressed the group of men in front of him. "I am here to let you know that we are happy with our mating and do not intend to separate but instead call for an immediate joining."

This was said with such finality that the room was silent for a moment. Some scanned the group, as if trying to decide how to take this announcement. Wheaton had certainly stunned some of them.

Demascus broke the silence.

"What gives you the idea you have the authority to make such a demand or go against a Council edict?" he asked as if he were offended on behalf of all of the Councilmen sitting around the table.

Unfortunately, when he said this, Poppy noticed some nods to his statement from the jerks on his right side.

"Council members, I would not go against a ruling if I felt it was the correct one to make for the good of our race." Linking his fingers through Poppy's, Wheaton smiled reassuringly. "This match is perfect in every way. We are compatible and have developed feelings for each other that would make it impossible for our match to be dissolved." Moving his gaze from one man to another and meeting their stares head-on, he then continued, "We are also physically compatible as well and it is in not only our best interests but the interests of the breeding pact to keep our union as binding."

A Council member whom Poppy had yet to meet watched her with kind eyes and addressed Wheaton. "Physically compatible? Does that mean that you have had sexual relations with your bride?"

As if realizing that he had asked a very personal question, he then shifted his attention to Poppy. When Wheaton stiffened at her side, Poppy stroked her thumb along his palm to let him know it was okay.

"Miss, I am sorry for the personal questions. Let me introduce myself. My name is Kaine and I am a brother to Wheaton. Most of us are wanting this program to work while others still have concerns. This mistake with the matches is a major concern for the entire program and has given us doubts if this is the best way to approach the breeding of our race. We are hesitant to let your match stand. All indications are pointing to Wheaton being matched to another female and you even had another warrior match. The original profiles were designed to find our most compatible mates and I cannot see how, if the system made a mistake, you would be happy to stay with Wheaton."

Poppy could see the kindness and understanding on Kaine's face and figured she was now allowed to talk considering that he had spoken to her directly.

"Councilor Kaine, I am unsure how the system made a mistake. From everything that Wheaton and I have learned about each other, we know we are compatible. It was an adjustment at first but once we got over the hurdles of a new relationship and started communicating, we realized that we cared for each other. We had developed feelings for each other, strong ones." Shooting Wheaton a smile, she continued, "I know for sure that there is no one else for me. Over the past couple weeks, we have bonded and if I were to leave him, I don't believe I would ever find another person to make me feel as he makes me feel."

"Feelings. Ha," Demascus scoffed. Gesturing around the room, he raised his voice as if trying to get the group on his side. "I am sure that you feel sexual attraction." He smiled snarkily at Poppy. "The profiles do not match though. There cannot be any other compatibility other than a physical attraction that you feel for Wheaton. Whatever he feels toward you is most likely due to being without a female for such a span of time. He simply needs to spend some time in the Pleasure Sector to cure himself of these feelings he has for you."

"Do *not* speak to my bride in that tone of voice, Demascus!" Wheaton seemed not only angered that Demascus had dismissed their match as based on sexual attraction only, but to say that Wheaton needed to "get laid" to cure himself of their attraction was offensive.

Poppy could feel Wheaton's hand shaking in anger by the time he finished biting out the sentence. She wanted to punch the guy out herself and easily imagined Wheaton shared the same feelings but didn't want do it and get into trouble.

"Poppy and I have made our decision," Wheaton said flatly.

"Not so fast, Councilor Wheaton," Demascus interrupted. "You have no grounds to keep your union intact. The decision has already been made."

"The Council is unable to interfere with our decision. We have brought along Poppy's liaison and she has the paperwork to support us in this situation." Gesturing to Valerie, Wheaton handed her the floor. Obviously hoping this would be the final argument that they received, he sat back in his chair.

Half the Council members had understanding on their previously unreadable faces. The others appeared as though they would follow Demascus out of sheer fear.

Poppy waited for Valerie to speak. Valerie seemed unfazed by the abundant amount of jackasses in the room, scanning the room and smiling at the men in front of her while she readied the paperwork that would hopefully pull their fannies out of the fire.

"Council members, according to the trial period clause within the contract that everyone has signed, you are only able to remove Poppy from Wheaton for the following reasons…" She started going through the contract and pointed to the paragraphs that held their saving grace.

Poppy could tell that the wind had left Demascus's sails but was positive he wasn't finished. He no longer seemed to be searching for backers but instead Poppy could see the wheels turning in his head as he tried to come up with a reason to get rid of her.

"And so according to your own paperwork, Poppy is here for good. Unless the honorable Phaeton Council is willing to go back on a vow." Valerie ended her speech with another smile.

A couple of the Councilmen were grinning back at Valerie and giving her appraising glances. Out of the corner of her eye, Poppy noticed that Thorne didn't seem to be too happy about the attention Valerie was getting.

"I concede that you seem to have found a way to keep your trial period intact for the time being, and for your human to stay on the ship," Demascus started.

"Thank you, Councilor Demascus." Wheaton stood up, his relief obvious.

"Please let me finish what I was saying, Council Member Wheaton." Demascus leaned back with an expression that made Poppy want to smack him. "Since we had already decided that Poppy was leaving, we took the opportunity to send for your *new* bride."

"Excuse me?" Poppy said at the exact same time that Wheaton yelled, "What?"

"We have explained that your match was incorrect and I believe you were notified that another bride had been matched to your profile. The Council took the initiative and brought her up to start her trial period immediately, which is in agreement with the contract *you* signed when filling out your profile for the warrior pool.

According to our paperwork, you are required to serve out a trial period with the bridal match that the system has generated. The system has given you another bride and you are expected to entertain her."

With this statement sitting like a lead weight in her stomach, Poppy sat back in her chair with her palm now sweating in Wheaton's hand.

"Well, send her back. I do not want her and it does not matter what the matching system says." Wheaton said this to the Council, but Poppy could tell it was also directed to her.

Apparently Demascus wasn't finished raining on her parade, because his next statement made her cringe on the inside.

"She is your match in every way. She is in politics. She is also very beautiful." This was followed by a sneer in Poppy's direction. "She understands how important your place on the Council is and she is highly educated. Her sexual compatibility also scored near identical to your own profile regarding your preferences. From what we have gathered this match is a far more appropriate one."

As if he had just won the battle, Demascus crossed his arms over his skinny middle and leaned back in his chair.

"I will repeat myself again so the entire Council can hear me since apparently you did not the first time," Wheaton said in a voice that wiped the smile off Mr. Smarmy's face. "My union to Poppy will stand. It will also be finalized with the bride contract as soon as we are able to file the paperwork." Pulling on Poppy's hand for her to stand, he tugged her up.

"We are done here. Council members, hopefully you can get this new woman back to Earth with no problems and we will hear no more about this. I can understand if any of the other warriors are having problems with their matches but mine is perfect and I will complete it." Starting toward the door, he stopped when Demascus spoke out again.

"Your correct bride is unable to go back to Earth. Our ship is moving toward the home world and you are aware that a shuttle cannot make that distance. Per your signed agreement, of which I have a copy here"—he laid a sheet of paper on the table in front of Wheaton—"you are required to start your trial period with your new bride, whose name is Hannah Talbot. Sounds fitting for a Council member's mate, does it not? Much more dignified than 'Poppy'," Demascus stated, as if he had won the lottery.

Kaine slid the paper in front of him and quickly glanced at the paragraphs that Demascus had indicated. Poppy felt sick that her luck in being able to stay with Wheaton had also inadvertently resulted in the other "bride" not being able to leave.

"This does state you are required to adhere to the Phaeton Code according to this contract," he said to Wheaton. Regarding them with understanding eyes, he then said, "If you insist on us recognizing the validity of your signature on one document then we must do the same to another. I am sorry, Wheaton." His sad smile showed Poppy he was indeed regretful for what he'd had to point out.

"Your new bride will be taken to your quarters and you should start getting to know your new wife. Furthermore, during this trial period, you cannot bind to another," Demascus decided to tack on.

"I don't want her anywhere near me. I am sure she is a wonderful woman but she is not my bride."

Wheaton looked as if he couldn't believe what a mess this was turning out to be. He reached for Poppy again to pull her into his side.

Poppy hugged him back, trying to reassure him without words.

"So we both live with you? I don't understand what has to happen now." Poppy felt her eyes sting as if she were about to cry. The last thing she wanted to do was shed tears in front of a man who seemed to take pleasure in other people's pain.

"I believe the Council will agree with me that you need to spend the same amount of time with Hannah that you did with Poppy to be fair regarding the situation." Demascus glared around and received some grudging nods from the other Council members. "We can find other quarters for your first human while you get acquainted with your true bride."

"Poppy does not leave my side." Wheaton moved to make a threatening step toward Demascus, as though he could strangle the man.

"Councilor Wheaton!" Kaine interrupted his advance. "I understand your frustration but do you want two women in your quarters? It might be painful for Poppy to see you interact with your matched bride. I would like to spare her that." Addressing Poppy, he continued, "We can find temporary quarters for you until you are able to rejoin Wheaton, and you will be in no way kept from him. I simply doubt keeping you in the same living space as the new female would be wise."

Swallowing hard so she didn't choke, she said to the kind warrior, "Yes, I see how that would probably not be a good idea. Can Wheaton and I have a moment to discuss this? We came in here with the thought that we would be going home together."

The handsome warrior smiled at her softly and said, "Of course. We will clear the Council room and give you a few moments." Leaning forward he said softly, "I believe Demascus has already moved this new woman into Wheaton's rooms, so I will make arrangements for your new quarters while you speak."

As the room emptied, Poppy noticed that more than half the warriors were giving her understanding looks while some seemed to completely ignore her. Demascus walked out with a satisfied swagger, seemingly happy with the chaos he'd been able to cause in the span of a few minutes.

As the door slid quietly shut, Poppy gazed up at Wheaton's face. Seeing the emotion playing across his features stunned her. She had seen him happy, aroused, amused and now, because of Demascus, even angry. His face was the epitome of heartbreak. He seemed completely torn, as if unsure what to do next.

"Okay, big guy, this is what's going to happen. I'm going to stay in the other room until they say I can come back and we get rid of this Hannah chick. When she's gone, we finalize our bridal contract. Nothing changes. Understand?" Reaching up, she cupped his cheeks.

Leaning down into her embrace, he breathed out harshly, "I do not want another bride. It doesn't matter what the computers say. You know this, correct?" Wheaton's eyes searched hers and his hands covered her own on his face.

"I know. We just need to get through this little span of time and then we're golden." Taking his hands into hers, she gave him a squeeze. "Now let's go get my stuff moved. I want to check out this new bride."

CHAPTER SIXTEEN

After saying a major thank-you to Valerie for her help, Poppy watched as she and Thorne headed toward their quarters. Walking with Wheaton and Dathrow to what she now considered her home, Poppy's stomach twisted. Dathrow had agreed to take Poppy to her new quarters that were located close to his own on a different level of the ship. The whole situation made her have flashbacks to when she first arrived and was pawned off on various warriors.

Almost to the door, she slowed her pace, causing Wheaton to glance at her questioningly.

"Poppy?"

"I need to breathe for a minute before I meet Miss Perfect," Poppy said with a small smile.

"Her name is Miss Talbot, not Miss Perfect," Wheaton said with a grin, finally starting to catch on to the way Poppy said things. He chucked her under the chin and planted a sweet kiss on her lips.

"Everything will be fine, Poppy, I promise." Kissing her again, he turned toward the door and waved his bracelet over the sensor.

Seeing perfect Hannah Talbot was not good for Poppy's morale. This woman was exactly what she expected a politician's wife to be like. Her blonde hair was styled in glossy, effortless-looking waves and she pulled off a gorgeous all-white although completely impractical pantsuit. She walked toward Wheaton with a ready smile on her face and her hand out to shake but stopped when she saw Poppy standing there.

"Hello...I'm Hannah Talbot...your bride," she said in a melodious voice while glancing questioningly at Poppy.

"I am Wheaton, and *this* is my bride, Poppy," Wheaton said in a calm voice, motioning to Poppy.

"I don't understand…" Hannah began with a confused expression. "I was told the previous matches were wrong and you were now my match. We're supposed to start our trial period immediately. That's why I'm here." Her gaze darted back and forth between the two of them as if she thought this was a big prank.

Wheaton leaned down close to Poppy's ear and whispered, "This is the type of woman whom I had originally expected to be matched with." When Poppy immediately stiffened, he continued. "She may *seem* perfect but you *are* perfect for me. Do not doubt that."

"Hannah, we're happy with our match and have decided to finalize it. We had actually just got done telling this to the Council members when we found out that you were here. Wheaton is obligated to have his own trial with a second bride," Poppy explained in hopes Hannah was actually going to understand the situation and not get a good view of the man she was going to be missing out on. She had to admit, if someone put Wheaton in front of her and then jerked him away, she would have been pissed. Her attraction to him had been immediate and the same for him to her, she believed.

From what she could tell with a quick glance, Wheaton wasn't giving Hannah any appraising stares. His expression was more polite than anything. He had on his "meeting" face. It was his poker face he used when she'd seen him speak to other warriors and Council members to show he was listening but remaining neutral.

"I'm not quite sure I follow. Councilor Demascus assured me that my match to Wheaton was perfect and we would be one of the most successful matches made," she stuttered out, obviously having been lied to by King of the Smarmy.

"Demascus was incorrect, Hannah. We ask that you please respect our decision to stay united, and we will try to make the next few weeks as comfortable for you as we can. Your trip back to Earth will not be possible until we move the ship back to Earth's orbit," explained Wheaton, his voice firm as if she would have no other option but to agree. "We are required to live in the same quarters but the decision has been made. Poppy has agreed to stay elsewhere to make this situation more tolerable but that is as far as we are in agreement with what the Council has forced upon us."

As Wheaton spoke, Hannah walked to the kitchen area and was now partially leaning against the counter as if she needed the support.

"I have given up everything for this... Everything..." she started mumbling to herself, which caused Poppy some concern.

"Hannah. Hannah. Are you okay?" Poppy walked forward to better hear the mumbling that was now starting to scare her.

"Of course I'm not okay! I have given up my entire life to move up here! I decided to withdraw from the city Council race to be one of the first political couples in space. I completely adjusted my five-year plan for this!"

Okay, Hannah was starting to really lose it. Poppy could deal with sad but crazy wasn't something she was ready to handle. Stepping back to stand at Wheaton's side, she kept her eye on the once perfectly styled woman who was now turning into a mascara-running mess.

Wheaton cast a worried glance at Poppy, completely unsure how to deal with what he was seeing.

"We are sorry, but we simply do not agree with the new matches and are more than satisfied with the original match. I understand why you are upset; however, it will change nothing. Poppy and I will complete our bridal contract despite the wishes of some Council members," Wheaton said in a calm voice.

"Wait...wait..." Hannah blinked her now raccoon eyes and held up a manicured hand. "The Council has ruled against your match but that means I still have to leave?" Her eyes dried almost instantly. "Explain please."

Oh no, Poppy had a feeling this had taken a turn for the worse. Judging by Wheaton's face, he could see the problem stirring as well.

"We are staying together, Hannah. I am not sure if the Council can rematch you, but you will not be matched to Wheaton," Poppy said with a finality that she hoped was convincing to Hannah.

Smiling at Wheaton, Hannah batted her eyelashes. "So, Poppy, you're staying in another apartment while Wheaton and I stay here?" she asked.

Uh-oh. Poppy could see the wheels turning in Hannah's pretty head and had a very bad feeling about this chick. She should have fought harder to be able to stay with Wheaton or have all of them moved to a bigger apartment. Poppy felt slightly nauseous at the thought of leaving him alone with Blondie.

"Yes, I'll be staying in another apartment but will keep you company during the day while Wheaton is attending to Council business." Poppy smiled, figuring that keeping an eye on Hannah would be probably be a good thing.

"Oh, no need to worry yourself about me. Councilor Demascus said that I would be welcome at the Council meetings with Wheaton so I could adjust to the politics of the Phaetons as a politician's wife." She smiled back, waving her hand to dismiss Poppy's suggestion.

Yep, definitely keep her close. Poppy's instincts were screaming at her that this whole situation with Demascus and a "political bride" seemed like too much of a setup but their hands were tied. Beside her, she saw Wheaton clenching his jaw again. Clearly he wasn't too happy with the situation either. Hopefully this time would fly by and they'd be able to get Hannah home sooner rather than later.

Wheaton couldn't stop the helplessness that came across his face. Hoping that Poppy kept faith in him and their union, he knew he had no choice but to follow the Council edict.

The door chimed, interrupting their tense moment. Letting go of Poppy's hand to answer it, he opened it to see Dathrow ready to escort Poppy to her new apartment. Panic rising in his chest, Wheaton wanted to shut the door in Dathrow's face and whisk Poppy away from everything.

"Poppy, I am here to walk you to your new quarters. They are close to my own so I can be of assistance if Wheaton is not available." Dathrow nodded to Wheaton, letting him know that he would be there to help Poppy if needed.

"Dathrow, is it? My name is Hannah. We appreciate you escorting Poppy to her new home. I am sure Wheaton and I have much to discuss." Hannah smiled sweetly at Wheaton and walked closer to his side.

Poppy decided in that moment if she had to witness Hannah hit on Wheaton she might pull out every strand of her Barbie-like hair. Councilor Kaine had been smart to see beforehand that the two women would have never been able to cohabitate. He had probably foreseen murder charges when he realized that Hannah was already in their apartment. Walking over to Wheaton, she then gave him a quick hug and kiss. He took comfort in her short embrace and seemed to relax.

"Don't forget to come and say good night to me before you go to bed." She leaned into him even more and gave him another quick kiss.

Tugging on her hair, he smiled sadly. "I will miss you, my Poppy," he whispered softly, meaning every word he said.

Eyes watering, she turned toward Dathrow. Standing with his arms crossed over his chest, he eyed Hannah with obvious distaste.

"Let's hit the road, Jack." When Dathrow gave her a questioning look she simply shook her head, not in the mood to explain it was a figure of speech.

Walking through the door and hearing it swoosh closed behind her, the distance between her and Wheaton seemed to grow in miles with each step. Her room was not too far away really, even though the walk felt like a mile. Dathrow was silent as he guided her down the hallway, making her peer over at him.

"Everything will be okay, right?" she asked the somber man beside her.

"Poppy, I want to talk to you but would prefer we do it where we cannot be monitored," he said in a quiet voice that made her stomach turn.

Reaching the door to what she assumed was her new quarters, she waited for him to open it while she held her small bag of personal items. Once inside, she noticed that it was almost identical to Wheaton's apartments but seemed much colder. Apparently Wheaton himself warmed the space that she had called home, she thought sadly.

Dathrow gestured to the kitchen area. "Would you like me to fix you something to drink? You have had a hard day and I could ask for the sweet tea you normally consume."

Poppy shook her head, "No thanks, but help yourself." She leaned her elbows on the counter. "What did you need to say that you couldn't tell me in the hall?" she asked apprehensively.

"I have heard rumblings about Wheaton's new bride. The news that I have heard may not be easy for you to hear," he muttered while slowly stirring the cup of tea he had fixed for himself.

His behavior was making Poppy very nervous. Dathrow was generally someone who didn't show any emotion and she noticed he seemed too nervous to continue.

"And?" she prompted when he didn't go on.

"From what I gather, the human Hannah is Wheaton's perfect political match," he said with a grimace as if unsure his statement would hurt her feelings.

Poppy admitted that it did sting hearing the words out loud. She had already seen the polished woman was someone a politician would be proud to have on his arm.

"Thorne secretly pulled her profile from the bridal match and he was impressed with her past political career. She is very accomplished and we were surprised that she gave up her career on Earth for a bridal match. It seems almost too perfect though. Thorne suspects Demascus had a hand in the match somehow but we were unable to find out how." He paused and added, "If we can find out he was able to influence the match, we can end the trial period early and hold a tribunal to make him accountable for his actions."

Poppy felt hope blossom in her chest but it faded fairly quickly.

"Dathrow...I want you to answer a question and be honest. Okay?" she said, not knowing if she wanted an honest answer or not.

"Of course. It is not in our nature to lie." Placing his cup down, he met her gaze head on.

"Is Hannah a better match for Wheaton?" she rushed out. "I vote when we have elections on Earth but I have never considered myself as being involved in politics. Wheaton has never actually even talked to me about what he does when he leaves during the day." Closing her eyes to brace herself for his answer, she waited and then reopened one to peer at him when he didn't respond.

She realized he'd been waiting for her to look at him. Opening both her eyes, Poppy focused on him. Kind brown eyes seemed to study her as he answered. "Politically, she *would* be a better match," he said plainly.

"However… Warriors need more than a match based upon our breeds. You make Wheaton behave in a way I have never seen. I cannot recall a time when he has been so quick to smile." Reaching across the counter, he touched her hand. "Poppy, you make him complete. He seems more relaxed and animated with you. When you are apart he shows how happy he is by talking about you to either Thorne or myself. He mentions you constantly when he has an opening to do so, almost to the point of irritation to some of the warriors. If you were to leave him, I don't think he would be able to cope. It was as if he were simply alive before, and now he is living." Picking up his cup, Dathrow grinned across the counter at her.

"I am actually jealous of his match," he admitted.

"Why? Aren't you in the warrior pool for a bride?" Taking a sip of the tea he had made for her despite her refusal, she smiled back at him. His words had lifted her spirits for the time being.

"Yes, but Councilor Kaine said there was a problem with my match and I needed to wait for a full briefing. I have realized that I am not a patient man. I was jealous when Wheaton was selected first. Meeting you has made me even more impatient. You are a wonderful bride, Poppy. You are beautiful, funny, smart and most of all you make Wheaton happy. I want that." Finishing his drink, he turned around to place his now empty cup into the sink.

"I must be going, but I wanted to let you know I programmed the second button on your door to ring to my quarters if you need anything and Wheaton is not available. I am unsure of his schedule for the next few days and want you to come to me if you need anything. Either myself or one of the other warriors will escort you wherever you may need to go."

Pausing at the door, he turned back around. "Make either myself or Wheaton aware if Demascus makes an attempt to approach you. I would not listen to anything he says if he does come to you. Remember, he is a cunning politician and can say things that people start to believe if repeated enough."

"Don't worry, Dathrow. That man has been high on my bullshit meter ever since I met him." Patting him on the back as he walked out, she said good night and turned to her silent new quarters. Tonight was going to be tough by herself. She had grown used to having Wheaton around and this room reminded her of her first week on Squadron One.

In the bedroom, she found that her larger bags had been stacked next to the bathroom door. Unpacking her items, she spread out her stuff the way she'd had it back in the apartment. Only thing missing was Wheaton, she thought with a sad smile. When her stomach growled she was reminded of how late it was. Figuring she would be dining alone tonight, Poppy made herself something to eat and sat down to flip through channels on the view screen. The ship had basically any and all channels she could ever imagine and when she logged in it had her most recently watched movies.

"Let's avoid anything that will make me reach for the Kleenex." Talking to herself again, she grimaced. It was going to be a long night.

CHAPTER SEVENTEEN

Waking up with her face stuck to the leather couch was not the best start to her morning. Rubbing her eyes, Poppy tried to think of what had happened after she'd started her movie. She surveyed the room for any signs that Wheaton had come by after she had fallen asleep. Figuring that he would have carried her to bed, she guessed he hadn't been able to come to her new quarters last night.

Hoping she was early enough to catch him before breakfast, she went to the door to buzz their old room. Not getting an answer, she decided he must have already gone to his morning meetings. Seeing the second button down and remembering what Dathrow had said, she went ahead and pushed it.

"Yes?" Dathrow's deep voice came through the speaker.

"Dathrow, I couldn't get hold of Wheaton. Do you know where he might be?" Poppy asked.

"Poppy, he was called to an early morning meeting with the Council. Did you need anything? I can send him a message if needed."

"No, don't do that. I just woke up and wanted to talk to him. Have you had breakfast yet?" Poppy figured she might need to find some company so she didn't go completely crazy. She hadn't been around Dathrow too much and felt like he might actually be a friend she could use while they waited for this double-bride problem to resolve itself.

"I have not had my morning meal yet. I will be right over," he replied in a pleasant voice.

With a beep ending the call, she quickly got ready. Dressed in her standard yoga pants and long tunic, she slipped her shoes on after pulling her hair up into a bun. Makeup today would consist of a little mascara and some lip gloss. The effort of putting on more of a face today seemed too much of a chore right now.

Poppy raised her eyebrows in surprise when the doorbell beeped. That was quick. Opening the door, she swept her arm back as if she were welcoming royalty into her quarters. Dathrow smiled at her and bowed as he entered.

"Thank you for the invitation, Poppy. I normally eat alone or go to the cafeteria for meals so I have company. Eating alone is not very fun."

"Don't you worry, Dath. You'll have a bride soon enough. One who will drive you just as nuts as I drive Wheaton," she said while moving around the kitchen counter. "Do you want the standard eggs and bacon? Wheaton really likes the pancakes that I have programmed to my band too. Have you ever tried those?"

"I love eggs and bacon but have not yet tried pancakes. I would like to though." Scooting his stool out so he could sit at the small bar area, he sent her a questioning glance. "Why did you call me 'Dath'?"

"Oh, sorry…I should have asked you before I shortened your name. I often give nicknames to people who I become friends with. Valerie became Val, Pixie is Pix and now Dathrow is Dath. Is that okay?" she asked, handing him his plate that was now filled with a stack of pancakes.

"You call Wheaton his full name, though. Why is that?" he asked. Dathrow stared at his plate, obviously trying to figure out how to eat the flat cakes.

Pouring syrup on her own pancakes and then on his, she motioned with a knife and fork and showed him how to cut off pieces.

"Well, 'Wheaton' can really only be shortened to 'Wheat', and that's a type of food on my planet. It would sound a little silly," she said with a wry grin. "But I have called him 'sweetie' and 'babe' a couple times. He reacted funny until I explained it was a term of endearment. He was insulted when he thought I was calling him an infant." Giggling at the memory, she looked down at her food. She didn't realize how hungry she was until she started shoveling her food into her mouth as if she were in a competition.

"You mentioned Pixie—that is your sister, correct?" Dath asked his question nonchalantly although Poppy read more into it.

"Yes, she was with me when we first met. Remember?" Hiding her smile, she took another bite.

"Is she mated?" he asked, his face slightly red.

"Well…yes and no."

When Dathrow looked up at her confused, Poppy went on. "She's been dating a man for a few years. They aren't married or engaged. Personally, I think he's too boring for Pixie. She is so full of life, ya know? When she first started seeing him it was all good. He seemed to pay a lot of attention to her and she was so happy. Then the longer they dated the more I noticed she seemed to change. It was the little things at first like her changing her hair or the type of clothes she wore. Believe it or not she had a collection of yoga pants that rivaled mine. Now she seems… I don't know. I guess dull would be the word I would go with. She thinks he's going to propose but a part of me is hoping that he doesn't do it yet." Poppy made a face. "That sounded awful, didn't it? I just want her to be happy and I haven't really seen a *happy* Pixie for a while now."

Poppy sat silent for a moment before gesturing back to the food they both had seemed to have forgotten. "Eat up before it gets cold. Or worse, soggy. Soggy pancakes are nothing to joke about."

Nodding his head and chewing his food, Dathrow made "mmming" noises while eating half his plate in record time.

"Good huh?" she asked with a smile.

"Wonderful! I could eat this every meal. Can this liquid be poured over other food items?" he asked while licking syrup off his lips and studying the bottle.

"Only if your name is Buddy the Elf," she quipped quickly and then began laughing at the confused expression on his face.

"That was a joke, Dath."

"Ahhh." Still not getting it, he was quiet for a moment before he asked, "Does Wheaton call you anything special?"

Remembering some of the sweet names he had called her recently made her heart hurt.

"He has called me his 'Little Flower' before," she said with a sad smile.

"Because Poppy is a flower...and you are also little," he said in understanding.

"Wheaton asked me when we first met if I was named after a flower." Smiling, she went on, "And I wouldn't be so little if you warriors weren't a million feet tall."

Laughing, he helped her clean their plates and put the syrup away in the cupboard.

"We are the standard height for most warriors. Wheaton and I are both under seven feet. Skrammon warriors are actually taller and I have not seen many under seven feet. Since they are a warrior breed, they use their height and bulk to their advantage when fighting," he explained.

"I haven't had a chance to see many of them on the ship. Are they around?" Poppy asked.

"We have warriors from each delegation on the ship but a majority of the Skrammon congregate in the rec area and spar during their free time. If you have no plans today, I could take you around the ship," he suggested as he moved from the kitchen area.

"Ummmm...sure. I'm assuming Wheaton will be in meetings all day and I can't keep hiding in here so yeah, let's do this." She clapped her hands together and followed him to the door.

Walking side by side down the corridor, she paused slightly when they reached the apartment she'd shared with Wheaton. Wondering where Hannah was if Wheaton was at a meeting made her completely stop in her tracks.

"Dath, if Wheaton got called to a meeting then why didn't Hannah answer my call this morning?"

"Hannah accompanied Wheaton to the Council meetings this morning," he replied.

"Wait—she went with him to a meeting? The same type of meeting that I'm not able to even hear about, much less go to? I realize Demascus gave her permission, but I just can't believe

Wheaton went along with it." Apparently her anger was starting to come out in her tone of voice, because Dathrow turned to face her.

"She has a background in politics, and I assume that Wheaton would rather have her occupied during the day where he can keep an eye on her. I do not believe he trusts either Hannah or Demascus." Frowning at Poppy, he realized she was really upset.

"So, it was okay for me to sit by myself when I got here? I wanted to bang my head against a wall from boredom it was so bad. Yet Hannah gets to follow him around and be a part of his daily life?" Poppy took a moment from her hissy fit and noticed the frightened look on Dathrow's face.

It wasn't fair to take out her anger on the poor guy. She wasn't even that angry at Wheaton when she thought about it. It was the entire fucked-up situation that had her wanting to spit nails. Keeping Hannah under a watchful eye made sense but she still felt left out. Considering he refused to even talk to her about his work, it was like a stab to the chest. One day on the ship and Hannah was able to see how the Council worked. Clenching her jaw, she tried to smile through her anger at the poor warrior in front of her.

"Sorry, Dath. I'm not mad at you. I'm not even mad at Wheaton. I just need to talk to him about some things. It isn't fair for me to take out my frustration on the messenger," she admitted.

"I appreciate that, Poppy," he heaved out on a relieved sigh.

"Come on and show me this ship. Wheaton gave me the bare bones tour, then more in-depth tours after a week or so. I watched him spar in the rec room with Thorne but we never spent much time around any of the common areas. I would like to meet some other warriors and maybe see if there's anything I can do around here. Do you know if anyone needs help with paperwork or odd jobs?" Glancing over at her new buddy, she went on, "I wouldn't even expect to be paid. I'm just bored when Wheaton isn't around and I can only watch *Sixteen Candles* so many times before I set fire to something."

When she mentioned "fire" his eyes got wide. Almost laughing at his expression, she quickly said, "Well not really, but it's better not to let me get bored." He would need to get used to her joking if he was going to hang around and keep her company. Looping her arm through his, she bumped his side as they turned the corner to the common area.

"We can check with the med center and see if the healers need any help. They are always receiving new supplies, and with the men sparring daily, they rarely have time to check the stock and catalog them," he suggested.

"That would be great. I actually worked in a doctor's office on Earth," she replied with a happy smile.

Deciding to show her the med center first, Dathrow suggested that they take the lift to another floor of the ship. Poppy realized that every floor appeared identical, and if he hadn't been guiding her around, she would be hopelessly lost. When she had toured with Wheaton, she must have been paying more attention to his fine ass as he walked than her surroundings. Making sure to pay attention, she kept her eyes peeled walking with Dathrow.

Pointing out the doors that led to the common area bathrooms, he explained that there were specific ones designated for the new brides who would eventually live on the ship. Poppy had a mental image of going to each floor and slapping a sticky note on the gleaming walls to help her remember which were the men's and which were the women's. Walking into the men's room while a warrior was doing his business did not seem like a good way to learn which was which.

"Dath, is there a reason why nothing is labeled? How do you know which doors are for the bathrooms and which is for the rec room? Will I just need to count my way down the corridor and try to remember each time?"

"There are small symbols illuminated on the side of the door that tell you where we are." Pointing to the small symbols, he explained which one was female and which was male. "I know you haven't had a chance to learn to read our language yet and the translator only works with the spoken word so maybe I can go over the most common symbols to help you learn them," he replied.

"That would be great. I hate taking up so much of your time. If I'm keeping you from a job, please don't feel you need to entertain me," she said when they approached the med center.

"I have been assigned as one of your escorts so it is not a problem, Poppy. I enjoy talking to you. Let's see if you can get a job here so you can avoid setting fires." He smiled as he let her enter the gleaming doors ahead.

* * * * *

On the other side of the ship, Wheaton was having an awful morning. Trying to extricate himself from a clinging Hannah had proven harder than he had expected. Last night, he'd answered endless questions while she sat staring at him with wide, adoring eyes. In the past, he would have been flattered by the attention of a beautiful female. Instead of feeling any type of attraction to his newly assigned bride, he had instead kept comparing her to Poppy the entire evening. It had been exhausting to try to keep as much physical distance between them as possible. She had chosen to sit as closely as possible to him no matter how far he tried to maneuver away.

He had been relieved when a few key Council members had come by the apartment to meet his new "bride" later in the evening. The addition of the Council members in his apartment had seemed to distract Hannah's efforts to get close to him. Unfortunately they had stayed so long it had been too late to visit Poppy when they left.

Hoping to have some reprieve from Hannah's company today had proved fruitless as well. The Council had instructed him to bring Hannah with him today to his meetings. Her constant chatter was making his head ache. Gritting his teeth, it took everything in him to not yell at her to be quiet. Shaking his head in frustration while rubbing his temple, he knew one thing. He missed his Poppy.

CHAPTER EIGHTEEN

The med center visit was a success. Meeting Tamin and Rodin, two of the Brakken warriors, had been very interesting. Both men were just as tall as Wheaton and Dathrow but they had shorter hair and small tattoos on their upper temples that ran up their foreheads and traced their hairlines. Noticing that their tattoos were identical, Poppy figured they were a warrior designation. The pair wore leather pants similar to what Wheaton had in his closet but they wore tops shaped like a tunic or loose-fitting sets of hospital scrubs. Each was equally muscled so she assumed that in addition to patching up those banged up from sparring, they spent just as much time on the mat.

Apparently the men had wanted to meet the human brides on the ship but none of the husbands had brought them by so far. As doctors they were curious regarding any physical differences—even though their research had shown that everything was compatible, they wanted to see it firsthand. Declining a physical exam, she did try to answer all the questions they had. When they started asking questions about her monthly cycle, Dathrow made a point to excuse himself for a couple minutes and check on a message waiting for him in the system. The questions they asked her about her period did make her realize she was going to be needing "supplies" fairly soon and wondered how she could go about asking that.

"Tamin, are you technically my doctor or will a human doctor be brought up from Earth if I need one?" Poppy asked curiously.

Rodin chose that time to pop into the conversation that had been led by the other doctor until then.

"We will be your doctors while on Squadron One if you need medical assistance. As of right now, we are too far from Earth to get a human doctor even in an emergency," he said.

Not wanting to be left out, Tamin spoke next. "Also, the Council decided that any Phaeton children will need to be monitored by our own race so all pregnancies would be seen to by either Rodin or myself while you are here."

"Why? Are you feeling unwell? Do we need to summon Wheaton for you?" Rodin asked.

"Ummmm…no. I just wasn't sure who I should talk to about getting supplies when I need them—to deal with feminine issues," she said while trying not to feel embarrassed. Talking to these two hunks about her period had not been on her mental to-do list today. Poppy had a male doctor at home but Dr. Stevens was about sixty years old with twenty grandchildren. He wasn't anything like these two babes in front of her and she wasn't quite sure how much they knew about periods or the supplies that were needed when they came.

"Of course, of course," Rodin answered with a nod, understanding what she was asking.

"We had planned on having a human nurse here to assist the brides when the time came but our ship was called away before we could finish the interviews. We did get enough 'supplies' though, for your stay to be comfortable, if needed. I can show you the supply closet next where those items are kept. You can choose what you need and let us know if there is something specific you would like. We can make notes for future orders regarding your preferences," Tamin finished.

Following Tamin down the small hall that led to the exam rooms, Poppy peeked around the rest of the small medical center. Walking past the open exam rooms, she glanced around in awe. Instead of normal hospital beds they had long pod-like structures in the center of the room. Pausing outside one of the doors, she was bumped by Rodin, who was following close behind.

"Oomph. I'm so sorry, Rodin," she said as she was jostled by the big body behind hers.

"No, I am sorry, Poppy. I admit, I am anxious to hear your questions and hopefully have you explain some of the supplies that we received. After studying the packaging we were able to understand what the purpose of some of them were but we are confused about an item that has wings. It does not make sense to us why wings would help during your menstrual cycle," Rodin said as he backed up a few paces.

Oh great. Poppy was not looking forward to explaining tampons or pads with wings to this big guy. His expression became similar to that of a kid in a candy store the more he spoke to her. He seemed as if he were soaking up every word she said. She had a flashback to her sixth-grade health class, when all the girls were separated from the boys and had "the talk" about menstruation. Picturing herself standing in front of a white board holding up various objects and explaining how they were used caused her to grimace. Deciding now was a good time to distract the doctors, she gestured to the open room.

"What are those?" Poppy asked, pointing at the weird pod objects that were where she expected exam tables to be.

Gesturing for Poppy to enter the room, Tamin and Rodin followed and walked to the center of the room.

"This is your standard regen bed," Rodin explained with a sweeping motion of his hand.

"Sugar, nothing you guys have up here is 'standard' to me. A regen bed? As in, regeneration?" she asked, walking up to the white pod with bright blue buttons. It appeared as though someone would lie on it and the sides and top would close when it was turned on. The result was something that resembled a space-age coffin.

"Exactly. When a warrior seeks our services, this is the quickest way to diagnose the problem. It takes vitals, searches for injuries and can provide a diagnosis within minutes as to what the problem is. When we have medical screenings, we use it to generate information for medical records." Tamin hit a button so the pod closed in a *hum*.

"It can also heal broken bones and most internal injuries. The duration it takes to heal different injuries varies depending on what it needs to fix or regenerate. The more complicated the injury the more time it may require." Rodin was leaning against a cabinet that held medical instruments more familiar to Poppy than the sci-fi bed in front of her.

"I would actually like to get a baseline on you if we could, Poppy. That way we will have your stats on file in case you need future care," Rodin said, nodding toward the pod.

"Ummm sure, but how long does that thing stay closed? It seems a little claustrophobic. As in a coffin type of claustrophobic." Poppy was apprehensive and braced herself. She was being silly. At some point she would need to get over using their medical devices.

Tamin hit a button that opened the pod up, and motioned for Poppy to lie down.

"It should only take thirty seconds for it to gather the readings and then it will open automatically. After opening it will give us the information within five minutes of a standard exam. When we have to heal bones or injuries, it can take hours to finish a treatment. The patient will fall asleep shortly after they enter depending on the diagnosis and wake as if they had been taking a nap. There really is nothing to be frightened of."

Poppy hopped up onto the bed after slipping off her shoes. It was actually quite comfy. Since the warriors were bigger than her by quite a bit and by default would need more space, it seemed much roomier than she'd expected once she stretched out. Judging the size to be similar to a twin bed but longer, she held her breath as Tamin hit the button for it to close. Cocooned in the pod, she appreciated the calming blue glow that lined the inside of the white tube. She lay wide-eyed inside, listening to the tones the machine was making. Was she supposed to stay absolutely still? Would it zap her if she moved? Crazy thoughts flew through her head as she stiffened her body, freaking out a bit. Before she knew it, the door and sides slid open on a *hum*. Well, that was anticlimactic.

"That's it?" she asked, not wanting to move in case it hadn't had a chance to do its futuristic mojo on her.

"Yes," Rodin said with a smile, helping her sit up. He brought her shoes over so she could slip them back on before stepping down onto the cool white floor. "Let us show you the supplies we acquired while we wait for the regen bed to make a report."

Dathrow chose that moment to walk into the exam room.

"Poppy, we need to head back to your quarters. Wheaton contacted me and he has a break in meetings so he is free for a small amount of time. He would like to speak to you." Dathrow nodded at the two doctors.

Poppy noticed the disappointment on their faces and felt bad that their time was cut short. On the other hand, she was grateful that she was able to successfully dodge the wings conversation.

"It was so nice to meet you both."

"Likewise, Poppy. Please come back when you can. We could use your assistance, if you have the time to spare," Tamin said, and held his hand out to shake.

"Yes, please come back. We would greatly appreciate your input on what other items we may need to acquire for your comfort, and would love to have your help here," Rodin agreed when it was his turn to shake hands.

"Oh wait, my regen report… Is it done yet?" She gestured back to the room she had just left.

"Not yet. It is still working on the report. I can contact you if we have concerns regarding your vitals once it is finished. We have the standard chart for where humans should be reading at so we will know if something is a concern as soon as it is printed out."

Poppy grimaced. Hopefully their charts didn't include the BMI portion. She knew for sure that result wouldn't be within the "standard" reading for a woman her height. Maybe she should make use of the rec room that she had toured earlier. Following a fast-moving Dathrow drove that point home. Poppy breathed heavily as she hurried to catch up. The speed he was moving showed her that maybe a little jogging wouldn't be out of the question also. Apparently, he was as anxious for her to see Wheaton as she was.

Walking down the gleaming halls, she again tried to pay attention to the doors and where the elevator was located. The sliding doors to the lift and the doors to the other rooms were all the same size and shape. She was going to make it a priority to learn the standard symbols for the areas she wanted to visit. She asked Dathrow if he could make her a guide for the symbols she needed, including the symbols for numbers. At least she assumed the strange hieroglyphics in the elevator were supposed to be numbers.

Reaching her apartments, Dathrow turned to her.

"Wheaton messaged that he should be here shortly. He will be able to lunch with you instead of the Council, but I am unsure how much time he will have before his meetings continue," Dathrow said before he bowed and turned to walk away.

"Dath?"

When he turned back and looked at her, she continued, "Thank you so much for keeping me company this morning and showing me around. I truly appreciate it." She reached up to give him a hug.

Hugging Dathrow was like hugging a tree. She must have startled him, because he stood stock-still with his arms hanging at his sides. She wasn't giving up on him, she decided. His cheeks had turned a little red. Smiling at him, she waved and turned to go into her quarters.

Deciding not to waste any time, she prepared a quick lunch. As she moved around the kitchen to get their food ready, she saw the notification light on the door blinking. Dreading that it was Wheaton calling to cancel her lunch, she jogged over to listen to the message.

"Poppy, this is Tamin. We received your readouts from the regen bed and we need to speak to you about the results. Please come back to the med center as soon as you are able."

Well crap. Maybe the regen bed wasn't as familiar with human bodies as the doctors had expected. Or maybe they had questions about her dental fillings. Did aliens have fillings? A tone at the door sounded. She was so anxious to see Wheaton that she practically ran to the opening, tripping over her shoes on the way. Knowing that her smile was gigantic, but not caring, she signaled for the entry to open—and felt her smile fall.

"Hey, Dathrow, what are you doing back?" she asked him.

"Poppy, I received a message from Wheaton once I reached my quarters. I am sorry but he is unable to escape the Council for the noon meal." He cringed as he broke the bad news to her.

"But why didn't he call here to leave me a message?" she asked.

"I am assuming that he thought I was still escorting you back when he called. My band alerted me that I had a message waiting but I assumed it was regarding another matter so I did not check it until I was back in my own quarters," he explained. With a sad smile, he gestured to the countertop where the lunch she'd made for Wheaton sat.

"Do you mind if I join you or would you rather have some time alone?"

"Well, sure, Dath. I could actually use the company now so I don't dwell on my disappointment too much. Once I go down that rabbit hole nothing except for an obscene amount of ice cream can lure me back out." She sighed. "I hope you like hamburgers." She tried to smile even though she wanted to cry a bit. She'd never thought she was a crybaby and usually couldn't stand whiners. But dammit, she had wanted to see Wheaton and talk about last night's no-show, as well as the fact that Hellacious Hannah was able to go to the Council meetings.

Lunch ending up being quite pleasant with Dathrow's company and he had time to answer questions that Poppy had from the morning tour. Between bites, Dathrow was able to draw her up a legend of all the symbols on the doors she would need to remember when walking around on her own. He laughed and almost choked on his burger when she mentioned going around and placing sticky notes everywhere.

Poppy picked up their plates. "Thank you for the cheat sheet. Hey, I don't want to just wait around until Wheaton calls. Can you walk me back up to the medical unit? Tamin called and said he needed to go over my regen bed reading with me," she explained.

"Of course, I will walk you there but will not be able to stay. I have been called to a meeting this afternoon. If you take your cheat sheet with you, you can try finding your way back, but I am sure that Wheaton will assign another escort for your return trip. He has informed me that he wants an escort with you at all times unless it is unavoidable," he said with a smile.

That was one thing nice about Dathrow—he was always smiling at her. It had taken her a couple days to squeeze the first smile out of Wheaton but Dathrow had smiled the day they met. Knowing he was a great catch made her wonder when he would be assigned his bride. Hopefully the bridal snafu worked its way out sooner rather than later.

She followed him out the door. Before leaving she called and left Wheaton a brief message. In case he was able to sneak out, it would be a good idea to let him know where to find her. Their walk to the med center took them past her old apartment. Pausing for only a moment to toss a sad look at the door, she decided she definitely needed something to distract her. The med center seemed a good place to start.

CHAPTER NINETEEN

Tamin and Rodin were extremely happy to see Poppy, judging by their huge smiles. Their reaction made her anxious for some reason. They had stopped looking at her with their normally friendly glances and now were studying her as if she were an experiment. Images of them using pegs to pin her down to a board and dissect her flitted through her overactive imagination. She kept an eye out for chloroform and scalpels, just in case. The men ushered Dathrow out quickly once Poppy was in the room with promises of keeping her safe and secure until he was able to send an escort to walk her back.

Poppy turned to the guys with an expression she was sure would let them know she was getting antsy to have them staring at her as if she were a frog in a high school biology class.

"Ummmm, guys…what is it we needed to talk about? You're making me nervous the longer you stare at me."

Rodin turned to Tamin and they shared a secret smile. After a few seconds, Tamin nodded to the other doctor.

"Spit it out, guys!" Poppy snapped, unable to hold back any longer.

"Tamin would like for you to have another scan. We are unsure if we received a false reading today and need to run a new scan before we discuss the findings," Rodin said, ushering her into the closest exam room.

"Yes, Poppy, I do not want to cause alarm if the regen bed readings are incorrect." Tamin opened the quietly humming bed while Poppy toed off her shoes to climb in.

"Okay, guys, just an FYI for future reference though… You're freaking me out and need to work on your bedside manner if you'll be assisting brides. You're eyeballing me like I'm going to sprout wings and take off," she said grumpily as she lay back.

As the door slid closed, Tamin quickly said, "We still need to discuss wings when you have a chance."

Oh Jesus Christ. They were back to the fucking pads again.

The thirty seconds for the scan passed quickly, but once Poppy had climbed out, the following five minutes seemed to last forever. It didn't help that both doctors were hovering over the screen at the end of the regen bed waiting for the results to pop up. Both of them were ignoring her completely, instead choosing to stare at the pod as if waiting for a pot of water to boil.

Tapping her toes on the shiny white floor, she fiddled with her bracelet, wondering if it was working correctly since she hadn't had a message from Wheaton all day. It was supposed to light up with an indicator when she had a message waiting in the system but nope, no blinking light and she was starting to get pissy the longer it stayed unlit. Banging it against the palm of her hand a couple of times, she stared at it harder. Nope. Nada. Nothing. Damn.

Five minutes had passed at an agonizingly boring pace when Tamin gave an excited yip. He was hugging Rodin like they'd just won the World Series. Seeing they were happy was a huge load off her nerves. Hopefully that meant that she wasn't dying or anything. Right? Whatever it was that had shown up earlier that had scared the men must have been a false reading,

"So can I go now or do you need me?" she asked, completely dismissing the medical chart printing out.

Rodin and Tamin both faced her with huge smiles, while clutching her printouts and gesturing to the paper.

"Poppy, we want to be the first to congratulate you and Wheaton!" Rodin said as he put out his hand to shake.

"For what?" she asked stupidly, automatically shaking the hand in the air.

"Your match has resulted in the first human hybrid baby in a new line of warriors!" Rodin said in an excited rush. "We did not want to presume that you had started sexual relations, but from your scan we can tell you that they have been successful," he said, while pumping her hand.

The words seemed to echo in her head. Sexual relations. Successful. Successful sexual relations. Oh dear god, they thought she was pregnant. It took a minute or two but she realized that her hand was now hanging in his grip and he was staring at her with a face filled with panic.

"Poppy, you have lost all your color and are swaying on your feet. Let's sit you down." Putting an arm around her shoulders, he led her to the chair next to a desk in the room.

"Tamin, please call back Dathrow. She may need a friend's counsel right now. I do not want her to go into shock," he instructed the other man.

"No…no…don't call Dath. I just need to sit for a minute and wrap my head around this." Rubbing her hand down her face, she took a few deep breaths and realized her mouth was dry.

"Can I have a glass of water?" she said in a weak voice.

"Of course, Poppy. Let me get that for you," Tamin said as he quickly moved to get her a drink.

Once he was back in the room and sitting down, she turned her chair slightly to face both of them. Feeling slightly better now that she wasn't standing, she focused on breathing evenly.

"First, how the hell can you tell I'm already pregnant? Our 'relations' didn't happen until a couple days ago." Now was not the time to start blushing so she willed her cheeks to cool while she eyeballed the two docs in front of her.

"Well, the regen machine is extremely sensitive and can detect changes in the body almost immediately. New life is growing in your womb. It is in the beginning stages but can be detected," Rodin explained.

"Wow. Okay. Wow." Poppy sat stunned. Realizing she was still holding a full glass of water, she took a couple gulps and felt a couple drops dribble down her chin. Wiping her face with her hand, she didn't care if she came across as a hot mess.

"Okay, fellas, let's have a chat, okay?" When the men leaned forward as if she were going to share secrets, Poppy smiled at them both. These two were so excited about this pregnancy. She had a feeling she was going to be followed around every second of the day for the remainder of this pregnancy.

"I don't want to burst your bubble, but this pregnancy is so new it may not take. On Earth women are told not to share news of a pregnancy until they're out of their first trimester. Miscarriages happen all the time and I have had many friends have them."

Poppy didn't want to be a Debbie Downer but she had to be realistic. Right now, whatever was there was so new there was still a chance it might not develop. She remembered an unexpected pregnancy Pixie had had a couple years ago. At first, her sister had been in shock but quickly come around and embraced the idea of becoming a mother. When she had miscarried at nine weeks, it had been heartbreaking. Pixie had been devastated and Poppy had felt the pain right along with her. That was when she had learned the first trimester was always the trickiest, with the chance of miscarriage being the highest.

Poor Pix had spent some time blaming herself for the miscarriage. It had taken an intervention from Poppy with the statistics for her to understand it was extremely common and she hadn't done anything wrong. It had been hard for Pixie to move on emotionally from the miscarriage and Poppy was sure she still thought about it from time to time.

"I'll tell Wheaton about the baby but I don't want anyone else to know as of right now, okay?" she said, noting the disappointment on the men's faces.

"But, Poppy, I am sure that the Council would be pleased to know that we have had a successful pairing," Tamin sputtered out.

"Right now, the Council can go fuck themselves," she muttered softly but apparently loud enough for the men to hear her.

"You *do* have some allies on the Council, Poppy and this may help your case with the undecided," Rodin said.

Poppy had to admit that Rodin had a point. She really wanted to keep this news just between them until she was further along, but if this would get Hannah the Horror out of Wheaton's apartment then it might be a good idea to let them know about it sooner rather than later. Leaning back and closing her eyes, she took a moment to think. No. It would be better to wait no matter the chance of it giving her bonus points.

"No, my decision is to wait. It's still too early and, guys…" She paused, hoping that they understood where she was coming from. "What if something happens?" Poppy asked in a sad voice. "If I lose this baby, they may have more reasons to get rid of me than they do right now."

"That is a valid point," agreed Tamin reluctantly, nodding at his friend.

"We will wait," Rodin added.

Still leaning forward, she felt like they were in a huddle at a football game and were strategizing their next play.

"Okay here's the plan, guys. I'm going to start volunteering here and you can monitor what's happening with Wheaton Jr. without anyone knowing I'm pregnant. Okay? That way you can see me every day and make sure everything's doing what it needs to do. When we get to the point where it's safe to share the news, we'll go from there. I'll tell Wheaton as soon as I see him next but I want this kept on the down-low."

When the men gave her quizzical faces, she added, "I want to keep this between us, on a need-to-know basis and nobody but us and Wheaton needs to know…got me?" She gave both guys a serious look, willing them to agree with her.

"That sounds like a plan, Poppy," Tamin said with a grin.

"We already have your vitals on record, but I would like to scan you every day if you are able to be here. According to our research, you should have a similar pregnancy cycle that humans have on Earth but we want to guarantee that you have the best care possible and also check for any differences between human-to-human pregnancies and human-to-warrior ones," Rodin explained.

She nodded in agreement. Not wanting to take any chances with the possibility of a baby, she knew these guys would take care of her the best they could. "Wait, the scanning won't cause my baby to grow any extra legs or anything right? It's safe to do it every day?"

"There will not be any extra appendages, we promise," Tamin vowed, holding his hand over his heart.

They all stood and Poppy leaned toward Tamin first and then Rodin for hugs. After somewhat hesitant embraces, mainly because the men did not understand why she was touching them, she leaned back with a sweet smile.

"Thanks, docs. Now show me more of this place and let's get crackin'. If I'm supposed to be working, then you might want to show me the supply room we never got to earlier." Leading the way, she tossed back, "And y'all need to relax...I'm a hugger. Get used to it." The men's chuckles followed her from the exam room.

The rest of the afternoon went by very quickly. Poppy checked her messages throughout the day but no messages from Wheaton so far and she was starting to get bitchy. Not trusting the bracelet's indicator, she scanned the message center every hour but nada...zip...zilch.

Tamin and Rodin took turns keeping her company during her inventory and exam room supply check while they worked on their tablet computer devices. Every once in a while they asked her if she needed anything and how she felt, which would cause her to make fun of them a little.

They had become familiar with her sense of humor and had been joking around with her all afternoon. Both men seemed to be really nice guys and had mentioned their opinions on the bridal match program. Apparently neither of them had entered to be selected in the first group of warriors in the lottery. They were biding their time, absorbing as much information on human interaction as they were able to. The two warriors seemed like two halves of a whole, which made Poppy think there might be more to them than they let on.

They actually did a great job of distracting Poppy from the fact Wheaton had not messaged her yet. Every time she went to see if she had a message, they would ask her questions about her childhood or her sister. Pixie ended up being discussed quite a bit, and her antics had both men laughing loudly when Poppy explained how they were similar but Pixie was a bit more "spicy".

They both had expressions of horror on their faces when she realized that they didn't understand the word "spicy" wasn't referring to cannibalism. That resulted in the next hour being spent going over phrases or words that would not translate correctly to their translation devices. Poppy smiled thinking about how she'd had to explain the word "fuck" to Wheaton, which of course made her check her bracelet for messages again.

Damn that man, where the hell was he? Feeling a hand touch her shoulder lightly, she jumped before she realized that Rodin was standing behind her.

"Are you all right, Poppy? I have been talking to you and yet you seemed so far away," he asked with a concerned tone in his voice.

"Sorry, Rodin. I kind of lost myself in my own head for a minute there," she said, shaking her head to clear it. "What did I miss?"

"We were considering reaching out to the brides still on the ship and asking to see if they would all have physicals. So far, we have been waiting for their warriors to bring them to the medical unit but we have only met you and one other when they received their translators," he said with a grimace. "Tamin and I believe that the warriors are possessive of their females and have decided to keep them away from most unmated males as a precaution. Of course with the news of the matches being incorrect we are unsure who will be staying and who will be taken back to Earth. Regardless, it is still a good idea to get them scanned just in case."

Rodin seemed to think for a moment before coming back to the present. "We were actually surprised that Wheaton gave you a tour of the ship after you first arrived. I realize he did not bring you to medical because we were unavailable but he did take you around."

Tamin entered the room as they were talking and passed Poppy a fresh glass of water.

"We believe that the other bride who came by initially would not have visited again if she had not accidentally cut herself and needed medical attention, which in her case was what you would call a bandage," Rodin added.

"Her warrior was beside himself with worry. I believe that is one of the other pairs that has also decided to fight the Council's decision of separation," Tamin said with a smile, obviously recalling how amusing it must have been to see a normally cool and calm warrior lose his mind over a small cut.

Poppy sat there for a minute, completely stunned that she'd forgotten for even one minute there were other women on the ship. *Human* women. Human women who were most likely in the same position she was in.

"How soon can you contact them, doc?" Poppy asked, her excitement building the more she thought about it.

Rodin smiled at her exuberance, studied his tablet for a moment and pressed some buttons.

"I just sent messages to the warriors to approach their brides and request a medical screening. When they contact me to set up a time, I will indicate that we have acquired another bride to assist during the exams. It will help in making them more comfortable while here in the center," said Rodin.

After talking about what might be needed for the women's visits, Poppy realized it was getting late. Tamin and Rodin had finished up their paperwork, or in their case, tablet work. While she had been taking inventory, there had been a couple warriors who had come in to be treated for various sparring injuries. During both of those occasions, Poppy had been shielded from the warriors' questioning glances, and the men were moved quickly through the med center. It was obvious that the doctors took her protection very seriously.

Stretching from where she sat on the floor organizing a low shelf, she stood and swung her arms over her head to get her blood moving again. Her bracelet caught her eye as she moved. It was blinking! She scurried over to the wall to check the system for a message. How the hell had she missed it flashing?

"Poppy, I apologize for today. I spoke with Dathrow earlier and he said that you were going to the med center to work…I am glad you are staying busy." Wheaton's voice paused on the recording as if he were unsure how to continue. "It seems that my work with the Council will prevent me from joining you for our normal evening meal. I am sorry but will speak with you as soon as I am able to. Just remember what I told you when we were last together."

Poppy realized she was on the verge of crying as the message ended. Why the hell was she so weepy? When she'd been in previous relationships, going a couple days without seeing her boyfriend had never been an issue. She wondered if the fact Hannah was taking her place in the apartment was bothering her more than she'd originally thought. It wasn't that she didn't trust Wheaton. Over the last couple weeks she'd felt closer to Wheaton than she'd ever felt toward a man. He had become an anchor in her strange new home and she felt somewhat lost without him. It didn't help that he *had* acted possessively toward her and she hadn't learned much about her new surroundings before this whole mess started. She could see his point. She was one of a few women on a ship of a couple thousand men. Men who didn't have female companionship. She would have been an idiot to not see the danger in that situation. But now that Wheaton wasn't here by her side, she felt as if she'd lost her life preserver. Leaning on Dathrow and now Tamin and Rodin had been a little hard since she hadn't really had much contact with any of them prior to a few days ago. Lucky for everyone that she made friends quickly, she thought.

Deciding she should get back and figure out dinner and maybe a movie, she spoke with Tamin about getting an escort to her quarters. It was at that moment Rodin came in with a couple bleeding warriors. Apparently sparring sessions were pretty intense on this ship. The men appeared as if they'd been in an ultimate fighting championship and she figured they'd need a bit of time in the regen beds. Grimacing at the angle of one of the men's arms hanging limply at his side, she quickly got out of their way.

Rodin tried messaging Dathrow for an escort but had no luck. It seemed as if she would be stuck in the med center for a while. Poppy was getting comfortable when she heard Rodin say her name.

"Poppy, this is Behyr," he said, gesturing at the tall, grim-faced man beside him.

Behyr was an extremely large warrior, mighty fierce with his long dreadlocks and somber face. He was actually very striking in appearance. If she could compare him to anyone, it would be that guy from *Game of Thrones* who married the dragon lady. He was big, with long hair and piercing eyes and didn't crack a smile or soften his face at all during their introduction. The only thing he was missing was the war paint and naked chest. Both of which, she was honest enough to admit, she wouldn't mind seeing.

"*Bear*, as in the animal?" she asked. Sticking her hand out for a handshake, she was surprised to be met with a gentle grasp.

"It is spelled differently in your alphabet but pronounced the same," he said in a deep voice that fit the packaging perfectly.

"Nice to meet you, Behyr." Poppy smiled up at the big guy, then over at Rodin. Why was he choosing now to introduce her to another warrior when he had seemed to act as a barrier to the ones who had come in all day long?

"Behyr has consented to walk you back to your quarters. He is a senior Skrammon warrior and has guarded Wheaton on missions when needed. Is this acceptable?" Rodin asked.

"Ummm sure," she said with a slight hesitation. If Rodin trusted this guy then she should too, right? Maybe his being so much bigger was throwing her off. She had seen some Skrammon warriors in passing but this was the first time she'd actually talked to one and she could see why this was *the* warrior breed. Behyr was intimidating as hell.

"I already contacted Dathrow and he explained he was caught up in a meeting and unable to leave. He is the one who sent Behyr for your escort," Rodin said with a reassuring smile when he noticed Poppy staring at the large man.

"If you would rather wait for me to be available, I should be able to walk you back in the next hour or so. We have a couple warriors with broken bones we need to get started in the regen beds."

"Yeah, I saw the guy with the hanging arm. Don't mind me, I've just never met a Skrammon before and was taken off guard by the differences between the warriors." She glanced up at Behyr and smiled. "Come on, big guy. I'm starving and my back hurts from organizing those shelves. I haven't been this sore since I decided I was going to start a garden. Now I remember why my plants died." Rubbing her back to ease some of the stiffness, Poppy gathered her stuff.

Waving to her friends, she promised them she'd be back the next day as soon as she finished breakfast. Following Behyr out of the door, Poppy took a good look at her new companion and his outfit. His suit was similar to Wheaton's everyday wear but was a dark red-brown instead of the black that Wheaton wore. Wondering if it was a warrior class uniform, she asked him questions and was surprised when he answered patiently. Behyr explained that certain colors designated different tiers in the Phaeton class system. Behyr's red leather designated his status as a senior Skrammon warrior. The Brakkens wore shades of blue leather while most Healson warriors wore black.

The short walk back to her quarters seemed much quicker since they spoke almost the entire way.

"Thank you for allowing me to escort you, Poppy. Dathrow said he may need me to escort you when either he or Councilor Wheaton is not available." With a short bow, Behry turned to leave.

"Behyr?"

"Yes, Poppy?"

"Thank you for walking me back and also for answering my questions," she said with a friendly smile. For someone so big, he was actually very quiet and gentle.

"Have a nice evening meal, Poppy. I may see you tomorrow." Bowing to her once again, he walked quietly down the hallway.

She might be smitten with Wheaton but she had to appreciate the way Behyr filled out his combat outfit. That man was a beast. He was a beast in the best way possible, if you could judge by the way he filled out his leather pants. Damn these warriors were mighty fine.

After making herself a pizza and finding a movie, she rattled around her apartment. Having the time to herself, she couldn't stop thinking. How exactly was she going to break the news of the pregnancy to Wheaton when she saw him? Was she actually going to see him tomorrow? She *hoped* but with her luck he would be busy again. Maybe she should do a couple runs of saying she was pregnant so she didn't stutter when she finally had the opportunity. Standing in front of the bathroom mirror, she practiced a couple times using different phrases. No matter how silly she felt doing it, she did feel better. After ten different times she smiled widely. She. Was. Pregnant. And not only was she pregnant, she was really *happy* about it.

"Wheaton, you're going to be a daddy." Yep, that sounded perfect.

CHAPTER TWENTY

The next few days were awful. Absolutely awful. After having such high hopes the day she'd found out she was pregnant, she was now not so happy with her circumstances. One call after another with excuses from Wheaton was getting really fucking annoying. First it was back-to-back meetings he absolutely had to attend. Then, when he had sought her out, she'd been in the med center and he didn't have time in his break to find her. She'd started relying more and more on the new friends she'd made to keep her company. Her daily schedule seemed to keep her busy.

She spent most of her day joking with Tamin and Rodin in the med center. Meals were usually eaten in her new quarters with Behyr and Dathrow. She was slowly starting to feel less lonely every day. The men often laughed at her antics and requested she play her music whenever they were around. It was often playing in the background now when she was present. She couldn't imagine having a life without music or art. From what she was able to find out, their society had been very staid and all the men absorbed human culture like sponges. Big, strong, delicious-looking sponges.

Dathrow had kept her up-to-date on the Council proceedings but there had been no new developments regarding her bridal status. Whenever she asked about Hannah the Hellhound, he would close up and change the subject. Of course that made her worry Hannah was fitting in better with Wheaton's way of life than she ever did. Behyr was a superb sounding board. He was still very quiet and she had yet to make him smile but he had laughed a couple of times at something she'd said before covering the sound with a cough. Her new mission was to make him smile and loosen up a little bit.

During one of their afternoon discussions, she had her mind blown when they described their childhoods. Apparently warriors were raised in what she would describe as an orphanage. The men who ran the schools were older warriors who were no longer able to serve in active warrior society. They took warrior babies and raised them in cold, sterile housing to be trained in the ways of their breeds. There were no art classes, music appreciation or hugs and smiles from their teachers. The warriors were raising the next generation the way they were raised. It all seemed so sad to Poppy and she actually teared up when they explained it all.

None of them seemed upset about it. Why would they be? They didn't know any other way. Rodin and Tamin had rushed to get her tissues when she started crying, staring at her as if she were losing her mind. Of course that was when Behyr had come to pick her up and decided to flip out. Apparently, seeing her crying made him angry, especially when Tamin and Rodin were unable to explain what had upset her so much.

After she'd dried her tears and stopped hugging the men in a round-robin hug fest, she told them as plainly as she could why she had broken down.

"That's just soooooo sad!" she blubbered, crying all over again.

Behyr, who was still in the dark about why she was crying in the first place, decided to give her his first unsolicited hug. Judging by his face, he was extremely uncomfortable but perhaps thought that since she had needed to hug them to calm down then this was the way to do it again.

"Why are you crying, little one?" he asked, awkwardly patting her back. Over the top of her head he was shooting death glares at the other two men.

"We did not do anything to her but talk, so please stop acting like you want to kill me, Behyr," Rodin said, his voice dry.

"Well, one of you made her cry! She was smiling when I escorted her to the med center this morning," he said angrily.

"No no no…they didn't do anything," Poppy said, her words muffled into his leather shirt.

"Please explain," Behyr requested, handing her a tissue.

"The boys were explaining to me how you were raised in the warrior houses. I can't imagine it, Behyr. You didn't have anyone to kiss your boo-boos, or sing you songs when you were sad…or give you hugs when you needed them." Poppy's voice still sounded teary but she had stopped crying enough that Behyr felt comfortable stepping back.

"And?" he prompted, perplexed as to why she was upset still.

"Don't you guys get it?" By this time, she was becoming upset with them for not understanding how fucked-up their childhoods had been.

"Children need love and attention," she said, pointing at the men. "Not barracks and classes to train them to be warriors when they're only kids."

"But, Poppy, this is our way," Tamin explained with his eyebrow raised in confusion.

"No. No! I will not let Wheaton Jr. be raised like that. This shit needs to be figured out before my baby gets here." Cuddling her belly, she was in such a tizzy she didn't realize what she'd blurted out. Behyr's mouth dropped open. He turned to Rodin and Tamin in disbelief.

"She is carrying a child?" he yelled.

Tamin and Rodin both held their hands up to calm him down. As the men argued about her pregnancy being a secret, she sat down while her mind whirled.

How was this baby going to be raised? Her apartment on the ship was small and could only accommodate a couple. Were there bigger apartments on the ship that could house a family? She would never turn her defenseless baby over to be raised in an orphanage. Was that what the Council expected? Did Wheaton just expect them to hand over their baby when the time came for it to be raised, and then start on another one? So many questions filled her head. So few answers seemed available.

The men stopped their chatter and stared at her.

"Poppy? Are you okay?" Behyr asked, concern evident in his voice.

"Guys, what's going to happen once I have my baby? Will they expect me to just turn him over to your warrior houses?" Seeing the men glance at each other, she realized they had no clue what step two of the plan was either. Fuck. That didn't help her at all. Propping her hands on her hips, she stared them down until they at least faked an answer for her.

"Honestly, Poppy, we are unsure what the plan is for the new generation of children," Tamin said with a grimace.

"The ship would not be ideal for raising a small warrior either," Rodin agreed, shooting a glance at Behyr as if hoping he might have something to add.

"We know no other way, little one," he admitted.

"Well, guys, we need to get on the ball because we are on a deadline now and they are *not* taking my baby away to raise it to be a cold warrior," she said in a voice that invited no argument and then continued, "I can tell you right now, the other brides are going to be on my side on this."

As they all sat down to try to figure out possible solutions, they came to a conclusion. The men explained that most warriors traveled on ships a majority of their lives, so the ships would have to be retrofitted to allow for family quarters instead of couples' quarters. Another thing discussed was the extensive baby proofing of the ships that would be needed. That issue would be a huge project by itself. Warriors on the home planet apparently resided in barracks, so family homes would need to be constructed there when the babies started coming. According to the men, only high-ranking Council members had their own areas in the barracks but they served as office spaces as well as living quarters.

As the list of "things to do" kept getting longer and longer, Poppy yawned widely. She had not realized how tired she was getting.

"Behyr, I am assuming the whole reason you arrived an hour ago was to escort me back to the apartment." At his nod she admitted, "I'm getting tired and hungry. How about we all think on this tonight and we can talk more tomorrow?"

The men realized they'd kept her well past her normal time and jumped up to help her gather her things.

"Poppy, tomorrow we want to perform another scan and check the progress of the pregnancy. Can you arrive early so we can make sure no other warriors are present?" Tamin asked.

"Of course I can. I'll let Dath know to come earlier for breakfast so we can get here maybe twenty minutes earlier. Would that be enough time for you to run the tests you need?"

"That is more than enough time," he agreed.

"And if you can bring those muffs again, we would appreciate it," Rodin chimed in.

"You mean *muffins*, Rodin, and yes, I will bring more tomorrow," she replied with a smile.

Walking back to her apartment, she noticed Behyr was standing even closer to her than normal. He acted as if he were on guard, like something was going to jump out and get her. Linking her arm through his, she smiled up at the big man beside her.

"Behyr, are you okay? You seem more tense than usual," she asked.

He gave her an uncomfortable look. "I am nervous, Poppy. Before this afternoon, I was responsible for just you. Now I am responsible for you and also the first of a new line for our entire race," he admitted. "What if you fall? What if you do not get enough food to eat? What if you have a problem in the middle of the night and no one is there for you?" he asked.

Reaching her door, she patted his hand and turned to face him.

"I'm tougher than you think. And, yes, I might be a klutz but unless it's a really bad fall I should be okay. I have food at my fingertips whenever I'm hungry, and I can call for help whenever I need it almost immediately, thanks to my nifty bracelet."

"But…" he continued, still concerned.

"Behyr, I'm scared enough for both of us, believe me. I think about it every day. I don't have Wheaton here to talk to about it and that makes it worse. He doesn't even know there *is* a baby yet because I wanted to tell him in person and now with everything I found out today, I'm really freaking out," she admitted, tired of the situation she had been forced into.

"Don't freak, Poppy. All will be well," he assured her in a serious voice.

Poppy began giggling. Apparently hearing the tone of his voice along with him telling her not to "freak" tickled her funny bone enough to make her start laughing. Pretty soon his face added to the hilarity when he appeared so completely confused and she laughed even harder. Obviously having a case of the giggles was contagious, because for the first time since she'd met him, Behyr started smiling. And it wasn't a small smile that he covered up with his hand. No, it was a full-on, teeth-showing smile accompanied by a booming laugh. That was when she noticed something that made her gasp.

Behyr had fangs. *Fangs*. Not gigantic vampire fangs, but they were definitely there. And they were sexy as hell. Before he knew what she was going to do, she reached up and touched his cheek. Her manners were the only thing holding her back from prying his lips open to investigate further. That and the knowledge that if a hug made him stiffen up, then checking his teeth as if he were a horse would totally scare the shit out of him.

"You have fangs! Why didn't I know you had fangs? Is it a Skrammon breed trait?" she asked while he stood completely still, letting her touch his face.

"Yes it is. We are fighters and sometimes we use our teeth in hand-to-hand combat. They are intimidating to our enemies as well," he said, flashing them again for her to see more clearly.

Nodding now in understanding, she let go of his face and he relaxed. Not wanting to lose the moment, she held his hand in hers.

"Is that why you don't smile?" she asked.

He nodded while still appearing slightly uncomfortable. "We also do not have much to smile about, Poppy. You seem happy all the time…this is new to many of us. I do not remember the last time I laughed before you arrived." His voice had lowered as if he had finally realized what she had been trying to explain to them about raising her children.

"*What is going on here?*" The booming question came from a couple feet away.

"Wheaton!" Poppy yelled, launching herself at him. Practically climbing his body in an effort to reach his lips for a kiss, she felt his arms come around her and squeeze tight. She saw Behyr, was now standing at attention with all emotion wiped from his face. Hands folded behind his back, he resembled a soldier standing at perfect attention. In her excitement at seeing Wheaton, she hadn't realized how pissed-off he was. Now she did. She saw him glaring at a warrior who had once been a friend, but who, if he didn't step back from his bride, would be a dead warrior.

"Don't you dare yell at me, Wheaton!" she said, climbing off him.

"I do not like the familiar way you were speaking with Behyr," he argued.

Oh hell no. Wheaton was delusional if he thought he was going to dictate who could be her friend and who could not.

"First off, Behyr is my *friend*. Friend. That is all. Understand?" she said, poking his chest. The action startled him enough for him to step back and focus his entire attention on her.

"Second, I haven't seen you in *forevah*, so if you think you have any right to be angry with *me*, then you're nuts!" she hollered with another hard poke as he moved even farther. Soon he had retreated all the way to her apartment door.

"And third…" she continued only to be interrupted.

Wheaton threw up his hands to ward off more pokes. "You are right, Poppy. I am sorry. I just have not seen you in days and I did not like how comfortable you seem to have gotten with another warrior," he rushed out, apparently realizing that he needed to dig himself out of a hole and do it quickly.

Glancing back, Poppy saw Behyr was still standing at attention. The only thing relaxed in his stance was the small smile he now wore. Poppy smiled back at him. "I will message you later about my schedule for tomorrow, okay?"

"Of course, Poppy. Have a nice evening." With a bow to both her and Wheaton, he walked away.

Poppy waved her wrist to open the door Wheaton was blocking.

"Come on, big guy, we have a lot to talk about."

Clutching his hand and tugging him into the apartment, she figured they couldn't waste any time in case he got called away again.

CHAPTER TWENTY-ONE

Once in the apartment, Poppy found herself in his arms before she could be sure the door had even closed behind them. Losing herself in his kiss, she breathed in his musky scent. Wheaton released the clip from her hair, causing it to fall in curls down her back. With his hands tugging at the strands like that, a shiver crept down her spine and goose bumps popped up on her arms. Holy hell, this man could kiss. His mouth was so warm on hers and she thought she would melt into a puddle as he sucked at her lips and tongue. Her hands were being wasted, gripping his shoulders, so she moved them to his hair. His shoulder-length hair was silky smooth and she tugged a handful of it, causing him to moan into her mouth.

Wheaton moved his mouth from hers, trailing it across her cheek to her ear and nibbling a bit before placing sucking kisses down to her neck. Fisting her hands in his hair now, she dragged his head back as she tried to clear her own. Wheaton fought her direction and kept his mouth moving lower.

"Wheaton, we need to talk." Rasping out the words, she gasped to pull air into her lungs.

"Talk later," he mumbled into her cleavage while trying to pull her vee-neck T-shirt down.

Pulling at his hair again to get him to tip back his head, she noticed his eyes had turned a dark green. The same dark green she anticipated whenever they got frisky. Before they'd begun fooling around, she would gauge when they needed to call a halt to their foreplay by the color of his eyes. If they were any indication right now, then she needed to put the kibosh on things now before she caved in and straddled him in the entryway.

"Wheaton, *not* later. Now. It's important."

He groaned at the serious expression on her face and straightened back up, his hard body skimming hers.

"Okay…let us talk quickly then," he said with a grimace as he tried to adjust his leather pants that now had absolutely no room to spare.

Gripping his hand, Poppy led him over to the couch. Before she was able to get comfortable, he pulled her onto his lap and settled her over his erection. Wheaton groaned at the pressure and wiggled his hips to a more comfortable position.

"Talk. Please. Quickly," Wheaton bit out, obviously losing his struggle for patience.

"Okay…here goes." Poppy had practiced this multiple times over the last week but her palms were still sweating.

As if sensing that whatever she was going to say would be something important, Wheaton opened his eyes and stared into hers.

"I'm…we're…" she started.

"Yes?" he asked when she paused.

"Wheaton, I'm pregnant," she rushed out, staring into his eyes.

Nothing. No facial expression. No words. He sat there as if she hadn't even spoken. He was stock-still and from what she could tell, not even breathing. Maybe he hadn't heard her.

"We're having a baby," she tried again.

Wheaton blinked a couple times, sitting completely still now. She could feel him holding his breath.

"A baby?" he echoed with a stunned look on his beautiful face.

"A baby." She nodded with a smile.

His mouth was open and she could see him breathing now. The hands that had been tightened on her waist were now moving up to push up her T-shirt and hover over her belly.

"A baby?" he repeated again.

And there was that smile she'd been waiting for. His smile was so big she couldn't help but mirror it.

"Can I feel it? When did you find out? Have Tamin and Rodin examined you yet?" he rushed out while rubbing her belly.

Apparently so many thoughts were running through his head and half of them seemed to be worries he had for Poppy and the baby she was growing in her belly.

"Well, you can't feel anything yet. I'm barely pregnant but the scan picked it up. I found out right after this whole Hannah thing started. And yes, they have checked me over. Everything so far is progressing great but they want to rescan me tomorrow morning. They wanted to scan every day but the med center has been so busy we haven't had any privacy to do another one. I want you to be there tomorrow for the next one," she said to answer his rapid-fire questions.

He had lowered his gaze to the area that he'd exposed. Seeing his dark, strong hands cradle her belly was so sweet. Before she'd met Wheaton, her belly had been something she had sucked in when it was getting attention while naked. Shortly after they'd started fooling around, Wheaton had asked why she was holding her breath. At that moment she had a mini come-to-Jesus meeting with herself. Figuring her relationship with Wheaton needed to start as she meant it to go on, she admitted to him that she was a little self-conscious of her belly and the flab that seemed to glare at her when she scrutinized herself in the mirror.

Normally it didn't bother her but in their intimate moment, it had made her nervous. What if she didn't turn him on? She had been insanely attracted to him to the point of panting—what if it was one-sided? At that point, he had asked her to point out the areas she didn't like. When she pointed to the waddle under the length of her arms, he stroked that area and gave it a line of kisses. When she next moved to her love handles and belly pooch, he ran his rough palms over her stomach and sprinkled kisses there. Once it moved to the area below her waist, she had finally figured out that he didn't mind her soft areas. From the size of his erection he had been sporting, he liked what he saw.

The next morning when they had woken up, he spent the next hour showing her again what he loved about her body. Wheaton explained that many warriors had shown preferences toward softer body types. Poppy figured it was because everything around them was hard, so maybe they needed something soft around them for a change.

Feeling his palms move, she shivered. His hands were on a seek-and-find mission of her sweet spots. Time to celebrate their baby.

Wheaton apparently did not want to make love to the mother of his future child on the small white couch. Picking her up, he carried her into the bedroom with her giggling and kissing his neck the entire way.

"I am so happy, Poppy," he whispered as he laid her back against her pillows. "A baby. We are having a baby. Maybe a little girl with hair like yours? Or a boy who will be a strong warrior to help protect his family. It does not matter to me really. I simply still cannot believe it."

"Me too," she whispered back.

Leaning down to nip at her lips, he turned a sweet moment into a much more sensual one with just a kiss.

Moving her hands back to his hair, she pulled him into a longer kiss. One that involved lots of tongue and teeth. Giving her one last peck, he moved back far enough to jerk her T-shirt over her head. She laughed when her hair flopped over her face, blocking her vision. Blinded momentarily, she could only gasp as she felt his lips on her now bare stomach. His tongue lapping at her waistband, she was about a second from losing her pants. Wanting to watch him as he proceeded to undress her, she leaned up on her elbows.

"Down to my underwear, babe, and you're still fully dressed." Poppy pointed out, motioning to his still-clothed body.

"Easily rectified, Little Flower."

Moving to the side of the bed, he jerked his shirt over his head. Seeing his torso exposed, she licked her lips. Apparently he noticed her lip licking if his groan was anything to go by.

Putting his hands to his waist, he unfastened the built-in buckle on his pants and pushed them over his hips. They were skimmed down his legs along with his underwear. Once his feet were free of his pants, he sat back down on the bed next to her and reached for her bra to undo it. Freeing her breast caused him to lick his lips and then it was Poppy's turn to groan. Leaning forward to catch one pebbled nipple in his mouth, he gave it a wet suck before looping a finger through the straps on each side of her hips. As he tugged her panties down to bare her mound, her underwear barely cleared her pussy before he moved to her cleft. His hand skimmed down into her wetness. Finding her opening with his fingers, he probed. Poppy tried to open her legs wider before reaching the limit of the stretch in her panties.

"Take them off," she moaned.

"I want to tease you more," he whispered in a husky voice. Taking his time now that he finally had her where he wanted her.

"No more teasing, Wheaton. I need to come. Now." Wiggling her hips to try to move the panties down farther, she was halted when his hand came down on the fleshy side of her hip. The light smack made her moan softly, and she gazed up into his eyes.

"You liked that, my Little Flower?" he asked.

"Yes, more of that, and less talking. Now," she ordered.

"Of course, love." His hand squeezed where it landed and rubbed once more before lifting up to give her another smack. When she moaned again, he reached down and pulled her panties down even farther.

Sucking at her nipples and rubbing his face in her cleavage, he delved his hand again between her legs to spread her wetness around her clit. Sparks lit up behind Poppy's eyes, which she again had closed. Putting her own hand on his, she moved his fingers where she wanted them the most.

Wheaton moved over her to lie on top of her in the cradle of her legs. Spreading herself wide open to make him more comfortable and hopefully give him a hint as to where she needed this to go—sooner rather than later—she dragged her hands along his back. Her nails might be short but she was able to scratch them up and down while he moved his hips in a circle. The tip of his cock started a steady and firm pressure against her mound and she opened her legs even farther to allow it to kiss her wet opening. Teasing her with the hint of penetration drove her crazy. She couldn't help but tilt her hips even farther so the head would enter her.

"Poppy, stop moving or I will finish too soon," he rasped, trying to hold her hips still.

"I can't. I need you in me now." Canting her hips toward him made his cock move a little deeper.

"That's it. Get on your hands and knees." He leaned up and moved to his knees. Poppy could see his dick was now wet from her and probably from him a little also.

"My knees?" She smiled up at him and decided to tease him a bit. "Have you been sneaking porn again and saw something you wanted to try?" she asked with a giggle.

Laughing, he helped her flip over and pulled her up onto her knees. Wheaton let out a groan when she flashed him a clear view of where she needed him. Hunger burned bright in his eyes as he stared at what she had exposed.

"No porn but yes, I do want to try this," he said huskily as he gripped her hips with one hand while the other moved behind her to hold his cock steady.

Poppy had always been a fan of doggy-style, the position being able to get her off the fastest. She was anxious to experience this with Wheaton. She rocked her hips a bit in a teasing motion. His hand tightened on her hip as the head of his dick began to stretch her opening. He accompanied the movement with a swat on her ass. Starting a rhythm that made all teasing comments come to a halt, he moved with firm, sure strokes. The only sounds that were coming from either one of them were moans, loud breathing and the thud of his hips against her ass. After a couple more smacks, both of his hands moved to grip her hips and pull her into his thrusts. One hand let go for a second and rubbed her lower back, pushing her torso down. The submissive position she was in allowed him to hit an even better angle and she soon had her breasts flattened against the bed. Poppy had never before been this turned on. The control he exhibited over her body made her burn for more.

Knowing what her body needed to come, her hand moved to her clit. Wheaton must have felt her adjust and realized she was playing with herself as he thrust in and out of her.

"Rub yourself for me, love. Make yourself come. I need to feel it," he groaned out.

"So close, babe, so close," she panted, feeling her channel tighten around the piston pumping back and forth inside it.

Making his strokes shorter and harder, he reached up and pulled a fistful of her hair. The slight tug was what Poppy needed to push her completely over. As time seemed to stand still except for the clenching of her pussy, Poppy heard moaning and realized it was coming from her. Wheaton was rumbling so loudly behind her she could feel the vibrations against her ass as his abs tightened when he came. Peering over her shoulder, her cheek pressed against the bed, she saw him throw his head back and heard him give a shout. The pulsing of his cock seemed to go on and on as he rumbled loudly to the ceiling.

"Wow," she breathed out, trying to catch her breath.

Wheaton lowered himself back onto his heels but did not let go of her hair or hips. Allowing her body to follow his shift in position as he relaxed, she was cradled into the curve of his kneeling body. Unclenching his fingers in her hair, he rubbed her back soothingly, his breathing slowly calming. Still inside her, he nestled her more securely into the curve of his body, wrapping his arms around her torso. He cradled her breast before moving his free hand to her neck. Turning her head so he could reach her lips, he gave her a hot, open-mouthed kiss.

"Yes, wow," he said when the kiss ended. With him still cradling her in a dominant way, she felt completely at his mercy. Poppy nuzzled his cheek. She would have been happy to stay like this forever. Her hips however were starting to protest. He gently lifted her off his lap and reclined behind her in spoon fashion. Sweeping his hand down her body as he cuddled his front into her back, he rested his hand over her stomach again.

"I am so happy, my Little Flower," he whispered to her, seeming not yet ready to break the little bubble they had created.

"I am too, babe. I am too," she whispered back.

After lying there a long while, Poppy had a thought.

"Are you able to stay the night, or will you need to go back to the apartment?" she asked, not really wanting to hear the answer if it wasn't going to make her happy.

"I want to stay. I plan on staying. Let me check my messages quickly and then I will come back and hold you."

As he stood, she realized she needed to tidy up. Good sex, it seemed, was a messy affair.

After she finished up in the bathroom, she found him the kitchen area with a glass of water. He was standing completely naked while chugging it. Poppy took a moment to appreciate the nude vision in front of her. His cock had just finished making her come but it was still long and thick as it rested against his thigh. His throat worked as he gulped, causing her own mouth to water. The strong line of his neck was calling for her to nibble at it. Lowering the glass, Wheaton shot her a sexy grin. His thoughts were obvious, if his hot stare was anything to go by.

"Did you check your messages yet?" she asked to distract herself from climbing on top of him in the kitchen.

Handing her a refilled glass of water, he walked over to the computer and waved his bracelet. The system told him he had one message and he quickly asked for it to play. His shoulders had stiffened so she figured he was anxious to make sure that he wasn't being called away yet again. The voice that came over the speaker wasn't a fellow Council member, though; it was Hannah.

"Wheaton, I figured that you would be back late and wanted to let you know that I am going to go ahead and go to bed. Don't worry about waking me up when you come to bed, just try not to turn on the light or steal the covers again. I was cold last night," said a voice that sounded more like a wife letting her husband know she couldn't wait up for him than just a mere roomie.

He turned around to walk back to Poppy with a swagger but she was still processing what she'd just heard.

Putting her hand out to halt him in his tracks, she couldn't hold in her reaction any longer.

"What the fuck!" she yelled at Wheaton.

"What?" he asked, perplexed.

"Don't you 'what' me! Are you sharing a bed with Hannah?" she asked, hoping that his answer would be "of course not".

"Well…yes. What is the problem?" he answered, confusion evident on his face.

"Wheaton, we have a *big* problem. You're sharing *a bed* with her. That is *not* okay. *Not. Okay*," she repeated.

"The apartment only has one bedroom, Poppy. I am unsure why you are angry," he said with a shake of his head.

"Because we are *together*, Wheaton! Have you fucked her?" She could hear herself losing her shit and tried to breathe through her nose to calm down. What she really felt like doing was pitching the glass that was still in her hand at his head.

"No, we have not had sexual relations." Hands held up as if in surrender, Wheaton moved closer.

"Have you messed around with her? Kissed her? Touched her? Has anything happened *other* than sleep, Wheaton?" she bit out, now furious.

The guilt on his face made her stomach drop. Oh dear Lord, she might puke. Turning to the kitchen bar, she placed the glass down calmly. Walking through the bedroom, Poppy understood her next stop was to be the bathroom. Locking the door quickly behind her so he wouldn't see her toss her cookies, she leaned over the toilet and breathed heavily. Stomach turning to acid, she tried to concentrate on calming her nerves.

Wheaton hadn't realized that Poppy would have such an emotional reaction. Yes, he had kissed Hannah. At the time, Hannah had argued and explained that maybe he *was* feeling closeness to Poppy because she had been the only available female. He knew that was not the case but Hannah seemed insistent that he test her theory. He kissed her and quickly proved that it was not true. Kissing Hannah had been like a shaking of hands. Cold and unemotional with no stimulation sexually. Wheaton could actually say with a certainty that he'd felt more emotion by simply speaking with Poppy than he had felt when kissing Hannah.

"Poppy? Poppy, open the door." The doorknob jiggled. Poppy checked quickly to make sure she'd engaged the lock firmly.

"We need to talk face-to-face…open the door please," he pleaded.

"Fuck you, Wheaton. Fuck. You," she cried out, not being able to stop a sob. Feeling that the nausea had passed, she stood up straight and moved to the sink. Splashing water on her face, she tried to stop her tears.

"Poppy, it is not what you think. Open the door, Little Flower, and let me talk to you." Hearing him talk close to the door, she knew he was not going to leave until she let him speak. She opened the door so quickly he had to step back or get whapped with it.

"Talk, asshole," she bit out with her arms crossed in front of her.

"Hannah kissed me. I did kiss her back." Seeing Poppy's face get even redder than it had been before, he rushed on, "However, it was more for the peace of mind that I had made the correct decision. I felt nothing for Hannah. No attraction. Nothing," he explained.

"Peace of mind? Are you fucking kidding me?" She walked over to the bed where just moments before she thought they had shared something special.

"I wanted to make sure that my attraction and feelings for you were genuine." At her look of disbelief, he continued, "Hannah said that I might have overestimated my feelings for you, since you were the only human woman whom I had been exposed to. She suggested that we kiss or touch to test the attraction, for both of us to make sure that what I feel is true," he explained calmly.

Poppy was having one of those moments where nothing made sense anymore. Before today, she'd had a goal. She knew what she was fighting for. But apparently Wheaton wasn't sure if he should even *be* fighting for her, not if he felt the need to go around kissing people to "test their attraction". Knowing that she was never going to be a pushover or a woman of weak will, she decided to make him see what she was feeling and there was only one way to do that.

Walking over to find the nightshirt she'd thrown on the floor the previous day, she slipped it over her head. Snagging a hair tie off the nightstand gave her a few more seconds to figure out what she was going to say. Wheaton had not felt the need to get dressed and sat as naked as he'd been before. Sure that her face conveyed her feelings, she stared at him for a few moments, waiting for him to look her in the eye. When he finally made eye contact, she saw him flinch. Whether it was the pure anger and disappointment on her face or the tears that had dried on her cheeks, she didn't know for sure, but he definitely flinched.

"Wheaton...I want you to listen very carefully to me, okay?" She waited for his nod before she continued. "I'm going to repeat what you just said, so I know I didn't hallucinate or misunderstand what happened."

Pausing, she stood a couple feet in front of him and laced her fingers in front of her.

"You've been sleeping with Hannah in *our* bed. Yes or no?" Keeping her gaze on his, she waited for his reply.

"Yes...but there is no other bed in the apartment. You are aware of this."

"Just keep it to 'yes' or 'no' for right now." She held up her hand and closed her eyes for a second to hold back the tears she knew were going to start again once she said what was next.

"You've kissed Hannah...yes or no?" She was unable to keep a tear from rolling down her cheek.

"Yes, but..." His voice halted when she held up her hand in a *stop* motion.

"The reason you kissed Hannah was to test your feelings for me...yes or no?" she continued.

"Yes...it seemed like a logical plan," he argued.

"Okay, now that we're both clear on that, I have one more question." This was the one she didn't want to ask, because it could seriously break her heart.

"Other than that one kiss, have you been intimate with Hannah or touched her in an intimate way?" Poppy didn't want to meet his eyes but knew she would need to when she heard the answer. Holding the stare of the green eyes she had come to love, she whispered, "Yes or no?"

Realizing what Poppy thought had happened made Wheaton feel about ten inches tall. Did she really think that he would have sex with someone else? Did she have so little faith in him that she expected he would be given a new bride and forget about the one he wanted?

"No," he said clearly, hoping that she believed him.

Poppy felt relief it had gone no further, but she needed to drive her point home, especially since he was giving her the hurt-puppy-dog face right now as if he'd done nothing wrong. Now was the part where she made him realize what she'd felt when he dropped the Hannah bomb.

"Using your logic, I should be able to test my own attraction with other warriors to make sure that my feelings for *you* are real. Yes or no?"

Boom. She saw what he felt the minute he realized what he'd done. His eyes got huge and his mouth dropped open as if he were stunned. He took a step toward her and gripped her arms as if getting ready to give her a good shake.

"*No!*" he shouted in a voice that made her wince. It seemed Wheaton couldn't help but feel intense rage at the thought of another warrior kissing his woman, but Poppy kept talking, not caring he was about to lose his mind.

Feeling a calm that wasn't actually there, she asked steadily, "Why not?"

Keeping her arms in his strong hands, not squeezing, just restraining, he stood stock-still. His mouth opened a couple times as if he had the correct answer to her question but was unable to say it. After what seemed like a lifetime, he slowly released her arms and took a step back.

"Because it would hurt me to have you kiss someone else," he whispered in a raw voice. She saw the understanding on his face and wanted to make sure he knew how much his actions had hurt her.

"Wheaton, it hurt me for you to even doubt what we have. When we made love the first time, I was showing you how I felt. How committed I was for this to work. The fact that you felt you needed to even 'test' that hurts me. It makes it worse that you decided to do that with Hannah, the bride Demascus the Douche seems to have handpicked for you."

Wheaton nodded in understanding, obviously still reeling from the idea of Poppy kissing another male.

"We are going to make a list of deal-breakers, okay?" At his confused expression, she pushed him back until his knees hit the bed and he sat down. Sitting beside him, she held out her hand and started counting off items that would cause her to call this whole thing quits.

"First off, no cheating. If you *ever* cheat on me in the future, *we are done.*"

She waited for him to nod.

Nodding quickly, he said, "Agreed."

Holding up another finger, she continued, "Second, no abuse…mental or physical. Don't fuck with my head and play games, and I won't do it to you."

"Agreed," he repeated with another nod and took the hand that she was counting off her fingers on and linked his fingers with hers.

"Poppy, are you going to test your compatibility with other males?" he asked in a rough voice, the thought clearly making him sick to his stomach.

Then, before she could even answer, he continued with an angry shake of his head and a squeeze of his hand.

"No. You will not. I will kill any male that comes near you." He bared his teeth. "Part of me wanted to pull Behyr's arms off and beat him with them when I saw you both smiling at each other," he admitted.

Taking her free hand, Poppy cupped his cheek. She realized that this big, stupid man had made a mistake and finally figured it out. Leaning forward to give him a hug, she basked in his closeness again.

Poppy sniffed through her now-stuffy nose. "You aren't off the hook yet, big guy. I am still disappointed in you for having doubts." Rubbing at her nose, she gave him a serious look.

"And I am pissed the fuck off at that bitch, Hannah. She's a human woman and would know how much that kiss would hurt me but also how that message sounded. I have a feeling she wanted me to hear it."

That quickly, Poppy's emotions shifted from sadness to anger. Jesus, it felt as if she were going through every single emotion in the world today. From complete bliss when finally able to see Wheaton, then sadness, anger, confusion. Anger at the other woman was clearly winning in the emotional wheel of fortune. She definitely needed to have a sit-down with Hannah the Whore, and hopefully it wouldn't end with her pulling out every single strand of her silky blonde hair.

"There will be no more sleeping in the same bed. You should have been on the couch or the floor the first night the problem came up. I don't care how uncomfortable it is." Seeing he was going to argue, she continued with what she knew would make him understand.

"Can you imagine how you would have reacted if you had found another warrior in my bed? Even simply sharing the same space? When Behyr found out I was pregnant, he didn't want me to spend my nights alone in case there was an emergency. It took quite a few talks to make him understand I didn't need him monitoring me during the night."

Breathing out heavily, Poppy said, "From now on, when you come across a situation like this, I want you to ask yourself one question."

"What is this question?" he asked.

"The question is, 'How would I feel if Poppy was in my place?' Get it?" she said with her brow raised.

"I believe so," he replied with an expression of mild confusion.

"Okay, let me give you a 'for instance'… Ask yourself how you would feel if I shared a bed with another warrior. A warrior who had been assigned by the Council as my new mate?" she asked with an innocent smile, as if she didn't know what his reaction would be.

"I now 'get it'." His face was murderous as he responded to her question.

"Good." Taking off her nightshirt and throwing it back on the floor in the corner, she turned to face him.

"Now, let's go to bed. We have an early appointment to see Wheaton Jr. tomorrow morning." Walking over to her side of the bed, she glanced behind her to see Wheaton watching her ass sway with every step.

"And no nookie. You're still on my shit list for a bit," she pointed out.

Giving her a disappointed but understanding grimace, Wheaton lay down beside her and hugged her close. As he snuggled up to her back and put his hand over her belly, he whispered to the top of her head. Unable to hear what he had said, she adjusted so she could see his face.

"What?"

"I said I am sorry I fucked up. Is that the correct wording?"

"Yes and yes, you did fuck up. I'm still angry but I understand you work on logic and not feelings so you get one free pass. Don't fuck up again, because we'll have problems if you do. I won't be able to forgive and forget a second time. No matter how much I love you."

Making sure that her words sank in, she leaned up to give him a quick peck. "Now go to sleep, big guy, we have a busy morning and I am emotionally done with today."

As Wheaton hugged her close and tried to relax, he thought to himself, *Thank your god for second chances.*

CHAPTER TWENTY-TWO

The next morning, Poppy woke up completely entangled in Wheaton's arms. First thing she noticed was how hungry she was. She'd missed dinner last night when Wheaton had surprised her at the door. Squeezing out from underneath the arm and leg he'd thrown over her, she made a pit stop in the bathroom before heading to the kitchen. If there was ever a day that called for pancakes, it would be this one. When the food generator beeped, she pulled out her plate, prepping one for Wheaton as well. Hearing him stir in the bedroom, she peered through the doorway to see him pulling on a pair of pants beside the bed.

"Babe? I have breakfast ready once you get cleaned up, and then we need to head to the medical unit," she called out.

"Let me use the facilities and we can eat before we go back to the other apartment. I will need fresh clothes before my meetings today," he called back.

Taking a moment to enjoy the flavor of her pancakes and chocolate milk, she wondered if Hannah was going to be at the apartment when they stopped by for clothes. She didn't necessarily want to have it out early this morning, but she also knew that until she spoke with Hannah, she would keep thinking about the shenanigans the blonde had tried to pull.

Wheaton joined her and before sitting down at the bar, he leaned over and kissed her.

"Good morning, Little Flower," he said, giving her another kiss, and then licked his lips. "You taste good."

"So do you. Now eat. We have lots to do today and the guys asked me to get to the medical unit before it gets busy this morning. They want me in the regen bed before the warriors need it," she said with a smile, loving how his eyes lit up at the mention of the med center. She was just as excited to get more information on her pregnancy.

Quickly devouring his plate of pancakes, he didn't speak much other than mumbles of "so good" and "I have missed these". When his plate was empty, he helped her clean up and then went to get her shoes from where they'd been kicked off the night before.

"Let me help you, love," he murmured, holding them up for her to slide her feet into them. Patting his shoulders before he stood up, she ran her hands through his shoulder-length hair. Giving the strands a tug so he would tip his head back, she stared into his eyes.

"I love you, Wheaton."

She held her breath, unsure if he would respond to her declaration.

"I feel love for you too, Poppy."

Hearing the words come from him made her eyes well up with happy tears. Hoping he truly understood what he was saying, she leaned down for a quick kiss. He ran his fingers under her eyes to wipe away the tears that had spouted. "These are not sad tears, correct?"

"No, these are very happy tears. Very happy tears." Smiling widely, she puckered her lips for another kiss.

"No more kisses, woman! I want to see our baby and those lips will lead to us being late." Pulling her to her feet, he swatted her butt before ushering her quickly out the door.

Poppy played through different scenarios in her mind. Her nerves were amped up with the thought that she would be able to finally speak to Hannah. This could go either of two ways. She could be calm and collected. Letting Hannah calmly know she was on to her tricks and it wouldn't be happening again was the first option. Option two consisted of her jumping on the tramp like a spider monkey, taking out her aggression on her perfectly coifed hairstyle. Hoping she could act like the sensible person she was, she would take route one over a brawl in their old apartment.

Once at Wheaton's apartment door, Poppy tugged on his hand for him to wait for a moment. Taking a few breaths to calm herself, she pasted on a fake smile and then nodded at Wheaton to go ahead and open sesame.

The apartment was pretty much like it had been the night she'd left. There were papers on top of the coffee table, most likely Hannah's since Wheaton used his tablet for everything. Other than that, no personal touches had been made to what she still considered her home.

"Hannah?" Wheaton said, clearing his throat.

"Yes, dear?" came from the direction of the bedroom.

Oh fuck no. Was that the way Hannah was going to start her morning? Gripping Wheaton's hand tightly, Poppy smiled up at him as he squeezed back. She prayed for the patience not to strangle the bitch and knew Wheaton was silently urging to keep calm too.

Hannah appeared in the doorway in what Poppy could only describe as a silk gown she had seen in movies, accompanied by little kitten heels with puffs on the toes. Her hair was tousled as if she'd just had a satisfactory night in bed. Rolling her eyes, Poppy was grateful that Wheaton had been with her all night. If she had walked in to see him stumbling out of the bedroom behind Hannah dressed like this, she would have lost her shit. As it was, she was having a very hard time not marching forward and grabbing a hank of that blonde hair.

Another squeeze of her hand made her glance away from Hannah back up to Wheaton.

"I did not require that she be naked in our bed…unlike with you," he pointed out quietly.

"Well, at least that's something," she murmured back sarcastically with another eye roll, this time in his direction.

"Oh! Good morning, Poppy," Hannah said with a fake smile, acting surprised to see her nemesis.

"Good morning, Hannah," Poppy said back with just as fake a smile. "We need to talk."

"Oh, of course. Let's make some coffee and we can chat while Wheaton gets ready for our day." Her face was frozen in a plastic-looking smile.

"I'll have tea with sugar instead of coffee but yes, let's get comfortable," Poppy agreed, moving to the counter.

Wheaton stared at both the women as if unsure it was safe to leave them alone.

"Wheaton, why don't you go get ready before I take you to the med center to show you what I've been doing? Hurry back though so we can make sure we're all on the same page." Poppy gave his back a push toward the bedroom.

"Of course, let me change. I will be right back." Wheaton gave Poppy a pleading glance that she interpreted as *Please don't hit the bitch.* Poppy wasn't going to make any promises though until she figured out where Hannah was coming from.

"Yep, you should probably hurry." After he walked away, she turned to Hannah and dropped the fake face. It was starting to hurt her cheeks to pretend to like this woman.

Taking the mug Hannah passed her, she took a few seconds to study the woman. When the silence was too much for her to take any longer, Poppy spoke, unable to contain herself.

"Soooo…Wheaton told me you've been sleeping in the same bed."

Hannah's mouth popped open. Poppy figured she didn't expect Wheaton to have been honest with her.

"And he explained you two have kissed."

Hannah cast a glance at the bedroom door. Was she hoping Wheaton was a speed dresser and would suddenly appear to save her? Hannah cleared her throat delicately, her discomfort apparent, but she still remained silent.

"Which was your idea," Poppy finished.

"Ummmm…well…" Hannah stammered, obviously unsure what to do or say.

Liking the fact that she had the normally well-spoken woman stuttering, Poppy decided to lay all her cards on the table and let her have it.

Setting down her cup, Poppy kept her voice as calm as possible. "Listen, Hannah, I get it. You came here expecting to have a husband and saw Wheaton. I know how *I* felt when I first saw him," Poppy admitted. "However, the crap that you pulled was *not* okay. Wheaton told me about it and he now knows it's not okay. I expect you to respect our relationship and back the fuck off. *Comprende?*" Poppy's voice had risen with each word out of her mouth, and she sat glaring at a stunned and slightly scared Hannah.

"Well…" Hannah again cleared her throat, as if trying to come up with something to say.

"Well what?" Poppy asked curtly.

Hannah pushed her silky strands behind one ear and tapped her fingers against her mug of coffee.

"Isn't that Wheaton's decision?" she countered with a lift of her chin. Poppy was surprised at the question. Apparently Hannah had just grown some balls.

"What decision? You approached him with logic and he agreed at the time, which I understand and accept. It's the way these guys' heads work. What I don't get is why. Why would you try to steal a man who is obviously in a relationship? Is that the type of person you are? Do you even care that it hurt someone? Wheaton and I are happy—hell, you *know* we are happy—but that didn't stop you from worming your way into our bed or tricking him into kissing you."

"I never—" Hannah started.

"Never what? Tried to break us up? You knew when you started sleeping next to him it would be a problem. You knew that kissing him was wrong, and yet you fucking did it anyway," Poppy said, on a roll.

Hannah took a sip of her coffee again and set the cup down. The way she avoided Poppy's eyes showed how uncomfortable she was. Had she not expected Wheaton to be honest with Poppy, or even get called out about it? Too damn bad for her then. Poppy was not the type of person to roll over and take shit from anyone. Especially when the fight was for her future.

"My intention was not to get in the way of your relationship…if that is what you truly have. Councilor Demascus had mentioned that

Wheaton might have been starved for attention and acted too quickly on meeting you without knowing he had options," Hannah blurted out.

"Well, that was your first mistake. Fuck that asshole. Listening to Demascus is going to be nothing but trouble for you. That guy is a tool," Poppy said plainly. "And yes, we truly have a relationship. What I have with Wheaton may have happened quickly but it's real. As real as it can get."

Hannah seemed as if she could cry, which surprised the hell out of Poppy. She had not expected the well-put-together woman to have emotions, much less show them to someone. If Poppy didn't know better, she'd have assumed she was a fem-bot considering how perfect she seemed.

"Listen, Hannah. I was really fucking pissed last night when I found out what had happened," Poppy explained. "Wheaton and I have talked and worked out the situation but I am letting you know right now that shit stops now."

"Okay…if Wheaton really is sure," Hannah said in a tearful voice, as if Poppy had just kicked her puppy.

"I am very sure, Hannah."

At the voice coming from the door, both women turned toward the bedroom. A refreshed Wheaton stood in the opening with his arms folded across his chest. He apparently had been listening for a bit so he knew where they all stood.

"I am sorry, Wheaton. I really did want you to make an informed decision," Hannah explained.

"My decision is final. It was final before you even showed up in my quarters," Wheaton said while keeping his gaze on Poppy's face.

"Yeah, I get that now," Hannah admitted, shooting glances between Poppy and Wheaton with what seemed more like understanding than the manipulation it had been previously.

"So, are you ready for the meetings today? We have quite a bit to go over before they start," Hannah said, obviously deciding the situation said and done.

"I am going to escort Poppy to the medical unit this morning but should be able to join you in Council meetings before lunch," he said now from Poppy's side while he rubbed his hand up and down her back.

"But we—" Hannah interrupted.

"I *will* escort her. Missing the first meeting will bring no harm and I am not yet ready to let Poppy go. You understand, correct?" His tone brooked no argument.

"Of course." Hannah backed down with that kicked-puppy look again.

Poppy had an idea. One that would take care of her problem with Hannah and allow her and Wheaton to spend more time together.

"Hannah?" Poppy's voice stopped Hannah as she was walking to the bedroom to get dressed for the day.

"Yes?" she said without turning around.

"How about when it's lunchtime we all get together? I'm sure the other warriors on the Council are pretty dry and I've met some great guys while I've been working in the medical unit. It would be a good thing to meet some new people and make friends."

It would give Hannah someone else to set her sights on, although Poppy didn't say that out loud. Waiting for Hannah to think for a moment, Poppy was surprised when she was witness to what she assumed was a "real" smile from her.

"That would be wonderful, Poppy," she answered, showing all her perfect teeth in their gleaming glory.

"All right, big guy. Let's leave so she can get ready and then you can escort her to lunch later this afternoon," Poppy told Wheaton.

Wheaton stopped Poppy with a hand on her arm.

"Who are these 'great guys' you were referring to?" he asked with a huffy expression on his face.

"Seriously, Wheaton, you leave me alone for two weeks, and now you get pissed because I made friends? Tone it down, Tarzan, or we're going to have our second fight in twenty-four hours. You should be happy I didn't knock Hannah the Horror flat on her ass. Not asking me stupid questions." She emphasized her words with a finger point.

"Okay, okay…no fighting. Just remember we agreed on no kissing these other warriors. No matter how great you think they may be."

Bumping sides while they walked, Poppy couldn't help but think that her discussion with Hannah had gone better than expected. Now to just make sure that she found someone new and stopped eyeing Wheaton as if he were a juicy steak and problem solved. Feeling much better, Poppy threaded her fingers through Wheaton's and his hand tightened on her shoulder.

As they reached the medical unit, Wheaton slowed.

Concerned, Poppy asked, "What's up, babe?"

Wheaton glanced up at the shiny ceiling in the hallway, confusion on his face.

"Not *up*, up… I meant what's wrong?" she asked, smiling.

"Oh, I find I am nervous to see you have a scan today," he admitted.

"Why?"

"What if there is something wrong with the baby? I am still feeling that we have been too lucky in our match."

"Lucky? What about our situation has been lucky lately?" she asked.

"We were matched together. It is a perfect match. We enjoy sexual intercourse. Quite a bit, I might add." His grin was infectious, and she couldn't stop herself from mirroring it.

"And now we have made a baby. We are very lucky," he explained.

"And?"

"What if there is a problem? So far we have had nothing but this 'easy breezy' way you always say. I am nervous that this cannot last." His worried demeanor immediately shot straight to her heart.

"Wheaton, nothing about you is 'easy breezy'. Remember when you ignored me the first few days here and I got all weepy and played Adele? And also, we can't forget the mess we have with this whole second-bride fucktastrophe. Believe me—*not* my definition of 'easy breezy'."

"I do not believe I will ever forget Adele and her sad songs. Still, we are lucky to have each other," Wheaton countered.

Giving him a side hug, she nudged him the last few steps to the door.

"Are you ready for this?" she asked before waving her arm over the door.

"As ready I will ever be," he replied, looking like he'd be blowing chunks at any moment.

CHAPTER TWENTY-THREE

Tamin and Rodin seemed both excited and surprised to see Wheaton when he walked in with Poppy. The men came up and gave him an arm shake accompanied by a manly back pat. After she hugged each of the men, which was accompanied by a growl from Wheaton, she clapped her hands together and said, "Let's get this show on the road."

The men obviously figured that she meant to get the scan started, and followed her into the exam room. Familiar with the drill by now, Poppy kicked off her shoes and hopped onto the regen bed. Blowing a kiss to a still queasy-looking Wheaton, she lay back and prepared for the doors to close.

Wheaton bent over the bed with an anxious glance, causing Tamin to smack his arm and mumble, "Calm down, warrior."

Poppy giggled when she saw Wheaton whip his head around to glare at Tamin, who pretended to be busy with his tablet.

One minute later, the door slid back open. Sitting up, Poppy glanced at a very concerned Wheaton.

"What the hell is your problem, Wheaton? You know these beds are safe. You're acting like it was going to kill me or something," she teased, trying to put him at ease.

"I explained that I am nervous, my Little Flower," he reminded her while helping her out of the bed.

Poppy witnessed Rodin mouth, *"Little Flower?"* to his friend. Both men smirked at Wheaton, their amusement obvious. Wheaton paid no attention to the other men as he helped her slip on her shoes once more. Waiting for the results seemed to take forever...or at least it seemed that way with Wheaton hovering over the readout screen at the end of the bed. Every thirty seconds he would pace back to Poppy and put his hand on her shoulder or smooth her hair back. Then he would trek back to the regen bed and stare at it, waiting for it to do something.

Tamin and Rodin tried to distract him but gave up when they were unable to get a response. Soon they began chatting with Poppy about the previous day's activities. When she explained about the situation she had with Hannah, they were furious on her behalf.

Once Wheaton overheard the phrases "that idiot Wheaton" in addition to "not deserving her", he finally joined in the conversation.

"I *was* an idiot and *do* deserve her. I have fixed my errors so mind your own business," he bit out, not at all willing to humor the men trying to rile him.

"Well, if for some reason Poppy changes her mind, then we know many a warrior who would snatch her up in a second," Rodin chipped in.

At those words, Wheaton lunged across the room and held Rodin up off his feet by his scrubs.

"What warriors are they?" he demanded, angry as hell.

Although Poppy had moved as quickly as she was able to help her friend, she wasn't fast enough to make it before Wheaton had Rodin in a death grip. Trying to get Wheaton to loosen his grip on Rodin, she was pulling on his fingers when the machine signaled it had completed its cycle. In an instant, Rodin was released and fell back to the wall behind him, still staring wide-eyed at Wheaton. With one last glare in Rodin's direction, Wheaton moved toward Tamin, who was standing by the bed.

Tamin snatched the information the regen bed spit out as it printed, and was scanning it quickly while Wheaton stared him down. Between him casting angry glances at Rodin for what he had said, and glaring at Tamin as if he needed to hurry the fuck up with his reading, Poppy just tossed her hands in the air and sat down again.

"Rodin, I need your eyes on this. Something seems…off," Tamin said, keeping an eye on Wheaton, who appeared as if he were ready to strangle someone again.

"Off? What does 'off' mean?" Wheaton asked, his voice hoarse. "If there is a question about Poppy's health then you do what must be done to fix her. No matter what the cost. Understand?"

"Yeah, guys, what does 'off' mean?" Poppy's voice rose to match Wheaton's.

The two men mumbled quietly to one another while Wheaton strode back to Poppy, pulling her into a hard hug. Holding her tight, he whispered, "Do not worry, Poppy. We will handle whatever has happened and make sure that you are taken care of."

As they huddled in their little circle while the men talked, she could feel Wheaton take deep breaths. Her mind whirling with possibilities, all bad of course, as to what could be "off". Moving her arms lower on his body to hug his waist, she leaned against him and felt him lean into her as well. With him kissing her ear and hugging her, she felt whatever the problem was, they would really be all right. The strength that he lent her was powerful enough to get them through anything as long as they were together.

"Poppy? Wheaton?" Rodin said.

Turning in Wheaton's hold, Poppy was startled to see the men smiling. What the hell? What was there to smile about??

Poppy's nerves shot, she snapped at the men. "Spit it out, doc. I feel like I'm either ready to cry or puke. Neither one of those options is pretty."

"I am sorry to have upset you. I wanted Rodin to confirm what I believed from the changes on this scan versus your previous scan," Tamin explained.

"And?" Wheaton asked anxiously when the doctor paused. He was just as much on pins and needles as she was. Poppy needed the doctors to explain what was happening before he started punching people for answers.

"Well, from the readings today, compared to your previous scan, it seems you are due in eighteen weeks," Rodin said with a smile.

"Wait. What?"

"Are you sure?"

Both Wheaton and Poppy had spoken at the same time.

"Hold the phone, people. Human pregnancies are normally forty weeks for full term. There is no *way* I'm due in eighteen weeks," Poppy said in disbelief.

"Well…it appears as if you two are compatible for breeding but Wheaton's cloning genes have taken over the gestation period," Tamin explained, as if that made total sense to a confused Poppy.

"Uh?"

Wheaton turned toward Poppy and took her hand. Gesturing for her to sit down, he explained, "When warriors are cloned, they are engineered to have a gestation period of only twenty weeks. This is to speed up the process. It must have influenced my own genetics when reproducing naturally with a human."

"But wouldn't I be showing more if I were due so soon? Will the development still be okay considering the timeline is short and the baby is only half Phaeton?" Poppy's voice sounded panicked even to her own ears.

Rodin walked closer to the couple, holding the readouts in his hand. "The findings are showing a healthy fetus for the time frame listed. Development is showing on par with what we would expect for a cloned incubator fetus with no signs of distress." As if embarrassed, he paused a moment before continuing, "Your…weight may be hindering our ability to see more of an obvious swelling of the abdomen. Do not worry though, you are completely healthy and we have no worries. It will not be long though before your pregnancy is apparent to everyone. We have been lucky so far that you haven't been showing considering your desire to keep your condition a secret."

"Now that I recall clearly, you are not as soft in your stomach as you were a few weeks ago. I did not notice it until I caressed you though." With Wheaton running his hands over her stomach, Poppy had to admit that she didn't feel as squishy as she had before.

"My baby, you are really having my baby," he whispered. "I still cannot believe it."

Poppy was having a surreal moment of her own. She had just gotten used to the idea they'd need to get everything baby ready in forty weeks and now her timeline had been cut in half. She was going to be a mom sooner rather than later and it was freaking her out. Flicking her gaze from one man to another, all she could hear from them was *"whaa whaa whaa whaa"* and wondered if this was what someone felt right before they passed out. As she lost consciousness, her last thought was *please don't let me hit the ground.*

Trying to open her eyes, she heard loud voices above her. Blinking, her eyes hurting at the bright lighting, she saw that she was lying in the regen bed with the men arguing whether or not to scan her again to see what was wrong. Not one of them had realized she had come to again and were starting to yell at each other.

"Guys? Guys. *Guys!*" she yelled to get their attention.

"Poppy, you worried us. How are you feeling?" Rodin asked, sweeping a handheld scanner up and down her body.

"I'm fine. I think I just got overwhelmed there for a minute," Poppy said weakly. Sitting up, she put her hand on her head to clear the cobwebs a bit. "Can I have a glass of water?"

Rodin rushed water to her so fast, she was amazed he didn't go skidding across the floor.

Wheaton was hovering over her as if she would pass out again any moment, and Poppy was feeling claustrophobic.

"Back up, guys, I need some room to breathe," she said, pushing Wheaton back a step or two. The hurt on his face made her heart twinge, but she really needed to not have three uber-tall warriors hovering over her right now.

Wheaton felt as if his heart had stopped when he saw Poppy droop in the chair. Realizing she was no longer conscious, he panicked. The first thought that ran through his head was to get her to the regen bed. Noticing both doctors seemed frozen, he lifted her out of the chair and laid her gently down in the unit. Tamin was hitting buttons on the machine when Poppy moved her head and fluttered her eyes as if trying to wake up. When she didn't immediately wake, he had demanded the doctors do their job. It was not until Poppy started giving orders that Wheaton felt relief. His Little Flower acted like a senior warrior sometimes in her temperament.

"Rodin. Tamin. We have a ship to baby-proof and plans to make regarding houses on the home planet," Poppy murmured once her head cleared. Plan mode was always her go-to for dealing with stress and this would not be an exception.

"As you would say, we have a lot of shit to do and not much time to do it in. Correct, Poppy?" Rodin asked with a relieved smile.

"Exactly, my friend. Exactly," she replied with a matching grin.

The men took that as their cue to help her up and start going over the plans they'd made earlier with Wheaton regarding how to get quarters prepared for when the baby arrived. Knowing that they were on an even tighter timeline seemed to give them a new energy for how things needed to be done. They all agreed that Poppy should be able to tell people about the pregnancy sooner rather than later considering the accelerated growth. The scan had come back showing a very healthy, if not speedy, baby.

Wheaton grilled the doctors about what she should be eating, doing, and reiterated she needed to have an escort at all times. Although he wasn't too fond of how close Behyr had grown to Poppy, Poppy figured Wheaton understood his fellow warrior was still the most logical choice considering Behyr already knew about the baby and he had become friends with Poppy.

After Tamin and Rodin had explained, repeatedly, that everything was fine and Poppy was safe with them, he agreed to head to his morning meeting.

"I wish I did not have to leave you yet," he whispered, hugging her for the umpteenth time as he prepared to leave.

"Me too, babe. Don't forget to come back for lunch and to bring Hannah with you. I want to introduce her to some eligible warriors and get her sights locked on someone other than you."

"That sounds like a good idea. She has been spending too much time with Demascus during breaks. I have a feeling he has been feeding her lies and false hope. Her meeting other warriors will benefit all of us," he agreed.

After a couple more kisses, where she could see Tamin and Rodin making fun of Wheaton by making smoochie faces, she finally kicked his butt out. Turning to the men who had become her close friends, she shook her finger at them. "Knock it off, will ya? He is going to kill you both if you keep teasing him."

Both men laughed at her statement but agreed with her. They each took turns giving her hugs and she was surprised when Tamin whispered, "I was not kidding when I said that another warrior would take his place if he was stupid enough to let you go."

"Really, Tam, who are you referring to?" she asked with a teasing smile.

She wasn't prepared for the completely serious expression that came over his face when he replied, "I know at least three." Then he turned and walked back to the supply room.

Rodin nodded in agreement. Well, that was interesting.

CHAPTER TWENTY-FOUR

Poppy might have warned Hannah off Wheaton but she wasn't going to be so dumb as to look like crap when the time came for lunch. Excusing herself to the bathroom to freshen up before they arrived, she stared at her reflection. Comparing herself to Hannah would do her no good. Where she was dark and curly, Hannah was platinum and sleek. It was apples and oranges. Thank goodness Wheaton preferred her apples. Smiling at herself, she smoothed her hair, or as much as she could. Hearing voices in the hallway outside the door, she listened closely, wishing she had just a bit more time. The male voices were muffled just enough for Poppy to be unable to make out who'd arrived. Slicking on some lip gloss and straightening her top, she opened the door to see that Behyr had arrived.

"Hey, Behyr!" she said, giving him a big smile in greeting that was followed by a quick hug. Of course he stiffened up again when she hugged him, which caused her to add in a whisper, "Remember I'm a hugger and this torture will not stop."

At his low chuckle, she stepped back and gave him a serious face, which caused him to still, most likely thinking that something was wrong.

"About last night—" she began, only to be interrupted.

"No worries, Poppy. I was out of line showing you my teeth. I can understand Wheaton's distress and it will not happen again."

His face was so serious she was afraid he was actually going to go back to being Mr. Cold on her.

"Oh no, Behyr! He wasn't mad at you, not really... We were both frustrated with not seeing each other for days on end, and you were convenient for him to get mad at." Noticing his disbelief, she went on, "I'm serious. You have become a great friend." Turning to the other men in the room, she glanced at all of them in turn. "In fact, you have all become amazing friends, and I don't know how I would have survived this past week without any of you. Wheaton is going to need to accept that humans need friends and that's exactly what you are to me."

Nodding her head at the men who watched her while shaking their heads, she continued, "Really, you guys have kept me sane. I have had fun this past week instead of staying in my room crying…and that's all thanks to you guys."

The men were silent for a couple moments before Behyr stepped forward and spoke.

"Poppy, Wheaton may not be comfortable with that. We value your friendship as well but Wheaton is a formidable warrior and I would not want to be on his bad side." Both Tamin and Rodin nodded their heads in agreement.

"Don't be such a pussy," she said jokingly while patting Behyr's arm.

Noticing his perplexed expression, she waited for it…

"A cat?"

When the question popped out of his mouth, she giggled.

"Not *that* type of pussy. There are many meanings of that word in our language. I was using it to replace 'being scared'," she said between giggles.

"That is not nice, Poppy. I am scared of nothing," Behyr said in the most affronted voice she'd ever heard him use.

"Well then quit acting like it, Behyr. In fact, all of you need to knock it off. Don't freeze up when he's around. It took me a while to get you comfortable and joking, and I don't want to go back and have to start over." She followed up her edict with a shoulder nudge to Tamin.

Walking from the room with the others following, she glanced back and asked to anyone who would want to answer, "Who's bringing the food?"

"I believe Wheaton and Hannah will be bringing lunch," Rodin replied.

Behyr was apparently out of the loop, because he stared at Poppy as if she'd sprouted two heads. "Isn't Hannah..." he started.

"We've decided to make nice and have lunch together today." Making a funny face at the men, she went on, "My goal is to distract her with other beefcake options, and she'll move on and leave Wheaton alone. Any ideas of who might be waiting for a bride?" she asked with an eyebrow wiggle.

"Is she anything like you?" Behyr asked with obvious interest.

Poppy couldn't help but sputter out a laugh at the thought of being compared to Hannah.

"Oh no, my dear friend. We are *nothing* alike. In fact, I can safely say she is the exact opposite of what you see standing before you today." Sweeping her hand up and down her body like a *Price Is Right* model, she laughed again.

"Well then no, I would not like to distract her," Behyr said with a straight face while the Bobbsey Twins nodded in unison.

Poppy was flattered by their compliments. "Aw shucks, you men sure know how to make a gal feel good about herself."

The door to the med center swished open and she turned to see Hannah and Wheaton enter with platters in hand. Walking up to Wheaton and taking the tray in exchange for a quick kiss, she turned to greet Hannah. Poppy was surprised Hannah actually gave her a genuine smile. Looking back at the men, she cleared her throat and gestured toward the large plate that Hannah was carrying with a *help her, you morons* expression on her face.

"Hannah, I would like to introduce you to Behyr. He's been my escort this past week while Wheaton was busy."

Behyr nodded and stiffly bowed when introduced.

"And these two great guys are the doctors here in the medical unit. This is Tamin and this one over here is Rodin." She waved them over to Hannah to shake hands. "Men, this is Hannah."

Tamin and Rodin greeted her with cool smiles. Apparently all the talking about Hannah this and that had sunk in, and she had a feeling the "bros before hoes" motto was sticking with them…Poppy being a "bro" in this scenario.

"Let's eat and you two can tell us about your morning," she suggested when nobody seemed to move.

At a round table in the common area of the medical unit, they dished out sandwiches and pasta salad. Of course, silence had descended on their group. With Wheaton sitting next to her, she gave him a nudge with her foot to hopefully get someone speaking. He obviously didn't get her "talk about something" nudge because he took a huge bite of his food. The men seemed happy stuffing their faces but Poppy could tell that Hannah was uncomfortable with the silence. Picking at her food and casting glances around the room, the blonde appeared nervous.

"So, Hannah…do you like attending the Council meetings?" Poppy asked in an effort to open up dialogue.

Hannah smiled at Poppy in what could only be interpreted as relief to be able to talk about work instead of something personal.

"Yes I do. With the recent situation, I believe I have become quite helpful calming down the Council."

Wheaton agreed with a nod as he chewed.

"What recent situation?" Poppy asked, while looking at Wheaton for clarification. Hannah was the one to answer though since she wasn't the one currently with a mouthful of sandwich.

"Well, when the ship started moving toward the home planet, the US government panicked."

"Why the panic? I'm sure they didn't expect the ships to stay in one place too long."

"They're aware that ships will be traveling back and forth, but they had some visitors on the ships who were not cleared to be taken out of reach."

At Poppy's confused face, Hannah went on, "Valerie for instance is being viewed as a hostage since she wasn't given an option to return before the ship started moving. When she did not return home her family filed a police report and have essentially used the word 'kidnapped'. Her parents are very conservative regarding their views of the Phaeton situation and don't seem to even support her work here." Hannah ended with a frown.

"Oh no, I haven't had a chance to see Val all week. Every time I tried to message her she wasn't available. Is she doing okay?"

Concern for her friend was now running through her head. When she hadn't been able to get in touch, she'd just assumed that maybe Thorne was keeping her company or something. She hadn't considered that Val was stuck on the ship—and possibly in trouble for it.

"Wheaton? She isn't in trouble, right? I mean, she came up here to help us out with the bride stuff, and I would hate to have brought this trouble on her."

Wheaton patted her hand to calm her down and said in a soothing voice, "Do not worry, Poppy, Hannah has actually made great strides in talking to your government and explaining the situation as to why Valerie was needed on the ship. It took a few days, but with Val sending messages to her parents assuring them that she was safe, she was able to convince them that we were not harming her and she would be returned safely as soon as possible."

"Whew." Poppy released a sigh of relief. Turning to Hannah, she smiled gratefully, "Thanks, Hannah, I'm sure your previous political experience helped the situation a lot and now I can see why you were needed at those meetings all week."

Wheaton cast Poppy a glance that she interpreted as relief on his part as well.

"This is what I do. Being a City Council member, I had to deal with some crazies…not only crazy but we had a lot of lawsuits for no reason other than miscommunication." She shrugged as if it wasn't a big deal.

When Hannah had explained her part in helping the warriors avoid conflict, Behyr had sat up and started studying her with a more appraising gaze than the weary one he'd had on his face earlier.

"Behyr?" Waiting for him to drag his eyes from Hannah, she smiled when he finally paid attention to her. "How's your warrior training going? Any there any more sparring sessions that we're going to need to prepare for in the medical unit?"

"You train the warriors here?" Hannah asked, casting her own appraising glance at the big man sitting across from her.

As the conversation continued, mostly with Behyr and Hannah talking, the rest of the group finished their lunches. Seeing that Hannah was starting to glance at Behyr with familiar big doe eyes while he talked about what it took to train the men, Poppy smiled inwardly. Mission Distract with Beefcake complete.

Since nothing was left on the platters, they were able to quickly clean up. Noticing that Tamin and Rodin had gone into "doctor mode" to prepare for their afternoon patients, she decided now was a great time to sneak in a little Wheaton time. Nodding her head for him to follow her, she led him down the small hallway to pull him into an empty supply closet where she wrapped him in a full-body hug. He returned the embrace and upped the contact with a full ass grab as he breathed in her scent.

"I have missed you, my Little Flower," he whispered huskily.

"I missed you too, babe," she said quietly back. "Why are we whispering?"

Smiling down at her, he said, "Because I don't want this moment to be rushed and I am hoping they forget we are here."

"I am sure at some point they'll need to come in for a supply or two," she joked.

Gripping her butt just enough to lift her onto her toes, he ground his hips into hers. "We can throw what they need in the hall."

This man made her engine go from zero to sixty in six seconds. Her skin had already begun to tingle and she wiggled even closer to him. At his rumble, she rubbed her hands on his chest as she leaned up for a deep kiss. Moving her hands to his neck, she ran her fingers through his hair and then back down.

Pulling down on his shoulders made him stoop slightly. Now she was able to give a slight jump, using him as leverage. When he caught her weight with his palms on her ass, she wrapped her legs around his waist. The rumble got louder when her crotch met the hard plane of his abdomen. Now face-to-face with her quarry, she nuzzled his mouth with hers. As he met her kiss and deepened it, she realized she'd never been this physically confident with any man before. She wasn't a small lady but Wheaton was able to handle her as if she were a doll. He always seemed to be surrounding her and sheltering her, which made her feel smaller than she actually was. That in itself was a huge turn-on.

Getting lost in his kisses while he kneaded her, she rubbed against him. Dear god, she was humping Wheaton in a closet. And not only was she humping him, she was extremely close to getting off. His chest rumbles had the effect of a vibrator against her clit. Dragging her mouth away to catch her breath, she shivered when Wheaton bit her earlobe. Poppy's eyes rolled back in her head as she took one step closer to coming.

"Wheaton?" she mumbled.

"Hmmm?" Still nibbling, he ground her pelvis into him harder.

"Undo your pants. Now," she said in a voice bordering on being able to qualify as a sex phone operator.

"Pants….can't…have to get back to work," he mumbled, while nipping harder at her ear and neck.

"No work. Cock now." Letting go of him, she wiggled to be let down. With a groan of disappointment he complied, obviously not hearing the "cock now" portion of what she'd said.

Slithering down his body, she went all the way to her knees. His eyes widened as he realized what she was about to do.

Poppy saw a doubled-over exercise mat in the corner. Dragging it to her, she lifted up enough to put it under her knees. The padding was thick enough to give her knees relief from the hard white floor and also thick enough to help her reach his cock easily while kneeling.

"Are you going to…" he asked with his eyebrows raised.

"Yep," she said with a wicked grin. Unsnapping the buttons on his leather pants, she licked her lips.

"I have seen this on the vids but I didn't expect…"

"I know, babe, but I want your cock in my mouth right about…now." She gripped his length and tilted his cock down slightly to meet her open lips. Swiping her tongue across the precome that had begun to collect, she smiled against his tip at his sucked-in breath.

"Shhhh…remember to be quiet. We don't want the guys barging in here," she teased.

"Uh-huh."

Poppy took a moment to soak in the beauty in front of her. Wheaton's hair was in disarray from her earlier run-through and he was still fully dressed in his leather shirt and pants. The only naked part was his erection that she'd pulled free from the opening in his pants. Meeting his gaze, she leaned forward and very deliberately gave him another teasing lick.

"Don't tease, Little Flower. Suck me."

Reaching the top of her head to pull out her hair band, he let her hair down to thread his fingers into the curls. Catching her hair in his grip, he used that as an anchor to move her closer to his cock. She could feel the heat coming off his body. With him gripping her hair, she became even more aroused. If a previous boyfriend had tried to push her head down, it would have instantly killed the mood. When Wheaton did it, all she felt was the overwhelming urge to do whatever he asked. Never before had she thought herself submissive but he apparently brought that out in her. Taking his guidance, she allowed him to move her mouth where needed and at that moment, he needed her sucking.

Opening her mouth as wide as possible to not scrape him with her teeth, she breathed through her nose as she moved up and down in a quick but deep rhythm. Unable to go too far for fear of gagging, she braced one hand on the root of his cock as he shuttled in and out of her mouth. Twisting her hand every so often, she moved it to follow her lips as she pulled almost completely off the head and then back down. Once she got close to the base, she gave him a squeeze and her efforts were rewarded with a loud groan as his grip tightened in her hair.

Feeling him get even harder in her mouth, she could hear the blood rushing between her ears and dropped her free hand between her thighs. Thank god for yoga pants. They were thin enough for her to feel the pressure of her fingers as she pressed against her clit and started humping her hand.

Using his grip on her hair, Wheaton tilted her head back to meet his eyes. She saw him realize she was rubbing herself. The knowledge that she was pleasuring herself while he was in her mouth threw him over the edge. He gave one loud, continuous rumble and the muscles in his thighs tensed up. The cock in her mouth pulsed to a quick beat. She didn't have long to prepare herself before she tasted his release on the back of her tongue and then was swallowing fast to contain it all. She had never been a swallower before but pulling away from Wheaton seemed like a sacrilege. As his hands loosened in her hair, she pulled slightly away to lick the remains of his come from his still-hard cock.

The beautiful cock in front of her was starting to relax. She savored the taste of his release in her mouth as she stared up at his body. His large plum-shaped cock head, shining with her saliva, slowly deflated before her eyes, his member still long and wide as he took big, gulping breaths. Poppy wiped her swollen lips and sat back on her heels for a moment. Her own orgasm at the tips of her fingers was forgotten as she took in the satisfied male in front of her. Wheaton took that time to tuck himself, still half-hard, back into his leather breeches and reached down to help her off her knees. Tugging her up and into his embrace, he hugged her hard.

"Let me return the favor, Little Flower. I am thirsty and I believe you may have something to sate me," he murmured.

"Why yes I do," she said with a wink as she shimmied her pants down her hips. Just then, there was a knock at the door.

"Excuse me, Poppy? Wheaton?" It was Hannah's voice that came through the door.

"Yes?" Wheaton asked, his voice still rough from his earlier groans and moans.

"We need to get back to the Council. We're running late but you seemed...busy." Even through the door, Poppy could tell Hannah was blushing. To be honest, that blush probably matched the color on Poppy's face.

For a moment there, she'd completely forgotten there were others in the med center. At least the supply closet was at the end of the hall so hopefully they hadn't heard too much. Poppy wasn't a prude but she wasn't one for public sex or even semipublic sex.

Wheaton gazed down at Poppy with disappointment in his eyes. "I have to go. I forgot that we needed to get back so quickly."

Poppy laid her palm against his cheek. She couldn't stop herself from smiling when he closed his eyes and relaxed into her hand. She reached up and gave him a deep kiss.

"I understand, babe. Just remember I have something for you to drink tonight." Winking at him when he groaned and adjusted himself in his breeches, she fixed her own clothes. Finding her discarded hair tie on the floor, she swooped it back up into a messy bun.

Leaving the closet was fairly embarrassing. Hannah was bright red as she waited for Wheaton. Tamin and Rodin wouldn't meet her gaze and Behyr just nodded at her with a small close-lipped smile.

After the door closed behind them, she turned to her three friends and held up a finger.

"Not one word," she said in the sternest voice she could muster.

This caused all three males to start laughing, first softly and then louder when she joined in herself a moment later.

CHAPTER TWENTY-FIVE

The rest of the afternoon was fairly boring for Poppy. Tamin and Rodin had expected the other brides to visit the med center but nobody had shown up yet. Poppy decided to keep to the supply closet for a while to make sure they would have things handy for when the brides did happen to show up. She also made sure to tuck the exercise mat back where she'd moved it from. That would hopefully come in handy again.

Behyr had been called away to the training rooms after lunch but showed up at the end of the day looking disappointed.

"What's up?" she said, not really wanting to hear the answer.

"Wheaton has been held up in the Council and will not be able to walk you back to your quarters or meet for dinner." Behyr was studying her and obviously trying to gauge her mood.

"Well...that sucks." Poppy couldn't stop the disappointment that swept through her, but she was sure it was out of his control. She realized this meant they would also be unable to finish what they'd started in the closet at lunch.

Behyr was still staring at her as if she might burst into tears at any given moment. Knowing she needed to reassure him before he panicked, she shrugged.

"I guess this means I'm free for dinner. Want to join me?" Her question was delivered with a sad smile.

"That would be nice, although I received a message from Thorne that Valerie was wanting to see you also. Would you like to invite them to your quarters for a meal? Thorne suggested it when I spoke to him earlier."

"Sounds like a plan. Company should help keep me occupied." As she gathered her belongings, she yelled to Tamin, who had been fiddling with an instrument in the exam room, "Tamin, I'm heading out."

"K.O.," was yelled back.

"It's 'okay,' you big goofball," Poppy replied with a giggle.

Deep laughter was followed by, "See you tomorrow morning, Poppy."

She was excited to see Val again. From what she had been told earlier, Valerie had been occupied with Council work all this time. If the glances Thorne had kept tossing Val's way were any indicator then Poppy would bet he'd been Val's shadow while she was on the ship.

As they entered the apartment, Poppy decided a shower was in order. Her time in the closet this afternoon with Wheaton had been enough to make at least a change of clothes necessary. "I'll be quick, feel free to watch one of the movies I have uploaded."

"I can wait until you are finished to start the vid. I was thinking of watching something that we have already seen."

Hanging out these past couple weeks, Poppy had introduced him to some of the films she loved. Behyr had quickly gotten addicted to any movie with Simon Pegg. His current favorite was *Hot Fuzz* and they'd watched it four times so far. Seeing where this was going, she quickly shot down another night of that movie and had him choose something else.

"But it is so entertaining, Poppy," Behyr said with what sounded close to a whine.

"No."

"But—"

"No. No more *Hot Fuzz.*" Poppy put her foot down.

Hearing him grumble as she left the room, she almost laughed out loud. Poppy tried to finish quickly so she was ready when Val arrived. Just as she had entered the living area with still-wet hair, she heard the tone at the door.

Waving her hand to open it, she smiled big when she saw a very flustered-looking Val and Thorne. Well well well. It appeared as though her pal Val had been participating in a make-out session recently, judging by the whisker burn on her neck and cheeks.

"Hello, my long-lost buddy."

Catching the knowing smirk on Poppy's face, Valerie grinned and stepped into the room to hug her.

"Hey, lady, there's so much we have to talk about," she said.

Poppy still hadn't told Val of her pregnancy so she agreed with a quick nod. "Maybe we can talk real quick in private though?"

"Of course." Valerie nodded at Behyr on the couch. "Gentlemen, could you excuse us for a few seconds? We need to chat." Not waiting for a response, she left Thorne at the door and dragged Poppy by the arm into the bedroom. As the door shut with a *whoosh*, she turned and said, "Spill it."

Poppy was unable to speak for a moment. Her nervousness at telling Val about the baby wasn't due to trust. Poppy knew she could trust Val with anything, especially after what had happened with the bridal matches. It just hit her that the more people she told about the baby, the more real it seemed to get.

"Well…I'm pregnant." The words seemed to tumble out of her mouth.

Val reached behind her to feel for the bed before sitting down with a flop.

"Pregnant?" she asked, shock evident on her face.

"According to Tamin and Rodin and that nifty regen bed, yes. Apparently Wheaton was virile enough to hit a homerun our first time at bat," Poppy confirmed with a grin.

"Wow. That's just…wow." Apparently Val was a little stunned because she didn't say anything for a few moments. Just sat still, as if shell-shocked.

"You doing okay, Val?" The expression on her face had Poppy worried. Valerie was always on her game. Now she seemed out of sorts and the color had drained from her face.

"Um yeah, I guess I expected the brides to take longer to get pregnant. Not sure why, maybe it's because they were cloning so much I figured that their juice wouldn't be as potent," she rambled as though she was nervous.

"No…that's not all. I can tell. There's something more that's bothering you," Poppy said, calling her out. "It's your turn to spill it. Now."

Valerie flopped back farther onto the bed with a groan and scrubbed her hands over her face.

"Mmmpffftherbnnn," she mumbled.

"What?"

Taking her hands from her face, she let them drop to her sides on the bed while staring up at the ceiling.

"I said…I slept with Thorne," she repeated with a groan.

"*What?*" Poppy yelled.

"Keep your voice down!" she hissed, leaning up on her elbows. "I don't want the whole ship to know!"

"You slept with Thorne?" Poppy whispered to a miserable-looking Valerie.

"Yes." Sniffling as if she might cry at any time, Val continued on, "And it was amazing."

"Then what's the problem, Val?" Poppy asked, unsure where this was going.

"Well, according to the bun in your oven, I might have one of my own baking." And there it was. A tear slid down Val's face.

"Well…fuck." Unsure what the ramifications were of Val being with Thorne, she didn't know what else to say.

"Yeah, 'fuck' is right." Standing up to pace, Val went on, "What if I'm pregnant? I'm pretty sure Thorne put his name into the pool to be selected for a bride. What if he wants to be matched with Miss Perfect and doesn't want whatever it is we have going on?" Stopping to stare at the door with a sad face, she went on, "We bicker all the time and this wasn't something I planned…it just happened."

Always one to see the bright side of a situation and make a plan, Poppy thought for a couple seconds.

"Okay, let's break this down… First, you slept with Thorne when he might have a bride being matched. You just need to talk to him ASAP and see where he stands on the bridal match now you've hooked up. I'm not saying he's all hearts and roses over you, but from my experience with these big guys, when they see something they want they go after it. In this case, it was you. And I'll tell you something right now, Thorne was looking at you pretty hard the first time you visited me."

Seeing Val nod at her with a hesitant smile, she continued, "Second, you may not even be pregnant. Wheaton and I may have just been extremely lucky on our first shot. Just because I'm knocked up doesn't mean all of them are this fertile." Poppy noticed Val blushed and her gaze skittered away.

"Why do I have a feeling there is more to the story?" she asked.

"Well, it wasn't just one time…" Valerie admitted in a soft voice. "We've been going at it like bunnies this whole week." Her face was now completely red.

Poppy let that sink in. "Okay. Still, it could be bad timing. Don't start picking out baby names until you visit the medical unit for an exam. That regen bed they have can pick up a pregnancy almost immediately. As my mom used to say, there is no point in borrowing trouble."

She gave Val a half hug and moved over to the door. "Now let's eat, this baby is starving." Seeing Val glance down at her stomach, she laughed. "I know, I know. I'm barely pregnant, but since I am, I've decided I'm going to blame every donut or hamburger on this baby and say fuck it."

Their dinner ended up being relaxing considering all the shenanigans going on around them. Poppy noticed Thorne seemed to touch Val or smile at her throughout the night. The slight touches on the shoulder or a quick brush of hair behind her ear managed to make Poppy slightly jealous. These were the small things she hadn't been able to share with Wheaton since Hannah had arrived.

"So, I had lunch with Wheaton and Hannah today." Noticing Val's mouth drop open, Poppy admitted, "She actually isn't that bad. We had a moment when I thought I could have happily pulled out every strand of her silky hair while cackling like a mental patient, but I think that's been taken care of." Val was now staring at her as if she had lost her mind. "Really. I think I may have diverted her attention to another warrior anyway."

Poppy noticed Behyr's gaze snap up when she added that last part. Trying to hide her smile, she turned to wink at Val.

"What warrior?" Behyr's question came out gruff and demanding.

"Well, it seemed as if she enjoyed lunch today with the guys so I'm hoping there may be romance in the air." Not wanting to give too much away, she hinted to Val and noticed her catch on to a possible match in the making.

Val figured out what Poppy was doing and offered her own observations. "She is very attractive," she said, while nodding at the men. "I'm sure she'll get snatched up quickly, considering we're unsure when more brides will be called. Right now, it's like a supercharged season of *The Bachelorette*."

Behyr quickly picked up his plate, taking it to the kitchen bar. "I have business to attend to." With a slight bow to the girls and then Thorne he strode to the door. "I will see you tomorrow morning for our walk to the med center, Poppy. Please contact me if you need anything later tonight since I am unsure when Wheaton will be available," he said as an afterthought as he left.

The minute the door closed, the women grinned at each other, bursting into giggles. Thorne sat, confused as to what had just happened.

"What is so funny?"

"Men. Men are funny. It seems it doesn't matter if they're human or alien." Poppy was still trying to control her giggles.

"Yes, they are. Did you see how quickly he lit out of here? It was like his pants were on fire." Valerie was still laughing and then laughed harder when she noticed Thorne was still completely lost.

"Thorne, your face right now is funny. Let me explain to you what just happened." Taking her bottle of water and shaking it at him, Poppy said, "I noticed Behyr and Hannah had some chemistry at lunch today. There was quite a bit of heat between the two of them. I have a feeling that mentioning the good doctors as possible competition was just the nudge he needed to make his move."

"Or he may have just had business to attend to." Thorne shook his head at the women.

"Okay, let me put it this way… If you found out that another warrior was interested in Val, what would you do?" Poppy continued.

The expressions that ran across his face went from understanding to anger quickly.

"That is not going to happen." Biting out those words, he put his arm around Val's shoulder and squeezed.

An angry look came over Val's face at that statement. "Are you saying that another warrior would not be attracted to me?" she asked tightly.

Judging by Thorne's face, he must have realized how that had sounded. He quickly sputtered out, "That is not what I am saying. I simply meant that you are mine."

By this point, Val and Thorne had created their own little bubble and Poppy felt as if she were watching a soap opera. Wishing for popcorn, she kept silent and waited for Val to respond to Thorne's declaration. This was better than Netflix.

"I'm yours?" Val asked with a teary but happy smile.

"Of course you are. I believe I have shown you that this week." He leaned closer to give her a soft kiss on the lips. "Multiple times."

"Oh." Val turned to Poppy and smiled widely, her eyes sparkling with happiness. "We have to leave now."

Poppy couldn't help but give herself a little pat on the back for helping that situation along.

"Yeah, I can see you totally need to leave," she said with an eyebrow wiggle that made Val and Thorne laugh. Poppy walked them to the door.

With hugs to both of them, she took the moment to whisper into Val's ear, "You really should drop by the med center and see me soon." Leaning back to make sure that Val understood what she was saying, she was happy when Val nodded back.

"I'll try to come tomorrow. I'm going to talk to Thorne a bit more and make sure we're both on the same page. I'll suggest he comes with me just in case the tests are positive."

Knowing that Thorne would want to be there if Val found out she was pregnant made Poppy feel a moment of sadness. She had found out about her baby without Wheaton there. It was a moment she would have loved to share with him. Hell, there seemed to be a lot of things they were missing out on considering he hadn't been able to even join her tonight. The bonding time they had once shared was no more and Poppy missed that. She missed their shared dinners. During those times they had talked about her previous life on Earth or things that were trivial, like movies or music. They had talked about subjects that were unimportant but that at the same time were instances that made up who they were as people. It was during those relaxed times that Poppy had felt able to connect with Wheaton the most.

Wishing she could simply hear his voice before she went to her lonely bed, she paused when she heard the tone at the door. Had Val forgotten something?

Opening the door and seeing her beautiful man standing in front of her had Poppy grinning like an idiot. She felt like crying but didn't want to scare him off so she settled for launching herself into his arms.

"I thought I wasn't going to see you tonight." Her words were muffled by his leather shirt.

"Nothing could keep me away, Little Flower." Wheaton hugging her in return, his hand running down her back to cup her ass and lift her so he could walk into the bedroom. As they walked, he kept talking. "Behyr came as the Council was letting out and asked Hannah if she would share a meal tonight, so I escaped while I could."

"He asked her to dinner?" Poppy smiled, clinging to him.

"Yes, why do you sound so surprised?" He lowered her until her feet touched the floor.

"Because he had a full meal here not even an hour ago," she said with a smile as he whisked her shirt over her head.

Unbuckling his pants, he quickly shucked them down his legs. After he was done with most of his own clothing he helped push her pants down.

Poppy grinned at Wheaton. "I have a feeling that Behyr may take Hannah off our hands," she said, eying the now half-naked form in front of her.

Dear god, this man was pretty. She would never tell him so—that would probably ruffle his feathers—but he was so beautiful to her it made her stomach clench. She was pretty sure that her stomach wasn't the only thing clenching. Leaning forward to nip at his muscled chest, she heard him hiss, and flicked her tongue out to follow the nip with a lick.

With his chest fully rumbling, Wheaton leaned down to grip her under her now naked thighs. Walking her to the bed, he tossed her backward. Poppy let out a laugh at his playful mood and his hot gaze on her pussy as she lay back and opened her legs.

Wheaton clenched and unclenched his hands while breathing in her scent. Leaning down with his fists on either side of her hips, he smiled sexily at Poppy.

"Little Flower?" he rasped.

"Yes?" she said with a now-dry mouth.

"I am thirsty."

That was her only warning before he pounced.

CHAPTER TWENTY-SIX

Poppy stretched in bed and groaned loudly as her back popped. She felt the bed move next to her as Wheaton chuckled at her actions.

"What?" Poppy turned over with a smile.

"Nothing. I am just happy." Wrapping one arm around her shoulders to pull her closer, he kneed her legs apart.

"I'm happy too. In fact, I can safely say I don't think I've ever been happier than right now."

The bedroom had simulated sunlight during the day and dimmed automatically at night. Right now, the light was reflecting perfectly off Wheaton's sculpted face. Poppy stared at him for a moment and absorbed his handsome visage. Brushing his long hair away from his eyes, she cupped his cheek.

"I love you, Wheaton." Following the declaration with a kiss, she nuzzled his cheek.

"I love you too, my Little Flower."

Meeting his gaze head-on, Poppy had no choice but to believe he meant what he said. She'd had fears at first that Wheaton would not be able feel love to the same depths as she did. Those fears had been unfounded. He was capable of love and she was the lucky girl he felt it for.

"And I love our little baby." Moving down the bed, he stopped to nuzzle at her soft belly.

Poppy raised an eyebrow at him. "You realize I'm going to get fat, right?" she admitted. "Well, I guess it would technically be 'fatter,' to be honest."

Poppy was actually someone who believed being fat was okay. People came in all shapes and sizes. She just happened to be more padded than some. She also didn't mind the word *fat*, which surprised people. She loved her body. There was a time, around high school when she'd hated the teasing and would wear baggy shirts to hide what she thought were lumps of unattractive fat. At some point she'd started not caring and had embraced the word *fat*. It made the bullies realize that being called names didn't bother her. Eventually, when they wouldn't get the reaction they wanted, they left her alone. She would never be able to run a marathon and that was okay with her. And if it was okay with her, then anyone who it wasn't okay with could go fuck themselves.

Truthfully, there were some things she would change about her body. She didn't know one person who would say differently. Honestly, she would love it if her arms didn't resemble bat wings. Was she willing to order that stupid shake thing she saw on TV to make it go away? No. In her opinion, nobody should look that stupid exercising. Sweating was punishment enough. She would wear tank tops and let her arms jiggle with pride and give the skunk eye to those who she saw judging her.

The extremely baggy jeans and tops had left her closet, and she'd started wearing yoga pants and fitted T-shirts. The jeans she did have were expensive and fit well, but she just hadn't had a chance to really wear them much since she spent so much time at home. Poppy tended to dress for comfort but she had come to realize very quickly that there was a difference between dressing for comfort versus dressing to cover up what others viewed as flaws. She'd admit that when she'd first been naked around Wheaton it had taken every ounce of courage she had. Being comfortable in your body was one thing. Hoping that your body sexually aroused a man who could be a body double for a god was another. He had shown her quickly that he didn't have a problem with her form and in fact craved it. Generally as naked as he could get her.

"I love your body," Wheaton said with a smile. He could obviously read her face well enough to realize she wasn't being disparaging to herself.

"Well, big guy, I'm glad you love my body, because after years in it, I have come to the realization that it's not going to change much." She grinned mischievously. "Now, on the other hand...if you lose any of your muscles, we may have a problem."

Laughing out loud when he caught her grin, he nipped her belly and tickled her sides. "Oh really?"

"Yes sir. I am going to be counting those ridges on your abdomen daily to make sure you don't start slacking on me." Between laughs as he tickled her, she was finally able to gasp out that he needed to stop before she peed herself.

"Wheaton! I'm warning you. Seriously!" At her frantic tone, he literally rolled off her—and right onto the floor. Of course, this caused her to laugh even more as she hurried off to the bathroom.

Relieved she'd been able to hold off having an accident, Poppy laughed at herself. Well, that would have killed the romance quickly, she thought while washing her hands.

"I have a few meetings scheduled with the Council today but I should be able to come and join you for lunch in the med center," Wheaton offered as he finished his breakfast.

"Anything important I should know about?" Poppy asked, hoping he had news regarding their match that he would share with her.

"Just some minor items are scheduled for today's talks. I believe we have the majority of our negotiations with Earth complete. We have only a few more days before we reach Phaeton Major and then I can show you around," Wheaton said, sipping coffee.

"Hey, that reminds me. One of the guys explained that warriors live in barracks on your home planet," she interrupted.

"Yes." Raising an eyebrow in question, he waited for her to elaborate.

"How are these warriors supposed to have families if they live in barracks? In fact, that brings up the question regarding our baby. Where are we going to live?" When he opened his mouth, she held up her hand. "And before you say it, if you even suggest that we let our innocent baby be taken away to a training house, I will literally kill you with my bare hands." She was completely serious.

"I admit that we might not have thought the family aspect through very well when it comes to housing but this is easily solved." Standing up to hug her, he whispered to the top of her head, "And I would never let anyone take our baby."

"Good. Now since you believe this is so easily solved, let me know what your plan is." Poppy highly doubted that he was able to figure out a solution when both she and the guys had been unable to do so. Their new timeline only added to the problem.

"First, we have many cloning centers. I would suggest we start turning those into housing for warriors who have been granted brides. Since the cloning has not been satisfactory for a few cycles, the centers should only contain machines that would need to be moved out. The same goes for a few training centers. We recently had some young warriors cycle out to be assigned to posts. Those buildings will be vacant as well."

Seeing the surprise on her face that he did indeed have a plan, he continued with a smile. "By my calculation we should have fifteen to twenty buildings available for us to transform into housing as soon as we have Council approval."

"Okay, Mr. Smarty Pants, I have something I doubt you've thought of yet." At his look, she continued, "What about baby-proofing the ship? I'm assuming you'll be on Squadron One quite a bit and would want us with you... How are you going to solve that one?"

"You are correct. That is something I never thought of." Wheaton tapped his fingers to his chin, unable to immediately handle that question. "I admit that the housing on Phaeton Major would not be ideal for the Council since we do have to travel quite a bit. And I do want you with me while I am traveling for my duties."

Wheaton smiled when he saw the glee on her face at having stumped him. Laughing at her little victory dance, he swung her up into his arms, hugging her hard before setting her back down on her feet.

"You got me, Little Flower. I will think more on a solution today while in the Council meetings and let you know what I can come up with. Now give me my last morning kiss before I have to leave you."

Leaning forward to steal some kisses, Poppy pulled back before it got too hot and heavy. "Let me know if you can do lunch," she whispered against his chest, taking the cuddle time to breathe in his scent before she would be deprived of it for the rest of the day.

"Of course. I should know what the Council schedule is within the hour." Walking to the door, Wheaton gave her one last hot smile before he left.

Poppy was bored out of her mind for the rest of the morning while waiting for Behyr. She had tried to call Pixie a few times to video chat but the interference was wicked. It seemed the farther they moved away from Earth, the more static was a problem. During the initial Hannah situation, Poppy had emailed Pixie a few times back and forth. Her sister had been sufficiently pissed-off on her behalf and had threatened to "hijack a ship and whip some alien ass".

After Poppy explained everything that had happened, Pixie had calmed down but was still holding Wheaton responsible for hurting her baby sister. She demonstrated her anger at Wheaton by thumping her fist into her palm a few times and reminding Poppy of what had happened in high school. As if she would ever forget that memory-worthy tidbit. According to Pixie, she was "about to kick ass and take names" at work but hadn't said anything more regarding what was happening. Instead she had said that it was too much to email and she would rather explain things face-to-face.

Annoyed by having to sit and twiddle her thumbs, Poppy realized that the whole "escort" thing was actually starting to grate on her nerves as well. Before she had been familiar with the ship, being shown around had made sense. Now she felt like a little kid constantly waiting for someone to come and fetch her from one place to another. Deciding she would talk to Wheaton later that day at lunch about her need for a chaperone, she made a mental note not to forget to show him her cheat sheet. That should placate him if he brought up the issue of her getting lost. She was sure there were things the warriors needed to do other than walk her around all day anyway.

The tone at the door indicated that her "babysitter" had arrived and Poppy took a second to stick her tongue out at the closed door.

It wasn't fair to kill the messenger so Poppy pasted a smile on her face for whoever the lucky guy was today. Opening the door, she greeted Behyr, who appeared to be a little ruffled.

"Hey, Behyr, how's it hanging?"

Behyr took a moment to inspect the doorway above him, searching for something hanging down.

"What?" he asked.

Confusion was evident on his handsome face and as he glanced around, she saw a noticeable hickey on his neck.

"Wowza." Not realizing she'd said it out loud, Poppy jumped when he repeated her exclamation, his tone one of bewilderment, and she realized her attention had been focused solely on his neck.

Trying to drag her gaze away, she smiled wickedly as Behyr tugged the neck of his shirt up.

"Oh nothing," she continued, in response to his puzzled look. Gathering her items busied her hands for a moment. "Nothing at all." Biting her lip to contain her laughter, she slipped on her shoes and studied him closely. The poor guy seemed so out of sorts compared to his normal put-together manner that she wondered what exactly had happened last night with Hannah. Unsure if she should ask him how things had gone, she followed him silently to the med center.

As they approached the med center door, she paused. "Behyr, how was your second dinner last night?"

Behyr stopped so quickly he almost tripped over his own feet. As he turned toward her, he had a slight blush on his cheeks. Sensing that she was enjoying his discomfort, he smiled down at Poppy.

"You liked that, didn't you?" he said. Laughing at her expression of innocence, he shook his finger at her. "Do not act like you did not enjoy catching me off guard. Wheaton must have mentioned that I took Hannah for a late meal last night, did he not?" Rubbing his hand up and down the back of his neck, he grinned down at Poppy widely enough for her to catch a glimpse of his fangs.

"Why yes he did…and I noticed your close encounter with Hoover Hannah." At his questioning glance, Poppy motioned to his neck.

Now with his face completely red, he pulled his leather collar up higher and flashed her full fang.

"Do not call her that and yes, we had a wonderful night." Walking the last couple steps to the doorway, he swiped his hand across the wrist plate and continued, "She is not anything like you described her before."

Poppy made a face at him and folded her arms across her chest before she smirked and dropped the bomb she was sure he wasn't aware of yet. "Oh really, well then I guess I shouldn't have hated her for a while because she kissed Wheaton." Turning, she walked through the med center doors as Behyr sputtered behind her.

"What?" Obviously shocked, he didn't move for a moment and the door closed with him on the other side.

"Oh, you hadn't heard that part of the story?" Poppy asked when the door opened again and he still had his mouth open.

"No, I did not. Explain the story please."

"Yeah, apparently your new girlfriend decided to test out her seduction skills on Wheaton before I made her realize it was a bad idea." When Behyr's face fell in disappointment, Poppy realized that she might have ruined the idea of Hannah for him. She clutched his arm and tugged him into the room so he wouldn't be shut out again.

"Don't make the gloomy face. She was testing the waters, and I don't have a problem with her anymore…at least as long as she keeps her eyes off Wheaton as potential mate material." Winking at him and nodding to his neck, she went on, "Plus, I think she may have someone new on her mind."

Poppy patted Behyr on the arm as she went to see where Rodin and Tamin were. Checking the exam rooms, she noticed that everything was empty even though the machines had been booted up. She heard footsteps behind her. Behyr had followed her as she'd searched for the doctors.

"Maybe they were called down to the training centers." Behyr was already moving to check the computer for messages. "Well…it doesn't say where they are but it does say here that we are to expect four brides today for checkups. At least, that is what the schedule has recorded."

"Really?" Poppy practically skipped to the message center, she was so excited to meet the other brides who were on the ship.

"Yes, it says here that they are to arrive this morning after Valerie has a scan." Pausing to glance around the center again, he shot Poppy a questioning gaze. "Is she sick?"

"Ummm...I think she wants to get a baseline in the system. You know, since she's stuck here and everything."

Not wanting to tell another's secrets, Poppy tried to make herself busy by gathering the welcome bags she'd prepped for the brides last week. They weren't much but she figured that any human female would appreciate a bottle of lotion and familiar soap along with some other female products they may have forgotten to bring or run out of by now. Poppy smiled, remembering Tamin's look of disbelief when she'd asked if they had ribbon for her to make bows. He'd ended up shaking his head but provided her with some blue medical string from the supply closet. She was happy she was going to be able to give these out and meet some of the other ladies.

"Poppy?" Behry's deep voice penetrated her thoughts.

"Oh, sorry. I've just been anxious to meet these women. It seemed like it was never going to happen." Smiling at him reassuringly, she put the bags back down. "Come to think of it, I should become friends with as many as I can, right?"

Behyr nodded, peering at the bags she had set down.

"What are these?" Picking one up, he read the bottle that showed clear through the cellophane wrapping. "Peaches and cream?"

"It's lotion." Taking up a basket that had the loose extras for more bags, she flipped open the top of a similar tube. "For some reason, when Earth sent supplies for the brides, they put in a large shipment of scented lotions for the women." Holding the tube up to his face, she puffed some air out and a glob popped out the opening to hit the tip of his nose.

"Aaack!" He jerked back with such a reaction of disgust Poppy couldn't help but laugh hysterically.

"It's only lotion, you goofball, not acid." Reaching for a tissue to help him clean off his face, she found he'd already done so with his hands and was sniffing them.

"This smell is…pleasant." As if he didn't know how to describe it, he kept sniffing his hands. "Could I have one of these packs for Hannah?"

Smiling at how sweet he was toward Hannah, she held out the basket. "Of course you can. There are different scents, though. Do you want to smell them all to see which one you like more?" Reaching for another bottle, she giggled when he snatched it from her.

"I'll do that. You seemed to laugh so much before that I think you may have done that to me on purpose."

After going through the bottles, he settled on one that was a vanilla-sugar blend. Noting his pick, Poppy figured it wouldn't be a bad idea to let Hannah know he preferred that scent over the other ones that were available.

Behyr stuck around long enough to help Poppy prepare everything, since the docs still hadn't arrived. He seemed to ask about everything human-related and Poppy got a kick out of pointing out the different things human women might like or need. Behyr became obsessed with a shower pouf and kept rubbing his thumb over a foot pumice stone, but when Poppy pulled out a box of tampons, he dropped the items and quickly found something to do in another room. If he did end up taking Hannah for a bride he would need to get over the squeamishness of the female cycle. Remembering she'd had to explain it to Wheaton and what had happened made her smile to herself. Wheaton had been curious when he had found her empty birth control packet and asked if they were vitamins. When she explained it regulated her cycle and prevented pregnancy, he had been full of questions. Apparently the warriors had been given information on human anatomy and how the body worked but he hadn't fully understood all that it entailed.

Stacking boxes of tampons and pads hadn't been on Poppy's to-do list for the morning but she was so excited to meet the other brides she decided it was a good idea to stay busy so she didn't get too nervous. Hearing the tone at the med center door, she almost jumped out of her skin and couldn't help the disappointment that came over her face when she realized it was just Tamin and Rodin.

"Thanks, Poppy. I can see you are thrilled to see us." Rodin smiled at her and rolled his eyes. A habit he had picked up from watching her do it so often.

Feeling bad that she had let her emotions show so clearly, she went up and gave him a hug.

"Where is mine?" Tamin spoke from behind Rodin.

"Well, I can't forget one of my favorite doctors, now can I?" she teased back.

Both men seemed to have their hands full so she took a box, only to have it snatched from her hands quickly by a scowling Behyr.

"You are not supposed to lift anything heavy." Setting the box down on a table close by, he mumbled, "Wheaton will kill us if he finds out you did that."

"Oh c'mon now, guys, he's not that bad." Crossing her arms over her chest, she pouted for a second. "Plus, that wasn't even heavy."

The men all paused and stared at her in disbelief.

"He's not that bad?" Rodin said, almost choking over the words.

The men glanced at each other and burst into laughter in unison.

"What's so funny?" Poppy thought to herself for a moment and couldn't come up with a time when Wheaton had tried to restrict her since the baby news.

"Poppy, the first thing Wheaton did when he found out that you were pregnant was give us a list of what was acceptable and not," Tamin said while moving more boxes out of her reach.

"And this was *after* we explained that working here wouldn't harm you at all. At first, he wanted to keep you in the apartment all day until I explained that it made more sense for you to be here in case there was an issue and you needed medical attention." Rodin was smiling now as he explained. Pointing at her stomach, he smiled and went on, "Don't even ask me how many questions he had regarding sexual intercourse and your baby. He was sure that he was going to poke the baby while he was enjoying your—" Obviously embarrassed, Rodin had to search for the right word before he settled on, "attentions."

Poppy was full-on laughing by now at how Wheaton must have been freaking out a bit. She had to give him props though. He had never let on that he was scared something would go wrong since their original scan…or that he had been worried if sex was okay. Deciding to give him a little extra attention tonight for being so darn cute, she held up her hands.

"Okay, guys, boxes are off-limits. I'll just go over here and make sure these gift packs are ready for the millionth time." Sarcasm was apparently lost on the warriors because they nodded like that was a good idea and went back to sorting through the boxes.

"What's in there, anyway?" Casting a glance back at her favorite supply closet, she tried to peek into one of the boxes that Rodin had opened and was digging through.

"We received some more supplies from a shuttle mission today. Phaeton Two is close enough for a shuttle to send supplies back and forth and since we have brides aboard and they do not, then we received some of their excess."

"But I thought we were in deep space?" Poppy asked, confused.

Rodin nodded and handed her a couple more bottles of lotion out of his box. "We are. Phaeton Two is heading to Earth and we are heading to our planet. While we are passing the other ship it will be within shuttle distance for a couple of hours."

"Wait, why are they going to Earth?"

"Part of our agreement is to always have a presence near Earth." Seeing that he had confused her even more, he tried to explain, "Part of it is for protection."

Behyr interrupted Rodin, watching Poppy with one of the more serious expressions that she had ever seen him have. "We are not the only ones that exist in space, Poppy. There are dangers that even Earth is unaware of."

"Earth is safe, right?" Concern for her sister was the first thing that popped into her head.

"Yes, most other life forms will not openly attack Phaeton warships or anything that we consider ours…and Earth is something that we consider ours." Behyr had never seemed more like a warrior than he did now as he was speaking. "Many of the other life forms are peaceful and not as technologically advanced. That or they are in trade."

Poppy winced when she remembered how Wheaton had had to explain the Pleasure Sector to her. That had been an uncomfortable conversation all around. Wheaton had become embarrassed explaining about the life forms that worked in the "skin trade". Realizing he was talking about visiting space prostitutes hadn't sat well with Poppy either. And then Wheaton had suggested that she might even like going to the Pleasure Sector when they had a chance. Even going as far as to say that he had enough credits for her to pay for anything she wanted.

Her immediate reaction had been to jump to the conclusion he was suggesting a threesome. Her face had showed her disgust and he had laughed at her assumption. At her expression of disbelief, he had quickly told her that the port also dealt in spices, jewelry and craft items that they sold in the marketplace. He explained that it would be a nice place for her to pick out a gift for her sister if she wanted to find something unique. Grateful he hadn't been suggesting an alien orgy, she agreed that Pixie would flip out if she got a gift from space.

Remembering that conversation, she could admit now that it had made sense that these men, who lacked any physical outlet, would visit the equivalent of a space whorehouse. She understood it, but she didn't have to like it. Wheaton had explained that when ships were close enough, they would have shuttles going back and forth for the men to take advantage of what was available for purchase…and that included sex. When she had asked why they simply didn't use these women as brides, Wheaton had said they were not a compatible match for reproduction with most of the species available. A majority of the female species were sterilized as a work precaution. When she had cast him a glare of disgust, he had tried to reassure her that they were not similar to human women at all. The races that sold themselves were born and bred for prostitution. Many of them were engineered to be as physically attractive to as many alien races as possible. That had actually made her even more grossed out.

Unable to stop herself, she'd thought of the *Total Recall* chick with her three boobs. Poppy had held out her palms in a "don't say anything else" pose and told him that what was in the past was forgotten, but if he ever even thought about visiting the Pleasure

Sector again, for anything other than items in the marketplace, she would neuter him. That had pretty much ended that conversation. Realizing that the men were staring at her while she had her mini-flashback, she smiled at them.

"I get it, guys. Wheaton had given me a run-down on some of the other species that you encounter when traveling. As long as my sister is safe on Earth then you don't need to say anything else."

The men, realizing that she had been made aware of what "trade" was, busied themselves with the boxes and spent the next hour organizing the new supplies they'd received.

Something had been in the back of her mind and she took the quiet time to ask. "Has anyone seen Dathrow lately?"

He had not been around the last couple of days and Poppy missed her friend. At first she had assumed he had been called to the Council meetings but Wheaton had not mentioned him recently.

"Did Wheaton not tell you?" Rodin asked, surprise on his face.

"Tell me what?

Behyr held out his hand to stop the other two men from talking. His movement quieted them almost immediately.

"I will tell her. Why don't you two make sure the regen beds are up and running? The brides should be here any minute."

Seeing the glances of sympathy the two men cast her way as they were leaving made her stomach churn a bit. What the hell had happened to Dathrow?

"Is he okay?" Poppy's worry increased when Behyr seemed more uncomfortable the longer he stood silently in front of her. "Spit it out. Is. He. Okay?"

Behyr obviously realized the more he stalled, the more anxious Poppy grew. "He is fine," he started, only to stop when she waved her hands for him to keep going. "Quit flapping your hands at me. I will tell you what I know, but I need you to listen to all of it and not interrupt. Agreed?"

Poppy was instantly relieved to find out Dathrow was okay but now Behyr was making her more curious by the moment with the cloak-and-dagger treatment. Nodding her head, she waited for him to spill the beans.

"Wheaton was concerned when he found out that you were being shadowed so closely by Dathrow when you were initially separated." Holding up his hands again to stop her from talking, he went on, "This was made even more of a situation when Dathrow approached the Council and explained that if Wheaton *did* choose Hannah over your own bridal agreement, then *he* would step forward to claim you as his bride."

"*What?*" Poppy was stunned. Utterly stunned.

Dathrow had been so sweet and never let on he was interested in her, other than a couple comments such as, "I would be grateful for a bride like you" or "Wheaton is a lucky warrior". Poppy had thought those moments were just him trying to cheer her up when she was bummed about what'd been happening. She never took it as a serious interest in her as his bride. Feeling awful for him possibly getting in trouble with Wheaton, she had to ask.

"Behyr, is this my fault? Should I stop hugging you guys or something?" And then a thought popped into her head. "Oh no, did Wheaton hurt him?"

"No, for the most part Wheaton was understanding. After all, Dathrow was your second warrior match." Behyr shook his head as if trying to let her know she wasn't to blame. He didn't realize the bomb he'd just dropped.

"Wait—*what? Dathrow* was the match the Council mentioned when we had our meeting?" Holy smoke, she needed to sit down. Her mind was whirling around and around. No wonder she had felt so comfortable talking to him. According to the computer program, she and Dathrow should have been comfortable around each other. They could have possibly been mated, for crying out loud. Even though she had never felt the pull to him that she did for Wheaton, she took some of the blame on herself. For him, she would have been the ideal and everything he had said when they were sharing meals or laughing together now made sense.

"So where is he? Was he told to stay away?" Feeling upset about something out of her control had always grated on her nerves. This was one of those situations.

Behyr noticed her sad face and came close to pat her arm awkwardly. "He understood the Council's standing and Wheaton's feelings. Dathrow asked for a transfer to Phaeton Two until a decision regarding your match was made. I believe he was on one of the first shuttles this morning once we were within transfer distance. If the Council dissolves your union to Wheaton, you will have the option to join him there. If the Council abides by your decision to stay with Wheaton then Dathrow will be matched to another bride."

Seeing that Poppy was still upset, he continued. "It is not your fault, Poppy. You are a beautiful, smart, friendly woman and all of us are slightly jealous of the luck Wheaton had when he was made your match." Tipping her chin up, he continued, "You make all of us smile by just being with us. You are kind to everyone you meet and I cannot imagine a better friend to have. Dathrow was tempted to try to claim you for his own and he let Wheaton know before anything went further."

Pausing, he gazed at her with a completely serious face.

"He is a good man. I might have done the same thing if I knew that we had been matched—Wheaton or no." Chucking her chin in a friendly way, he smiled, showing his fangs. "Plus, you are one of the first to not be frightened by my teeth."

Realizing he was trying to joke to defuse the situation, she grinned back and asked, "Oh really? What did Hannah think about those awesome teeth of yours?"

Behyr laughed and turned back to the boxes. "You are a curious thing, aren't you?"

"Why yes I am. It's a fault, I know. Curiosity killed the cat and all that jazz."

Hearing the tone indicating that someone was at the med door was the only thing that stopped her from trying to weasel any more out of Behyr regarding his time with Hannah. Jogging to the door, she bounced from one foot to the other as the men laughed at her antics.

"They're here! They're here!" Poppy was obviously acting like an idiot at the prospect of meeting some other women but she didn't care. She took a deep breath to calm herself and then let it out on yet another disappointed sigh when the door opened and it was just Val and Thorne.

"Oh, it's just you guys."

"Well gee, best friend, thanks for the welcome," Val said sarcastically, giving Poppy a little arm punch.

"Sorry. I was just hoping you were the other brides who were supposed to come by today. I have been waiting to meet them for what seems like for-e-vah." She frowned, realizing she'd forgotten Val's appointment was first, and that the brides would be a while longer.

"Just us...so sorry to disappoint you." Sticking out her tongue at Poppy, Val held Thorne's hand and grinned at the doctors. "We're here to run the test on the regen bed, yes?"

Sensing why Val was asking to be scanned, they ushered her quickly back to the exam room.

Val grinned behind her and said to Poppy, "Want to come in and show me how this works?"

"Sure thing." Poppy smiled back at Val. She could tell that Val was nervous. And by the look of Thorne, he was equally on pins and needles.

"Plus, you can keep my big guy calm while we wait. He's more nervous than I am if that's possible," Val whispered to Poppy once she'd caught up to her in the exam room.

CHAPTER TWENTY-SEVEN

Val's screening was just as easy as Poppy's had been. As they waited for the results, Poppy tried to distract Thorne with questions.

"So…I thought you guys were going to be here earlier this morning. What took so long?"

Thorne jumped when Val elbowed him to get his attention, and then appeared sheepish as he realized that Poppy had been talking to him and he had ignored her.

"Sorry, I am just…anxious," he explained.

"So, where were you?" Noticing his gaze still hadn't left the doctors who were staring at the screen of the regen bed, she tacked on, "You know that watching them like a hawk won't make it go faster, right?"

"Of course, of course. Sorry. We were held up in Council meetings." Surveying the room now, he seemed to realize something. "Where is Wheaton?"

Now Poppy was confused. "What do you mean? Wheaton was at the Council meeting all morning."

The weird expression on Val's face didn't make Poppy feel too good about what was coming next.

"No, he wasn't, Poppy. Both Hannah and Wheaton were absent this morning," Val replied, squirming under the scrutiny.

Poking her head out of the exam room, Poppy yelled, "Behyr!"

He came running into the room, which he scanned as if he were checking for an enemy. Finding no one was in danger, he relaxed slightly. "Why did you yell for me? I thought something was wrong."

Waving her hand at him, which she knew he hated, Poppy brushed off his words. "Where is Hannah today?"

She could see he was confused at her question but he answered, "At Council meetings," then became confused at both Val and Thorne shaking their heads at him.

"Apparently not. These two just came from the Council and said that neither Wheaton *nor* Hannah were there this morning." She nodded to the pair.

Now everyone was confused. But at that moment the regen bed beeped, letting them know the scan was complete. Thorne practically barreled past Poppy to get to the doctors. If Poppy could guess based on the smiles on their faces, she had a friend to schedule playdates with. Her suspicion was quickly confirmed when Thorne turned and raced across the room to lift Val up and hug her so tightly that her back should have popped.

"So yes?" Val whispered.

"Yes," Thorne answered in a soft but happy voice.

"Yes!" Poppy couldn't help but exclaim with a fist pump into the air.

"Yes what?" Behyr asked, watching everyone apparently celebrate, but not knowing why.

Thorne turned with his arm around a beaming and slightly crying Val and announced to everyone within earshot, "Valerie is having my baby!"

The entire scene made Poppy laugh. Thorne seemed pleased as punch that Val was pregnant. Val was happy as well if her beaming smile was anything to go by. The docs were patting each other on the backs as though they personally had had a hand in the baby-making while Behyr was stunned, his confusion apparent on his face.

"You and Valerie?" he said, pointing between the two of them. "But you weren't matched…" Unable to get out what he was trying to say, he stopped and then asked, "Does the Council know?"

Thorne nodded and hugged Val tighter to his side. "We met with them this morning and explained the situation. I have petitioned for a match with Valerie and it has been approved. Now we are waiting for the paperwork to be signed." He sent Poppy a grateful smile. "Poppy had suggested that we point out it would be to the benefit of the Council to have a liaison stationed here and it worked to our advantage. They did not want an unattached female on the ship permanently, but a liaison who is also a bride was perfect."

Walking forward to give hugs and congratulate the couple, Poppy whispered to Val, "I'm so happy for you."

Sniffing back her tears, Val laughed a little. "It's a bit hard to take it all in. I mean, I came up here to help you out and then go home. Instead I met Thorne, we're getting married and now we're pregnant. I'm overwhelmed but so happy I feel like I could burst into confetti at any second."

"No bursting please." Poppy laughed, wiping her own eyes that had teared up. "Speaking of bursting," she added, "We should ask Tamin or Rodin about something to ease morning sickness. That shit can hit you quick but they might have something to deal with it."

"Yeah, that's a good idea," Val replied, holding her hands up to her smiling cheeks as she took a deep breath. "Do you ever feel like things happen for a reason?"

Poppy took a second and then nodded at the men in the room. "Yeah...I do."

While Thorne grilled the two doctors about what Val could and could not do, it seemed like the ideal time for Poppy to steal Val away to the main medical room. Behyr followed them, obviously having some questions and knowing that he wouldn't be able to get answers out of Thorne for a little while now.

Poppy ushered her now-pregnant friend to a seat at a round table where they all made themselves comfortable even though Behyr seemed tense.

"So, where the hell are Wheaton and Hannah?" Poppy blurted out, trying to solve the puzzle in her head.

Valerie shook her head. "I'm not sure, Poppy. When Thorne and I arrived at the Council meeting, we looked for Wheaton. We wanted him on our side when we broached the subject of our mating with the Council. After asking a couple Council members, we were told that neither he nor Hannah were available this morning." Glancing back at the exam room, she frowned. "Now that I think about it, one of the members whispered something to Thorne but I didn't hear what was said. I was too nervous about our petition to pay much attention at the time. Maybe they told him something they didn't want me to hear?"

Now Poppy was hoping Thorne would hurry the hell up before she had to yell again but Behyr beat her to it.

"Thorne!" Behyr's voice was so loud Poppy had to shake her head to stop the ringing.

Smacking his arm, she frowned at him. "Warn a girl next time, will ya? You almost blew out my eardrums."

He sheepishly grinned as Thorne shot into the room as if there was a fire.

He ran immediately to Val and twirled her around in the chair.

"Is everything okay with the baby?" Thorne's hands were cupping Val's nonexistent belly.

"Yes, big guy, everything is fine." She motioned over to Behyr with a nod of her head. "They want to know where Hannah and Wheaton might be."

Thorne grimaced and glanced between the two of them. Letting out a sigh, he sat down at the table next to Valerie.

"Well, a Council member said they were discussing their bridal agreement with a few senior members and finalizing some paperwork."

Poppy jumped when Behyr's fists hit the table with a hard *thump*.

"That is not possible," he gritted out with a clenched jaw, his fangs showing slightly.

Never having seen Behyr angry before, Poppy now understood how scary the fangs were when you took in the whole package of a furious warrior of his size with teeth bared.

Thorne raised his hands to show Behyr he wasn't a threat. To calm him down he said, "I am not saying that they were upholding the contract, my warrior brother. It could be that they were finalizing it being dissolved."

Keeping a protective arm around Val, Thorne watched the Skrammon closely before speaking further. "Demascus was also absent from the morning meeting," he added.

Behyr stood quickly and nodded at all of them. "I am sorry if I scared you, Valerie, but I could not help my reaction." He pledged, "I will control myself better when around your female. I am sorry I upset her."

Valerie shook her head. "It's not a problem, Behyr. I would have had the same reaction if someone had hinted Thorne was possibly mating with someone else," she assured him, giving him a quick peck.

"If you will excuse me, I am going to find out where Hannah is at," Behyr said. He paused in his path to the door when Poppy called out to him.

"Can you tell Wheaton to check in please? I want to make sure everything is all right," Poppy asked. She knew everything had to be okay. She wasn't sure how she would deal with things if it wasn't.

Nodding his head in agreement, Behyr left quickly. As the remaining three friends sat around the table, both Val and Poppy teased Thorne about what questions he might have asked the doctors and why it had taken so long. Thorne turned bright red when Poppy hinted that maybe he had been asking sex questions. At his telling blush, both of the women started giggling like crazy.

"We are going to work on an information packet explaining how to handle a pregnant bride," Rodin declared, entering the room with Tamin following closely behind.

At his statement, the group around the table burst into laughter. Both of the doctors jumped, startled before Thorne explained what they had been discussing just moments before.

Val and Poppy had some suggestions when it came to what needed to be on the list and it included foot rubs and lots of chocolate, which the men took seriously and jotted down on a sheet of paper. As the women glanced at each other with smiles on their faces, they seemed to both be thinking the same thing: *it couldn't get any better than this.*

After a while, the doctors had to get back to more serious work and disappeared into the exam rooms. Thorne reluctantly admitted he had more work to finish and excused himself, leaving Val in Poppy's care.

"If I am not back in time, then I will meet you back in our quarters. Do not leave without an escort. That is an order," Thorne said seriously, making sure the pair nodded before he left.

Upset that the brides were going to be no-shows for their appointments, Poppy couldn't help but wonder what the deal was. This was the first time they had all scheduled actual appointments and had not canceled nor let anyone know they wouldn't be able to make it. Tamin and Rodin had messaged their warriors, trying to see what was causing the delay, but had not received any responses. It was odd but the doctors both shrugged it off.

Poppy and Val were unable to hide their disappointment, so Rodin took pity on them and tossed a couple of pregnancy books onto the table for them to read. Poppy had to admit that the *What to Expect* book was full of information she didn't know. For instance, were they getting all the nutrients the baby needed to grow right? She wasn't sure how the replicator worked but assumed that some of the ingredients were legit. At the very least she hoped she wasn't feeding her baby space slime disguised as a hamburger.

Busy flipping through the books, the women were surprised when the door chimed two hours later. They hadn't realized how much time had passed as they'd been chatting about their futures.

"My butt can definitely tell how long we've been sitting, Poppy. I think one of my cheeks fell asleep," Val joked while rubbing her behind.

"No kidding. I think my foot is asleep too. Remind me to request some cushions for these pieces of space plastic they call chairs." Picking up the books and tucking them away from prying eyes, Poppy then went to the door to answer it, to be greeted by two warriors she did not remember having seen before.

"Hey, guys, do you need to see the doctors?" Poppy asked as she stepped aside to let the men into the med center. Usually when a warrior arrived, he came in with something bleeding from a sparring session that had gotten out of control, but these two appeared fine.

"We are here as an escort for Poppy." One held out his hand to shake.

"I'm Poppy and this is Valerie," she said, shaking the first warrior's hand and smiling.

"I am Cannon and this is Leo."

The warriors smiled back at both of the women while shaking hands for longer than necessary. Poppy thought she should maybe suggest a human-warrior relations class to teach them how to shake hands properly. Handshakes with the new guys always seemed either too quick and jarring, or hard and slow. Filing that away to talk to Wheaton about, she hollered to Rodin.

"Rodin, I'm heading out for the day. I'll see you tomorrow."

He mumbled a goodbye from the second room, and Tamin poked his head out of the first room.

"Later, gator. Tomorrow I'll bring donuts."

Tamin smiled at the promise of a treat and waved back.

Oh, the warriors hadn't mentioned escorting Val back to her apartment.

"Can Val come too? I would appreciate it if you could walk her home once you're done with me so she doesn't have to wait for another escort," Poppy asked.

Both men nodded as one but only Cannon spoke when he said, "Of course."

Poppy grabbed her bag and swung around to speak to Val. "You ready to blow this popsicle stand?"

Both men seemed worried by what she said.

"It means leave. I asked if Val was ready to leave." With that said, she linked her arm through Leo's and walked with him out the door as Val followed, talking to Cannon.

Leo stiffened slightly when she touched him but started chatting with her as soon as she started with her "get to know you" questions. Poppy was so engrossed in talking to Leo and finding out what type of warrior he was she didn't realize they were on an unfamiliar floor. She paused and looked around. Gripping his arm, concerned that they had gotten lost, she stopped in her tracks and caused Val and Cannon to bump into them.

"Are we going to Val's first?" Poppy asked.

"Ummm, Poppy, I'm only one floor beneath you. This is a completely different part of the ship," Val replied, sharing in the confusion.

Leo shook his head at the women. "We were instructed to escort you here, not your quarters, Poppy."

Poppy noticed more warriors here than she usually encountered while walking the halls. Most were carrying parcels or bags and seemed to be moving very quickly. In fact, most of the warriors paid no attention to the women, which was strange as Poppy was used to the stares of interest she got when moving about the ship from one place to another.

"Where is 'here' exactly?" Poppy asked while continuing to walk, this time at a slower pace.

"The intake floor. We received orders from the Council that you were to have a meeting here and they sent us to escort you. During the meeting, you will be briefed on life on Phaeton Prime and how to adjust." Nodding behind him at his friend and Val, he added, "We will escort Val to her quarters once you have been dropped off."

For some reason, Poppy's Spidey-senses started tingling. The warriors seemed nice enough but not knowing where she was going was triggering something inside her. That combined with not having heard from Wheaton all morning didn't sit well. Trying to remember where they were walking and how to get back if needed, she started paying attention to the symbols on the doors she passed. This was one of those times she wished she could pull out the cheat sheet Dathrow had drawn for her.

Reaching the door to their apparent destination, Poppy hoped to see Wheaton on the other side of it, but was disappointed when she was shown into an empty room.

"We were told to have you wait here, Poppy," said Cannon. He turned to Val, who had followed Poppy into the room, and held out his arm for her to take. "We can now take you to your apartments, Valerie."

Seeming uncomfortable with the situation, Val looked from warrior to warrior and then back at the empty meeting room. "Actually, I think I'll wait here with Poppy and keep her company.

After all, I'll be going to Phaeton Prime too, so any information she needs then I'll need as well. I'll have the next escort take me back to my rooms when they walk Poppy back."

Both of the warriors seemed fine with her request. Bowing quickly in unison, they nodded at each of the women.

"It was nice to meet you, Poppy," Cannon said.

"And you too, Valerie," Leo added, then turning as if he had forgotten something, he paused. "We were told that there is an antibiotic that you need to take. It's there on the table. It's just a precaution. You should find a pill inside the small cup."

Walking to the table at the back of the room, he picked up two medicine cups from a long row of them sitting on the table. He handed both women one. They both had a purple pill inside.

Valerie glanced at Poppy before asking the men, "What exactly is this for?"

"We were instructed that it is an antibiotic that humans need to take prior to arriving on Phaeton Prime. Something to do with a disease that you may catch that we are immune to. Since you will be accompanying us to our home planet then you should take it as well, Valerie." Cannon walked back to the table and found two water bottles in a cooler beside the table. He handed each woman a bottle and the warriors excused themselves and left the room.

Alone in the empty space, Poppy and Val stared at each other.

"This is totally weirding me out... Do you think this is safe to take while pregnant?" Poppy asked, staring into her cup.

"Something doesn't seem right," Val agreed. She shook hers around. The pill made a small tinging noise in the little plastic container. "Let's wait to ask Rodin or Tamin before we take any meds."

She reached for the pill Poppy hadn't taken and shook it and hers into a tissue she pulled from her pocket, which she then put into her messenger bag. "I'll hold on to them until we get the okay from the docs." Dropping the empty cups onto the table, she opened her water bottle and took a swig. Valerie walked to the table in the corner of the room and picked up a file folder.

Poppy nodded at the papers Val was leafing through. "What is that?"

"These are consent forms for something—"

Both women stopped their snooping when the door beeped. Without either them opening it, it swished open, revealing Demascus with four warriors.

The bad tingles that Poppy'd had in her stomach earlier moved to full-on earthquake mode when she saw him smile.

"Oh great," she let out on a soft breath.

Val was standing so close to Poppy that when she gripped her arm, Poppy could feel her whole body tense.

"I don't like this," whispered Val out of the corner of her mouth.

Nodding in agreement, she was about to ask Demascus what the hell was going on, when he spoke in the nasally voice she'd come to hear in her nightmares.

"Well hello, ladies." Giving Poppy a toothy grin, he walked far enough in for the other men to follow and the door quickly closed behind him.

"What are we doing here, Councilor Demascus?" Val asked in an authoritative voice.

"Valerie, so nice to see you." Nodding to the men at his side got them flanking the women, which caused Val and Poppy to move even closer together, like sheep being herded by dogs.

"This is actually a bonus. I had just summoned Poppy but here you are... How do you refer to it, two birds with one stone, I believe?" He walked forward to take the folder out of Val's hands. He cast a brief glance at the table, from where a warrior had retrieved their cups, which were now missing their pills.

"And you have already picked up the consent forms too? How nice of you to get started without me." He walked to the table and took a seat, flipping through the papers.

"I don't get it. Why are we here?" Poppy asked nervously. Anything that had to do with Demascus could only be bad and his warrior thugs were definitely making her uncomfortable.

Demascus leaned back in the chair and arched his eyebrow. "Poppy, you know I do not like you." At her surprise, he paused and smiled. "What? You think I am not going to be blunt now?" When she was silent, he continued, "I think you and your human species are going to spoil everything that the Phaeton race has strived to be."

"It doesn't matter what you think, does it?" Poppy shot back. She wasn't going to just stand there and be bullied—especially by a dickhead like Demascus.

Standing quickly, he walked toward the women. "No, it doesn't. However, now that Wheaton has a new bride you are no longer needed." Nodding at the men who were standing at their sides, he went on, "These warriors are here to transport you to Squadron Two." Pausing when Poppy let out a gasp, he smiled again then glanced at Valerie. "And you are a bonus. We will be able to let Earth know you will be back in orbit for transport to home within days. This is in fact a most wonderful bonus," he said, clapping his hands.

Strong hands gripped her arms and Poppy struggled against the hold.

"You can't do this, Demascus. I'm mated to Wheaton and Val is mated to Thorne." Hoping to get through to the warriors who were apparently doing his bidding, she sent a beseeching glance to the one nearest to her.

Demascus grinned toothily. "Oh yes I can. And don't worry, I explained to these men that you have been acting out of character since Hannah arrived and Wheaton showed her favor over you." He whispered, "Who are they going to listen to…an emotional human or a senior Council member?"

Then he turned to Val.

"Unfortunately, I never received a bridal agreement from Thorne since I have been out of the meetings all day. If that is the case, then we will have no problem with Thorne going through the proper channels to retrieve you in a few short weeks."

Valerie began to struggle with all her strength against the warrior at her side who was gripping her arm to pull her forward. Poppy fought the arms holding her still, kicking her legs at any body part they could reach. She was almost loose when one of the warriors reached forward with a silver cylinder and pressed it to Val's arm. As Val went limp, Poppy cried out in concern.

"What the fuck was that?" she yelled, still battling to get to Val who was now being whisked away.

"That is something to make the transport a little easier for you ladies. Don't worry, we have one for you as well."

Demascus gave a nod, and Poppy didn't have time to fight before she felt a small prick on her arm—and then darkness.

CHAPTER TWENTY-EIGHT

Feeling as if she were waking from a hardcore nap, Poppy could just about make out Val saying her name over and over again. Shaking her head to clear it, she immediately felt woozy and regretted the action.

"Fuuuuuuuck. What the hell happened?" Poppy asked.

Opening her eyes, she saw Val leaning over her. The bright lights peeking behind Val's head caused Poppy to squint. She risked moving her hand up to rub her eyes and forehead, hoping to alleviate some of the pain centered there. But her wrist was too light, something was off.

"Where did my band go?" Poppy rubbed her wrist. It was red in one area, as if she'd been pinched.

"Here, drink this." Handing Poppy some water, Val gestured to the room. "All of us are missing our bands. I think they must have been cut off."

Val helped her to sit up on what Poppy now realized was a cot. She noticed six other women contained with them in what resembled a jail cell. One side of the room consisted of plain metal walls with cots in a row against it, and a toilet. The other was lined with bars that ran the length of the room. Past the door to the cell, Poppy saw the standard entry door and message panel on the wall. Looking at the women, she tried to figure out how they'd all gotten there. A few of them were huddled into balls on their cots, moaning and crying. At least she hadn't reacted that badly to whatever it was that Demascus had injected her with.

"Where the fuck are we and what the fuck happened?" Poppy asked, trying to make sense of the scene around her.

Val took the glass back once Poppy had drained the water, and nodded to the other women.

"That is Melanie and she helped me wake up about twenty minutes ago." Letting out a huff of air, Val seemed as if she were seconds away from crying. "It seems that only two of them were able to avoid Demascus knocking them out."

Poppy nodded to the women in acknowledgment, figuring that now was not the time for handshakes.

"Poppy, while we were unconscious, we were shuttled to Squadron Two. I think we're on our way back to Earth." Barely giving Poppy time to let that sink in, Val blinked and tears fell down her cheeks.

"Valerie, it's okay… They'll come for us." Moving closer to the women around the room, she saw most of them were crying or had been, if their puffy eyes were anything to go by. "Everyone needs to stay calm. Our husbands will come for us."

When one of the women on the cots cried out, Poppy jumped and went to see to her. "It's okay. Your husband won't let you be taken away. I'm sure they're searching for us right now." Brushing the hair back from the woman's forehead, she noticed the pretty redhead was sweating. Her cheeks void of any color, she had taken on almost a gray tone.

"What's wrong with her? Did the shot do this? Could she be having an allergic reaction?" Poppy demanded of Val.

"No, Poppy. The shot didn't do that." Valerie swallowed hard and motioned at the woman with pity. "She's losing her baby." It came out as a whisper, but Poppy heard it clearly.

"What?" Poppy asked softly in horror. What had happened while she'd been knocked out? She winced over the woman crying on the cot and her stomach tried to revolt again. Holding back her nausea, she struggled again to figure out what was happening.

Valerie walked toward the cot and tried to calm down the bride, smoothing her hair back from her damp face.

"The pill…that fucking pill they gave us… The women who were pregnant started bleeding almost immediately after they were brought here," Val said, both anger and sadness making her voice husky.

Melanie was a pretty blonde who was so small a stiff wind could knock her over. She stood with her arms across her chest. "I was the first to wake up and it was to those three crying out in their sleep," she said. "I couldn't help but notice the blood. Their pants are completely soaked through. At first I thought maybe they might have been…raped. It wasn't until she started crying for her baby that I realized what was happening." Swallowing hard, she was unable to keep talking and simply bit her lip.

"These three have been bleeding heavily and holding their stomachs," another woman added. "The rest of us just felt sick to our stomachs and hungover. I can only assume it's because we weren't pregnant."

Another woman got up from a cot on the far side of the room and made her way over to Melanie. Rubbing her shoulder to bring her out of the haunting memory, she smiled sadly at Poppy and Val. "My name's Andrea. I didn't fight when they told me that I was being transferred…I guess I didn't even think to. My groom and I decided to part ways since we didn't seem compatible. Once I saw the rest of these women carried in unconscious, I realized that not everyone was leaving on their own."

She raised her voice so everyone could hear her better. "We are definitely on a different ship now though. We were all transferred to shuttles and then brought here once that docked. There were four warriors who took turns carrying you guys in while a smaller guy gave orders."

After Andrea finished speaking, everyone introduced themselves and included whether they were happily mated or not. So far Melanie and Brandy were both happily matched; Andrea was attached and then there were the three women who were on the cots. From what they could gather, the women who had taken the "antibiotic" and were pregnant were also happily mated, but other information wasn't easy to gather. They just kept asking for their husbands between bouts of tears.

Witnessing what could have happened to herself, Poppy felt her body go numb and cold. Val, who had obviously seen her face, helped her stand and walk to the toilet in the corner of the room. "Go ahead, Poppy. Between the shot and seeing how close we were to this, I got sick too."

After retching a few times with nothing coming up, Poppy felt dizzy, but no longer as if her guts would come out of her mouth.

Leaning into Val, she took a look at the other women. "Val, what the fuck are we going to do?"

"I don't know, Poppy…I don't know. But I do know that they will come for us."

"I know that. I mean, how are we going to help those poor women?" Nodding to the women in obvious pain, she couldn't help the stray tear that rolled down her cheek. She felt completely helpless.

"Well, if Tamin and Rodin were here, they would probably say to keep them calm and still. That's the only thing we can do until we get medical help. Maybe it's not too late?" Val said in a hopeful voice.

"Well, if you're the praying type, now's the time to do it," Poppy murmured. Where the hell was Wheaton when she needed him?

* * * * *

Back on Squadron One, Wheaton and Hannah were leaving for the medical unit after an afternoon of meetings with the Council. Thorne had arrived at the midday Council meeting after his morning in the medical unit to share his baby news with Wheaton. He took great pleasure in relaying the message that Wheaton might be "up a shit creek", according to Poppy, if he did not get in touch with his bride. Hannah was also told that Behyr was looking for her, which caused her to blush in front of both the men.

Leaving Thorne behind at the Council meetings, they headed to the medical unit. Wheaton was surprised to find that an escort had already arrived for Poppy. Confusion showing on his face, Wheaton waited for Tamin to explain further.

"An escort arrived earlier for her. I was busy in one of the exam rooms but she shouted that she was leaving and Val would be accompanying her as well," Tamin ended.

"I wonder where they went," Hannah said, wondering out loud to Wheaton. "Did she leave you a message?" The question prompted Wheaton to check his band yet again.

"I have not received one. I had a message from Behyr saying that Poppy was still in the medical unit and he was searching for you but that was earlier." Wheaton was stumped as to where Poppy might be.

Moving down the hallways, they halted when they heard Rodin yelling Wheaton's name.

"Thank goodness, I caught you!" Almost completely out of breath, Rodin took a moment before he was able to speak again. "I am missing meds from today's shipment."

"What does that have to do with me?" Wheaton asked, confused.

"There were at least a dozen doses missing of Hefnon 12." When Wheaton showed he was not catching on, Rodin bit out, "It's the med that we were supposed to deliver the next time we went to the Pleasure Sector." Still not getting the reaction that he needed, he yelled, "It terminates pregnancy!"

Everything inside Wheaton stilled. "Tell me everything you know," he said quickly.

"I became suspicious shortly after Poppy had left with the escorts you sent."

"I never sent any escorts!" Wheaton argued.

"We did not know that, Wheaton." Rodin said defensively.

"Continue." The word came out as an order.

Rodin nodded. "I received a message from a warrior questioning why his bride was not back yet. When I explained that I had never even *seen* his bride, he said that she had been escorted here earlier for her exam. Then I received another call and then another until I got six calls, all to do with the brides who had missed their appointments today. Thorne just messaged saying that he is unable to find Valerie in their apartments. When she left she was with Poppy and the escorts who had arrived."

Staring at a now terrified Wheaton and a stunned Hannah, he said, "Six brides missing plus Poppy and Val…Hefnon 12 doses that were cataloged but are now missing. I am not liking the way this is adding up."

Wheaton gripped the front of Rodin's lab coat and lifted him onto his toes. "What does the medicine do exactly?" he hissed through gritted teeth.

"It causes cramping, bleeding and then the body will abort the fetus if left untreated. Usually within a few hours. It's extremely efficient, which is why the pleasure workers ordered it on our last visit."

Hannah reached up, trying to calm Wheaton enough to let Rodin down. "Wheaton, now is not the time to fight. We need to find Poppy and Val."

Nodding his head and trying to breathe, Wheaton let Rodin down and unclenched his fingers. "Grab whatever you need to help the women and come with me. If I find them and they have taken the doses, we will need medical there to help." Pushing the doctor to hurry him along, he added, "Have Tamin message Thorne and let him know the situation."

Rodin ran back to the med center, and Wheaton started furiously tapping his band.

"What are you doing?" Hannah asked.

"I am sending out a protection code. It is a protocol that we put into place when the women were brought onto the ship. It alerts the warriors that there may be a human in danger, to stay aware and if needed to step in and protect."

When she frowned at him in confusion, he explained, "We have not had access to women before, Hannah. Bringing females aboard a ship with a starved male population was recognized as a risk. The Council established a system to alert warriors on the ship of a possible threat to a bride, even from one of our own." Nodding back to where Rodin had disappeared, he continued, "According to him, we have eight humans missing and in possible danger so we need all the eyes we can get."

An orange light began blinking along the hallway walls.

"Is that part of your protection code?" Hannah asked.

Following Hannah's gaze, he nodded stiffly. "Yes, it will continue until everyone is accounted for."

Some warriors had come out when the alarm went off, checking up and down the corridor. When they noticed Wheaton with Hannah, they nodded to him.

"Who is missing, Councilor Wheaton?" the warrior closest to them asked.

"We have eight brides who are unable to be located. They were escorted by warriors to an unknown location and we need to find them immediately. If a bride is spotted, message me immediately." Wheaton spoke loud enough for all the men to hear him. Hannah could see Rodin pushing his way through the gathering of men with his medical bag.

Not waiting for Rodin to catch up with them, Wheaton started running down the hallway to the lift. They had wasted enough time as it was. Hannah paused for a moment to kick off her heels to run barefoot behind him, trying to keep up.

"We will check floor by floor until we find Poppy," Wheaton declared in a determined voice.

"And Val," Rodin panted as he jogged beside them. "Val was with her."

"And Val," Wheaton agreed with a grim nod.

CHAPTER TWENTY-NINE

Poppy and the missing brides bided their time on the second ship, trying to take care of the women crying on the cots. As they tried to make them as comfortable as possible, Val noticed that the sick women's fevers were starting to fade but the women were still in obvious pain. Poppy was trying to keep everyone calm but couldn't stop her own anxiety from rising.

"They need medical attention. Why hasn't anyone been back to check on us?" Poppy asked, glancing at the door on the other side of the cell.

"My only guess is that Demascus doesn't care. He seemed crazy, Poppy. The few times I've met him in Council meetings he seemed like an ass, but today he was really off his rocker." Val motioned for Melanie to come closer so they wouldn't disturb the women on the beds.

"Melanie, was Demascus the one who transferred you?" Poppy asked, wondering if he'd had a hand in all the brides being taken.

"Yes, it was weird. I was supposed to be escorted to the medical unit for an exam today but instead I was taken to a room where Demascus was waiting for me. He told me I would be getting a briefing on Phaeton Prime to be able to acclimate and he gave me a pill. I didn't realize what was happening and ate it like candy."

Melanie grimaced, as if realizing how stupid she had been and continued, "Andrea apparently is the only one who was told why she was actually escorted to Demascus. Since her union was being dissolved, she signed some forms and followed his goon squad without a fight. She just thought she was hitching a ride home. It was only when she realized that not all of us were here of our own free will that she started asking questions. I think he hit her, if the red mark on her cheek is any indication."

Hearing their whispers, Andrea left Brandy to take care of the sick women and joined them standing by the cell door.

"Yeah, that little asshole backhanded me when I went to help Staci," she said, nodding to the brunette on the first cot. "It was obvious she wasn't herself when the warriors strapped her into the shuttle. When every one of you seemed drugged, I realized not everyone had signed up to dissolve their bridal contract."

Motioning to Brandy, who was wiping the brow of one of the women, she continued, "Brandy wasn't drugged either. I asked her what was going on but she wasn't sure. The idea of her fighting four warriors wasn't an option in her opinion so she didn't struggle."

"Andrea, I hope I'm not being too nosy, but why did you dissolve your contract?" Val asked quietly.

"I'm curious too. I can't even imagine leaving Sorin," Melanie admitted.

"When I met Zane, I felt attraction, but as we got to know each other, I realized I thought of him as more of a brother or best friend than a possible husband." She grinned wryly. "I friend-zoned him pretty quick."

"Was he pissed?" Poppy couldn't help but ask.

Andrea smiled at the women and shook her head. "No. We talked about it and have actually become really close while I've been here. When we found out some of the matches were incorrect, it seemed to make sense that ours was one of the mistakes. I think he may have been relieved, honestly. We act more like siblings than anything else."

Glancing at the women who had calmed enough to fall asleep, Andrea whispered in a hushed tone, "We may not have wanted to marry but I'm sure he's wondering where I am now. I was actually pretty bummed that I couldn't just stay on the ship and work. We became pretty close. He's like the big brother I never wanted."

She shrugged. "I thought I was going to the medical unit today for an exam since I was going to be around a while longer until I was able to go back home. I'd never been to the med center so when my escort led me to Demascus, I followed him, not knowing it was the wrong direction. All of a sudden I was in a room with Demascus and he said I was being transferred immediately."

"Hey, Melanie said that she was supposed to go to the medical unit too." Catching Val's gaze, Poppy saw she'd caught on too. "That's what happened to the appointments today."

Both women were lost and waited for Poppy to explain.

"I work in the medical unit with the doctors and we were expecting all the brides," Poppy explained. "When none of you showed up, we weren't sure what was happening. Rodin and Tamin left messages for your warriors. If they received the messages then they must have realized by now that you never made it."

"Which means that someone will already have realized we are missing!" Valerie finished for Poppy.

"Exactly!" Poppy was so excited at the thought that someone had to have noticed their disappearance that she almost didn't catch the glance Andrea sent her way. "What?"

"You've been working at the medical center?" Andrea asked, cocking an eyebrow at Poppy.

"Yeah, why?" Still unsure where this was going, Poppy studied Andrea's face. She didn't seem mad at Poppy, but more curious than anything.

"I was a nurse on Earth," Andrea explained. "I had been hoping to help out on the ship but never got the chance to make it there. Zane even suggested I ask the Council if I could possibly stay and work here permanently."

Poppy realized now why Andrea seemed to naturally want to hover over the incapacitated brides. Her training must have been helping her care for them as best she could. It explained all the forehead touching and pulse checks Poppy had witnessed her doing off and on all day.

Thinking for a moment, Poppy studied Andrea with all-new eyes. "Andrea, how would you like it if I took you to the medical unit and showed you around once we get back?" Seeing Andrea's eyes light up with pleasure, she tacked on, "The place also comes with not one but two handsome doctors who are in the market for brides."

Andrea couldn't help but laugh. "Well now, I'm not sure I'm ready to jump into the dating pool again so quickly." When Poppy's face fell, she added, "But I would love to see the medical unit. Zane told me about some of the cool stuff they have and I admit I can't wait to get my hands on a couple things."

Keeping her fingers crossed that Andrea would rethink her stance on dating, Poppy grinned when her new friend started asking all sorts of medical questions. The smile dropped off her face when she heard the all-too-familiar tone at the door. They were apparently about to get a visitor.

The person who walked through the door was not the one Poppy wanted to see. Demascus smiled thinly at the women and his grin deepened even further when he noticed the women on the cots.

"So I see that only three of you were actually pregnant." He whistled through his teeth, apparently pleased with himself.

Clenching her hands into fists, Val hissed, "You knew this would happen, didn't you?"

"How fucking evil are you?" Poppy yelled as she approached the bars of the cell. If he got close enough, she was going to reach through and grab his skinny little neck and strangle him herself.

Keeping back from the cell bars, Demascus glared at each of the women before again smiling thinly and folding his hands in front of him.

"I see you as a plague, Poppy. Nothing more than an insect that needs to be smashed." Motioning to the women on the cots, he smiled. "At least I know that we have stopped the abomination of cross-breeding with you humans."

Poppy reached beside her to where Val was standing and squeezed her arm to warn her and keep her quiet. Lord only knew what Demascus would do if he realized that they hadn't taken the pills. Trying to figure out his plan, she needed to keep him talking.

"How do you plan to get away with this?"

"Very easily actually." Pacing in front of the bars as if he didn't have a care in the world, he stated casually, "I am going to be leaving Squadron Two shortly on a shuttle to join my true warrior brothers."

"You're going to the Verge?" Poppy remembered what Wheaton had explained to her and Val earlier. "Wheaton said you were so far down on the totem pole you couldn't be a Council member if you joined them...are you going to be a lackey?" Smiling when she saw Demascus freeze in his steps, she took a step back when he turned to her with hate in his eyes.

"Actually I have been assured a Council position now that I have been able to carry out my plan, you stupid human."

As Demascus spoke, he moved closer to the bars. Overcome by anger at his words, Poppy acted before thinking. Moving quickly, she struck like a snake. Grasping his tunic between the bars, she used all her strength to pull him into the unforgiving metal. Grunting when her arms were wrenched from the action, she hit any part of his body she was able to reach. The warriors who had been with Demascus had not seen her attack coming but quickly moved to save their leader once they realized he was trapped. Before they were able to free him, Poppy latched on to a chunk of his greasy hair and was furiously trying to separate it from his scalp. Banging his head against the bars separating them, she stopped when a warrior pulled out the now familiar silver cylinder. *Dammit!* She'd wanted to get in a few more licks before the cavalry made their move. Letting him go, Poppy tossed hair she had managed to free from his nasty pinhead to the floor.

"Who's the stupid one now, fuckhead?" she goaded.

"You surprise me, Poppy," Demascus wheezed. Adjusting his tunic and trying to smooth his hair, he forced a smile. "Do not worry though, I have a surprise for you as well."

"And what's that?" Poppy asked, her voice trembling with anger.

"Not only have I gotten the brides away from their husbands, but I was able to plant a virus in the matching code. What took years for the Council to accomplish with the profiles has been destroyed in seconds. The Phaetons have no need for Earth if they are unable to make bridal matches."

Poppy couldn't believe the crazy man standing in front of her. The only thing missing from making the sight perfect was him cackling like an evil villain and vanishing in a puff of smoke.

"Our husbands will come for us, you moron. When they do, that means you're going to get your ass kicked." Melanie walked toward the bars as if she weighed a lot more than the hundred and thirty pounds Poppy guessed her to be.

"Seriously, little human, what exactly will your husband come here for? His profile said he preferred tall redheads with large breasts…and you are anything but." Seeing Melanie physically deflate before his eyes at the sting of his words, Demascus laughed in her face.

"You see, none of you are what the warriors wanted. Or even needed for that matter," he continued, turning to walk out the door. "And now they can move on from this stupid idea of human brides."

"Demascus?" Poppy called out. When he paused to glance back, she smiled at him. "Wheaton *will* find you."

"Poppy, I wouldn't worry about him finding me. I would worry about him finding you." With those parting words, Demascus swaggered out the door.

CHAPTER THIRTY

Poppy huffed out an angry screech. If it was the last thing she ever did, she was going to pop that asshole in the eye.

"C'mon, ladies, we need to figure out a way out of here," Poppy said, determined not to let him win.

As the women started to take a catalog of what they had in the cell that could be used as tools to escape, Poppy ran through different scenarios in her head. The cell was fairly big and had four cots, three of which were taken by sick brides, a toilet and a sink. An inspection of the lock showed them it was electronic and the bobby pin Val had found in her bag wouldn't be any help in picking it. Poppy suggested using Val's lighter and some paper to set a small fire to try to call someone's attention. That idea was quickly thrown out. The women felt it was possible nobody would respond to the room and they could suffer from smoke inhalation or worse. After further inventory, they realized they didn't even have anything they could use as a weapon.

At the cell door, Poppy took out her frustration on the bars and gave them a good kick. She would have done it a second time too but decided she didn't want a broken foot on top of the mess they were already in.

After what seemed like hours, even though Val's watch showed that it had only been about forty-five minutes, they heard another tone at the door. Shielding the unconscious women, Poppy, Val, Andrea, Brandy and Melanie waited anxiously. She didn't know what the plan was if it was Demascus again, but she was not going to go down without a fight.

Poppy's knees almost gave way when she was blessed with the confused face of Dathrow.

"Dath!" Poppy shouted out, rushing toward the bars. She reached out to touch him to make sure he was real.

"Poppy! What the hell is going on?" he asked. Checking behind him to make sure he was alone, he stepped quickly into the room and allowed the door to close. He tried to hug Poppy even though they were separated.

"Oh my god, Dath, you have to get us out of here." On the verge of happy tears, she gripped him tight. "Demascus has taken all the brides and transferred us here to go back to Earth."

He cast a glance at the beds on the far side of the room. "Are they okay?"

"They need medical attention. I think they're losing their babies." Poppy motioned for the women who were standing to come forward. "He kidnapped all of us and he said he'd sabotaged the computer's matching system."

"But why? It doesn't make any sense," Dathrow said, fiddling with the lock pad on the cell door.

"Maybe because he's fucking crazy! It doesn't matter why. Just get us out of here and to the medical unit now." Poppy was gripping the bars now as if her pulling on the door would spring it suddenly open.

"I do not have authorization to open this. I need to find a superior officer." Glancing at the door behind him, Dathrow was obviously torn as to whether it was safe to leave them to get help.

"Be careful who you trust. There were other warriors who helped Demascus to bring us here." Poppy was unsure if she wanted Dathrow to leave. Hoping that she wasn't making a mistake in letting the key to their safety leave, she pushed him from the cell door and motioned for him to hurry.

"Give me a moment. I will be right back with an officer who has clearance!" Turning and barely waiting for the outer door to open, Dathrow slipped through the small space as soon as his big body could clear it.

Before it closed, she yelled, "Message Wheaton and tell him where we are!"

Unsure if he'd heard her or not, she lingered by the bars for a moment longer before turning to the other hopeful brides. The ones who were awake had watery smiles on their faces.

"Thank god!" Val let out with a relieved breath.

Melanie was pacing and wringing her hands together. "I just hope whoever he goes to is on the good side," she said. "There have to be good guys out there, right?"

Nodding and encouraging Melanie was something Poppy found easy to do in this case. "Yeah, there are good guys. And Dathrow is one of them," she reassured her new friend.

The wait for Dathrow to return took only a few minutes but felt like hours. When the door opened again, he was there, accompanied by four warriors. None of the men were familiar to Poppy and she was relieved to see none of them were the thugs whom Demascus had had in his goon squad earlier.

As one of the warriors moved to open the cell door, Dathrow reached through the opening to hold Poppy's hand.

"Thank goodness I checked this room." Looking at the women behind Poppy, he whispered, "This area was marked as cargo to be transferred to the Pleasure Sector... You weren't meant to go home to Earth." Hearing Val gasp behind Poppy, he raised his voice so she could hear too. "My belief is that Demascus had planned for you to disappear there. I believe he was going to try to sneak you onto one of our shuttles transporting medical supplies for trade. The room next door is full of empty crates that could easily have fit two or three of you at a time."

"We were going to be dumped at the Pleasure Sector?" Val asked incredulously.

"As far as I can tell, that is where you were headed. As a human you would have fetched a high price in the brothels, once trained. The more exotic the workers, the more money they make."

"Are you fucking kidding me?" Poppy yelled.

"Poppy, I do not think we would have recovered you if that had happened. Some of the women are purchased and taken to other sectors during auctions. My guess is that Demascus planned for you to disappear."

"He wanted more than for us to disappear. That dickhead wanted us to suffer." She was now shaking with anger as she waited for the cell door to open.

"What an asshole!" Melanie burst out, punching her hand as though she wished it was a certain Council member's face. "Warn a gal next time you plan to go for the jerk, Poppy. I would have liked to have gotten in a few hits myself."

"Did he hurt you, Poppy?" Dathrow asked, concerned.

Shrugging his question off, Poppy asked, "Did you get a message to Wheaton?" She rushed through the open door as soon as the lock clicked, and gave Dathrow a full hug.

"That's the funny thing." Dathrow smiled at Poppy with raised eyebrows. "My band was still receiving notifications from the other ship. He must have raised the alarm searching for you ladies. I was able to message him and let him know that you are here. They were panicking because they were unable to find you anywhere on Squadron One."

Once the women were helped from the cell, the other warriors hurried in to check on the incapacitated brides on the cots.

"What is wrong with them?" one asked when he realized that they were not simply sleeping.

"I'll tell you what's wrong with them. That douchebag Demascus gave us all pills that made the ones who were pregnant lose their babies." Andrea was toe to toe with one of the startled warriors. Poking his chest with her finger, she yelled, "They need doctors! Now!"

Dathrow squeezed Poppy's arm in concern.

"The baby?" he asked, his panicked gaze falling to her stomach.

"Val and I didn't take the meds. We weren't sure if they were okay for us or not so we pocketed them. Demascus assumed we took them when he saw they were gone."

Before Poppy could say anything else she was pulled into a hug yet again. "Thank your god!" Dathrow whispered into her hair as he held her tight.

"Dathrow? We must move now."

Turning around to the warrior behind him guarding the door, he nodded.

"Right." After letting Poppy go, he walked to the warriors, issuing orders. "Pick them up gently. We need to hurry and move to a more secure location before Demascus is notified the cell has been opened."

The warriors lifted the women like babies and carried them out of the cell. The warrior guarding the door checked both ways down the corridor before gesturing for Poppy and the rest to follow.

Poppy felt as if she'd been cast in a spy movie as they silently followed the warrior leading them down a hallway and into a room at the far end. Recognizing a supply closet, Poppy moved as far into the room as she could to make room for the ones following.

"Are we seriously going to hide in a closet?" Poppy asked, confused.

"My main concern was moving you before Demascus came back. We now have a few moments to regroup." As the door swished closed behind Dathrow, who had been bringing up the rear, he spoke to the other men. "We need to figure out our plan. If Councilor Demascus had warriors help him abduct the women, I am unsure who to trust."

Not being the type to be discussed without her being actually part of the discussion, Poppy popped in her two cents. "I can always point out who I saw with him. My main concern is for the brides who are hurting right now."

When one of the men tried to speak, she held up a finger. "Is there a doctor on this ship?" She nodded to the woman he was currently holding. "We have to get them to help."

"I agree. The only problem is that both of our doctors are currently on the other ship for meetings. We have no choice but to shuttle back." The warrior paused. "I am not sure how much longer these women can hold on. I believe they may have been given Hefnon 12."

When Dathrow cursed under his breath, Poppy raised her eyebrows. "What the fuck is Hefnon 12?" Poppy watched his face go through a range of emotions while she waited for him to answer.

"It is a drug that we were supposed to transport to the Pleasure Sector. It is made for a species stronger than humans." Rubbing his hand along his jaw, he obviously wasn't sure how much he should say. "The intended purpose is to terminate and prevent pregnancies. I am afraid that it could possibly kill these women. It is a very strong medication."

A panicked Poppy clutched at his tunic. "That is not acceptable. Get us to a doctor and do it now. I don't care if we have to hijack a shuttle to do it."

Behind her, Melanie, Andrea, Brandy and Val all nodded in agreement. Knowing they had no choice if they wanted to save the brides, the warriors took a moment to speak quietly. After some murmuring amongst themselves, Dathrow nodded.

Standing by the door, he turned and spoke quietly to the others. "I will go and secure a shuttle. Once I have one prepped, I will signal Drake's band to lead the group to me. I can message Wheaton to make sure he has medical doctors ready and in the docking bay to receive the injured brides. Once I have a shuttle, you will need to—"

Poppy stopped Dathrow right there in his tracks. If he thought she was going to be okay to sit there and wait for another rescue, then he was nuts.

"Why can't we all go to the shuttle now? I don't think we should split up." She had seen enough scary movies to know that when people split up, throats started getting slit.

Obviously torn, Dathrow ran his hands through his shoulder-length hair and then pulled on the ends. "Because I don't know who I might run into out there, Poppy. What if Demascus is waiting in those halls? He could have already figured out you have been released and be searching as we speak."

"Dath, we're going to have to walk there eventually, right? It makes more sense for all of us to go now and stop wasting time standing here arguing or sending someone ahead."

Turning to the rest of the women for support, she was happy to see all of them were ready to run, if needed. "Plus, Demascus should be scared of *us* by this point. He tried to kill our babies and he might have succeeded with those brides." Pointing over her shoulder at the women being carried, she was ready to kill. "If I get my hands on him, I won't be responsible for what I do."

Brandy stepped forward and nodded to the men. "We're ready to go if you are." she continued, "Don't forget, we are warrior brides—we can do this."

Dathrow shook his head at the women. "I can see that," he replied. Readying himself to open the door, he glanced back. "Stick close and don't talk. Squadron Two did not receive the protection notification so we should not be stopped by anyone."

The women all tensed as the door opened, and they waited for Dathrow to walk through before following closely behind him. They linked hands and the warriors carrying the three unconscious brides brought up the rear as they all hurried down the empty hall. As she held on to the back of Dathrow's tunic to keep pace, Poppy felt his back stiffen slightly before he relaxed. Peeking around his shoulder showed her a tall warrior standing in their way.

"Dathrow? What is going on? I saw you receive a message and then leave quickly." The loud voice came from immediately in front of them, and Dathrow was shielding her as best he could.

"Raz, Councilor Demascus transferred these women here against their will. That was the notification I received earlier when I left abruptly. We are getting these brides back to their husbands on Squadron One. Three of them need immediate medical attention." Dathrow reached back to pat Poppy's arm when she tightened her grip on his tunic even more.

"It is okay, Poppy. This is Raz. He is a friend to Wheaton."

She peered around him to the big man in front who was blocking their path. If Poppy had had more time, she would have appreciated the hulking figure of the warrior but all she heard was that this was another man who could help them.

"Wheaton has talked about his good fortune with his bridal match." Raz bowed quickly to Poppy. Gazing past her, he blanched. "Those women do not look well."

Seeing the warrior's face pale, she cast her own glance back to the brides. They seemed to be barely breathing now. "We need to go *now!*" she demanded as she tightened her grip on Dathrow once again.

"Follow me," Raz ordered.

They started hurrying down the hallway again, this time with Raz leading the way.

"I just docked my shuttle from a run to Squadron One. It should still be available," Raz informed them.

As they reached the docking bay, the men tried to shield the women as much as they could from curious glances. Poppy saw a large hangar with small shuttles that were either being fueled or stocked with cargo. She stopped in her tracks when she caught a glimpse of Demascus. Poppy's first instinct was to attack on sight—her fingers itched to get hold of him again. Slipping from the grasp that Dathrow had on her arm, Poppy hurtled forward. Dathrow grabbed her shirt fast. Bringing her up short and pulling her back into place, he ignored her attempts to maneuver away from the group.

The scuffle drew Demascus's attention to them. When he spotted Poppy, he shifted to get behind his guards, relaxing only when Dathrow stopped Poppy's advance. As they made eye contact, Demascus nodded mockingly to Poppy and then slipped aboard a shuttle, all the while surrounded by six warriors.

As they reached their destination, Raz ran up the shuttle ramp and the others ushered the women quickly onto the ship.

"Strap down fast. I will run through flight check quickly. Dathrow, secure the door." Raz rushed out instructions as he moved to the cockpit.

As Poppy was buckling her belt and making sure the others were ready to go, she caught Dathrow's eye.

"I saw Demascus in the bay," she whispered.

"Is that why you tried to break from the group?" Dathrow hurried to the glass on the side of the ship and peered through, quickly scanning the open space. "Was he getting on a shuttle?"

Poppy nodded as she tried to calm her breathing. The fast walk from the closet to the docking bay had been so quick and nerve-racking and she didn't think she'd taken a breath the entire time. "He was getting into one with six other warriors. And for your information, if you'd let me go, I would have kicked major ass."

"He cannot stop us from leaving now. The shuttle is locked. We are almost ready to take off." Buckling his belt, he gave Poppy and the women a grim smile. "Knowing what I do, I can tell you that he would not have fought fair. If he knows what is good for him, then he will disappear. The husbands of those women are going to seek vengeance for what he has done."

Poppy leaned her head back against the seat and closed her eyes. "I still would have kicked his ass."

"Poppy, are you all right?" Val had taken the seat next to her and appeared as frazzled as Poppy felt.

"Yeah, I'm just overwhelmed and I think I might have a mini-breakdown," Poppy let out on a cross between a laugh and a cry.

"We're going to be okay." She clutched Poppy's hand, squeezing hard.

The women all sat in silence as if they were afraid to jinx themselves while the shuttle engines fired up. As they flew to Squadron One, Poppy tried to calm herself down. Raz had called ahead to the docking bay to request medical units prepared when Poppy's ears pricked up. That was Wheaton's voice coming through over the intercom. Tears immediately flooded her eyes. This whole ordeal was almost over.

"Yes, I have them all. Three are in need of serious medical attention," Raz repeated.

The static from the speaker and the roar of the shuttle engines made it hard for Poppy to hear what was being said from the other end. She could hear panic in Wheaton's voice even though she was unable to make out the words. Raz was obviously unable to hear him very well either, since he kept repeating the same sentence over and over.

"They need a doctor! Did you hear me? They need a doctor!" he shouted.

Poppy glanced back at the women strapped into the seats behind her. She knew one was Staci but hadn't been able to find out the others' names. All three were somewhat conscious. The awareness they showed reminded Poppy of someone who'd been heavily sedated but was awake at the same time. They were unable to sit up on their own and the only thing keeping them in their seats were the five-point harness safety belts. Unable to watch the woman any longer without losing it, she had to stare straight ahead.

From the large windshield in front of her, she soon spotted Squadron One as they approached it at a high speed. Quickly maneuvering through a tunnel that opened on the side of the ship, they coasted into what Poppy assumed was the docking bay. Her hands were shaking. They were almost home. They were safe.

Landing was quick and as soon as Raz unbelted himself, she did the same. The other warriors had unbuckled themselves and were assisting the sick brides. Before she knew it, they were carrying the limp women out of the opening and down the ramp of the shuttle. From her place at the top of the ramp, she could see the booted feet of warriors running toward the craft.

Scurrying down the ramp after the others, Poppy couldn't make out the voices of those shouting. Time seemed to slow. The noise from the docking bay and the angry shouts of warriors were covered by the sound of her blood rushing through her ears. As she stumbled the rest of the way clear of the ramp, she could see Wheaton running toward the ship in front of Tamin and Rodin. She tried to run to meet him but felt her legs grow weak. The last thing she remembered was seeing black spots and hearing Wheaton's voice yelling at her through a closing tunnel.

CHAPTER THIRTY-ONE

As Poppy came to, she was first aware of voices whispering and a bright light shining behind her eyelids. Feeling as though she was waking from a deep nap, she wiggled her fingers and toes. Tingles raced through her extremities, as if they were still asleep. The voices around her got closer as she opened her eyes.

"Poppy?" Recognizing Tamin's voice, she blinked a couple times to clear her vision. Why were the lights in the exam room so fucking bright?

"Where's Wheaton?" Her voice came out husky with sleep.

Feeling a hand grip her own, she turned to the other side of the bed and her breath caught in her throat. Smiling through her tears, she reached up to touch the strong jaw of the man who was leaning over her. Poppy had to admit she'd never witnessed a more beautiful sight than her big, strong warrior gazing at her with love in his eyes. Cupping his cheek, she pulled him down for a kiss. Wheaton's lips touched hers so softly that the kiss could have been her imagination. Not being one to settle for half efforts, she took her other hand and cupped his neck to pull him tighter into her embrace.

Poppy let the tears she had been trying to hold back drift down her cheeks. "Wheaton, you have no idea how happy I am to see you." Licking her lips to preserve his taste, she smiled against his neck. Poppy breathed in his unique scent.

"Poppy…do not ever do that again," he whispered as he peppered kisses across her forehead.

They were both silent for a moment. Out of the corner of her eye, she could see Tamin moving around the exam room.

"Tamin? Are the other brides okay?" she asked as Wheaton helped her to carefully sit up. She tried to read the doctor's face for clues of their condition.

Walking back to the bed where she was now sitting, he patted her shoulder with a grim look on his handsome face.

"The brides are fine, Poppy. You did a great job getting them here safely."

Wheaton had shifted his position to sit on the bed beside Poppy and folded his arm across her shoulders to pull her into a hug. Knowing he needed her touch as much as she needed his, she leaned into his embrace.

"What about…" Unable to finish the question, she hoped that he understood what she was asking.

"Their babies did not make it." The news was delivered with such sadness, she knew Tamin was struggling with the fact that he'd been unable to save them.

Allowing more tears to fall, she turned into the safety of Wheaton's hold. Having already assumed the worst didn't make it any easier for Poppy to swallow. She thanked whatever good juju that was out in the universe for the fact she and Val had not taken the pills.

"I do have a question though," Tamin continued. "How did you and Valerie not suffer from the same problem?"

"When they gave us the pills, we weren't sure if they were good for the babies or not. We put them in Val's bag to ask you or Rodin when we saw you next." At her words, Wheaton cursed under his breath and squeezed her hard.

"I almost lost you." Rubbing his hand over her stomach, he whispered, "Both of you."

Tamin gave her a sad smile and squeezed her free shoulder. "You amaze me, Poppy." Moving to leave the room, Tamin said, "I need to check the other brides. The regen beds should be finished soon and their husbands are anxious to see if we repaired the damage done."

"Damage?" Poppy asked. Stopping at the door, Tamin turned to her.

"The Hefnon 12 came very close to killing them. We were unable to save the fetuses and are unsure if the regen beds were able to repair the damage left behind." Shaking his head in anger, he gritted his teeth. "All of this...those women...the pain...I never realized how heartless someone could be."

As the door closed behind Tamin, Poppy gazed up at her silent warrior. Once she turned her head to him, he leaned his forehead against hers and breathed out roughly.

"I almost lost you." He repeated his earlier words in a broken voice.

"But you didn't." Kissing him softly at first, and then with more ferocity, she trailed her mouth to his ear as she hugged him hard.

"Wheaton?" When she heard his chest rumble, indicating he was listening to her, she smiled against his skin. "I love you."

The rumble between them got louder as he hugged her tighter. "I love you too."

She looked up at him with a question in her eyes. "Where's Dath at?"

"'Dath', is it?" Wheaton did not seem pleased at her familiarity with the other warrior, but as he smoothed the hair out of her face he seemed to decide now was not a time to be mad.

"He received some trouble for abandoning his post on Squadron Two, but we smoothed that over with their commander. When they found out what he had done, they were pleased with his actions. He may actually receive a commendation for his bravery today. Many a warrior would not have questioned such a senior Council member as Demascus."

"But where is he? I feel awful that he had to leave his home here because of me. I actually wanted to talk to you about that..." Unsure how she needed to broach the subject, she stalled.

"Poppy, he will eventually come back, but right now he has missions that he will need to complete on Squadron Two before that happens. He left shortly after we received medical reports on all of the brides. He wanted to make sure that you were okay before he went back to his post." Giving her an understanding smile, he tapped her chin. "You cannot help but be lovable, can you?"

"I'm sorry, Wheaton. The last thing I ever wanted to do was come between you and a friend."

"It is not your fault. If our situations were reversed, I can safely say that I would have done everything in my power to make you mine. He is a good friend and came to me with his concerns before making any inappropriate advances and for that he has my respect and friendship." He cupped her face and leaned down for a kiss that soon turned too hot to stop. Pulling back reluctantly, Wheaton said, "Now, we just need to figure out a way to get him a bride so he will leave mine alone."

They were lost in a string of kisses when they heard the noise of a throat clearing at the door. Raz stood in the opening, waiting for them to acknowledge his presence. Once they turned to him, he stepped farther into the room.

"Council Member Wheaton, he was able to successfully launch from Squadron Two."

Feeling Wheaton's whole body tense, Poppy knew immediately who "he" was.

"So Demascus got away?" This question wasn't really directed at anyone. Poppy was voicing what she already seemed to know.

"Unfortunately, yes. From our intel reports we learned the shuttle he stole has docked on a Verge Battalion ship." Nodding to Wheaton, he continued, "Council has been informed of his location. We have been advised that no action will be taken until we complete an investigation and determine the condition of the damaged brides."

That sentence raised the hairs on Poppy's arms. "Damaged brides?" Turning angrily to Wheaton, she couldn't control what was spewing out. "Those women are not damaged! They've been brutalized by Demascus, and he needs to pay for what he's done!"

"I know, Poppy, and I agree," Wheaton said in a calming voice. He informed Raz, "You can let the Council know that I agree with the need for caution but he must be held accountable for his crimes and I expect a formal Council meeting to discuss his charges as soon as all members can attend."

Raz bowed stiffly to the couple as he left the room. Poppy let out a tired sigh. She knew that she'd just woken up but felt as if she could sleep for a couple days at least. Give her a warm bed with Wheaton in it and she would have to be bribed out of it with either chocolate or pizza.

"I'm so tired, Wheaton."

"I can take you back to our apartments now but first someone wants to see you." He walked to the door and stuck his head out. "She is awake now and you may talk to her for a short amount of time. Then we will head to our apartment, where I expect no interruptions."

Unsure who he was talking to, Poppy was happy and surprised to see Val peek around his shoulder.

Standing up carefully, Poppy crossed the room and threw her arms around the other woman.

"Val!"

Hugging her back just as hard, Valerie laughed for a minute, overcome with emotion. It seemed like the better option than crying.

"Poppy, did you hear about the other brides?" Letting go of Poppy long enough to reach behind her and tug Thorne into the room, she gave her a sad questioning glance.

"Yes I did. Right now I'm just glad they survived." Poppy let out a relieved sigh and noted that Val had changed clothes.

Turning to Wheaton, she raised her eyebrow. "How long was I out?"

He took a moment to brush some hair out of Poppy's face. "A few hours. Rodin was monitoring you and everything seemed fine so we didn't want to rush you to wake."

Poppy turned as more entered the room, hoping to see some of her new bride friends. She was surprised to see Behyr tug Hannah into the room.

"Poppy, it is so good to see you awake and on your feet," Behyr said. Giving her a hug, he didn't flinch when Wheaton rumbled.

Scanning her group of friends, she remembered something. "Hey, where were you and Hannah this morning if you weren't at the Council meetings?"

Everyone grew silent and looked at the pair in question.

"Well—" Wheaton started, only to have Hannah interrupt him.

"Wheaton and I made it official this morning."

When Val gasped and Behyr smiled, Poppy was even more confused.

"Huh?" *Somebody better start talking now*, she thought.

"Hannah and I officially dissolved our trial period this morning," Wheaton said while he tugged on one of the curls that had escaped Poppy's messy bun.

"Thank god!" she shouted and flung herself into his arms.

Making a scene by peppering kisses all over Wheaton's blushing face, she eventually let go of him and scooted around to a very happy Behyr, who was holding Hannah's hand.

"And I can see I'm not the only one happy."

"Hannah, I don't really know what to say other than thank you...and I'm sorry for calling you a twatwaffle."

Val let out a burst of laughter behind her and Poppy turned to her.

"No really. I'm sorry," Poppy repeated as Val covered her mouth to try to hold in her laughter while the men were trying to figure out what a "twatwaffle" was.

"Um, Poppy? You never called me that," Hannah said with embarrassment clear on her face.

Smiling widely and winking at the red-faced woman, Poppy said, "Well, not out loud I didn't. I'm apologizing for all the things I called you in my head...except for when I found out you kissed Wheaton." When she tacked that on, Behyr tugged Hannah closer to his side and flashed his teeth at Wheaton.

Val walked toward everyone with shooing motions. "Okay, okay, everyone is best friends forever and blah blah blah. Why don't we get out of the med center and give Rodin and Tamin some time to focus on the others without us taking up space?" Valerie had resorted to using her "liaison" voice to usher them out of the room.

"Just a moment." Wheaton stopped everyone as they were walking toward the door. "With all of our friends here, I believe now may be the best time to do this." Standing in front of Poppy, he dropped to one knee.

"What are you doing, Wheaton?" Poppy was sure she was either still slightly loopy from their ordeal or not totally awake yet.

"I have watched many movies with you that have had this particular scene in them." Clearing his throat, he grinned up at her.

"Poppy, you are my perfect match. I almost lost you today and I did not realize until that happened how you have become more important to me. More than anything else in the universe. You are constantly in my thoughts when we are apart. You are the first thing I think of in the morning and are my last thought before I fall asleep. I cannot imagine my life without you. You are my Little Flower and I would be the luckiest warrior in the galaxy if you would marry me."

Finishing his speech, he pulled a ring out of his pocket and held it up to her finger, preparing to slip it on.

"Oh, Wheaton…yes. Yes!" Helping him slide the ring on her finger, Poppy leaned down to kiss him while he was on his knees. They continued to kiss as their friends cheered. The steady rumble in his chest indicated that they needed to stop before things got out of hand. When they parted, everyone came forward to hug Poppy and exchange slaps on the back between the men.

Wheaton kept a tight grip on Poppy's hand as they walked back to their original apartment. Poppy yawned when they reached their door.

"I know I slept for a while but I can't seem to stay awake."

"You have had a very busy day," Wheaton pointed out as they walked into their rooms.

Poppy kicked off her shoes and raced toward the bedroom. She tossed a sassy grin at Wheaton over her shoulder and said, "But I'm never too tired to have some attention from a particular warrior." She giggled when she was lifted and bounced in his arms. "So, you and Hannah dissolved your trial period?" Kissing his neck, she felt him nod.

"Why didn't you tell me that's what you were doing this morning?" she asked.

She caught him smiling.

"We wanted to surprise both you and Behyr." With a grim look, he added, "If I had known what Demascus had planned, then we would have done things differently."

"Hey now, don't think like that. I'm safe and the baby is safe. There's no point in thinking of how we could have changed things." Tapping her finger against his chin, she caught her breath when Wheaton nipped her fingers.

"I want you undressed," Wheaton muttered, his voice now gruff with need. Leaning forward for a quick, hard kiss before he set her on her feet, he whispered against her lips, "Right now."

"Ditto." Poppy had already started tugging her shirt over her head the minute her toes touched the floor. Wiggling out of her pants, Poppy glanced up to find a nearly naked Wheaton. She smiled.

"What?" Wheaton said, catching her grin.

"Nothing. I just like looking at you."

"I love you looking at me. I love looking at you also," he replied with a smile. Slowly advancing on her, he reached for her hips and tugged her nude body to his own. With his chest rumbling softly, he leaned down and rubbed it against her hardened nipples.

Poppy tipped her head back and let out a groan. "I love the feel of your body too."

Wheaton bent his knees to grip her ass to lift her up. Poppy wrapped her legs around his waist and swayed forward to nip at his chest.

"Biting now, are we?" he mused. He nibbled at the spot where her shoulder met her neck.

Wheaton turned so her back was to the bed and walked until his legs touched the edge. Laying her down, he stretched out on top of her.

"I want to hold you close for a moment. No clothes. No talking. Just us," he said while staring into her eyes.

Poppy reached her hand up to trace the area around his green eyes and smiled into his serious face.

"This is a good place, isn't it?" Poppy asked.

Taking her hand in his own, he kissed her knuckles. "It's the perfect place."

After a few moments of silence, Wheaton reached for her mouth with his own. Kissing had never been such a turn-on before. Deep and intense, she felt invigorated and yet out of breath while time seemed to stand still. Long, drugging kisses soon made her squirm under his strong, hard body. Running her hands down his back, she let her nails drag against his skin and was rewarded when he pushed even harder into her body. Wheaton shifted his weight so he settled into the cradle of her body and Poppy felt her legs open helplessly against him. Her body seemed to be on fire and the only thing he had done so far was kiss her.

He ran the tip of his tongue from her collarbone to her nipples, circling each in turn before he gave a hard suck to the tips. Bringing one hand to her chest, he squeezed and plumped each breast that he wasn't worshiping with his mouth. Once her nipples were almost too sore to get any more attention, Wheaton moved even farther down her body.

At her stomach, he stopped and scattered kisses over the area housing his baby. Seeing his eyes water with tears, she reached down to his face and cradled his cheek.

"I love you," Poppy couldn't help but whisper again.

Clearing his throat, he took a moment to calm his emotions. "I love you. Both of you." Wheaton kissed her stomach before moving lower. Widening her legs with his shoulders, he raised them until they were hooked over his shoulders. With her legs draped over his back, he began nosing into her folds. Poppy's head dropped back to the pillow. His tongue and teeth teased her nether lips before swiping at her fully.

Wheaton adjusted himself to bring his arms up around her legs. He managed to hold them wide enough to make a meal out of her. Panting and twisting on the sheets, Poppy couldn't seem to stop her body from simultaneously fighting and reveling in what Wheaton was doing. Her wonderful warrior was giving her no chance to catch her breath or move away from his mouth. His taking turns sucking and giving pointed licks straight to her clit had her panting. Getting to the point where she was sure she was going to pop his head off with her legs, she realized she needed to loosen not only the grip she had on his hair, but also her legs.

When he moved a finger to her opening to circle the entrance that had been treated to a tongue bath, she gripped the silky strands of his hair even harder. So what if she plucked him bald? She couldn't help herself.

When the telltale tremors started in her belly and moved to the rest of her limbs, she heard a voice she recognized as her own shout out. Not the standard "Oh god" or even Wheaton's name, she instead went with the "oooooooohhhh" that was all her brain could think to form as she was taken over with chills.

As Wheaton gave one final lick to her now too-sensitive clit and spread her juices around her opening to ease his way, he leaned up onto his knees and positioned his cock right where she wanted it. "Are you ready for me, Little Flower?" he asked, wiping his mouth.

"Fuck yes," Poppy whispered, getting an eyeful of what he was preparing to plunge into her. "Have I told you how much I love your body?" she asked huskily, running one hand down his abs and smoothing her finger down his member that was poised at her body.

"You can tell me more. Later. Right now I want you too much to talk." With that he leaned his weight forward and allowed his cock to fill her one inch at a time.

Once he was fully inside her, their eyes locked as if they each understood how perfect this particular moment was.

"I will never get enough of you, my Little Flower."

"Ditto," Poppy said softly with a smile that turned to a gasp. She arched her back as he started thrusting.

Still on his knees, he kept hold of her legs while he pumped into her over and over again. Not being able to reach his body easily, Poppy reclined and gripped her hands into the sheets under their straining bodies. As her knuckles tightened on the fabric, she knew she was close again. Wheaton's clenched jaw was now coated with beads of sweat. Letting go of the sheets, Poppy reached down between her legs to finger her still-hard clit. Wheaton must have felt her move, because when his eyes saw her hand, he groaned and started thrusting even harder into the cradle of her hips.

"Let me." He pushed her hand away and pinched her clit with a sharp flick of his fingers. As if he had his own personal switch to her body, she immediately detonated. Under her straining, open legs, she felt his thighs tighten as he pumped hard into her sheath. Groaning

out loud, his body stayed tense for a few more moments while Poppy
tried to catch her breath.

"I will never get tired of this." His voice was hoarse with passion,
and Poppy smiled at him through sleepy but satisfied eyes.

"That's a good thing." Reaching up to tug Wheaton down, she
cuddled him a second before turning over to wiggle back into the
curve of his body. As they lay there, damp with the passion they were
unable to control, she traced the muscle on the forearm that was
around her waist.

"What happens now?" she asked quietly.

"We will be happy, Poppy."

Smacking his arm, she said, "I know that, you goof. I meant, what
happens with everything else?"

Pulling her back into place, he settled his chin on the top of her
head. "We will try to have Demascus brought before the Council to
face charges. We wait for our baby to be born. We keep you safe." As
if those were the easiest things to do, he didn't pause with his answer.

"What about calling more brides? That's been ruined for so many
warriors." Poppy couldn't help but feel bad for the men who
wouldn't have a chance to find their mates. She'd made friends with
some of them and couldn't imagine them being alone until they fixed
whatever Demascus had done to the computer system.

"Actually, before Demascus installed the virus, we had already
pulled fifty more matches from the system." Leaning down to kiss
her hair, he paused. "Depending on what he was able to upload it
could take some time for us to fix the damage that he has done. The
virus he installed has managed to infiltrate so many parts of the
system. Our first step will be to see how far it was able to reach
before we can estimate the length of time we will be without new
bridal matches. One of the system engineers believes that Demascus
may have uploaded the virus earlier than expected. We will not know
for sure, but he may have been the cause of the system matching me
with Hannah. We suspect he may have infected the system first to set
up false matches and cause the Council to doubt our alliance with
Earth. When that did not work, he went to more extreme measures."

"What an asshole. I hope they can get it all sorted out. I feel so bad for all the warriors still waiting for their chances at getting a bride." Closing her eyes, she suddenly felt everything catch up with her. Yawning widely, Poppy snuggled closer and murmured, "Night, babe."

Feeling him nuzzle her ear, Poppy smiled when she heard him whisper, "Sleep well, Little Flower."

EPILOGUE

"E.T. phone home… E.T. phone home."

"That's still not funny, Pixie." Poppy stuck her tongue out at the video monitor that showed her sister's smiling face.

"Oh c'mon, it is totally funny." Wiggling her eyebrows back at Poppy, she gave her a pointed look. "How is my future alien niece or nephew? And tell me again why Wheaton didn't want to know the sex of the baby?"

"He or she is perfectly fine and you can blame it on watching too many movies. Apparently he wants the full 'surprise' experience. Tamin and Rodin have been sworn to secrecy to anyone and everyone who tries to weasel it out of them." She rubbed her stomach and leaned back so Pixie could get a glimpse of her rounded belly. She smiled. "By the way, it is so nice to see your ugly mug again. I was getting really tired of just hearing your voice."

Pixie grinned back. "I know. Being able to see and talk to you makes a big difference. Almost like we aren't too far apart. Oh and let me see that ring now!"

Waving her hand in front of the screen, Poppy showed Pixie the ring Wheaton had put there not too long ago. After Pixie's appropriate "oohs" and "aahhs" Poppy laughed at her sister and gestured for them to move on.

"So, what's been happening in your neck of the woods?" Poppy asked. Keeping one hand on her stomach, she realized it had become a habit to rub her baby belly. It weirded her out when other people touched her stomach but she was always comforted when she was able to massage the rounded-out area.

"Well…a lot actually," Pixie answered. The seriousness on Pixie's face caused Poppy to worry for a moment.

While Squadron One had gone to the Phaeton Prime for a few short weeks, they were currently zooming back to Earth to relieve Squadron Two due to ship malfunctions. The planet had been beautiful but Poppy was relieved they were going back home for a while. Hoping that the timeline matched up, she was crossing her fingers Pixie would be able to visit her for the birth of the baby. Thinking back to her time on the planet, she realized it had been rushed but wonderful. It was a beautiful place that Poppy had been enthralled with. She had even managed to get Wheaton to capture some images on a camera-like object so she could show Pixie.

When it had been time for Squadron One to move back into orbit around Earth, Poppy had talked Wheaton into moving back into their apartments. She figured that when the baby was still an infant, they could handle sharing the small space and one bedroom but once the baby got older, they would need to broach the problem of setting up a nursery.

"Hey, you still with me?" Pixie waved at the monitor to catch Poppy's attention.

"Sorry, baby brain has settled in. So what's so important that we had to wait for video chat for you to talk to me about?"

"I'm just going to start at the beginning and I don't want you to get mad, okay?" Pixie began.

Oh dear. With that start, Poppy braced herself, wishing Wheaton hadn't been called down to the sparring room, so he could be there. She found his mere presence had gone a long way in soothing her lately. The baby also loved being around him, because the little bugger usually calmed down and took it easy on her bladder when Wheaton caressed the skin stretched over her growing stomach.

"I broke up with Brian," Pixie informed her baldly.

Poppy searched Pixie's face for signs of sadness but amazingly didn't see any. "Ummm, okay…why?" She thought about the man her sister had wanted to marry, and wondered what had happened.

"Well, here's the kicker. Remember Brenda?"

At Poppy's nod, Pixie nodded too. "He was fucking her. *He. Was. Fucking. Her.*"

"No!" Poppy was truly shocked.

"Yes! Not only that but the woman who I thought was a friend and assistant was messing with my work to make me busier so she could get me out of the way so they could meet!" Pixie spoke as if she could truly murder someone.

"When did you find out?" Poppy asked, so stunned that she could only sit there with her mouth hanging open.

"I noticed mistakes that even an idiot shouldn't be making with the bookkeeping. One night, I decided to take home the extra work that she'd been making for me and found Brenda in bed with Brian apparently doing *her* extra work. Well, technically they were on the couch."

"No! Fuck! I loved that couch." Poppy made a disgusted face at the camera. "Now I feel the need to go and dip myself in antibacterial soap."

"Yeah, needless to say that is one piece of furniture I didn't take with me when I left."

"Fuck. Me." Unable to believe what she was hearing, Poppy reached for one of the donuts that was ever present at her side. As she stuffed her face, she waved her hand to get Pixie to keep spilling the beans.

"Nope, it was Brenda fucking Brian. Plain as day."

"What did you do?" Face stuffed with a donut, Poppy's words came out mumbled but Pixie got the drift.

"Well, I told her she was fired and I told him to fuck off."

"Wait…you asked me not to be mad earlier. What would I be mad about that for?" Wondering where this was going was making Poppy crave another donut.

"After I cleaned house at work and at home, I realized I was going to follow in my sister's footsteps." Pixie smiled at Poppy and seemed pleased with herself.

"I don't get it."

"I walked my happy ass down to the Intake Center and filled out a bridal application." Recoiling back from the screen as if she were waiting for Poppy to reach through and strangle her, Pixie waited a minute before opening her eyes and seeing what her sister's reaction was.

"You what!" Where were more fucking donuts when you needed one…or five? Poppy thought.

"Okay, I thought this through. I'm single. I knew that with the Brenda-the-bitch fiasco at work, my boss was not going to be okay with me staying on since I let her get away with fucking up for so long. The biggest thing though is…I missed my sister."

Pausing for a moment, Pixie seemed as if she were going to cry. "Poppy, I want what you have. I've never seen you happier than you are right now. You have a gorgeous man who adores you, a baby on the way, and you're living a life I'm truly jealous of."

"I don't know what to say, Pixie." Poppy truly didn't. Pixie had always seemed to have her shit under control and thought everything through to the point of obsession. Her path had seemed to be laid out from the time she started college: finish school, find a management job and marry the man she had been dating for years. Her two planned kids were scheduled to follow three years apart after the honeymoon was over. This seemed so out of character that Poppy hoped Pixie didn't end up regretting her decision.

"But, Pixie, I thought Earth received the press release from Phaeton that there would be a halt on bride matching. With the system down, they're working hard to get it going as soon as possible but it could be a while before you're selected." Feeling a tiny bit better that Pixie would have time to rethink her decision, she calmed slightly.

"Actually the whole Brian/Brenda clusterfuck happened a while ago and my application was matched before that asshole kidnapped you." Seeing Poppy wasn't understanding what she was saying, Pixie smirked and explained, "I was one of the matches that was pulled before the system went down."

"Oh." Not sure what else to say, Poppy sat there quietly for a moment. "Do you know who your future husband is?" Trying to stay positive, she thought to make the best of a situation that was worrying her.

"Yes I do, and the good thing is you know him too." Pixie had that look on her face she got when she had a secret.

"Oh really?" Consumed with wonder as to who it might be, she wished Pixie would just spit it out.

"Yep. We would have already started our trial period, but he's been too busy to come to Earth to fill out paperwork." Grinning widely, she clapped her hands together. "This means that I will be on Squadron One once you get close enough to Earth."

"Who. Is. It?" Poppy was sure Pixie was doing this on purpose. Even when they were little, Pixie would always drag things out just to drive her crazy. She loved her sister dearly but dear god she was ready to reach through the screen and strangle her.

"Okay, okay, okay, keep your ass calm before you go into labor." Pointing her finger at the screen, Pixie gave the order. "You'd better not have that baby until I get there, bish. I mean it!"

"Pixie! Who the fuck is it?" If she kept this up, Poppy was going to have her baby right before Pixie got there just to fuck with her.

"My future loving, gorgeous husband is…drum roll please…" Pixie drummed her hands on the counter in front of her.

Poppy folded her arms across her chest, not at all amused. "Piiiiiiixiiiiiie." Raising her eyebrows, she leveled her with a glare.

"Jesus, Pissy Poppy, you take all the fun out of things. I was matched with Dathrow."

"Oh fuck." Realizing she'd whispered it out loud when Pixie stared at her in confusion, Poppy stuttered, "I… I… I mean…ummm… Dathrow? Really?"

Not knowing what was winging through Poppy's head, Pixie smiled and nodded. "Yeah, you remember him, right? He was here with Wheaton when you first met."

"Of course I remember him." Figuring now was a good time to end the conversation before she said something that would freak Pixie out, she changed the subject and then told Pixie she couldn't wait to see her soon.

After logging off, Poppy sat in the chair for a little longer while she went over their conversation again in her head.

Pixie had been matched to Dathrow.

Pixie. Had. Been. Matched. To. Dathrow.

Dathrow, who had become one of Poppy's closest friends. Dathrow, who at one point had been a second match for Poppy. The same warrior who had gone to the Council and been transferred to another ship because of his attraction to her. That same Dathrow had been matched to her sister.

Getting up and walking to the kitchen for another donut, there was one thing Poppy knew without a doubt.

Things were about to get interesting.

About Leora Gonzales

I am an original Kansas girl who misses the Sunflower State every day. I spend my time reading and writing making sure my two kids don't kill themselves or each other. My addictions include tattoos, cursing, good food and good company (not necessarily in that order). I believe that tough moments in life can be combated with good humor, and I find a reason to laugh or smile daily.

Find me online at: www.leoragonzales.com
Sign up for my mailing list, follow me on Facebook and Twitter, or learn more about my other works.

Other works by Leora Gonzales

Warriors of Phaeton Series (Self-Published)
Bridal Pact
Bridal Bonds
Warriors of Phaeton: Dathrow
Warriors of Phaeton: Finch
Warriors of Phaeton: Hix (coming 2018)

Braving the Heat Series (Lyrical Press)
Melting Snow
Simmering Heat (coming 2018)